I0578370

GRAND SLAM

THE ERICA JEWELL SERIES - BOOK 3

KATHRYN LEDSON

PILYARA PRESS

ALSO BY KATHRYN LEDSON

Rough Diamond (The Erica Jewell Series - Book 1)
Monkey Business (The Erica Jewell Series - Book 2)

Copyright © 2019 Kathryn Ledson
All rights reserved.

No part of this book may be reproduced in any form or by any electronic or mechanical means, including information storage and retrieval systems, without written permission from the author, except for the use of brief quotations in a book review.

This is a work of fiction. Names, characters, organisations, places and incidents are either products of the author's imagination or are used fictitiously. Any resemblance to actual persons, living or dead, business establishments, events or locales is entirely coincidental.

ISBN: 978-1-925827-20-0
Cover Art by Kellie Dennis at Book Cover By Design

For my Mum and Dad

*R*ain pummelled my tin roof. It alternated between deafening and nothing, with some pitter-patter between. When it came it roared; a million tennis balls served at lightning speed. When it stopped the wind stepped up, raging in great bellowing gusts.

Something scraped my bedroom window. I got up, peeked through the gap in the blind at my tiny walled garden. The young pear tree thrashed around. In the dim street light I could see a tornado of leaves and paper, the clattering front gate, dark corners. Beyond all that, the sky was blacker than the night itself. Lightning approached; its thunder banging louder every second.

I tugged at the blind, pulling it to the side to try to cover the gap, as I'd done a million times before, also without success. I needed a new blind. I got back into bed.

At the back of my half-demolished house, I could hear Steve's tarps fighting for freedom. They snapped, up and down, a loud clapping sound. The back door rattled.

It was a warm summer night, but I snuggled under the doona. Put it over my head. Tried to think positively, like how lucky I was to have a roof that would probably stay put, unlike the poor buggers in

Western Australia, not knowing which direction the prowling Cat 5 cyclone would take on a whim, its eye on defenceless roofs and our oil rigs.

Axle was suddenly alert next to me; his body tense. I snatched the doona away from my face and in the increasing flashes of light, I watched him watching the window. He sat up, his long, black tail waving. I turned my head and together we stared at the pear tree's madly waving limbs, at its eerie strobing image through the thin blind.

I sat up, too. Axle lowered into a crouch, paws tucked under, tail twitching. Now he stared at my bedroom door.

'Bloody hell, Axle. You've slept through worse than this. You've slept through Jack's snoring.'

He didn't respond. I tickled his ear. He stared at the door. Against all usual desires I had about really big mice and where I'd like them all to go, I hoped that's what had his attention. But then I heard a sporadic thump, thump, thumping sound. I, too, stared at the bedroom door, holding my breath for a full minute.

I shook my head. 'This isn't helping.' I turned on my bedside lamp, threw off the doona and wiped the sweat off my face, scanning the floor, knowing but still not believing that big mice couldn't fit under the bedroom door. I pulled on my dressing gown, changed my mind and donned a raincoat and runners. I held the door knob, took a breath, yanked open the door. Nothing there but my passageway full of boxes and crap. Directly to my left was the front door. I checked all three locks. Down the passage was the spare room, then the bathroom, and that's where my house ended. Where Steve had temporarily placed the old back door. The cat flap blew in, horizontal. It dropped, blew up again. Too small for someone to crawl through. Too small for a big bad man, anyway. Not too small for a really big mouse.

I shivered in spite of the heat and tiptoed around the mess, arms out for balance. I stepped over a box of saucepans, stopped, picked up a small but heavy one. At the door, on my knees, I stared through the cat flap. No-one there. Hold on, wasn't I supposed to have a security guard? Didn't Jack say he'd put one there every night until I moved out?

I unlocked the back door and pushed it open. The wind snatched it off me, slamming it into the old brick wall that separates my house from its twin. Something smacked my face and I dropped the pan, reeling back, palm to my stinging cheek. A rope danced in front of me; one of the tarp's ropes, broken free. I grabbed it with both hands and it yanked me into the backyard, the rain, the mud. A wind gust flipped the hood off my head. The rope tried to shake me off. I looked for an anchor, somewhere to secure it. Above me was an exposed beam, its likely home. Too high for me to reach without a ladder. Too dangerous even if I had one. Should I call Steve? No, because he'd nag me to move out. I let the rope go, arms up to protect myself from its crazed flapping. I pulled the hood back over my head and squelched across the yard to the cyclone wire fence at the back. I checked the padlocked gates and pressed my face into the fence, peering up and down the narrow lane, full of nothing but quivering back fences, sleeping vehicles and torrential floods in the gutters. None of those cars contained a security guard, that I could see. Now I thought I should call Jack, but he'd definitely make me move out if there were noises keeping me awake and his security guy hadn't fronted. I'd rather risk my life than move to my mother's. Well, for a couple more days, anyway.

But what if the security guy had been murdered by bad men? Who were now waiting in the shadows? Waiting for a chance to get me. I mustn't think about bad men. I mustn't! It was hard not to, though. Shane McGann was now in jail because of Jack and me. His friends might want payback. That's what bad guys do, don't they? Dish out payback? Avenge their mates in some horrible, throat-cutting, body-dumping fashion? Tyre irons and boots of cars. Bottom of the river and all that?

Goosebumps crawled up my back. There was a movement behind me that I sensed rather than heard. My head snapped around and I stared at the square, dark space between me and the back of my house. Axle stood silhouetted in the open door, ignoring the leaping rope. I strode across the yard and through the door, slamming it behind me, unconcerned about my muddy shoes on the old carpet. I bent to pick Axle up but he hissed at me – hissed! – and streaked up the passage, his body low, to my bedroom. I followed, hesitated at the bedroom door. There was a new noise. I stepped up to the front door and peered through the peep hole, waiting for my vision to adjust to the darkness. But I knew without looking that my front gate, which was closed ten minutes ago, was now open, and banging against the wall. Somebody was out there.

I rushed into my bedroom, to the laundry hamper. I hadn't touched my gun since Jack gave it to me over a year ago. Back then I'd pushed it into a sock and dropped it into the hamper and covered it with a pile of clothes. Which were still unwashed because I'm scared to touch the gun. I reached into the hamper, changed my mind. I'd simply freeze if I had to use it. The bad guy would take it off me. I closed my eyes, took a huge, shuddering breath. I simply forgot to lock the gate, that's all. If it had been locked, no-one could have opened it. Unlocked, it was old and unreliable, like the rest of my house, especially in this weather. I relaxed my shoulders, rolled my head, opened my eyes.

From the end of the bed, Axle growled. It was a low, warning sound I'd never heard come out of him before. As I stared at him in horror, it took me a second to realise that he wasn't staring back at me, but rather past me, at the window, where I now looked, and where a sudden flash of light showed, in sharp outline, a human shape on the other side.

CHAPTER 2

*A*mazingly, I survived the night. After the human-shape-at-the-window incident, I'd hidden under the bed for twenty minutes, thinking about Shane McGann and the other enemies Jack might have who'd like to hurt me, just for the pleasure of pissing Jack off. But McGann's friends didn't come through my window and I gave myself a good talking to about being brave, finally working up the courage to approach the front door and flick the outside light on and off a million times to create an annoying disco effect for the intruder. Then I'd stared through the gap in the blind and the peep hole in the door for another twenty minutes before actually opening the door, venturing forth and shutting (and locking) the gate.

Back in bed, Axle and I discussed the plethora of possibilities around finding someone in a front garden in Richmond on a stormy night, the most likely scenario being a homeless person in search of shelter, which he/she had found until I scared him/her off with the disco effect. By the end of our conversation, Axle had curled up and slept again, and I lay there relieved of the burden of fear, which had been replaced by guilt at having scared off a poor, shelterless, homeless person. Unfortunately, guilt, like fear, can keep one awake.

So now I stood at Richmond station, yawning, waiting for the next train direct to Flinders Street, trying to focus on the moment, if not the day ahead. I watched the Punt Road traffic crawl in from the north. It was doing what it always does, and commuters were doing what they always do. Council workers mopped up after the big storm. This morning's weather was a balm on the memory of last night's horror. Hot, dry and still – my favourite. Good things happen when the weather's like this. The Yarra River would be glossy and teeming with rowers, lunch time picnickers on its banks. I imagined the lonely beaches of winter now swarming with crowds. Cricket was on at the Melbourne Cricket Ground – the MCG. I could hear the crowds from my house. My summery thoughts – acting with sudden positive fervour – turned to the approaching Australian Open tennis tournament, and that reminded me of Emilio Mendez who, on the international tennis circuit, is this:

- number one darling
- number two seed
- the hottest babe, ever.

And I was about to meet him. Which is why I'd spent hours on my hair, even though I was already sleep deprived without the extra early start. It had been a mighty effort to find my hair straightener; an extreme sport with my bathroom full of renovation dust, all my hair goodies in plastic bags scattered around what was left of my house, mostly in the passage under piles of cutlery and tampons. But worth the sweat and tears because my hair looked fabulous. If I hadn't straightened it, I'd look like a broccoli.

On the train I stood squished in the door, facing out so I could watch Rod Laver Arena glide by. My company's logo was everywhere, flapping in the breeze and stretched across billboards, all ready for the tennis. I couldn't help smiling at my good work, and looked around to see if anyone else was admiring it. Nope. Phones and iPads were far more interesting. The man next to me was reading about the cyclone in Western Australia. Maybe Dega Oil should have paid for some e-ads. Although you couldn't help but know who the major sponsor of the tennis was. It had been quite a coup for the company – an expensive one, but worth it, according to our CEO, John Degraves. Dega's reputation and share price had lagged last year but now, things were looking up. Among the neatly mown expanses I could see landscapers creating pop up gardens around great, white marquees. Tennis Oz staff would be working long hours. Like me. I yawned.

From Flinders Street station I crossed the Yarra, squinting up at the flashy Dega Oil building, its eastern side ignited by the morning sun. In the building I rode the lift to the 46th floor and crept to my desk as quietly as possible, knowing Rosalind would be in her office. She usually was. Maybe she worked through the night. I suppose when you're a vampire you don't need sleep.

Marcus was there – Rosalind's PA. He stopped by my desk on his way to deliver her coffee, sat one pert bum cheek on it.

I leaned close. 'Tell me again why my desk is closer to her than yours?'

'Good management on my part, darling. I love your hair.' He tucked a few strands behind my ear and I untucked it.

'Don't touch. This took me hours. I had to get up at five.' Not that I'd been asleep, anyway.

'I'm impressed with your efforts. You don't usually bother.' He made a sad face.

'Gotta look good for the "world's sexiest man".' I made quotation marks in the air. Not sexiest according to me, but some magazine. Second sexiest, according to me.

'Speaking of sexy men,' said Marcus, 'how's that *unbelievably* hot spunk of yours?'

'Which one? I have so many.'

'Very funny.'

'Actually,' I said, 'haven't seen him for about a week.'

'When you do, give him one for me.'

'I'm sure he'll be flattered.'

'You know, darling, he'll realise one day it's me he wants. I hope you're prepared for that.'

'And I hope you're not looking for commitment.'

Marcus gave me a wink and as he stood to leave, I asked if there was any more news on the cyclone.

'It's slow but still on course for Port Hedland. Next couple of days, they say.'

'Are we evacuating the rigs?'

'That's the plan, honey.' He carried on to Rosalind's office, and I threw a paper clip at his back.

I heard Rosalind say, 'Is that Erica?'

'Yep – she's been here half an hour.'

I both loved and hated him for that – posting me at my desk before I was really there but then telling her I was there, which meant she'd want to see me. No time to get coffee.

My phone rang as Marcus walked by and ruffled my perfect hair. I smacked his hand and picked up the phone, smoothing my hand over my head. It was Rosalind calling from her office, which is about three metres from my desk. Marcus's desk is next to mine and there's a partition between us. A paper clip landed on my head.

Pretending not to know who it was, I said into the phone, 'Media and investor relations. Erica Jewell speaking.'

'Why aren't you standing in front of me? I need to see you.'

My telepathy skills have been a bit off lately, I admit. With pen and paper, I passed through the gateway to hell, fixed a smile and waited for her to tell me if I was allowed to sit.

Rosalind's head was down as she examined the magazine on her desk. Her stiff black hair was fake, I was sure; the drag-queen disguise designed to distract people from the truth of her nature. They say, just by the way, that the creator of the vampire based the creature on the narcissist who, in her most vile form, is a psychopath. Apparently, the difference between a psychopath, sociopath and someone with narcissistic personality disorder is quite fuzzy. The psychopath may kill without hesitation or remorse, apparently, while the others have some semblance of conscience that prevents murder. Perhaps I exaggerate. Maybe the sociopath would murder if necessary. If she were pushed.

'You need to get to the hotel early.' She didn't look up from the magazine. There was a photo of Emilio Mendez on the cover. It was one of those action shots, mid-serve with shirt riding high, showing off those magnificent abs, his face contorted from the effort but still beautiful.

'I'll leave here at ten-thirty. Plenty of time.'

'We don't want the tennis player arriving without a host to look after him.' She tapped the magazine, looked up and scanned my body, just like my mother does. Unlike my mother, though, there were no comments about my clothes or hair. Rosalind's gaze landed on my jugular and stayed there.

'I agree.' I took a small step back.

'We need to be ready when the cyclone hits. It's a big one.'

'We'll be ready.'

'You might want to prepare a media release with the usual business. That all's well, our staff are safe, no oil spills, etcetera, etcetera.'

'I've got one ready.'

She shooed me. 'Off you go.'

I held my smile. 'See you at lunch.' And turned to leave.

'Erica.'

'Yes?'

She took off her glasses, stared right at me. 'God help us if it doesn't go well.'

'The lunch? The cyclone?'

'The *tennis*, Erica. The whole thing. God help us.'

CHAPTER 3

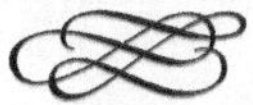

I'm not sure why I thought it was a good idea to walk to Crown Hotel. To slow time? Take my mind off Rosalind's vampire curse? Whatever had possessed me (Rosalind?) to do so, what I'd imagined was a pleasant stroll in the summer warmth, taking in the joyful morning frolics of office workers also claiming a few rare minutes of Melbourne's outdoor offerings. But halfway there, I hit a wall of cold. Our famous cool change. It's the reason Melburnians follow the forecast in summer. To know if the morning's forty degrees will later drop to twelve. The cool change is usually welcome when the weather's been so hot, but I didn't welcome it now. And I didn't see it coming. In my stressed and sleepless state, I'd forgotten to check the forecast.

My hair blew up. And so did my skirt. With one hand on my crotch and one on my bum, holding down the flimsy material, I cursed the icy wind to hell. The hot wind that last night had blasted in from the north had reached Antarctica and turned back. I staggered along the river promenade carrying a huge bag over my shoulder, the wind buffeting me. Something cold and wet hit my nose.

'What the —' I looked up. Oh, shit. Rain?

I ran as fast as my heels would allow, heading for Crown Hotel, which was the nearest building, anyway. I knew it was too late – I could feel the strands frizzing at my scalp. I could hear them! I fell through the door, found a loo and stood in front of the mirror.

'Oh, perfect. That's really great, Erica.' I dragged a comb through the strands, turning them into damp fuzz. 'You idiot.' I wet my hair again from the tap, resurrecting the broccoli, which was somehow better than fuzz. There was running mascara, too, which nicely complemented the lack-of-sleep dark circles.

I stamped my foot. 'Fuck it!'

A toilet flushed behind me. I hadn't realised someone else was in the room and I felt stupid for talking to myself. And swearing. What if the someone was a little old lady? In the mirror I watched the door swing open, and a man emerged. Not just any man. Emilio Mendez. I let out a gasp. He wore running shorts and singlet top. He, too, was wet, presumably from the rain, but more delicious for it, in the way James Bond was delicious as he emerged from the sea.

'*Hola!*' He looked around. '*Es este el cuarto de baño para hombres?*'

I looked around also in case I'd made a mistake. Was this the ladies' or men's? There was no urinal but maybe they don't have urinals in posh hotels.

Emilio stood next to me, washed his hands.

I patted my hair. 'Ah, this is the ladies' bathroom, I think.'

He pulled a paper towel from the holder and looked me over. 'You are caught in the rain, no?' His eyes fixed on my hair, then the mess of darkness under my eyes.

And I found myself transfixed by *his* eyes. Was that normal? For someone with such black hair to have eyes so vividly blue they looked like sapphire pools?

'No, I mean, yes. Caught in the rain.' I laughed, pulled at my hair, wiped pointlessly under my eyes.

'What is this weather? In Spain, when the sky is blue, it is blue. In Melbourne it is hot and blue, then cold and grey. How does this happen?'

'It's the cool change. Most people like it when the weather's been so hot.'

'I do not like it.'

I held out my hand to introduce myself. 'I —'

'You would like my autograph? I do not have a pen.'

'Yes, I mean, no. I mean —' I clamped my mouth shut.

He smiled. 'Do not be embarrassed. Most ladies are excited to meet me.'

Devastated, humiliated, mortified. Not excited. 'Ah, actually, I'm —'

'I must get ready for my lunch.' He checked his Rolex and turned to leave.

'Um. That's me. I mean, I'm your lunch. Your host!' Jeez. I held out my hand again. 'Erica Jewell from Dega Oil, at your service.' I smiled at the cliché but he didn't. Rather, he looked … disappointed.

'*Si?*' He looked me over again, shrugged. 'Well, I will see you there. In one hour, *si?*'

'*Si*. Yes.'

Emilio left, but not before thoroughly inspecting me again, head to toe. Mostly head.

WHEN EMILIO MENDEZ walked into the Palladium ballroom – half an hour late – all staff and guests fell silent, and paused in whatever they were doing to watch him. I'd seen that reaction from the general public before: when Jack Jones enters a room. Jack doesn't have the accompanying fame, though, and possibly not quite as much money. But he has magnificent looks and a presence that commands immediate respect and adoration. Also unlike Jack, Emilio noticed the attention he'd drawn and appeared to be enjoying it. He moved slowly into the room, arms held wide, giving little waves, soaking up the love, while the woman with him – presumably Teresa, his manager – walked ahead, seeking their table. I greeted her, introduced myself, and showed her the way. I went back to find Emilio, who'd been caught up in the crowd, signing autographs. I pushed ahead of the queue. The half-hour allocated for pre-lunch pleasantries and social-ising was well and truly up. He needed to sit.

'Emilio, hello again.'

He glanced at me, handed the signed paper and pen to a woman who was probably eighty and who stood on tiptoes to kiss Emilio's cheek, causing him to laugh out loud, give her a one-armed hug and announce, to the delight of his audience, 'If only I am ten years older!' They posed for a photograph together, the old lady cradling in her palm Emilio's famous lucky charm, which he wore around his neck.

Emilio turned to me. 'Ah, it is you, Emily. My host.'

'Actually, it's Erica.'

He inspected my face and nodded. 'Better.'

My hair, however, was a nightmare. In fact, if I'd *had* a nightmare about my hair looking awful at today's event, it wouldn't have looked as awful as this. I'd scraped it back into a short, wet ponytail. Not like that wet look models sometimes choose, when their hair is pulled into a tight bun, all glossy and smooth, showing off their high cheekbones and fine jawlines. No, my hair was lumpy, like I'd just been swimming and dragged it off my face to get it out of the way so I could, for example, concentrate on the supermarket shopping list. I cleared my throat. 'I'll show you to your table.'

We approached John Degraves, who was standing with his wife.

'Emilio, you remember John Degraves, CEO of Dega Oil.' It wasn't a question. Emilio and JD certainly had met before to discuss sponsorship arrangements – Dega was not only the major sponsor of the tennis, we were also one of Emilio's.

JD introduced his wife, then JD and Emilio chatted charmingly, sucking up to each other. Emilio needed his sponsors' money and, according to Rosalind, JD really needed Emilio to win the tennis so everyone would love Dega Oil again.

Sue Degraves said to me, 'And where's your gorgeous man today? Is he coming?'

I could feel the blush form. It started at my ears. 'Oh, Jack and I aren't really —'

'Of course you are.' She gave me a big smile.

In fact, Jack *had* been invited to today's lunch – not because of me but because he's on all social and business A-lists because he's so good-looking, filthy rich, owns successful businesses and a big, posh house in Brighton. He was also a secret 'business' colleague of JD's but not many people knew about that. Anyway, apart from the fact that he rarely socialises in public, he'd declined today's invitation because, apparently, he was busy with some new Team recruit. And no, we weren't really, you know. Well, we were, but we weren't. Like, we get together privately sometimes and in my head I call him my boyfriend, but, oh my God, if he knew I was thinking that way…

'Can I get you something, Mrs Degraves?'

'Call me Sue.'

'Would you like a drink, Sue?' I looked for a waiter.

She sighed. 'I wish you two would just get over yourselves and get on with it, you know?'

'We're really just friends.'

'Friends with benefits?'

Sue gave me a knowing smile, which was not all that unusual. She often gave me knowing smiles and I was never quite sure if they were about my so-called relationship with Jack, or about her husband's other business: the secret team of vigilantes JD founded to keep the streets of Melbourne safe. The "Team", whose operational leader is Jack Jones and for whom I also, occasionally, work.

First course was done. Time for speeches. I approached Emilio's manager, who was seated next to Rosalind. They seemed to be getting along well enough, polite conversation and all that. Rosalind had a fake smile she reserved for necessary sucking up. I knew it was fake because it was the only type she could muster. It was more like a grimace, where the mouth stretches wide but doesn't curve up, and those who don't know Rosalind might think she was in pain. Teresa looked about forty and I had no idea how old Rosalind was – a hundred and fifty?

Rosalind said, another glass of champagne poised dangerously between two fingers, 'Erica, don't you go flirting with Emilio. Teresa says he's irresistibly drawn to the wrong types but I assured her he wouldn't be interested in you. What happened to your hair? It looked half decent this morning.'

Somehow, my mother had infiltrated Rosalind. I turned to Teresa. 'We'll start the speeches shortly. Mr Degraves will speak, and then Emilio. I'll interview him and ask questions from the audience, then there'll be media photographs.'

Teresa nodded, sighed and checked her watch. 'You'll let him know, *chica?*'

'Right away.'

I interrupted Sue Degraves's chat with Emilio, who sat beside her. She was asking him about his love life and why he hadn't found just the right girl yet.

'Ah, they elude me, Sue. I find the most beautiful woman, but she is sometimes empty, and sometimes she is a *puta*.' He gave her a sad look.

'Excuse me, Sue, Emilio, speeches will start shortly,' I said.

Emilio said, 'You should try something different with your hair, Emily,' and gave me a wink.

I forced a wide smile. Much fake smiling and laughing at this lunch. 'Well, Emilio, I think you've been talking to my mother.'

He laughed. It wasn't fake.

EMILIO MENDEZ'S brilliance as a tennis player wasn't his only reputation. He was regularly photographed with some hopeful Spanish, French, Italian, American, whatever, girl on the cover of a trashy mag with headlines like, 'This One?'. Some people said he was a womaniser, others reported that he was just young and foolish, taking advantage of his fame and beauty with older women. It seemed to me, though, that he just fell in love too easily. Emilio was only twenty-three years old but had been engaged a couple of times already. Those relationships hadn't worked out. Maybe, now that he'd left Spain and his crappy father and was settled in Sydney with his mother, he'd meet a nice Aussie girl his own age.

I watched him at the lectern, relaxed and charming. Mature beyond his years in that regard. So comfortable with the limelight. He made corny jokes in his soft, sexy Antonio Banderas accent that had everyone either in fake stitches or swooning; he said nice things about Dega Oil, how he hoped we got a great return on our sponsorship. When he finished I asked him questions that I'd gathered from the audience. We stood side by side at the lectern, and he smiled at the audience as I spoke.

'Emilio —'

'Yes, Emily? You have a question?'

I heard Rosalind guffaw.

'I certainly do. Someone has asked —'

'To marry me? Is she very rich?'

Everyone roared laughing. I giggled, politely.

'I apologise for this nonsense,' he said into the mic. 'Please, continue.'

'Who are you most looking forward to playing in this tournament?'

He was suddenly serious. The pro. 'I hope to meet Vladimir Vavilov in the finals, and I hope that after, I will be the number one tennis player.'

Everyone cheered and clapped.

The questions carried on. He wooed the already-in-love crowd.

Finally, I asked, 'And how do you like Melbourne so far?'

'It is a very nice city and perhaps I will live here one day. Maybe I will meet a girl from Melbourne.' He winked at the audience and we paused for the laughter. 'But I do not like this strange weather of yours.' More raucous laughing.

When I thanked Emilio, said what a pleasure it was to interview him, he took my hand and bent low over it. 'It has been my pleasure to be interviewed by you.'

There were photographs with the media, and I was invited to be in the one with the Dega Oil executive team. Emilio stood in the middle and I ended up on one side of him with JD on the other. Emilio put his arm around my shoulders and I stood there all stiff and embarrassed. He gave me a squeeze, pulling me in closer, causing me to put a hand on his chest to keep my balance.

He whispered in my ear, 'All the women, they want to be you, Emily.'

After lunch I walked with Emilio and Teresa to the hotel lobby, reminding Emilio about the following Friday when he had a commitment with his chosen charity.

'Don't hesitate to call me.' I handed him a business card. He gave it to Teresa, took my hand again and kissed it, telling me that he thought I was very funny, and that I made him laugh, even though I hadn't said or done a single thing that was meant to be funny.

CHAPTER 5

My phone was ringing as I approached my desk and I ran to get it. Marcus was there, hands on hips, gawping at the fright that was my hair. I'd set it free from the ponytail.

I snatched up the phone, but before I could speak: 'Erica!'

Jesus H. Christ. 'Hi, Mum.'

'What time will you be home? It's fish and chips Friday.'

Home. Geez. 'I'm not moving until tomorrow.'

'Have you got plans tonight?'

No. I had no plans tonight. There was not one single invitation forthcoming from anyone. But there were plenty of things I'd rather do than spend an evening with my mother. I could meet Lucy and Steve after work, for example. Maybe hell would freeze over and Jack would invite me to some gorgeous, expensive restaurant for dinner. Maybe I'd sit on top of the Westgate Bridge and meditate.

'No,' she said. 'I didn't think so.'

'Didn't think what?'

'That you'd have plans.'

'I might have plans.'

'Well, tell me what you want so I've got it written down. In case your *plans* are cancelled.'

What to say? I found Mum's goading exhausting rather than irritating, and felt suddenly tired.

'Piece of flake?'

'You shouldn't be eating shark, Mum.'

'Potato cake? Chippies?'

'Look, I really don't think I'll be there for dinner. Please don't worry about me.'

'Tsk tsk.'

'I'll see you tomorrow, okay?'

We hung up and I called Steve.

'Have you finished my renovation?'

He laughed. 'I'm not there today. Why?'

'I'm serious. I haven't even lived there yet. I haven't even *been* there yet!'

'Your mother's? What happened?'

'She reckons I've got no plans tonight so I should go there for fish and chips. But she's right. I've got no plans.'

More laughing. The thing is, Steve has known my mother all his life. We were neighbours, in nappies together. Our mums were friends. His parents were the only normal people in our street. Steve knows what Mum's like. He used to laugh when we were teenagers, too.

'What are you guys doing?' I said.

'Charity dinner for Lucy's work.'

'Bugger.'

'What about Jack?' he said.

I shrugged, even though he couldn't see that. 'Dunno.'

'Spend the evening in your bathtub. It'll be your last opportunity.'

I told Steve about the loose tarp and he said he'd drop by and secure it.

'What time are you coming in the morning?' I said.

'Seven. It'll all be gone by nine. Be ready for a lot more dust.'

I DID in fact get a phone call from Jack. He needed his security guy for something else tonight, and I told him the guy didn't show up last night, anyway. I didn't mention the human-shape-at-the-window incident.

'He was there, Erica. Might have gone for a bathroom break … how do you know, by the way?'

'One of Steve's tarps came loose. I went out to check on it.'

'I really don't like you being there on your own, anyway. Your house isn't secure.'

'I'm not moving until I absolutely have to. Which will be tomorrow after Steve demolishes my bathroom.'

'I'd rather you move out today.'

Well then, maybe I should move to your house while Steve renovates. Or, maybe you shouldn't involve me with bad guys in the first place. 'I'm excited by the idea of dust, rats and potential for murder.'

'That's not funny.'

There was silence for a while, and then, I don't know why, but I said, 'Anyway, I'm going out tonight and want to be close to the city.'

'Where are you going?'

'To a really expensive restaurant.'

'Which one?'

'Um, I can't remember.'

'Who with?'

Who with? Who with? 'Emilio Mendez.' Good one.

There was a long pause. 'The tennis player?'

'Yep. We're his sponsor, you know. I have to look after him.'

'Okay, well, that's a shame. I thought you might spend the evening here, stay the night.'

I sensed this was an idea that had just popped into his head but still, bollocks on my stupid lie. I wanted to go stay at Jack's. It's the only way we got to be together. We never went out. I wasn't sure if that was because he wanted to keep our little affair quiet, or if it's because he just doesn't like going out because he's treated like a celebrity (because he's so hot), or if it's because he doesn't want me getting carried away thinking we might be in an actual relationship.

'Yeah, shame. Are you lonely? What about the new recruit?'

Pause. 'Out tonight.'

'What about Joe?'

'He snores.' I could hear the smile in his voice.

I laughed, but mentally kicked myself again. 'Well, we might catch up one day. You never know.'

'Erica?'

'Yes?'

'I thought you might like to go to the beach tomorrow. With me.'

The beach! Oh my God! An actual public appearance together. 'Sure. I'm moving to Mum's in the morning but I'll be free after that.'

We arranged for me to go to his house at lunchtime and hung up. And I sat there, cross with myself. An opportunity to spend the night in bed with Jack Jones tossed carelessly away. And it would have been the *last* opportunity because once I was living at Mum's I wouldn't dare be such a hussy as to stay overnight with a man who wasn't my husband. Maybe I should call him back and say my plans had been cancelled. But then, I rather liked the idea of getting all dressed up and having dinner somewhere posh. What was I thinking? I wasn't going anywhere posh. I was planning an evening in my grubby bathtub.

I waited half an hour and called Jack.

'You won't believe it. Emilio Mendez has cancelled.'

'He got a better offer?'

'No, he's … tired or something.'

'Shame.'

'But you know what I was thinking?'

'What?'

'I'd still like to go out. I'll buy you dinner.'

He laughed. 'You'll buy *me* dinner? I couldn't let you do that.'

'Good, so you can buy me dinner. Pick me up at seven?'

He didn't say anything for a really long time and I wondered if he was trying to think of a way to get out of it. I was tempted to tell him to forget it, that I'd just come over in my tracky dacks and spend the evening on the sofa drinking beer and eating pizza, but I kept pace with his silence a moment longer, holding my breath.

'Alright. Where do you want to go?'

'Oh. Ah …'

'Never mind. I'll make a booking somewhere. Somewhere nice.'

Wow. *Wow.*

'I'll pick you up,' he said and we hung up, and I did a little tap dance by my desk, just as Rosalind wafted by with a champagne-induced grimace on her face. Or was that a smile?

CHAPTER 6

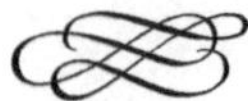

For the umpteenth time today, my hair had cost me. This morning it cost me time and sleep. At lunch, it cost me my dignity. And tonight, it cost me actual money because I'd been to my hairdresser after work to fix the mess. It was worth it, but surely there must be an easier way to have nice hair, daily, without all that sacrifice?

When I got home, first thing I noticed, as I opened the front door, was my footprints from the night before. I frowned, cursing the stupid fear that had sent me running from nothing into the house with muddy shoes. I headed for the bathroom and saw, still by the back door from last night, my muddy shoes. My stomach did one of those churning things and my skin prickled. I glanced into the bathroom, the spare room, and headed back to my bedroom at the front of the house. Nothing. I listened, holding my breath. Axle shot through the cat flap suddenly and dashed past me, into the bedroom and under the bed. Something outside? I crept along the passage, hesitated outside the spare room. The muddy prints got stronger as I got nearer the back door. I turned, placed my foot next to one. Similar size. Maybe they *were* mine. I was so stressed last night I couldn't remember what I did. I sighed, pushed open the spare room door.

Nothing out of place, it seemed. Hard to tell anyway with all the crap in there.

On my knees, I peeped through the cat flap. Daylight makes things so different. I opened the door and saw that Steve had been to fix the tarp. So they were *his* prints in the house. I'd have to tell him off. The fact that the prints were about half the size of Steve's boots, I chose to ignore. I crossed the backyard, which now contained a pile of concrete stumps sitting to one side, and checked the padlock on the gate. It was locked, but one of the gates had been pushed as far forward as the chain would allow. There was a gap big enough for a slim person to fit through.

I called Steve. 'I saw you fixed the tarp.'

'Yep. No harm done.'

'And you had the stumps delivered.'

'Uh-huh.'

'And you went into the house with muddy boots.'

'Didn't go inside.'

'But —'

'Watch your language, by the way. I've got the kids in the van.'

'Oh. Hi, kids.'

There was a chorus of chipmunks. 'Hi, Aunty Erica.'

I made appropriate kiddie conversation without bad language and we hung up. I looked at the gate, and the set of footprints leading from it to the back door. Probably some curious teenager, checking out the building site, I thought as I adjusted the gate. Yep, that's what it would have been, for sure.

JACK PULLED up out the front of my house in his sporty little Audi. He was fifteen minutes early, as usual. This was a nasty habit he'd formed, I suspected, after he was late for breakfast with his wife and parents in New York on September 11, 2001. They'd been waiting for him at the top of the World Trade Centre.

I watched him from my bedroom as he came through the front gate. My heart thumped and I felt faint. This is normal, of course. It's a wonder my body's survived it so far – the effects of seeing Jack. Tall with broad shoulders, the hottest body. Better than a footballer's. Eleven out of ten. Maybe twelve. I sat on my bed to recover.

Jack took me to a frighteningly expensive restaurant at Southbank, upstairs overlooking the river, Flinders Street Station and the lights of Melbourne, which were getting brighter as the orange sky faded, the ice-cold weather heading back to where it came from, having achieved its sole purpose: the destruction of my hair.

We sat by the window. Jack gave me the seat with the best view, my back to the restaurant. He ordered me a glass of French champagne and I sipped on it, sighing with happiness. Waiters moved about the room, all discreet and efficient. The tables had crisp white linen cloths and napkins, and soft candlelight. Jack had told me once that candlelit dinners were foreplay, always. He'd said that before we'd actually slept together, when I'd wanted to go to a candlelit restaurant in Sydney during our first secret mission together to prevent the Opera House from being blown up. It was so romantic.

'I don't think you and I have been out for dinner since Sydney,' I said.

'That can't be true.'

I shrugged. 'Can't think of another time.'

Jack's eyes moved from my face and fixed on something over my shoulder. There was a slight smile in those tell-tale eyes. 'Here's your friend.'

I whipped my head around, and was so shocked to see Emilio Mendez and entourage walk into the restaurant that I lingered with my staring. Emilio saw me, and grinned. I turned back, feeling the flood of heat course through me, prickling my face.

'He told you a fib,' Jack said.

'Where are they sitting?'

'Behind you. He's coming this way.'

Oh crap, oh crap. And then, Emilio was standing at our table. Without acknowledging Jack, he took my right hand and held it. 'You would like my autograph?'

He didn't recognise me? 'Oh, um, actually, you've already asked me that.'

'We have met before?'

'Well, yes, Emilio —'

'But I would remember such a beautiful woman!'

I thought I heard Jack's eyes roll. 'We met at lunch. I'm your host from Dega Oil, Erica —'

'Emily! It is you?' He released my hand and slapped his to his heart. '*Bella*! You have changed your hair like I suggested.'

I glanced at Jack. He was watching me with raised eyebrows.

'Ah … Emilio, this is my … friend, Jack Jones.'

They shook hands.

Emilio kept his eyes on me. 'A lucky man to sit with such a woman. *Muy afortunado.*'

Jack gave me a long look. 'Yes indeed.' He seemed suddenly impatient, like if someone didn't leave soon, he might.

Emilio said, 'Enjoy your meal, my friends. Emily, I will see you soon, yes?'

'It's Erica.'

He took my hand again and bent over it.

'Call if you need anything,' I said. 'You've got my number.'

'It is most definite I will telephone you.' His mouth hovered over my hand as he spoke, then he kissed the back of it very softly. And lengthily. He returned to his table.

'He didn't apologise for standing you up tonight, Emily.'

'Very funny.' I shrugged, remembering my lie from earlier. 'I don't care. I'd rather not be working tonight, anyway.'

'You'd consider that work? Dinner with Emilio Mendez?'

I glanced behind. Emilio had a line of fans waiting for his autograph. As he welcomed each one, another two arrived. 'Probably not. He's pretty cute.'

'He's got quite a reputation.'

'I don't think he's a womaniser like people say. He's just young.'

'You should be careful.'

A waiter arrived with a bottle of Krug champagne. 'Compliments of Mr Mendez.'

Jack waved the waiter away. 'We don't want it.'

'I do!'

I turned in my chair. Emilio was signing autographs but watching me. We smiled at each other.

I mouthed, 'Thank you.'

He gave me a wink.

Jack cleared his throat and picked up the wine list. The waiter poured me a quarter of a glass of champagne.

'Why don't they just fill it up?' I muttered.

Jack took ages with the wine list.

'What about a nice shiraz?' I said to hurry him up. 'You like red wine.'

Jack ordered a French gewürztraminer. 'I prefer white with fish.'

'Delatite makes a nice gewürztraminer. I've tried it.'

'I prefer French.'

Mr Prefer. 'Well, I think you should buy more Australian things.'

'I buy a lot of Australian wine.'

'What about other things? Your cars aren't Australian.'

'Soon there'll be no such thing.'

'True. But you could get one now. It'll be a collector's item.'

'What should I get? A Holden ute? A pretty green one?' He smirked.

'You could fill the back of it with your guns.' I'd said that way too loud.

Jack frowned. Neither of us checked to see if anyone had heard. I finished my champagne and stared at the waiter across the room, willing him to bring more. He got the message, returning with the champagne and Jack's *preferred* French wine. Jack tasted it and nodded to the waiter.

'I want some of that, too.' I pushed my wine glass toward him.

The waiter poured a good thimbleful and walked away.

I took a sip. Nice. But now I was ready for more. I stared at the waiter again. Said to Jack, 'I didn't think you spoke Spanish.'

'I don't. Not really. When did I speak Spanish?'

'You understood what Emilio said before. He said *afortunado*.'

'It's pretty easy to interpret. I speak other Latin languages.'

'And what does *afortunado* mean?' I felt pretty sure I knew exactly what it meant.

'It means fortunate, as in, how fortunate you are to be sitting here with me, in this wonderful restaurant with a magnificent view and stunning wine.'

'Yes, most *afortunado*.'

EMILIO AND CO left before us. In fact, they finished their meals within an hour and didn't linger over coffee or dessert. As they left, Teresa gave me a small nod and Emilio smiled at me. I smiled back. Jack didn't acknowledge them, and he went all quiet over his fish.

'How's business?' I said.

'Which one?' He frowned, glancing up.

'Any one. I'm just interested in what you've been up to. Conversation. You know how it works.'

He dabbed the corner of his mouth with his napkin and tossed it on the table. 'Pie business is going well. We've had a big order for the tennis.'

'That's good. I'll skip breakfast on tennis days.' If you don't like a Pee Wee pie, then you're not Australian, I reckon. Imagine my delight when I discovered Jack owns the company, whose office also disguises the Team's shooting range. Jack occasionally gives me freebies. Pies, I mean. I'm also allowed to play at the shooting range, which I choose not to do. 'And the *other* business?'

He looked around. I was so naughty tonight. We're not supposed to discuss the Team unless we're under the cone of silence. But I think I wanted to prompt some kind of response from him that wasn't … what? Bland. Always Mr Cool. Mr Understated. Mr *Prefer*.

'Quiet.'

'Business is quiet or I should be quiet?'

'Both.'

'Oh, well, that's good, if things are quiet.' No targeted baddies at the mo.

'Perhaps.' He leaned in. 'I've been thinking about tonight. About you being at home, alone.'

'And?'

'I want you to come home with me. Joe'll take you home in the morning.'

'That's nice of Joe.'

He didn't respond, well aware of the sarcasm.

'Anyway,' I said, 'I need to be home for Steve. He's coming at seven.' I didn't need to be there, actually, but Jack didn't need to know that.

'He'll get you home early.'

'Why can't you take me home?' Erica. What are you doing? Why make a fuss? Just go home with Jack tonight and be happy. You love his bed, especially when he's in it.

'I've got a training routine. Plus paperwork.'

'Well, I have to demolish my bathroom.' The devil sitting on my shoulder gave me a nudge. I lowered my voice to a whisper, leaned in. 'Besides, I'm safe because I've got a gun, remember?' Maybe I was a bit drunk.

Actually, I'd forgotten about my gun. I needed to do something with it. I couldn't leave it in my laundry hamper, but I couldn't take it to Mum's, no way.

Jack sat there for ages, looking at me across the table. He had his bossy-boots face on. 'I assume it's secure?'

I drank some champagne. 'Of course.' I had some wine.

'Where?'

'It's, um …' Where? '… in the drawer under my bed.' I hoped that was the right answer and made a mental note to move it over the weekend. Steve had built the drawer for me when Jack first gave me the gun but I'd never put it there because I was too scared to touch it once it was in the laundry hamper. The drawer sat snugly within a section of the bed frame, was lockable, and you really had to know it was there to find it. Steve thought the drawer was for secret girl things.

Jack considered that for a moment and nodded. 'That's safe enough. You shouldn't have it at your parents'.'

First thing in the morning, I'd move it to the drawer. After I'd used it tonight to shoot potential murderers. I just hoped the gas man didn't knock on the door at 3am wanting to read my meter.

It was after ten-thirty when we left the restaurant and I'd had most of Emilio's champagne and half the wine while the responsible driver opposite me had refrained. We walked to his car side by side. Well, I staggered a bit. I took his arm, and he tucked mine firmly under.

'Stay with me tonight. I'll take you home tomorrow.'

'*You'll* take me home?'

He nodded.

'Well, I'd like to but I need to be there for Steve.' I looked up at him. 'You could stay at my place.'

Did he wrinkle his nose? I stopped walking, staring at him, and he stepped away from me.

'What's wrong?'

'Nothing.' I kept walking. 'Let's take a raincheck.'

We drove the few minutes from Southbank to Richmond in silence and I brooded over the wrinkled nose. My house wasn't that bad. My bedroom was clean and tidy. Well, not that tidy. I crossed my arms, shitty, but couldn't help glancing at him, wondering what he was thinking, admiring his beautiful profile, that perfect mouth I longed to spend my life kissing. There was something about the way Jack kissed me that turned me to jelly, or set me on fire, sometimes both. But I wanted more than his occasional kisses, and I wanted them all for myself. Was that very greedy?

We pulled up outside my house. I wanted to invite him in – even for just an hour – but I couldn't trust myself not to say something mushy when we were in the throes of passion. Instead, I said, 'You still want to do the beach tomorrow?'

'Sure. Unless you've seen enough of me for now.' His mouth smiled but his eyes didn't.

'Hmm. I could stand looking at you a bit more.'

He got out of the car to open my door. Jack might be infuriatingly hard-hearted but his manners are impeccable. He wanted to come inside to make sure my house was secure. I opened the front door and he stared at the mess before him – my passageway full of boxes, dust, crap, muddy footprints, etc. Axle climbed his leg, as he's always done. It's his special Jack greeting.

'Jesus,' said Jack, lifting Axle by the scruff, holding him in front of his face. 'You're too big for this shit. I keep telling you that.'

'You're his favourite human, you know. Apart from Mum, who gives him roast chicken.'

Jack put Axle down, walked along the passage, out the back door (without looking through the cat flap first), and across the yard to the back fence. He peered up and down the lane, checked the padlock, came back inside saying everything looked okay. At my front door I stood on tiptoe to peck his cheek, but he turned his head and with his arm around my waist I couldn't escape the hard, closed-mouth kiss. Not that I wanted to escape it.

He released me abruptly and I stumbled back. He caught my wrist, righted me.

'Thanks for dinner.' I smoothed my hair, an attempt at nonchalance. I put a hand on the wall to steady myself.

'You're drunker than I realised.'

I tried to think of something a sober person would say. Nope. Nothing came.

'Goodnight, Erica.'

He stepped away, and I watched him walk out my front gate. He looked up and down the street several times, got into his car and drove away.

IT TURNED out I didn't need my gun overnight because I fell into such a heavy wine-and-lack-of-sleep-induced coma, I wouldn't have known if someone came in anyway. And besides, I forgot to take it out of the laundry hamper. But as my head hit the pillow, I thought that in the morning, before I did anything else, I'd secure my gun in my under-bed drawer. I'd definitely remember to do that.

CHAPTER 7

Steve swung his sledgehammer like a pro-golfer and smashed my dunny to smithereens. He emerged from the mist, pulling his mask and protective glasses off as I peeped around what was left of the bathroom wall.

'That's it,' he said. 'You're officially homeless.'

'Can't live here without a toilet.' I waved at the dust and coughed.

We moved to the spare bedroom, which had doubled as my kitchen and living room for the past week. What used to be my kitchen and living room was now outside. The plans for my house were laid out on the dining table.

Steve put the kettle on. 'Cuppa?'

'Sure.' Anything to avoid packing and moving. 'Or I could make you one.'

'This is a building site, buddy. My space now. I make the cups of tea.' He poured the water and looked at me. 'Get the hint? Time to move out.'

'Don't suppose I can stay here without a bathroom. Where would I throw up when I'm drunk?'

'You've got a hangover?'

'A bit.'

'What'd you get up to?'

'Dinner with Jack.'

'In public? Impressive.'

Steve handed me a cup of tea and as he examined the renovation plans, I stood there gazing around the dim little room. It was the room I'd put Jack in when we first met, after I'd found him in my garden, bleeding to death from a bullet wound. My front garden attracts all kinds, it seems.

'You know, I could live here and use the shower at work.' Axle circled my legs, rubbing against me. 'I've got this one for protection.'

'What about Jack?'

I shrugged. 'He's got some new Team recruit from Sydney staying at his house.' Steve knew about the Team. He didn't know about my gun. Which reminded me, I still hadn't moved it.

'There was a security guy out back when I got here.'

'Really? Jack said he didn't have anyone available last night.'

'I don't understand why you can't just live at Jack's while I do the reno. So what if his spare room's occupied?'

'He didn't offer.'

'He's worried you'll move in and never leave.' Steve grinned. 'You could stay at my place but I've got the kids most weekends. I know you hate them.'

'I don't *hate* them. I just don't understand the crying and vomiting all the time.'

'It's what little kids do. And it's not *all* the time.'

Steve took his tea and beckoned me to follow him outside, which now included the space where my bathroom had been an hour ago. The dust was still settling. We stood in the middle of the backyard, and I thought about the footprints, and he pointed to where my kitchen used to be, where the new one would roughly sit.

'The layout's not that different. You'll need to choose appliances. Stan needs them before he builds your kitchen. Or at least the specs.'

I checked my watch and sighed. 'I suppose I should get going. I've got a couple of trips to make.'

'I'd give you a hand but I've gotta get back to Mum. She's with the kids.'

'It's fine.'

'So, you'll move out today?' he said.

'Yeah.' Sigh.

'You'll like being back in Chadstone. Just think of the shopping.' He was trying so hard not to laugh, the bastard.

'Very bloody funny.' I turned and went inside, tackling the obstacle course to my bedroom.

'Say hi to your mum,' Steve called after me.

Without looking back I gave him the finger. I could hear him laughing.

I MADE a trip to Mum's with stuff to store in their garage. Dad's car was in the driveway in its usual spot, right near the gate, which made it hard to squeeze by, especially with armloads of stuff. The driveway is long, with a garage at the end, but he never puts his car up there in case someone parks behind him and blocks him in – I don't know who would do that – or in case he needs to dash out for Mum's prunes at three in the morning.

When I walked in the door, Mum flapped the newspaper at me. The *Herald Sun*.

'I suppose you've seen this, young lady.'

'No, but I'm sure you'll show me.'

Mum set the newspaper on the kitchen counter and opened it with flourish to the social pages. I had a guess at what might be in there. Emilio Mendez's first social appearance. Yep. And me, leaning into him, hand on his chest, looking surprised at whatever dirty thing he was seemingly whispering in my ear.

'This looks very unsavoury, Erica, I must say. What on *earth* did you do to your hair? Why are you in that photo?'

'We're one of Emilio's sponsors. That's the Dega executive team.'

'You're not an executive.'

'I'm looking after the tennis sponsorship. Just don't worry, okay?'

'But what will I tell the neighbours?'

'Tell them how proud you are of your daughter, that she's doing a wonderful job managing Australia's biggest company's sponsorship of the Australian Open, which is one of the world's biggest tennis tournaments. How about that?'

She pursed her lips. 'I suppose.'

Dad was watching *Mega Constructions*. I went to speak but he held up a hand. I waited, watching the telly. Wind rocked a bridge so hard it flapped like Steve's tarp, clinging desperately to the earth either side of a ravine until it finally gave up, let go, and plunged into whatever was below. An ad came on but still, it's important to be careful about interrupting. Your life might not be worth living if you dive in with a 'Hi Dad,' in the middle of an ad for *The Good Guys* or something.

Dad looked at me, his silent permission for me to speak.

'Can you move your car so I can unload mine in the driveway?'

Mum called from the kitchen, 'The car's broken.'

'What's wrong with it?'

'Something to do with the radio.'

'Radiator,' Dad mumbled.

'Are you getting it fixed?'

'No need for now,' Mum said. 'You can do the shopping for us while you're living here.'

Yeah, sure, just get me to do whatever because I've got so much spare time. I left to get the rest of my things. By the time I got back to Richmond, Steve had packed up and gone. I threw some clothes into a gym bag and looked for my favourite high heels. I might need them, I thought, if Jack wanted to have dinner again. It was ambitious thinking, wishful even.

But I couldn't find them. In my drunken haze, who knows what I'd done with them? Did I wear them last night? They were probably rolling around the floor of Jack's car, and he'd have them for me when I got to his house. I shivered with excitement at the thought of seeing him again so soon. With my bag packed, I left my bedroom and closed the door firmly against a potential change of mind. Living at my mother's for the next few weeks would be no picnic and I really was tempted to cancel, to keep living at home and just use the bathroom at work. But, quite apart from the potential for murder, the only running water now was from a tap outside, that used to be inside, and there was no toilet, which meant squatting in my backyard where the entire world could see me. Unless I got Steve to rig up a screen, but couldn't imagine having that convo with him: 'Hey, Steve, can you put up a screen over there so I can bury my poo in privacy?' He'd never go for it. He'd be too worried about my safety – and my sanity for suggesting such a thing.

I found Axle out back, crouched behind the pile of stumps, munching on a really big mouse. I felt suddenly happy to be moving out, with big mice now having easier access to my bedroom via the cat flap, but not so happy at the thought of Axle the big-mouse muncher sharing my single bed at Mum's. Maybe he could sleep with Mum.

As I PULLED up at Mum and Dad's again, Mrs Booth, their rear neighbour, drove by and waved. She looked like she was slowing down, maybe for a chat or to cast a spell, so I gave her a wave, a look of regret, and hurried on up the driveway. Not that I'm usually rude to Mum and Dad's neighbours but Mrs Booth was especially strange. The strangest of them all, even more so than Mary up the road, who is currently in minimum security prison for Tupperware thievery.

I walked in the front door carrying Axle in his cage. I put the cage on the floor and Axle dashed out of it, leaped onto the kitchen bench where Mum had roast chicken waiting for him. I wouldn't have minded a bit of roast chicken, too, but it wasn't offered to me. I unloaded my car, squeezing past Dad's with my stuff, then showered and shaved bits that needed it, ready for the beach. Or rather, for what might take place at Jack's house *before* the beach. With that in mind, I went to his house an hour earlier than we'd agreed.

CHAPTER 8

Jack Jones lives in one of the most exclusive parts of Brighton, which is one of the most exclusive suburbs of Melbourne. The house had originally been his grand-mother's, he'd told me, and when his parents were killed on that horrible day in September 2011, Jack and his sister had inherited the stately old home. But Jack's sister lives in New York, so it's really his. Not long after I first met him, when he recruited me to the Team about fifteen months ago, I stayed at his house to hide from bad guys. I've never met Jack's sister, but it was her room I stayed in. Now, on the odd occasion I'm invited to stay, it's in his.

I parked on the street. Joe was walking out the front door as I was about to hit the buzzer at the security gate. Joe works for Jack and lives at his house. If Jack were Batman, Joe would be Alfred and Robin all rolled into one. He's built like a brick shithouse, according to Steve, but I reckon he's just a big softy. A tattooed one who cooks delicious cakes. He also kills bad guys as and when required. I wished he was my big brother.

'Hey, Erica.'

'Hi, Joe. How's it going?'

'Good.' He released the security gate and held the front door for me. 'Jack's watching TV.'

'Thanks.'

Jack's house was like him: elegant, charming, well built. Totes impressive. He'd done the most tasteful (expensive) renovation. The house was Edwardian – not quite as old as my cute little cottage – and two storey, with the front door opening onto a grand staircase that led to two football-field-sized bedrooms upstairs, plus an office. I suspected those three rooms used to be more, but Jack apparently needs a monstrous boudoir. From the front, you'd never know the extent of its renovation, and internally, much of the front part of the house was in original condition, with double doors to formal living and dining rooms to the right of the entry, but to the left he'd installed a gym and beyond the stairwell, where I was now headed, the fully overhauled rear of the property caused a new visitor to gasp at its magnificence (also like when you see Jack for the first time). There was a grand, open and very modern kitchen, living and casual dining area with a ceiling the full height of the house, and a wall of glass that faced the manicured gardens of his backyard. To the left and right the house framed the lawn, with an extra-long garage on one side – hidden by creeping vines – and Joe's wing on the other. The wall of glass was open. It wasn't so hot, the weather trying to recover from yesterday's cool change, but in the sun it was warm and would be nice at the beach.

There he was, in one of his favourite possies – on the sofa in front of the television, wearing singlet top and shorts. I stopped walking and stared at him. His feet were crossed on the ottoman in front of him and those magnificent arms were hooked behind his head, accentuating the bulge of his biceps. My second favourite part of his body.

He gave me a small smile, and any semblance of self-control left my body. I strode across the room and straddled his lap. 'Hello.'

'Hello.'

'Thank you for the security guard.'

'You're welcome.'

I leaned in to kiss him but he said, 'Nice photo of you in the paper.'

I jerked back. 'What? You never read the *Herald Sun*.'

'Someone else in this household reads it.'

'Joe doesn't read it either. He wouldn't dare. You'd sack him.' I laughed, making light of it.

He didn't laugh, or even smile, so I resumed my seduction, which possibly resembled desperation. I tugged at his top, trying to get it off him, but he took my hands and held them still.

'I need a shower.'

'I like you sweaty.' I struggled against his grip. 'It's okay. Joe's gone out.'

'We've got other company,' he reminded me and I heard footsteps coming from the front of the house. Runners, squeaking on the timber floor. Of course. The new recruit. But they were light, quick footsteps – not ones that belonged to a big tough guy, surely.

Jack and I stared at each other as the footsteps approached.

'Hey y'all,' said an American woman's voice.

Jack's eyes crinkled at the corners – finally amused – as he clocked my expression.

I turned my head. A blond Amazon stood there, hands on hips, one hip cocked as she took in the scene, clearly surprised. Her hair was short and spiky. She was probably six feet tall, had an awesome tan and a six-pack that put Jack's to shame. She wore a teeny, tiny crop top and tiny, weeny shorts that had been sprayed on and showed, without a doubt, that she had no pubic hair.

'Jack didn't say he had a girlfriend.'

I lifted myself from his lap, trying to make myself as tall as possible. 'That's because he doesn't.'

She made one of those whoops-I've-upset-the-girlfriend faces and I approached her, slowly.

From behind me, Jack said, 'Sharon, this is —'

'Erica Jewell.' I held out my hand.

'Sharon Stone.'

'Of course you are.'

We shook hands and I discreetly nursed mine, which had been crushed.

She looked past me. 'Hey, Black Jack, I've got a new routine. Can I go over it with you?' She thumbed over her shoulder, presumably indicating the gym, not the stairs leading to her bedroom.

'Sure,' said *Black* Jack and I didn't look at him as he passed, joining Sharon Stone and heading to the gym. Or her bedroom. 'Make yourself at home,' he threw over his shoulder, 'you know where everything is.' Like I was just a visitor or something. Not someone who actually *lived* there. Not like Sharon Stone, who didn't need to be invited to make herself at home. I watched them walk away, looking at Sharon's muscled bottom, which I reckoned you could crack a coconut on. I felt thankful that at least her pert breasts were smaller than mine, even though she was physically perfect in every other way, with nipples that strained through the fabric of her top.

Jack was gone for fifteen minutes, during which time I'd lost my appetite for his body but found it for food. I made a cup of tea and helped myself to a slab of Joe's freshly baked banana cake and sat there brooding in front of the telly. The Sydney tennis was on, the tournament that precedes the Australian Open. Emilio had chosen not to play in it so he could be fresh and well prepared for the Open. For the first time since Dega's sponsorship deal was announced, I felt zero excitement about it.

Jack came back, eventually. 'Sharon's the new recruit.'

I stretched my mouth wide in an attempted smile, hoping it made me look happy, relaxed and generally pleased with the world. 'Great.'

He stood there, looking satisfied.

'She seems nice.'

'Come upstairs.' He held out a hand, seemingly pleased with his Erica-and-Emilio-in-the-paper payback and ready to return to a level playing field. 'Have a shower with me.'

'No.'

He let out a surprised laugh. 'Why?'

'Um. I feel sick from running ten kilometres this morning.'

'You don't run.'

'And a hundred sit-ups.'

I heard the footsteps again. Shaz appeared. 'What are y'all doin' today?'

Going upstairs to have sex in the shower.

'We're going to the beach,' said Jack.

'Can I come?'

CHAPTER 9

Of course Shazza's bikini was tiny. There wasn't much she needed to hide. Certainly no pubes hanging out. No bulging, bouncing boobs to worry about. The golden bikini was the same colour as her skin, so from a distance she looked naked. Men tripped over cricket stumps and soccer balls trying to get a look at her. They fell into holes dug by their kids. Women, on the other hand, were discreetly adjusting sunglasses and pretending to watch for drowning children so they could perv at Jack.

While I'd had visions of a romantic liaison at some quiet Brighton beach, Sharon had wanted to go to St Kilda along with the rest of Melbourne's population. I'd brought my beach hut – more for privacy than anything – but as no-one else had shade of any kind, I left mine in the car. I tried to join Jack and Sharon in their soccer game with a bunch of swarthy men, but I kicked the ball and hurt my toe, so limped back to my towel to watch instead. I realised that in competition generally, Sharon Stone left me standing at the starting post. Except for one thing. With my one-quarter Italian blood, I get a great tan.

. . .

I OPENED my eyes and sat up. Had I been asleep? Where were Sharon and Jack? Then, together with the rest of the beach crowd, I fixed my eyes on a vision emerging from the sea. They seemed to rise from the ocean in slo-mo; a James Bond moment. Daniel Craig and a blond Halle Berry, but better. Much better. And taller. Gleaming, tanned, perfect. As they approached, Jack frowned. Sharon seemed curiously satisfied about something.

'You're burnt.' Jack stood over me, hands on hips, water dripping from his hair. 'Didn't you put sunscreen on?'

'Ah …' I checked my arms and thighs. Yes, a bit burnt.

'We'd better get you home.'

'Yeah, I've had enough sun.' And enough beach time with Sharon Stone.

As I stood I swooned, and Jack had to support me. 'You haven't had any water, have you?' He checked out my full, untouched bottle.

'Yes. This is a new one,' I lied, but he didn't believe me.

BY THE TIME we got to Jack's and inside his house, the full extent of the burn, and the associated pain, and the dehydration, was starting to reveal itself. Joe was there, in the kitchen. He looked at me with shock, and then crossly at Jack, who seemed worried and guilty. I went to the bathroom, threw up, and stood in front of the mirror. I'd been aiming for a knock-out tan but instead, I was purple. My eyes were puffy with white circles around them from my sunglasses. At least the burn was only on my front, but it made me look even more ridiculous because my back was white. I wiped a hand across my mouth.

'You,' I told the mirror, 'are a fuckwit.'

When I came back to the kitchen, moving slowly so my top didn't rub the burn, Joe had snipped some aloe vera from the garden and was splitting it lengthways, exposing the gel inside. Gingerly, I pulled my T-shirt over my head so I was wearing just my bikini top and shorts. Joe handed a piece of aloe vera to Jack and told him to do my shoulders, which he did. I took some and rubbed the gel on my chest while Joe did my legs. But Jack kept slipping and scratching me with the barbs, which made me cry, so Joe waved him crossly away. Jack stood back to watch, and Shaz appeared from upstairs, freshly showered, smelling great. She wore a white singlet top and no bra. Sprayed-on shorts. The white showed off her deep tan exquisitely. And her nipples. Her hair was blonder.

'Hey, Black Jack.' She beckoned him. 'I wanna show you the new move I learned last night.'

Jack had the decency to hesitate. He looked at Joe. 'Do you need me for a minute?'

Did I?

Joe shook his head. I didn't get an opportunity to.

Jack went after Sharon, who was waiting for him on the lawn in the backyard.

'Black Jack?' I said to Joe.

'It was his call sign in the air force. No big deal.'

Joe stopped his aloe vera application and we watched them sparring. My mouth hung open.

'She's a kick-boxer,' explained Joe.

'Not much kicking going on there. Or boxing.'

Joe resumed his nursing. 'You don't need to worry about her, Erica.'

'I'm not.' I so was. But, I thought, seeing Jack and I aren't in a relationship, there's no reason why he shouldn't have another lover. Several lovers, in fact. Which meant I was free to do the same. Except I didn't want to.

After ten or fifteen minutes of pretend sex, the happy duo came back inside. I stood there, shiny and red, a glistening idiot in the kitchen. Joe worked around me, too polite to ask me to move. Shaz announced she was going for another shower.

Jack came up behind me and softly touched my shoulder, causing me to say, 'DON'T TOUCH ME!'

He jumped back, and I hobbled across the room to the sofa, where I very slowly sat on the edge of it.

Jack approached with caution, sat on the coffee table in front of me and reached for my hand. I glared at him. He took my middle finger between his thumb and forefinger, gave it a little squeeze. 'Stay the night.'

I huffed. 'No point staying. You can't touch me. Besides, you know what my mother's like.' I looked away.

'Stay for dinner, if you want.'

'No.'

'Why?'

Why … why … why? 'Because.'

He nodded. 'Alright.'

'I might just go home now.'

He nodded again and I didn't wait around, because I didn't want to see what Sharon Stone was wearing this time.

CHAPTER 10

Mum called me a silly little girl, told me she wouldn't be surprised if Jack called it off, and covered me with calamine lotion. She made me lie on my bed while she did it and I wasn't allowed to move for two hours. I don't know why two hours, but that's what she said. When I checked the mirror, the calamine lotion combined with the aloe vera had turned into a gluggy sludge. The sludge made it look like my skin was coming off in great, grey lumps.

By 11pm, I wanted to die. I googled sunburn remedies and roamed the house, looking for apple cider vinegar, cold tea-bags, listerine. I soaked my sheet in apple-cider-vinegar-laced water and wrapped it around me. I took pain killers. While my body was on fire, the sheet was freezing. In bed I turned, shivering, then checked to see if my skin had fallen off. The sheet became hot and clammy. I smelled like salt and vinegar chips. I got up, a hand over my mouth to keep the scream down to a squeak, threw the sheet into the bathtub and looked for another. I could find only a fitted cot sheet for some reason. My old cot sheet from thirty-plus years ago. Where were all the single sheets? I tucked myself into the cot sheet and fell asleep.

Axle woke me in the morning by sitting on my chest. His usually soft body felt like a belt sander. I screamed and he bolted.

Mum came in. 'What's wrong?'

'Sunburn,' I gasped.

'Silly girl.' She tsked. 'What in heaven's name are you wearing?'

I was lying on my back with legs crossed yoga style, cocooned in the tiny sheet. 'Cot sheet. Why don't we have any other single sheets?'

'I gave them to Saint Vincent de Paul.'

'Why did you keep the cot sheet?'

'You might need me to babysit. Your old cot's in the garage.'

'I don't have any babies.'

'One day you will.'

'Aren't my children allowed to stay here when they grow out of the cot?'

'Stop making such a fuss, Erica!'

Mum left. I unhooked my feet and shoulders, squeaking, and shuffled into the bathroom. My hair looked like a field mushroom. I set the shower to luke-warm and stood under it. Molten lava poured over me and I screamed. Mum didn't come to see if I was alright. After, I hovered the towel over my body, and checked the mirror. At least I was no longer purple. That was something. I took more pain killers and went into the kitchen.

Mum looked me over. 'What are you doing today?'

What was I doing? It was Sunday. I hadn't made plans with Jack and, actually, I didn't want to go to his house again. Not while Sharon Stone was staying there.

Mum plonked her old, hand-written recipe book on the kitchen counter. 'I could teach you to make my special secret recipe so you can hand it down to future generations.'

'What's your special secret recipe?'

She lowered her voice and cupped her hand around her mouth, protecting her secret. 'Spaghetti Bolognese.' She said it as though it were unholy, which perhaps it was to her with its foreign element, Mum being the illegitimate result of a one-night stand my grand-mother indulged in sixty-odd years ago. The man in question – my biological grandfather – had been a handsome, nameless Italian.

'What's so special about spag bog?'

'Really, dear, I wish you wouldn't use that kind of language.'

Please, God – I glanced at the ceiling – find me something else to do?

My phone rang – thank you, God. It was Lucy, my darling bestie, who told me she was helping Steve renovate my house and thought I should be there, too.

'What are you doing there? Hasn't he got the kids?'

'Nah. She wanted them back this morning.'

'Okay, I'll come. But I can't be out in the sun. I got burnt yesterday.'

'You idiot.'

I DROVE to Richmond and parked out the front of my house, shuffled down the passageway and through the back door. I took in the scene. Jack was there. Why was he there? I couldn't ask because I was speechless. He was shirtless, wearing a pair of old, ripped work shorts that fitted his bum in a way that was sinful and, oh my God, those thighs … The work he'd already been doing with Steve in the hot sun had caused him to sweat, which glistened on his tanned, bulging muscles and dripped down his face and, oh my God, those abs …

He gave me a smile and I swooned.

Lucy was sitting on a fold-out chair under an umbrella. I sat in the other, slowly.

'Hey, hon. Nice sunburn.'

'Ssh. I want to take in the view.'

'Gotcha.'

Mind you, Steve was also shirtless and pretty easy on the eye, but he's more like a brother than my brother, so I didn't perv at him. After a couple of minutes, we sighed in unison. I gave Lucy's leg a squeeze. 'You wouldn't believe what happened yesterday.'

'Try me.'

'Nope. You just wouldn't believe it.' I chuckled at the thought of

Lucy meeting Sharon Stone, knowing it was bound to happen one day and quite looking forward to it. I nodded at the boys. 'There's something very sexy about watching a man do what he's good at, don't you think?'

'Uh-huh.'

There was a concrete truck parked out the back, its massive barrel rolling, and the boys used a wheelbarrow to haul the concrete in and dump it in the holes. Steve gave instructions to Jack that seemed to involve not much more than a finger point and uttered word or two. I could imagine me there instead, needing detailed information – in writing, with colourful diagrams – before we started work and then stopping incessantly to confirm the instructions, blaming Steve when I got it wrong. And the concrete setting before any stumps got installed.

'I feel I should be helping.'

'Nah. For a start, you need to not go anywhere near that sun.' Lucy pointed at it, in case I wasn't sure which sun she was talking about.

'Why is Jack here?' I said.

'I couldn't manage the stumps.' She shrugged. 'Steve needed someone with muscles.'

'Jack's got nice muscles.'

'Almost as nice as Steve's.'

We grinned at each other.

'It's nice of Jack to come,' I said.

'Yep.' But it was a clipped 'yep'. Lucy does like Jack. She's saved his life twice (being the brilliant nurse she says she is) as he seems to regularly attain life-threatening, illegally-acquired injuries that require unofficial attention. But she worries he'll hurt me. And not just emotionally. My life's been pretty much in constant danger since the day I met Jack Jones.

CHAPTER 11

The boys finished their work so now my backyard was a forest of short, evenly spaced stumps upon which, Steve said, he'd attach things called bearers and on those, joists. 'Then I'll build the walls and lay the sheet flooring.'

I thought about the muddy footprints and as we watched the boys clean up, I told Lucy about it. But I didn't mention the human shape at the window because I was determined, possibly as a result of denial, that it was unrelated. 'It looked like someone had been inside.'

'Tell Jack.'

'No way! He won't let me leave Mum's. He'll give me an armed bodyguard.'

Jack and Steve had rivers of dirt down their arms and legs and all over their faces. They washed under the tap. I was glad I wasn't a guy, feeling obliged and even compelled to do such stinky work.

Jack took an empty bucket, turned it over and sat on it.

Lucy said, 'Erica said someone broke in here on Friday.'

'Lucy!'

Jack frowned. 'Why didn't you tell me?'

Steve sat on his esky, checked out my sunburn. 'You do know about skin cancer, don't you?'

'Let's all pick on Erica,' I huffed and crossed my arms tightly, which caused me to groan in pain. I uncrossed them.

'Tell me what happened,' said Jack.

'No-one broke in.' I gave Lucy a look, and told him about the footprints inside. 'It was probably some kid.'

'So someone broke in.'

'No, it wasn't like that.'

'Erica, I don't want you coming back without Steve being here.'

I pursed my lips, scowling at Lucy for dobbing on me. She gave me a smug smile.

Jack said, 'Understood?'

I looked away.

'Erica, I don't want you coming here without Steve or me. Is that clear?'

'Geez, okay. Bloody hell.'

Jack said to Steve, 'If you have any suspicions, call me. Or the police.'

Steve nodded, looking worried. Jack went inside to look for the footprints, which I'd vacuumed up.

Steve packed up his truck, shook hands with Jack. There was the added grip of the shoulder as well, which in bloke language I think means something. He swept Lucy out of her chair and she shrieked, 'Yuck! You stink! You're filthy!' but it was all said between coughs of laughter.

He carried Luce out to his car. 'Can you guys lock the gates? We're going home for a shower.'

Jack gave me a look that made my knees wobble, and made his way through stump-land to lock the gates.

And I remembered my gun, which was still in the bottom of my laundry hamper. Jack would surely want to check on it. I slipped inside, rushed to my bedroom and started rifling through the dirty laundry. As I was bending over the basket Jack snuck up behind me and gripped my hips.

I let out a stump-splitting shriek, bolting upright, causing me to shriek again from the sunburn pain. I turned on Jack. 'You scared me! I thought you were Shane McGann!'

'Why would you think that when I'm here and he's in jail?'

'I'm still traumatised.' I walked past him, heading for the door.

He snagged my top. 'I want to talk to you.'

'Let's talk out here.'

He pulled me close, but gently. 'I meant it when I said stay away from here.'

I glanced at the laundry hamper. 'Sure, no worries. Let's go.' I pushed away. He pulled me back. 'Ow! Sunburn!'

But he gave me a sexy smile. 'You, me, alone at last.' He nodded at the bed. 'Join the dots on that.'

'You hate my bed.'

'I love it. True.'

'You're all dirty.' I twisted out of his grip and headed down the passage, hoping he'd follow.

He did, but grabbed my wrist, spun me into his arms and kissed me. I had to pretend not to like it, groaning from the pain, or maybe it was pleasure. I kissed him back, unable to resist, my arms around his neck, whimpering. The pain and fear took priority, though; the fear that he'd find my gun in a purple sock in my laundry hamper, and I squirmed, pushing away but not hard enough to put any distance between us.

'Come on,' he muttered, 'you love dirty, sweaty sex.' He gently bit my lip. This was true – I did love dirty, sweaty sex with Jack Jones. Any kind, in fact, and under other circumstances he wouldn't have to work so hard. He wouldn't have had to work at all because I would have already thrown myself naked on the bed.

Holding my wrist, he towed me toward the bedroom.

I screamed.

He spun, hand on his heart. 'Now what?'

'There was a huge spider!'

He looked around, up at the ceiling. 'Where?'

'It went down there.' I pointed toward the back door.

'It's gone outside.'

'No, it hasn't. I'm sure it's hiding, waiting for me to move back in.'

'For God's sake.' He headed down the passage, inspecting the walls and ceiling. 'Here it is.'

What? I followed him, which I'd never normally do – move *toward* a spider – but I didn't believe he'd actually found one.

He opened the back door and threw something. 'All gone.'

'Let me see.'

He barred my way. 'It's gone.'

'I don't believe you.'

He put his hands on his hips. 'Are you avoiding me?'

'No!' I checked my watch. 'Mum's expecting me for dinner.'

'What time is it?'

'Three-thirty.'

He moved in. 'Plenty of time.'

'I've got sunburn. I've got my period!'

'Why didn't you say so before?'

'Um. I was embarrassed.'

'Why would you be embarrassed … ah, that explains it.'

'Explains what?'

'Why you were so touchy yesterday.'

'That's right! PMT.' I waved my hand. 'Can't fool you, Jack Jones.' I gave him a shove. 'Let's go.'

So I DIDN'T GET to move my gun, after all. I managed to push Jack out the front door without him asking about it. I think he had other things on his mind – a cold shower maybe. He followed me down Punt Road until I turned onto the freeway, and then I couldn't be bothered back-tracking. I went to Mum's and he went to his house. I'd considered just picking up my entire laundry hamper and bringing it with me, but I couldn't have the gun at Mum's. No way. Imagine if she found it! And she would, because she'd want to do my laundry. She'd think I wouldn't do it properly.

When I walked in the door, Mum said, 'Just in time. You can make the sticky date pudding. I'll teach you.'

She had a packet of dates spread out on the chopping board.

'They look like cockroaches,' I said.

'Oh, you always do that.'

Do what?

'Why don't you ever invite Jack for tea?' she said.

Poor Mum has never really understood my relationship with Jack. When we first met and he recruited me to the Team, I had to pretend he was my boyfriend. And the notion kind of stuck for people who know me, but don't know about the Team. Mainly because he keeps turning up in my life, and because I keep turning up in his bed.

'He can't. He's ... busy.'

'Not every evening, surely.'

'Yeah. He is.'

I walked away, ignoring Mum when she called after me, 'What about the sticky date pudding?'

STEVE AND LUCY came to dinner, which meant we were allowed to have wine, and having Steve and Lucy there distracted me from the horror of the things my mother says. And Dad's farting. When we were growing up, Steve spent as much time at Mum and Dad's as he did at his own place, and Lucy had appeared as my new bestie when we'd just started high school, only thirteen years old, so she, too, was comfortable there. Mum giggled like a schoolgirl with Steve in the room. I think she'd hoped I'd marry him when we grew up. But when you've seen what someone else has done in their nappy, it kind of puts you off. Likewise for him, no doubt. But anyway, Mum thinks Jack is perfect. Most people think he is. I know better, though. I know he's in pain. One day I'll sort that out, I'd decided.

'Why don't you get Lucy to show you how she does her hair?' Mum said.

'Are you talking to Steve?' I said.

Lucy laughed.

'I'm talking to you.'

'Really? Well, Lucy's hair is about as opposite to mine as any hair could possibly be.'

'Mrs J, my hair's so fine,' said Luce.

Dad turned the telly on, bless him. He keeps an old portable on the buffet in the dining room so he doesn't have to listen to Mum crapping on about whatever.

'We don't want the television, Tom. We're having tantalising conversation.'

'It's not tantalising, or even titillating,' I said. 'It's annoying.'

We watched the news. The cyclone was right up there with top stories, and there was a radar image of it; a great, white circle on an otherwise clear, dark blue background. Cyclone *Sharon* was still a Category 5, and still on course for Port Hedland.

Steve said to me, 'Have your rigs been evacuated?'

'That's the plan. It's a monster.'

On Monday morning I was exhausted from lack of sleep. I'd tossed, turned and fallen out of bed, which I forgot wasn't queen size, screaming from the sunburn pain.

Mum was in the shower when I wanted it. Why did she get up so early? She didn't have to go anywhere or do anything. I lay in bed with Axle while I waited, and she finally stuck her head in my door. 'You should be up by now! It's a work day, you know.'

'I'm waiting for the shower.'

'Well, you could be making your lunch while you wait. Plenty of things to do.'

Making my lunch? I think the last packed lunch I had was a Vegemite sandwich and apple, paired nicely with a box of juice.

I walked into the bathroom. Mum was putting her make-up on.

'Have you finished?'

'Just a few minutes.' She powdered her nose.

I sighed and went to the kitchen, made a cup of tea. Out the back I could see Mrs Booth's black cat sitting on the fence, staring at our house. It looked just like Axle, except Axle wasn't evil.

By the time I'd had my shower, dressed and come into the kitchen, Mum had her old orange crock-pot going with tonight's dinner in it.

She wore an apron, her hair was flawlessly coiffed, coral lippy outlined to perfection.

I put bread in the toaster, which had been a wedding present some thirty-five years earlier and still sparkled like a brand newie. I could see Mum's reflection in it. She stood behind me, watching, lips pursed.

'Hmm.'

I looked at her. 'What?'

'Nothing.'

'Oh, for God's sake.' I turned away, put the kettle on.

'I do wish you wouldn't blaspheme, Erica.'

I didn't respond.

'Alright, I'll tell you. It's your hair. You need to do something with it.'

I faced her, fiddling with a curl, standing under the full glare of her scrutiny. When Mum doesn't actually comment on my appearance I can pretend she's not giving me the thorough once-over, even though I know she is.

'What do you suggest?' May as well give her carte blanche, she'll tell me anyway. And, a rare thing, I agreed with her. Since the haircut from hell about eight months ago, I lost sleep over it. If I didn't tame it with a gallon of product, hello broccoli.

'I've been speaking with Joseph, my hairdresser in Carnegie. He says you can get hair extensions.'

I held up a hand. 'No.'

'You can get extra hair attached.'

'Not having this conversation, Mum.'

'Once it's attached, they perm it to match your curls!'

I turned my back, buttered my toast. 'Let's talk about the weather.'

'Well, if you won't get hair extensions …' I could hear her shuffling about behind me. I glanced over my shoulder. She pulled a Myer bag from her Tupperware cupboard. And from that bag, a wig. One that looked just like my hair before I chopped it all off. 'Ta da!' She waved the wig around.

'Did you buy that?'

'Yes, dear.' She held it out. 'It was very expensive, I have to say. But worth it in the long run, I think.'

'I'm not wearing it.'

'Just try it on.' She jiggled it. 'Look how bouncy!'

'No, Mum.'

'But this is how your hair used to look! I'm sure Jack would propose if you had long hair again.'

'I think I'm more than just a head of hair to Jack. He does actually like me as a person.' Maybe not. 'Besides, I don't want to get married again. I keep telling you.' I say it, so it must be true.

She came at me with the wig. 'Just try it on.'

I ducked out of her way. 'No.'

She tried to shove it on my head.

'Mum!'

She wouldn't stop. I ran away. She came after me. I grabbed my bag and ran out of the house. She chased me onto the street to my car.

'You haven't cleaned your teeth!'

I zoomed away, watching her in the rear-view mirror, standing in the middle of the road, arms forming a heart shape as she pointed to her head, like if she didn't point, I might not notice that she was now wearing the wig.

CHAPTER 13

I was at my desk before eight, a rare thing indeed. Marcus inspected my sunburn. 'It'll fade to a fab tan, darling.'

'What's the latest on the cylone?'

'On top of our rigs —' he checked his watch '— right about now.'

'Did we evacuate?'

'Uh-huh. Skeleton staff only.'

It was board meeting day – my favourite – so Rosalind would soon be disappearing upstairs. She called me into her office, and tossed a large envelope across her desk.

'This is the graduate. Her curriculum vitae.'

'Graduate?'

'You might want to read it. She'll be here at nine.'

I picked up the envelope and peered inside. 'What graduate?'

She clicked her tongue, rolled her eyes. 'We *discussed* this, Erica.'

We so didn't.

She informed me, with a big sigh and another eye-roll, as though she resented wasting precious oxygen on me, 'We have a PR graduate starting. I want you to look after her. Mentor her.'

'Hold on, is this the graduate position I'm meant to be interviewing for after the tennis?'

'Where *is* that document?' She flipped through the papers on her desk, already thinking about the next thing. 'She's starting today. Off you go.' She shooed me.

I dared to keep standing there. 'What about the other applicants?'

Rosalind glared at me. I turned and left, made a beeline for Marcus in the kitchen. I flapped the envelope in his face.

'Graduate!'

'I know, honey. Painful, isn't it?'

'Why wasn't I told?'

'Wait, you didn't know?'

'No! Last I knew, we'd advertised and were starting interviews after the tennis.'

'God, she's a cow.'

'She's not a cow. Cows are *nice*, Marcus.' I stomped back to my desk and opened the envelope with the graduate's résumé inside.

Charlotte Johnson was her name. There was a photo of the girl. She'd provided her age, which she said was twenty-five. Quite old for a PR graduate – and, in fact, she looked older than twenty-five – but then, people do go back to school. Her mousy hair was pulled back in a ponytail. She was without make-up and quite pretty in a plain kind of way. Charlotte had completed a Bachelor of Arts (Public Relations) degree and passed all subjects with high distinctions. She listed her 'interests and hobbies' as tennis and cooking. Well, there was one thing we had in common. Although I preferred to watch tennis than play it.

Marcus propped on my desk. 'I hate board meeting day. They're so demanding.'

I stared at Charlotte's résumé.

He gave me a tickle under the chin. 'Don't worry. I'll help keep her occupied.'

'Who did the interviewing?'

'Rosalind. While you were meeting with the Tennis people. But there was only one applicant.'

'What? Why? This role should have attracted heaps.'

He shrugged. 'One got sick, someone's dog died, another moved interstate…'

'Well, this one's certainly qualified.'

'Get her to do your filing.'

Great idea! In fact, I thought, Charlotte could do all the crappy things I don't like doing. She could pretend to be me and go live with my mother.

At 8:45am I got a call from reception: 'Charlotte Johnson here to see you.'

In the lobby, on the far side of the vast, granite space, Charlotte sat primly on the edge of an uncomfortable designer bench, hands clasped on her lap. She looked just as she did in the photo, with her hair in a ponytail and face without make-up. When she saw me approaching she stood, gathered her bag and mirrored my stride across the marble floor.

'Hi, Charlotte? I'm Erica. Welcome to Dega.' I held out my hand.

Charlotte gave it a good shake. 'Thank you for employing me,' she said with confidence but she was bright red in the face, embarrassed. Or maybe …

'Are you sunburnt?' I said.

'Yes. I went to the beach on Saturday.'

'Oh, me, too! Which beach did you go to?'

'St Kilda. You?'

'Same. Maybe we saw each other without realising.'

'It was pretty crowded.'

'Let's get you settled in, shall we?'

Charlotte followed me to the lifts.

'Did you drive?' I said as we waited.

'I came on the train.'

'I prefer the train.' I smiled at Charlotte and she smiled back.

The lift whizzed us north and we stood side by side, watching the numbers as they lit up in turn.

Charlotte said, 'I saw you in the paper.'

'Oh, right. Emilio's lunch.'

'You're lucky. Getting to meet Emilio Mendez.'

'I suppose.' We reached our floor. 'Here we are!'

At my desk I pulled up a visitor's chair and offered it to her. It was where she'd have to sit until I found another spot.

'Well,' I said and smiled.

'Well,' she said and smiled.

I stood and she stood. 'Let me show you the ladies'.' After a few introductions and a tour of the toilets, the kitchen, Rosalind's office, the rest of the media and investor relations team, including Marcus's desk where he carried on and I laughed and Charlotte laughed, it was nine-thirty. Only another eight hours till home time, during which Charlotte Johnson would presumably learn something.

I INVITED CHARLOTTE TO LUNCH, and made sure I had my corporate credit card with me. I'd booked a table at a café on the river, just down from the Dega building in Southbank. I ordered a glass of mineral water; Charlotte asked for Perrier. Gawd. Fussypants. We scanned the menu. I asked the waiter for his recommendation.

'The seafood risotto's really good.'

'Sounds good to me.'

'And me,' Charlotte said. 'But I want mine without mussels.'

'So, tell me about yourself. Your family? Where did you grow up?'

'East Malvern.'

'Really? Me, too. Well, Chadstone.'

'I loved living near the shopping centre.'

'It was the best.' Chadstone Shopping Centre – Chaddy – is the shopping mecca of the southern hemisphere, and I grew up walking distance from it. 'I'm living back there at the moment. My house is being renovated.'

She nodded. 'Lucky.'

I didn't mention the issues around living with my mother. Charlotte waited for me to make a move on conversation, so I prattled on about myself, telling her boring things about my family, including the issues around living with my mother. I told her how I got the job at Dega and all about my cat. I even complained to her about

Sharon Stone and she sat there, sipping her Perrier, listening politely.

Our meals came, I talked and ate, Charlotte listened and ate, and we'd just finished when I got a phone call from Rosalind, who was supposed to be at the board meeting.

'Hi, Rosalind?'

'You need to get back here *now*.' She hung up.

It wasn't unusual for Rosalind to speak to me like I wasn't worth the effort, and not even unusual for her to be abrupt, but it was unusual for her to leave the board meeting and want to see me. *Need* to see me. Something was very wrong.

CHAPTER 14

e walked into the building; the atmosphere had changed. Something gripped my stomach – a sense of thrill and panic at the same time. I planted Charlotte at my desk and shoved the company policy and procedures manual in her hands, telling her I'd be back.

I stuck my head in Rosalind's office. 'What's wrong?'

Her hands were flying over her desk. 'What's *wrong*? Do you live under a rock? A rig's blown up. One of *ours*! God, I don't need this. I don't need this!'

'An oil rig? Where? How? Was anyone hurt?'

'We need a media release. We need a miracle!'

'I'll call Laura.' Laura worked for the PR company we used when things were big. Bigger than we could handle. They were experts in crisis control.

Marcus rushed in with Rosalind's coffee and a sandwich. He gave me raised eyebrows and a pursed mouth. The board meeting had presumably been cancelled.

'Don't you go calling Laura,' Rosalind said, phone to her ear. 'John doesn't want them involved … Grant!' Her voice turned to honey. 'You're first on my list, of course …'

I went back out to find Charlotte sitting with the manual closed on her lap, watching me. I left her and went looking for Marcus, who was at his desk.

'Give me a quick run down.'

He turned from his computer, eyes shining, in love with the drama.

'Well, there was only skeleton staff, six people. We don't know yet if anyone was hurt but the explosion coincided with the cyclone, so that's what we're going with, honey. Better than admitting we might have done something wrong.'

'We're saying the cyclone somehow caused the explosion?'

'Uh-huh.'

'Do we know if that's even possible?'

Marcus shrugged. 'I love the name *Sharon* for a cyclone, don't you?'

I went back to my desk. My phone was ringing and before I could get to it, Charlotte picked it up. 'Media and investor relations, Charlotte Johnson speaking.' I snatched the phone off her. It was the *Herald Sun*.

'No news yet. Something to do with the cyclone. We're investigating ... you're first on my list when we get something ... no, skeleton staff only ...'

I spent the next hour on the phone with the media. I hung up from a call with *The West Australian* and watched my phone, waiting for it to ring again. The other two members of our team were taking calls from investors and the public. Rosalind would talk to the share registry people; JD and the chairman would handle the super VIPs, the major shareholders. My phone was silent.

I turned to Charlotte. She'd lined up the pens, paper clips, stapler, sticky-tape dispenser, post-it notes, etc. in neat, orderly rows. The paper clips especially were impressive. Little soldiers. Hmm. Useful. As I stood, my jacket swished across the desk, disturbing the line of paper clips.

'Sorry.'

Charlotte stared at her destroyed artwork.

'Have you read any of the manual?'

She looked up at me.

'Okay, well, why don't you put that away for now. You can watch how we handle a crisis.'

I explained to Charlotte what I knew about the explosion, adding that this wasn't normal, in case she worried about regular blasts and panic around the office. I sent her home at 5pm and started my day's work. Mum called my mobile at 5:45.

'I'm just dishing up.'

'Dinner? It's not even six o'clock.'

'Are you nearly home?'

'Mum, no, I won't … it's been a terrible day at work. I'll be here for ages yet.'

'Well, what time? Just so I know.'

'Mum, please.'

She huffed into the phone.

I drew in a deep breath. 'Just … please don't allow for me at meal times. I can take care of myself.'

We hung up, hopefully still friends. Taking care of myself would mean McDonald's drive-thru and I'd prefer Mum's cooking, but I needed her to back off.

At six o'clock, John Degraves, most of the company execs, a scattering of minions and the entire media and investor relations department met in the boardroom to watch the news. The explosion was top story. JD had been given a few seconds of airtime where he said the company was investigating the explosion, however, 'all evidence points to a terrible accident quite beyond Dega Oil's control'. What evidence? Because of the cyclone, no-one had been able to get out to the rig to investigate.

They'd interviewed Martin McGann, CEO of Australia's second biggest company, Mintin Mining. He also happened to be JD's arch-enemy and father of the very nasty Shane. Mr McGann despised John Degraves, for lots of reasons. JD had a bigger company, bigger house, better-looking wife, children who didn't go to jail. JD had won the major sponsorship for the tennis, when Mintin Mining had wanted it.

Martin was telling the journalist that this was 'clearly a cover-up'.

That responsibility and fault lay firmly with Dega Oil, and that 'cyclones do not cause explosions on oil rigs that are maintained to industry standards'. He'd added a brief laugh, as though the very idea of an explosion-causing cyclone was ludicrous.

But he had a point. How could a cyclone cause an explosion on an oil rig?

CHAPTER 15

*I*t was after ten o'clock when I packed up my desk. Marcus had left at nine. Rosalind was still there, probably waiting for everyone to disappear so she could hang upside-down from the ceiling. I stuck my head in her door and said I was going. She gave me a wave without looking up, and without a word of farewell.

In the car I got teary. It'd been a big day. We still hadn't had the full story from the oil rig because no-one had been able to get out there. *Sharon* was a slow-moving monster and hadn't yet crossed the coast-line; it was expected to do so overnight. Lots of people lived in that area. Someone had called in from the rig to say the six people on board were all safe, but they hadn't been able to check the damage from the explosion. So no injuries or deaths. There'd been a fire but the skyscraper waves crashing over the rig had apparently put it out. I'd been able to report all that to the media, and that was something. We wouldn't know about oil spills until maybe tomorrow.

I decided that ten-thirty wasn't too late to call Jack. I needed to talk to someone who'd understand about explosions and disaster. I wanted to hear his voice. I dialled his mobile and put mine on loud-speaker, resting it on my leg as I drove. It went straight to voicemail so I called the house phone, hoping I didn't wake Joe. I did wake Joe.

He was sleepy sounding. Maybe Jack was already in bed? Next door to Shaz. She was probably lying there, trying to decide if she should sneak into his room and jump on him. Like I used to do.

'Sorry, Joe, it's me. I woke you.'

'It's alright.' He yawned.

'Jack must be in bed?'

'I wouldn't know.'

Oh. 'Um, is he out?'

'He's in WA.'

'What? Why?'

Another yawn and I felt a bit guilty but not enough to let him go back to sleep. Not when I wanted to know what Jack was doing on the other side of the country.

'JD sent him to investigate the explosion.'

'Why? I mean, why Jack?'

'Because … it might not have been an accident.'

'You mean, deliberate?'

'Maybe.'

'Like, terrorists or something?'

'Something like that.'

'Shit.'

'Yeah.'

More brain chewing. I should let Joe go back to sleep. But the cyclone …

'Joe, how could he fly there with the cyclone?'

'They had to fly to Broome —'

'*They?*'

'— then Sharon flew them as close as they could get and they drove the rest of the way.'

'What do you mean she flew them?'

'Helicopter.'

'Sharon's a *helicopter* pilot?'

Yawn. 'Yeah.'

'Is that how she knows Jack? She was a helicopter pilot in the air force?'

'US Navy. She flew hornets.'

'What's a hornet?'

'F/A-18.'

Silence from me.

'Did you ever see *Top Gun*?'

Top Gun ... 'I'm going to kill myself.'

Joe let out a laugh. 'Like I said, you don't need to worry about Sharon.'

I TRIED to sneak into the house but Mum was still up, waiting for me in her hair rollers and dressing gown, defrosting the fridge. The same fridge she used to defrost when I came home after midnight when I was eighteen. She really needed a new fridge. A frost-free one.

Mum turned on me. 'You could have called.'

'I didn't know you'd still be up.'

'I thought you were dead!'

'Why didn't you try to call me if you thought I was dead?'

'What time do you call this?' She pointed at the clock, which said 11pm. 'Coming home from work at midnight!'

I plonked my bag on the kitchen bench. 'It's just ... this is what my work's like, Mum. Sometimes I need to work late.'

'Well, we may as well have a cup of tea.' She put the kettle on.

MUM HAD LEFT the wig on my bed. She'd laid it out with her favourite dress of mine, an empty body under the headless hair. She'd even set a pair of high heels on the floor so I could get the full picture. It's a wonder gloves and hat weren't included. I shut my bedroom door, picked up the wig and tried it on. I wriggled it around, poked my escaping curls under. It did look nice, actually. When my hair's long it looks pretty good. The weight of it pulls the curls out so they're soft ringlets, rather than tight little spirals as they are now. I should make more effort, I thought. I should straighten my hair. I wondered if you could straighten a wig. Why not? I could straighten the wig and wear it so I didn't have to worry about my own hair. It'd be so much easier. But if I turned up at work with hair suddenly twelve inches longer, people would guess it wasn't real. Imagine Marcus! He'd give me hell, unless he thought it looked real, and fab, then he might think it was okay. I suppose I could cut the wig to the length my hair is now and wear it. Maybe no-one would guess. I could get it done professionally at my hairdresser in Richmond.

I said to Axle, who was asleep in the middle of my bed, 'What do you think? Should I get the wig straightened and cut?' No response. I leaned in and tickled behind his ear. Without opening his eyes, he stretched his front legs and paws, claws extended, then curled up and went back to ignoring me.

'I bet if I was Jack Jones you'd have something to say.'

Nothing.

CHAPTER 16

I lay in the dark in my single bed, thinking about the wig and if Jack would notice or mind. I supposed he would if we were in the throes of passion and he accidentally pulled it off. Surprise! There was a bit of occasional hair pulling when we were in bed together. And spanking. Not really. Well, a bit.

I huffed a huge sigh. I missed Jack. Black bloody Jack and Sharon bloody Stone, on a romantic holiday together in Western Australia. I sat up, turned on my bedside lamp and opened my laptop. I googled images of hornets. A whole lot of bees came up. I googled 'hornet aircraft' and there they were. Images of F/A-18 hornets landing on big ships, taking off from big ships, bursting through the sound barrier. Those sound barrier pics were pretty awesome. So this was the plane Sharon used to fly in the US Navy. She was a fighter pilot. Holy crapping hell. Jack must be impressed. If I didn't hate her so much, I'd be super impressed. If he was Black Jack I wondered what her call sign was.

I checked the news to see the latest on the weather in Port Hedland. They were bracing for the other *Sharon*. Maybe not so romantic there at the mo. I checked the time. Nearly midnight here, so only 9pm in WA. Not too late. I tried Jack's mobile again. Straight to voicemail, but I didn't leave a message. I googled hotels in Port Hedland, and checked the images. Lots of photos popped up, even ones guests had posted. There was a close-up of a toilet with brown marks in it. Jack wouldn't stay there. I called the Esplanade. It looked like the best one. And it looked romantic.

Bingo. They put me through and as the phone in Jack's room started to ring, my heart started to pound. Why was I calling him? Because I wanted to make sure my friend was safe in the cyclone? Because I have Team business to discuss? Because I'm jealous and insecure?

'Hello?'

Sharon. Not the cyclone. Which means they put me through to the wrong room. The only explanation, of course. Both rooms were probably booked in Jack's name. Her accent was really annoying. I wondered what part of America she was from.

I cleared my throat. 'Hi, Sharon? It's Erica.'

'Who?'

'Erica, um, Jewell.'

Silence.

'Jack's … friend.'

'Oh, right.'

'They put me through to the wrong —'

'Stand by.'

There was a muffled, 'It's Erica Jewell,' and then I heard Jack say, 'Thanks, sexy, see you for breakfast,' and then he was talking to me. 'Hey.'

Sexy. I forced a smile, hoping it would penetrate the tone of my voice. 'Hi! How are you?' I tried to be chirpy, but I sounded like a baby bird.

'I'm fine. How are you?'

'Me? Oh, you know. Awful day at work.'

'I can imagine.'

'How's the cyclone?'

'Windy.'

'Right.' Now what should I say? Something sensible, something that sounds like, even though I'm terribly busy in my life, I've still got time to let my friend know I'm concerned about him? 'Sharon's a helicopter pilot?'

'She is.'

'Good trip?'

'Bumpy.'

Um ... 'Are you safe? In that hotel?'

'As safe as the others.'

'So ...'

He waited, letting me suffer through his silence. Waiting for me to get to the subject I was dancing around. The subject of him and Sharon being in a hotel together on the other side of the country. Don't do it, Erica. Don't go there.

'Joe told me about JD's theory. That it might not have been an accident.'

Good girl!

'Yeah. We're taking a look tomorrow.'

'You'll be able to get out to the rig?'

'Hopefully. Sharon's crossing the coast as we speak.'

Was he talking about the cyclone or was that a metaphor for something sexual?

'She should lose intensity,' he continued. 'We'll go out there first thing. I want to beat the locals to the scene.'

'You'll go in a helicopter?'

'That's right.'

'Does Sharon have her own room?'

'The cyclone?'

'Very funny.'

Silence.

'You called her sexy.'

'Sexy Texan was her call sign.'

'That's not very appropriate. She might get the wrong idea.'

'Erica, if Sharon and I wanted to have sex, we could do it at my house. We don't need to cross the country and stay in a four-star hotel.'

My mouth pursed of its own accord. I bet I looked like my mother right now. 'She doesn't have pubic hair.'

'Wha — How on *earth* would you know that?'

'It's pretty obvious. She shows it off.'

He burst out laughing and it took him about five minutes to stop. Finally, his voice warm and low, he said, 'You don't have much down there.'

'I've got *some*. I've got a landing strip.'

'So I know where to land? Maybe you should get landing lights tattooed on.'

'Ha, ha. It's not right, having no pubic hair. It's … indecent.'

'And now you sound like —'

'Don't you dare —'

'— your mother.'

I didn't say anything for ages as I sat there on my frilly pink bed, brooding, trying to justify my bad mood but unable to do so. He waited in irritating silence for me to speak. Eventually, I lightened my tone and said, 'So, it's not a nice hotel?'

'It's not Crown, no.'

I couldn't think of anything else to say that wasn't snippy and bitchy, so we said goodbye and hung up and I lay there thinking about Black Jack and Sexy Texan having sex in the cyclone. In the helicopter. On the oil rig. No, probably not on the oil rig.

CHAPTER 17

On my way to work the next morning, I was so distracted by everything I nearly got run over. It was so close, in fact, I had to throw myself back onto the footpath to avoid it. I landed on my bum, and my bag went sprawling, contents rolling across the pavement. I looked for the car in question, but it was peak hour, and the road was busy with traffic. A young guy helped me.

'That was close.'

'Yeah, I wasn't watching.'

'I saw it. I don't think the driver even realised you were there.'

'Hmm. Thanks.'

Maybe I was being paranoid but I couldn't help wondering if it was deliberate. Some enemy of Jack's? One of Shane McGann's friends? Although, if McGann wanted to hurt me, he'd do it in a much nastier way than hit and run. There'd be rape and throat-cutting, maybe concrete boots in the river. I thought I should tell Jack, but didn't want to worry him. He was probably flying out to the oil rig, anyway. I'd checked the weather earlier and it seemed *Sharon* had crossed the coast, had an orgasm, and was now lying back, calm and relaxed, with a cigarette. Sadly, a body had washed up on the beach at Port Hedland and they were trying to identify him. One of the cyclone's victims. There was also a dead dugong and I had to google dugong to find out what it was. Poor dugong. I hoped there wouldn't be more bodies – human or otherwise.

Charlotte was sitting at my desk when I arrived, busily typing something. She was fast, and used all her fingers.

'What are you doing?'

'Helping Marcus. He's overburdened with work.'

'Hmm. So am I. Could you help me with filing?'

'You'll have to wait.' And before I could respond: 'Your sunburn's looking better.'

'So's yours,' I said.

'I used calamine lotion.'

'Yeah? Me, too.'

WHILE CHARLOTTE HELPED MARCUS, I spent the morning on the phone with updates for the media, but the updates were only about the fact that the cyclone had passed and authorities could now access the rig to see what damage had been caused. I hadn't done any work on the tennis yet, and I needed to. After lunch, Rosalind called me in. She'd just returned from JD's office. She made me close the door and waved at the visitor's chair. I got pen and paper ready.

'We've just had news from the authorities. Three men were killed in the explosion.'

'But I thought —'

'And several of those sea creatures. The ugly ones.'

'Dugongs?'

'Once word is out, we're expecting backlash from the public about the dead people and from irritating environmentalists about those creatures. You need to be ready.'

'Who were the men? I thought our crew —'

'Fishermen or something.'

'Why would fishermen be out in a cyclone?'

She glared at me. 'How on earth would I know such a thing?'

'What about oil spills?'

'We don't know yet. Now, go write a media release.' As I walked out of her office, she said, 'That girl, the graduate – I like her.'

BY LATE THAT DAY, Dega Oil had announced the awful news that three fishermen had been killed in the explosion, and that Dega was very sad to advise also that some dugongs had been lost. We said the authorities were yet to determine the identity of the fishermen, and the cause of the explosion, but that Dega was encouraging the authorities to investigate the fishermen's reasons for being in a boat near our rig during a dangerous and well-publicised cyclone. I was busting to call Jack, but didn't in case he thought I was being clingy, which I was. I called Joe instead, who told me Jack had been out to the rig and was coming home tomorrow.

'Joe, are we thinking those fishermen had something to do with the explosion?'

'JD thinks so.'

'A terrorist attack?'

'Maybe.'

'Did you see what Martin McGann said on the news?'

'Yeah.'

'What does Jack think?'

'Too soon to make a call on it.'

I thought about it for a minute. Joe waited with inexhaustible patience, as he does. Finally, I said, 'It would be good if Dega wasn't at fault.'

'Yeah, but we don't want terrorists.'

'No. No, of course. Thanks, Joe.'

'See ya.'

He didn't mention Sharon. Joe's so wise.

CHAPTER 18

The next morning, something we hadn't expected happened: backlash from Tennis Oz. They called me, said if the tennis wasn't so close to starting, they'd sack us as sponsors. They didn't want to be associated with an awful, careless, environmentally unfriendly oil company. They were furious and said they'd be calling JD. I didn't know what they thought JD could do. No-one could undo what was done.

In the afternoon, JD wanted to see me in his office.

'More news on the explosion?' I asked him.

'Not yet, but that's not why I called you here. I wanted to let you know there may be an opportunity for you, and glean your interest.'

'For me? I thought —'

'That's right. You know that Dega has a succession plan, of course.'

'Ah, yes.' I suppose. I'd never thought that I might be part of it, though. I sat forward slightly.

'I'm looking at splitting the media and investor relations role. I want you to manage the public relations side of it. It would be a promotion for you, of course, and you'd report directly to me.' He smiled.

I didn't know what to say to that. I sat there mute, but inside I was fizzing. What about Rosalind? Who cares!

'It all depends on the tennis, though. As to whether the restructure goes ahead. Of course you'd realise that.'

'Of course.' Why?

He then launched into a speech about the explosion, telling me how terrible the whole business was, that the fishermen were very suspicious as far as he was concerned and he intended getting to the bottom of that. He repeated what I already knew about the outraged public and environmentalists because of the dugongs, blah blah blah, and now, to make things worse, Tennis Oz was calling for some kind of fix. But what could we do?

'There's an opportunity for us,' he said. 'A wonderful opportunity.'

'Oh?'

'Emilio Mendez.'

'Emilio Mendez?'

'That's right. As you know, Emilio's never won the Australian Open, and doing so would make him world number one.'

'Yes, everyone wants him to win.'

'That's right!' he said, like I was a child catching on to something important like tying shoe laces. 'Especially as he's now an Australian citizen. Imagine how wonderful that would be.'

'Yes. Wonderful.'

'And here at Dega, we also want him to win.'

'Yes. We're one of his sponsors.'

'Partly because of that. But mainly because it'll put Dega's name in a positive light, and distract the public —' he waved his hand, '— make them happy.'

'Oh, of course.' A happy public is better than an axe-wielding one.

'We're not getting very good press at the minute.'

'No. No, we're not.'

'Share price is low.'

'Yes.'

'The public is becoming more ... environmentally aware. Unfortunately, they're under the misconception that our type of business can simply be replaced. God knows what with.'

Sun? Wind? Water? I nodded.

'But of course that's a ridiculous notion.'

'Of course.'

'This country's economy relies on companies like Dega Oil!' He thumped his fist on the desk, stood and paced around his office. 'Do they realise how much we contribute to the health of this nation?'

Health or wealth? 'I'm sure they don't.'

JD returned to his chair, sat back in it, and made a steeple with his fingers in front of his face.

'I'll get to the point, Erica.' Thank God. 'Emilio and his managers are very upset about the public's overreaction to the explosion. Emilio can't focus on his game. He feels that the public associates him with Dega Oil.'

'Well, we're his sponsor —'

'And he's speaking with his lawyers about ending our association.' The mask slipped. JD's anxiety was now on full display, and I couldn't blame him. This was serious shit. He wiped a hand over his face. 'To be honest, Erica, we don't need this.'

'No. No, we don't.'

'We need to convince Emilio not to proceed.'

'How do you propose —'

'He likes you. See if you can talk him 'round. Help him understand that the business with the explosion will be dealt with quickly, and disappear. That he should concentrate on winning this tournament and leave the other business to us.' JD leaned in again. His voice hardened. 'I don't want to have to go the legal route. Emilio won't win. Our contract is watertight and it won't be pleasant for anyone.'

ROSALIND SURPRISED ME. She gave me a level look, one that almost made me feel she considered me human after all (which was actually worrying, considering the vampire thing). She sat back in her chair, looked away, thoughtful. Finally, she said to the wall, 'What on *earth* is

JD thinking, approaching you directly about this?' It was nice to see her angry with someone else, but then she narrowed her eyes, looking me over as though she might somehow find that the fault did, in fact, lie with me. 'I'll go see him.' She stood, wafted past me and out her office door.

I sat there for a minute, not sure what to do. She'd never left me like this, sitting in her office. Usually, I'd be dismissed. I stood cautiously, approached the door carefully, but she reappeared suddenly and silently, pushing past me to her desk, where she picked up a file and left again. Did she even see me there? Who knows? But her sudden reappearance had caused me to jump back, which caused me to bump the printer on the credenza, which had dislodged the paper sitting in the print tray and sent it floating to the floor. As I picked it up I noticed it was an email from JD to Rosalind. I didn't *mean* to read it, but one word stood out: 'relocation'. I checked over my shoulder, then read: ... *if all goes well with the tennis, I'd like to talk further about the role we discussed, which would require your relocation to Sydney* ... No chance to read any more because there she was again, standing at the door, glaring at me.

'Lucky I came back!' She snatched the paper from my hand.

'Sorry, it was on the floor —'

'That's all.' She waved her hand and as I left her office, I could hear her on the phone to Marcus, asking him to reschedule an appointment.

If all goes well with the tennis ...

Rosalind eventually went to see JD. Afterwards, she informed me that I needed to go see Emilio, pronto. Yes, I did want to see Emilio, but on the tennis court, or on the other side of a dining table. I wouldn't even mind getting a glimpse of him in the shower. But where I didn't want to see Emilio Mendez was on the other side of a boardroom table in a lawyer's office. I blew out sharply, felt the sweat prick my armpits. Bloody hell.

I CALLED TERESA, Emilio's manager, that afternoon.

She wasn't interested in pleasantries. 'We do not want meetings with your lawyers.'

'No, just me.'

'One minute.' She spoke with someone in Spanish. I heard her say 'Emily'. She came back on the line. 'Please come to this hotel tomorrow at eleven a.m.'

CHAPTER 19

In the morning I washed my hair and stood in front of the mirror. I felt exhausted at the thought of having to tackle it again so soon.

Mum came to the door. 'I need the bathroom, dear.'

'Can you wait? I'm going to be ages with my hair.'

'No, I can't wait! Aunty Betty's coming. I need to be ready.'

'I'm sure Betty won't care if you're not wearing lipstick.'

She looked at me like I might have lost my mind. I went into my bedroom. I couldn't turn up to my meeting with Emilio with horrible hair. I supposed I didn't have to go to work first. I could go straight to the hotel. I had time to do my hair properly. It'd only take, oh, four hours or so.

The Myer bag with the wig was still on my dressing table. I took it out and looked at it. And made a decision. I called my hairdresser on her mobile, waking her up. She knew how difficult my hair was. She was still fixing someone else's mistake from eight months ago. (That mistake may have been mine, made in a drunken stupor.)

'It's a matter of life and death,' I said.

'Hair always is, darling. Okay, I'll meet you at the salon in an hour.'

She was surprised when I presented the wig.

'Can you straighten it and cut it to match my hair?'

She shrugged. 'Okay.' And so she did.

When it was finished and fitted, I smiled at my reflection.

I KNOCKED on the door of Emilio Mendez's hotel suite. Beyond the door I could hear a man's voice, speaking rapidly and loudly in Spanish. The door opened and Teresa waved me into the room. 'Come in, Emily.'

'Actually, it's Erica.'

She shrugged. '*No importa.*' She pointed to the sofa. 'Please.'

But I remained standing, finding that my feet had suddenly taken root as I gawked at the vision pacing by the window, framed by Melbourne's skyline, shouting into the phone. He wore nothing but white shorts, a deep tan and his lucky charm. His glossy black hair was wild and like this, half-naked and probably straight out of bed, Emilio Mendez was absolutely beautiful.

He turned, saw me, and dropped the phone, which landed with a soft thud on the thick carpet. 'Emily, it is you.' He walked quickly across the room, gathered me in a tight hug.

My arms went around him, tentatively, and I patted his smooth back. 'Um, yes, I'm here.'

With his hands on my shoulders he held me away so he could look at me, let me see his anguish, then he pulled me in and kissed me on the mouth. It was a quick one, and possibly the way Spanish people greet each other, but it wasn't a dry peck either. Actually, it was soft and sexy enough to be inappropriate.

I stood there, a frozen kangaroo. Emilio's eyes were the blinding headlights: intense, full of fire, so *blue*, and I couldn't think of a single thing to say.

I blinked.

He released me. 'I am, how you say, disturbed by what is happening in the news.'

I cleared my throat, shook my head and tried to remember why I was here. I needed to talk to him. Talk about what?

'Come!' he said. 'We shall have herbal tea.' With a hand on my back, he pushed me across the room to the dining table where there was a china tea service. 'Please sit.' I sat. He poured me a cup of tea, speaking Spanish to Teresa. I took a sip. Camomile. Yuck. But it had the effect of smelling salts. It cleared my head.

Emilio said, 'You are wearing a wig, no?'

My head fogged up.

'Your hair is difficult, yes?' He gave me a quizzical look. 'I remember now.'

I fiddled with the ends of the wig and fumbled about for some words. 'It's … ah … I thought —'

'Tell me everything about yourself. I want to understand you.'

'Well —'

'I will tell you about me!'

What a fabulous idea. I sat back in my chair and let him talk. My senses returned in dribbles. Tiny spurts of intelligence arrived. But I did wish he'd put on a T-shirt. I found I was comparing his nipples to Jack's. The hair around them. Also, Jack has a series of fine scars on his left shoulder at the front, and a bullet-hole-shaped one at the back. Emilio had no scars that I could see.

'— and I am so happy to be living in Sydney now.'

'How nice.'

'*Si. Mi padre idiota* – my father – he make no life for *mi madre* in *España*.'

'Your mother's Australian, I believe.'

'*Si*. I hope, how you say, the testicles, they fall off.'

'Your father's?'

'*Si*.'

This was a great interview. I wished I'd taken this line of questioning at the lunch. 'Is your mother coming to Melbourne, Emilio? Will she watch you play?'

He muttered something in Spanish, looked away, waved his hand. 'It is fortunate I have Mother Teresa. And I have this.' He lifted the chain around his neck and showed me the renowned amulet. The one he purportedly couldn't live without. I leaned in to admire it. It was a flat gold disc with an inscription.

'This was a gift from *mi abuela* – my grandmama – for my sixteenth birthday. To bring me luck on the tennis court. It is *muy precioso*. Since I have it, I win! I cannot play without it.'

'It's lovely.' It looked like a one-dollar coin.

'It is, how you say, priceless.'

I nodded and smiled. Checked my watch. 'Well, Emilio, we really should —'

'Ah.' He put down his teacup and looked at me seriously. 'It is so nice to be with someone I can talk to.'

'I —'

'But now, we must discuss the business.'

'Yes. We must.' I glanced at Teresa, who was lounging on the sofa, reading a romance novel. One with a gorgeous topless man and a swooning woman in a Victorian dress.

Emilio took my left hand in both of his, leaned across the table. 'I cannot play the tennis. The people, they hate your company. And they hate me because I am your associate.'

I placed my right hand on his. 'Emilio, everyone loves you so much. The whole world wants you to win! This business with the explosion will go away soon enough. You know how the media works. It's headlines today, forgotten tomorrow.'

He nodded. 'Yes. Yes, that is how it works in the media. But people have been killed, Emily.'

'The deaths of those people are being investigated. We don't believe Dega Oil is at fault, not at all. We'll make sure this is public knowledge.'

'How can I play when the people, they are so angry?'

'But you'll make new headlines with your brilliant play! You support a wonderful charity and you're such fun for the media. In no time at all, the explosion will be forgotten. I promise.'

'Yes, I will make the headlines. The media, they love me.'

'*Everyone* loves you, like I said.' I gave him a big smile.

'You love me, Emily?' He winked, grinned.

God, those teeth were so perfect and white. 'What? Oh!' I giggled. 'Yes, I want you to win the Australian Open, more than anyone!'

'You are a very loyal person, no?'

'Ah, sure. Yes.' I sat back, gently removing my hand from his grip. 'You know what? I've got an idea. How about a game of tennis with someone … maybe a local celebrity? I'll make some calls, and we'll get the media there to record it. What do you say? It'll be so much fun.'

'I think that is a very good idea.'

'Fantastic! I'll go back to the office and make some calls. I'll let you know —'

'You will make the calls here.' He waved at the room. 'There is a telephone. You can sit there.' He pointed at the desk.

'Well …' I supposed I could call Marcus at the office, get him to email my contact list.

Emilio stood, took my hand again and pulled me across the room, to his bedroom. 'But first …'

I stopped, took my hand back. 'What are you doing?'

'You will help me decide what to wear, yes?'

'Me?'

'This one?' He plucked a white T-shirt with a Dega Oil logo off his bed and I rushed forward.

'Oh, yes, that one's perfect!'

Emilio sat on the bed, pulled on his shoes, and stuck a Dega Oil cap on his head.

While I waited for my contact list from Marcus, I stood at the window, pondering the life of the rich and famous and what it might be like. Imagine having staff! 'What would madam like for dinner?' And madam would say, waving her hand (with delicate portraits painted on each nail), 'Surprise me. But watch the carbs!' It'd be nice, I suppose. Could be like that, married to Jack Jones, lounging around, making calls when I wanted something. Or getting Joe to organise it. 'Joe, can you call my hairdresser to come urgently? My fringe needs a trim.'

'You will make the calls, Emily?'

'Huh?'

Emilio was standing there, adjusting his groin area.

'Oh, sure.' I sat at the desk, checked my phone. The contact list had come from my own email address, attached to a message from Charlotte telling me she'd finished taking shorthand from Rosalind and was typing some correspondence. Shorthand? Who takes shorthand? And who types *correspondence*? That's what my mother thinks still happens in offices.

I called Laura at our publicity company, asked her to find me a good-looking famous person to play tennis with Emilio Mendez, preferably today. She came back to me with a list of familiar names, most of whom were willing to drop everything for this opportunity. Especially the women.

'You're very popular, Emilio,' I said, holding up my handwritten list. 'You see? Everyone still loves you.'

'*Si?* They love me?' He sat on the edge of the sofa, elbows on knees, watching me, biting his nails. I wished he wouldn't. It was off-putting, having a beautiful man stare at me like that, sitting close, all wide-eyed. I felt an urge to give him a pat on the head.

I returned to my list and crossed off names of people who either weren't famous enough, weren't attractive enough, or weren't men. I chose a well-known Collingwood footballer, a super good-looking one. It was all set. Emilio Mendez and Robbie Dick would play tennis this afternoon, and the media would write about it, and everyone would forget the explosion, and life would be fantastic again. But as wonderful as it all sounded, there was a niggle in the back of my mind telling me that, although I shouldn't be alarmed, I should definitely stay alert.

CHAPTER 20

We arrived at Rod Laver Arena in a stretch limo driven by a chauffeur who looked like Danny DeVito. Inside the arena, Emilio introduced me to his coach.

'John, this is Emily.'

'Actually, it's —'

John the coach said, 'Fucking around with some slag again, Emilio?'

My mouth fell open.

'Come now,' said Emilio. 'Emily is no *puta*. You see? I will play the tennis with Robbie Dick and everyone will be happy.'

'This is bullshit,' mumbled John as he walked away.

Robbie Dick was being interviewed when we arrived at the practice court. I'd called all my Melbourne media contacts. There were lots of journos and photographers, even a television camera. Emilio certainly knew how to make an entrance, always arriving late so everyone could watch him walk into a room, onto a court.

'*Hola amigos!*' All heads turned.

I met Robbie Dick and, while I blushed at his size and beauty, he gushed over the chance to meet and play tennis with the great Emilio Mendez. The two men were interviewed together being all jokey and happy, and the ump called time for everyone to move off the courts so the game could begin.

The journos took their seats, photographers took up position and before I could find a shady spot to sit (there was none), Emilio approached, lifting his lucky charm from around his neck.

'You will take care of this for me, Emily?' He stood close. 'I cannot wear it when I play. I always leave it with someone I trust.'

'Oh, that's nice of you to say, Emilio.'

I held out my hand to take it, but he placed the chain around my neck. 'This is the safest place for it.'

'Alright. I'll look after it for you.'

Emilio kissed my cheek and before he could run off to play tennis, a journalist called out, 'What's your name, sweetheart?' A photographer stood next to him, camera aimed at us.

'Who, me? You don't need —'

'Emily!' said Emilio. 'Emilio and Emily!' He laughed and put his arm around me, posing for the camera.

'Actually —'

'Surname?' said the scribbling journo. I didn't know him. Probably from the *Herald Sun*, in place of my regular guy.

'You don't need my surname.'

'What is your surname?' said Emilio.

'Emilio,' I whispered so softly he had to put his ear near my mouth. 'I shouldn't be in these photos.'

'It is alright,' he whispered back right into my ear, then called out, 'Take your photograph.'

'Surname?' the guy asked again.

'Jesus,' I mumbled.

'Jesus!' said Emilio. 'Emily Jesus.'

'No! It's —'

'She is very religious, aren't you, *querida*? Very chaste. A good Catholic girl.'

'Actually —'

'And now!' said Emilio. 'I must play the tennis.'

ROBBIE DICK WAS a good tennis player, perfect for our purposes. He looked great, held his own but wasn't so good that Emilio couldn't relax and have fun with it. Emilio let Robbie win a few games, everyone laughed, cameras snapped away.

About an hour into the match, I got a call from Charlotte. 'Rosalind said you have to come back to the office now.'

'What? Why?'

'She said you shouldn't spend so much time with the tennis player and you have work to do here before you go home.'

'Oh, for God's sake.' This was typical Rosalind – sending me on an important assignment then pulling me away from it, changing the goal posts for her deranged pleasure. And, knowing her, there was probably something seriously important I needed to do but she hadn't issued details, hoping I'd screw up. She'd be able to say, 'But I *told* her to come back to the office!'

'Alright, I'll come.'

I found Teresa and explained that I was needed at work, and to please call me when the game had finished.

'We do not need you.'

Ouch. I glanced around the court, checked that everyone seemed to have what they needed, and left, taking a smelly taxi, not a stretch limo, back to Emilio's hotel to collect my crappy old car. So much for lifestyles of the rich and famous.

CHAPTER 21

$\mathcal{B}$ack at the office, Rosalind wasn't even there – she'd left early for an appointment. Charlotte had gone home. I checked my tidy desk for a note, message, something. There was nothing.

I said to Marcus, 'Rosalind wanted me, apparently.'

He shrugged. 'I didn't know about it.'

'Charlotte called me.'

He shrugged again. 'Charlotte's been Rosalind's good little secretary all day. I'm hoping I'll be made redundant so I can go on a cruise with your man.'

IN MY CAR on the way home, my mobile rang and I pulled over to answer it. It was Teresa, telling me that Emilio was very upset I'd left today with his special lucky charm.

Oh crap. I'd forgotten about that. My hand went automatically to my chest. I could feel the amulet under my top. 'I'm so sorry.'

'It is fortunate, that he did not notice until the end of the match that you had left.'

'I'll have it couriered to the hotel.'

'You will not. Bring it when you come for dinner.'

'Dinner? But I —'

'Come at six, please.' She hung up.

Six? No way could I get home and back to the hotel in time. I carried on home. Where Mum and Dad were watching the news.

'Is that you, dear?' Mum pointed at the image of Emilio decorating me with his lucky charm.

How perfect. The footage from today's celebrity match included a few seconds of the game itself, and a lengthy snippet of my romantic moment with Emilio.

'Yeah.' I sighed and sat.

'Did you go to the supermarket?'

'Supermarket?'

'There's a list. Didn't you take it?'

'I didn't know.'

She went to the kitchen. Came back with a shopping list that contained at least fifty items. 'Here it is.'

'Why can't you get it delivered?'

Mum looked hurt, like I'd just announced I wished she wasn't my mother, which I sometimes want to do.

'You said you'd help if you came to live here! Besides, I don't want those supermarket people handling my bananas.'

'Okay, well, can this stuff wait till tomorrow?'

'Yes, dear, except we're almost out of milk, so we need that plus your father's All-Bran. And I've run out of prunes and vitamin D. And Tim Tams. They're on special this week. Your father loves those. And —' she snatched the list from my hand '— we need this and this and this.'

'Alright.' Sigh. 'I'll do it tonight on my way home.'

ON THE WAY back to Crown Hotel, Lucy called me. When I pulled over and saw her number come up, I felt strangely relieved. Lucy was such a solid presence in my life, the sensible one, the nurse. The one who made choices based on intellect rather than emotion. She was tough and suffered no fools. A dose of Lucy was often what I needed.

'Hi!' I said, happy.

'Marry him.'

'Who?'

'Emilio Mendez.'

'Very funny.'

'You should. He's gorgeous, rich, famous. What more could you want?'

'He calls me Emily.'

'Emily's a nice name and besides, he might have finally met the love of his life. You know. *The one*. But don't sleep with him yet. From what I've heard, that's a deal breaker.'

J called Emilio from the hotel lobby. 'It's *Erica*. Erica Jewell.'

'Who? Ah, Emily! You are late. I wanted you here at six.'

'Sorry, I had to —'

'Come to my room, *querida*. I am not ready.'

When he opened the door to his suite, Emilio was seemingly alone, and wearing only his undies, which he filled very well. Mentally, I added to Lucy's list of gorgeous, rich, famous ... and mentally gave myself a slap across the face.

He looked me up and down, gave an approving nod. 'I like this dress.' He stepped back. 'You have nice legs.'

'Where's Teresa?' I peered past him.

'She has dinner in her room.'

'She's not dining with us?'

But Emilio's eyes were now on my chest, staring at his lucky charm, which I'd kept around my neck so I wouldn't, God forbid, lose it. 'Ah, *mi amuleto*. It suits you well.'

I went to remove it, hand it back, but he put a hand on my arm. 'Please, continue to wear it. It makes me feel ... *fortunado*. Lucky.' He beckoned me in.

'I'll just wait here.'

'But you must come in!' He opened the door wider. A housemaid walked past, spotted Emilio, looked me up and down, smirked.

'Bloody hell.' I walked into his room and sat on the sofa.

'Would you like herbal tea?' He stood in front of me, crotch at nose height.

'No, thank you.' I looked at my watch.

He bent forward, inspected my wig. 'What is happening under? It is a mess, yes?'

'I don't always have time to style it, you know?'

'Ah, *eres tan adorable*. You want to look your best for me.'

'Well ...'

'Do not be embarrassed. Most women want this.' He swept a hand over his body.

I smiled. Nodded. What to say?

Emilio took me to an Italian restaurant on the promenade near the hotel, overlooking the Yarra River. We sat outside, right at the front so Emilio could smile at passersby and be recognised. Some stopped to get a photo with him, others asked for an autograph. The waiter came.

I read from the wine list. 'I'd like a glass of —'

'Perrier,' said Emilio. '*Dos.*' He held up two fingers.

As the waiter walked away, Emilio sighed with happiness and sat back in his chair, hands behind his head, gazing across the table at me. 'Last year I earned over thirty million dollars.'

'Thirty million! I can't imagine what I'd do with that much money.'

'One day I will show you my wardrobe. And my cars. Then you will know how I spend it.'

'Don't you give any of it away? I mean, there's so much good you could do.'

'I have my charities. I give them my time. Tomorrow I have a lunch!'

'Such hardship,' I muttered.

'I want to know about your boyfriend.' Emilio leaned in with his elbow on the table, hand supporting his chin.

'You mean Jack? He's not my boyfriend.' I said it quite snippily. 'We're just ...' How to say bed-pals without sounding like a *puta*?

'You are *amigos*. Friends.'

'Yes. We're friends.'

'This pleases me.'

I was rendered suddenly speechless by the sight of Jack and Sharon Stone strolling along the promenade. She wore a short, tight-fitting white dress, and heels that put her pretty close to Jack's six feet four. People stared at them. All the people. Jack was looking at me. I realised my hand was in Emilio's – how did that happen? – and I snatched it away, throwing myself back in the chair, putting distance between us. Jack headed my way, followed by Shazza. I smiled up at him. The waiter came with our drinks.

'Mineral water,' said Jack, eyes fixed on my wig.

'Hey y'all.' Shaz checked out Emilio, eyebrows raised.

'Emilio,' I said, 'you've met my … friend, Jack Jones, and his, ah, friend, Sharon.'

'Well!' said Emilio. 'This is a very good evening! *Muy bueno.* You will join us? Emily was just telling me about you, *Yack*. That you are just friends, because I thought you might be her lover.'

'No.' Jack's eyes were on me. 'I mean, no to joining you.' He glanced at Emilio. 'Thank you.'

Sharon said, 'Can I have your autograph?'

'*Si*! You have a pen?'

While Emilio signed his name on the soft-yet-firm white under-side of Sharon's forearm, right next to a small rose tattoo, I asked Jack, 'How was your trip?'

'Alright.'

'Find out anything?'

'One or two things.'

'What are you guys doing?' I glanced at Sharon. Maybe she and I could swap places. She could stay here with Emilio and I could carry on with Jack.

'Working. And you?'

'Yep, working.'

'Undercover, Emily?'

'Ha, ha.'

'I'll leave you to it.'

I smiled. 'Bye.'

Jack touched Sharon's elbow. She said goodbye and they walked away.

'There is a magnificent couple,' said Emilio. 'Now I understand why *Yack* is not your lover, because he is Sharon's lover.'

A gushing fan arrived for a photo with Emilio and I watched the magnificent couple over my shoulder. They walked slowly, taking in the scenery; the lights on the river, the buskers. Like any couple, really, except they didn't hold hands or touch each other, unlike me and my new boyfriend. They stopped to admire some street art – a guy sitting on the pavement, drawing on it with chalk. Jack crouched before him and they spoke. The guy looked nervous, glancing around. Sharon discreetly stood on his hand with her stiletto. The guy's face contorted and he looked like he was shitting himself. I checked to see if anyone else had noticed. Apparently not; it all seemed pretty normal and casual from a distance. Sharon moved her foot and Jack placed what looked like a note in the guy's upturned hat. The guy took the note and pocketed it. They spoke a bit more, and Jack and Sharon walked on. Jack glanced over his shoulder at me. I gave him a little wave but he turned away without acknowledging it.

AT HIS INSISTENCE, I escorted Emilio to the door of his hotel room but not one step further, not even for herbal tea and whatever Lucy thought I should be doing to please my new boyfriend, not even to assist Emilio choose an outfit for the following day's charity lunch. Except he got sulky, so I said, 'I'll help you choose an outfit then I have to go.'

Emilio addressed his wardrobe. 'I have a very good feeling about you, Emily.'

'Actually, my name's —'

'Would you wear *mi amuleto*? Keep it safe for me?' He turned to me, gave it a little tap with his forefinger.

'What, forever?'

'Oh, no, *ángel*. For this tournament. I think you make me lucky.'

I blew out a relieved breath. 'Okay. Sure.'

'What time will you come in the morning?'

'Morning?'

'You speak English, don't you, *querida*? What time will you come to me in the morning? We have the important charity lunch.'

I didn't know what to say. I told him I had to go to work. I told him that JD and Rosalind would attend the important charity lunch. That she was more senior than me and it was so important, surely Emilio would expect the most senior executives of Dega to attend? Besides, I had other very important things to do. He sulked and put on his Gleam toothpaste T-shirt.

I took the lift to the ground floor. I'd intended going straight to my car in the car park, but found myself in the hotel lobby instead, staring out through the windows to the river promenade. I left the building and headed for the restaurant we'd been to earlier. The street art guy was still there. I stood in front of him, watched him draw. It was bleak. Buildings, all black and grey.

'I like your art,' I lied.

He looked up. 'Thank you.' Strong accent.

'Where are you from?'

'Melbourne.'

'I mean before.'

He looked around, but not at me. 'Why you want know?'

'I'm interested in people. Especially artists. What influences them,' I thought to add.

'Russia.' He shrugged.

CHAPTER 23

I drove along Dandenong Road, heading home, yawning, thinking about the weird day with Emilio and dinner and his lucky charm. *Guard it with your life, Emily. I cannot play without it.* Geez Louise. Seeing Jack tonight with Sharon Stone had been horrible. They *had* looked good together, the magnificent couple. And the Russian artist. I wanted to know what it all meant, but more than that, I yearned for my bed. Not even Jack's bed – that's how tired I was. It was almost ten o'clock, and I was done like the proverbial dinner. When I stopped at the lights, I checked my phone. Text from Lucy wanting to know about my dinner with Emilio. A million emails. One new voicemail, which I listened to: *It's your mother. Don't forget my prunes and your father's All-Bran.*

Carnegie loomed, and though I was tempted to just go home and do it all tomorrow, I worried about what it might mean if Mum didn't have her prunes and Dad didn't have his All-Bran. And, God forbid, Tim Tams.

Woolworths at Carnegie Central was moderately busy. Other stupid people were shopping instead of being tucked up in blissful bed. As I approached the lines of trolleys, I took out my purse and the few coins in there fell out. I bent to pick them up. Emilio's lucky charm swung in my face. There were no one- or two-dollar coins among the lot on the floor, so, no coin for the trolley. 'Bugger.' The service desk was unattended, so I couldn't get change. I fingered the charm. I wonder ...

Can't hurt, I thought, guiltily, as I pushed the trolley up the vitamins aisle. The gold chain swung from the coin slot, where Emilio's amulet snugly sat. A perfect fit, really. Despite my weariness, I managed a brief giggle at my audacity, although the chosen trolley was annoying, its sticky wheel forcing it to the right.

Vitamin D was on the list. I picked up a Mega B Exec Stress for myself and read the bottle. *Perfect for tired and stressed executives.* Lucy rang.

'I'm at the supermarket, if that answers your question.'

'What question?'

'About whether or not I slept with him.'

'I know you wouldn't be that stupid, hon. He won't marry you if you have sex with him.'

'Quite apart from the fact that I *only just met him.*' I struggled one-handed with the wayward trolley, then I saw Mum's rear neighbour, the extra strange one. 'Uh-oh. Mrs Booth's here.'

'Ooh. Creepy.'

'I know.'

'What's she doing at the supermarket so late?'

'I know. *So* weird.'

When we were kids, Mrs Booth wore her hair long and black, floor-length purple skirts with mirrors all over them; sandals, even in winter. If she cornered me, she'd ask questions like, 'How's school?' and the way she looked at me was like she knew something about it that I didn't. I always wanted to say, 'Why? What do you know?'

'Ask her to cast a spell on Emilio so he'll marry you.'

I smiled when Mrs Booth spotted me. Through gritted teeth I muttered, 'She's coming this way.'

'What's her hair like?'

'She's chopped it all of. It's short and frizzy. With grey bits.'

'What's she wearing?'

'*Matching* tracky pants and top. Aqua.'

'Weirdo.'

As Mrs Booth approached I indicated the phone at my ear, giving her a look of regret that I couldn't stop and talk.

She nodded in understanding, mouthed, 'Hello to Mum and Dad.' Then she turned and looked behind as if expecting someone to be there. I gave her a smile and wave and hurried on. Mum and Dad would rather move house than see Mrs Booth, I felt pretty sure of that.

'She's gone,' I said to Lucy.

'Remember how we thought she'd murdered her husband and buried him in the basement?'

'Yeah,' I said. 'Steve and I went down there once.'

'Really?'

'It was so scary and dark but we didn't find a body.'

'Maybe it's still there.'

'Yeah. Maybe.'

I hung up from Luce but kept spotting Mrs Booth, who always looked like she was trying to find someone. Me? So I kept the phone at my ear and pretended to be talking. By the time I reached the checkout, I had a crick in my neck.

In the almost deserted car park, I loaded up my boot. Just as I was finishing, Mrs Booth appeared with her trolley, and I squatted behind my car. I left the trolley, crept to the driver's door, opened it and crawled in. I could see Mrs Booth standing at her car, again looking around. I started my car, crouched low, and drove slowly out of my spot. I peered over the steering wheel. Mrs Booth was loading her bags into her car. I put my foot down, sped through the car park and checked my mirror. Mrs Booth was waving. I wound down my window and waved back. She wouldn't mind, I was sure. Maybe she wouldn't notice my rudeness. I hoped not. She might cause something horrible to happen. But I couldn't have stopped anyway. I had to get Mum's prunes to her. The ice-cream would have melted if I'd stopped.

Mrs Booth would have asked me questions about my life, my boyfriend status, why I was living at Mum and Dad's. It would have been hard to know how to answer all those questions. Besides, I needed to get to bed.

I was thinking all those things, and it wasn't until I was almost home that I remembered Emilio Mendez's precious lucky charm – the one he can't live or play tennis without – that was, I prayed, still sitting in a supermarket trolley at Carnegie Central shopping centre.

I LOOKED for the trolley near where I'd left it. There were two stuck together but no lucky charm, so I assumed neither was mine. Good old denial. Maybe someone had taken my trolley to the trolley parking place where I should have put it, or maybe an employee collected it. I trawled the car park, looking for abandoned trolleys. I searched every trolley return and I went into the supermarket and searched there. I walked the aisles, peering at the trolleys people were using. I waited at the service desk for someone to come and I asked her, 'Anything handed in to lost property?' She said no. I asked every employee in the store. I stood in every line and asked the checkout people. I returned to the aisles, harassed customers, asking about the lucky charm. I didn't believe them when they told me no, they hadn't seen it. Someone must have seen it. Surely if someone had found it, they would have handed it in? Why would someone take something like that? Why would someone steal another person's lucky charm? In the middle of the supermarket fruit and vegie section, I yelled out, 'Has anyone seen a trolley with a lucky charm in the coin slot?'

The manager asked me to leave.

Back in the car park, I saw a young trolley guy pushing a mile-long line of trolleys toward the supermarket entrance.

'I'm looking for a trolley I used before,' I told him.

'What'd it look like?'

'Um…'

'Full size or half size?'

'Full size.'

'New or old?

'How would I know that?'

'Black or silver?'

'Oh. Silver. Old. Actually, it had a sticky wheel and pulled to the right.'

'Why didn't you say so in the first place?' He scratched his chin and looked around.

'I left a … coin in the slot.'

'Someone woulda grabbed it.' He continued pushing. 'Kids always looking for money in the trolleys.'

I followed him. 'It was a special coin. On a chain. I really need to find it.'

'Actually, have a look at that one.' He nodded at two stuck-together trolleys parked across the way. 'I think that's old Bessie.'

They were the ones I'd seen before and checked already. My stomach churned. Shit.

'Not that one?' said trolley guy.

'I think so, but the coin's gone.'

'She's a real bugger, that Bessie.' He continued on.

'Okay, well, thanks.'

I slumped to my car, and the trolley kid called out, 'Mrs?'

'Me?'

'There was a lady. I just remembered. I thought she was a bit weird.'

'A weird lady?'

'Yeah. She mighta nicked your coin.'

Weird. Right. Mrs Booth.

So, should I knock on Mrs Booth's door and ask if she took my lucky charm? I didn't want to. I definitely didn't want to. She had a black cat. Okay, so, Axle is black, but Axle doesn't do weird things. Okay, he does weird things, but he doesn't sit in the window and just stare at people like Mrs Booth's cat does. Maybe he stares, but he's not, like, Mrs Booth's.

As I sat in my car in the Carnegie Central car park, I called Lucy.

She yawned as she answered. 'Someone better be dying.'

'You know how Emilio gave me his lucky charm?'

'Uh-oh.' She was quickly alert. I imagined her sitting upright in bed. 'What have you done with it?'

'It was a perfect fit in the supermarket trolley.'

'You left it in there.'

'I did.'

'And now it's gone.'

'It is.'

'Holy *shit*, Erica! You *always* leave the coin. Didn't you think you'd forget it?'

'Of course not! It's too important!'

'Oh, my God. What are you going to do?'

'I think Mrs Booth took it.'

'That's *so* the kind of thing she'd do.'

'I know.'

It was times like these I wanted Luce to just take charge and fix it. She's good at that. And she's so brave. Much braver than me. 'Will you go to Mrs Booth's and ask her for me?'

'No!'

'Please?'

'No way!'

'I'm scared she'll use the charm to put a spell on Emilio to make him lose the tennis.'

'She might.'

'Shit.'

'Yeah.'

My mother's screeching woke me from the two hours' sleep I'd managed. The noise invaded my nightmare, getting closer and closer until it finally burst into my bedroom and sent Axle scampering with a howl. Mum hurled the newspaper at me. Some of it fluttered around the room, but most of it landed on me. The *Herald Sun* – a weighty tabloid. Mum had it delivered daily so she could finish the crossword before Mary up the road, who has to wait for jail-time newspaper delivery, giving Mum a distinct advantage.

'What's wrong?' I yawned and stared cross-eyed down my nose. There was something on it. Peeling skin. I rubbed it.

'You know very well what you've done! Imagine if Jack sees this! What will he do? He'll break up with you, that's what!'

Mum stood there with a cat's-bum mouth, arms crossed tightly, toe tapping wildly, while a slo-mo replay of the previous day trudged through my mind. I sat up and pulled the scattered bits of newspaper onto my lap. Mum snatched the front page off the floor and flung it at me. Front page. I flattened the paper across my lap. The headline read: EMILIO IN LOVE … AGAIN.

The full-page pic showed a photo of Emilio standing with his arm around me, his head bowed as he listened to whatever mushy thing I was whispering in his ear. A reversal of the last photo of us together, where he was doing the whispering.

A few pages later there were a couple of smaller photos showing Emilio and me holding hands at dinner – the photo seemingly taken from the middle of the river – and one of Emilio decorating me with his lucky charm. The one I'd had a nightmare about – that it was still in the shopping trolley coin slot, but now, in my nightmare, at the bottom of the Yarra River.

'You are such a hussy!' Mum wailed and stormed away.

'It's not me! It's …' I checked the name in the paper. 'Emily Jesus!'

On the bright side, there were also photos we'd wanted. Of Emilio's tennis match with Robbie Dick.

I sent Jack a text: *It's not how it looks.*

I waited ten minutes, staring at the phone. Nothing. I went for a shower. When I came back to my room, there was a reply: *What are you talking about?*

Herald Sun.

You know I don't read it.

Well, if you do happen to see today's, just ignore the silly little article on the front, ok?

You mean the one about Emilio Mendez's new girlfriend?

You've read it!

No.

Bloody hell. *Ok. See ya.*

No response. Well, that was that. After last night's performance at the restaurant and then today's front-page thing, I'd probably done my dash with Jack. He'd surely run off to Switzerland with Sharon Stone. Or Paris. Mum was right. And that was the most annoying part.

My phone started ringing and didn't stop. Journos, wanting to interview Emilio Mendez's new girlfriend and wanting to know why I'd given a false name. They'd lost all interest in the oil rig explosion. Mission accomplished, albeit not in the way I'd planned. *The Saturday*

Morning Show wanted me to participate in a group interview with other WAGs of famous sporting stars. Mostly Aussie Rules football girlfriends, they said.

'So can you come in on Saturday morning?' said the producer.

'No, I —'

'Could you offer some fashion advice to our viewers as well?'

'Fashion?'

'Emilio seems pretty smitten. We're pretty excited about it here.'

'Oh, no …'

'See you at five-thirty a.m. You know where our studios are?'

'No, I —'

'I'll email the details.' She hung up.

I checked the time. I needed to get to work. Lucy had left a message. I called her.

'Geez,' she said. 'You're all over the media.'

'*The Saturday Morning Show* wants me to offer fashion advice.'

She laughed and wouldn't stop. I hung up.

She called me back. 'Sorry, hon, what's happened?'

'I don't know what to do about Mrs Booth.'

'Just call and ask her if she's got the charm.'

'I'm scared.'

'Get your mum to do it.'

'She's not talking to me.'

'Why? Oh, the *Herald Sun* article. Well, you'll just have to do it.'

'I suppose.' I hung up, sat on my bed and stared out the window at Mum's camellia bush. I didn't want to ring Mrs Booth. Instead I snuck out to the backyard via the laundry, to avoid Mum. Dad was in his vegie patch. I said hello as I picked my way through the towering tomatoes, and stood on the bottom rail of the timber paling fence. When I peered into Mrs Booth's backyard, shivers scuttled up my spine in memory of the childhood terrors of her house, which she and Mr Booth had built in the '50s. It was American-style, with a basement and attic. Steve and I had been drawn to it, in the way you're drawn to look at a car crash when, really, it's the last thing you want to see. We'd climb the fence and sneak around the garden, hiding behind the giant pine tree and getting stuck in the nasty rose bushes. We'd peer in the windows and sometimes we saw her having a séance with Ruth, her daughter, by candlelight. We'd watch as the cup moved around the Ouija board. Ruth was hugely fat from eating so much chocolate and she had pimples and greasy hair that stuck to her face. I still wondered if Mr Booth was down there in the basement.

A shadow crossed Mrs Booth's kitchen. Dad farted. I dropped off the fence, ran back inside and called Lucy.

'I can't go in there. It's too creepy!'

'Call her!'

'What would I say?'

'Just ask if she took the thing.'

'What if she didn't?'

'You won't know if you don't ask.'

'I wish I could just go to a shop and buy another one.'

'Actually … hang on a minute.'

I could hear Lucy moving about. 'What are you doing?'

'Googling. There's a shop with imitation Emilio Mendez lucky charms.'

'Really?'

'Here we go. *La Joyería* at Chadstone. They're running a promotion for the tennis. They're good ones. Gold. Two hundred bucks.'

'I'm going there now.'

'You can't spend all that just to get a necklace.'

'Watch me.'

Standing in the lift at work, I patted my chest which, under my suit jacket, was covered by a high-neck T-shirt. And under the T-shirt, my fake Emilio Mendez lucky charm. They really were quite good quality. Quite nice, in fact. I wondered if Emilio would be able to tell through the T-shirt that it wasn't the real charm? My life would be over if he did.

Charlotte was already there, diligently rearranging my paper clips. She was dressed like me: gunmetal grey suit and T-shirt; hers was black, mine was white.

'Journalists keep calling. I gave them your mobile.'

'Gee, thanks.'

'They think you're his girlfriend.' She gave me an accusing look.

'It's not like I meant it.'

I checked my watch. Not much time to get work done before I had to meet Emilio. The charity lunch was to be held at Rod Laver Arena itself, in one of the giant corporate marquees. JD had insisted I'd enjoy it, after Emilio had called him first thing this morning to complain that I wasn't giving him enough attention, even though he was very happy with the newspapers this morning. JD was also very happy with the newspapers this morning, and wanted me to continue on my brilliant PR mission to distract the public from the human and environmental horrors caused by our company.

I also had an email from *The Saturday Morning Show*'s producer with details for tomorrow morning, and one from Rosalind suggesting my real hair would be "less tacky" to wear to the lunch. I wore the wig.

Emilio wanted me to meet him at his hotel so we could go together, and he told me I was privileged to be sitting at his table – which meant I couldn't sneak off. At least it was for a worthy cause, so that made me feel a bit better about everything. That I was helping raise money for kids in third-world countries who had no food or tennis courts.

Emilio opened the door to his suite and stared at my nose. 'What is wrong with your face?'

I put a hand on my cheek. 'What do you mean?'

He leaned right in. 'There is something wrong with your skin.'

'Oh, that. I'm peeling. Sunburn, you know.'

'It is very unattractive, Emily.'

'Actually, it's Erica.'

His gaze dropped to my chest. 'You are wearing *mi amuleto?*'

'Oh yes.' I patted my chest. 'Safe and sound under here.'

'I like to see it. It makes me feel … how you say … secure.'

'It's there. Don't worry.'

'I want to see it.'

Teresa came to my rescue. She appeared from her room next door and called out, 'Let us go, my darling!'

INSIDE THE MARQUEE there were giant posters of Emilio with a forced smile, surrounded by laughing, grubby children. He was a very good actor. I was sure he'd rather have been somewhere else. Somewhere like the massage room at Crown.

I sat by Emilio's side listening to boring speeches, remembering with relief that time was, in fact, moving forward, which meant that every second, I was closer to the end of the tennis tournament.

Although, thinking about that also meant thinking about the real lucky charm and that I needed to get it back. And I thought about the work I wasn't getting done while I was sitting there. And Charlotte Johnson, who had said to me, 'Just give me instructions and I'll get on with my work.'

'Instructions … instructions …' I'd looked around for inspiration. Finally, I'd sent her to the canteen to see if she could help there.

JD had bought a table at the charity lunch, and so had Martin McGann, which I thought was strange, considering what Martin had said on the news about Dega and the explosion. Maybe he was there to show the media he had no hard feelings, but sometimes when I looked in his direction, I caught him staring at JD's table or mine, and never in a friendly way. I wondered if Martin had had a bad relationship with Shane, and that's why Shane turned out so awful. But then, look at me and my mother. It's a wonder I didn't turn out rotten.

JD gave a speech, saying how proud Dega Oil was to be Emilio Mendez's sponsor, and how proud he was of Emilio's choice of charity, to whom Dega had donated a shitload of money. He didn't say shitload. I snuck off to the loo and checked my silenced phone, listening to messages. I had some from media wanting responses about the explosion; other media wanting an interview with Emilio's new girlfriend; from Marcus, telling me that Charlotte had finished making scones in the canteen; from Rosalind, wanting to know where her stapler was; from Steve, asking how I got on with the appliance shopping; from Mum, wanting to know if I wanted fried or grilled flake with tonight's fish and chips order. (Doesn't she *know*? Doesn't she know I always have grilled? And that I don't eat shark?) But not from Jack. No messages from him.

I got back to the table in time for Emilio's speech. When he was called to the lectern by the MC, Emilio gave my hand a squeeze, stood and smiled broadly at his adoring audience, then bounced up the steps to the stage, his ebony hair slicked back and tied in a ponytail, looking for all the world like Antonio Banderas in *Zorro*. But better. A mask would have completed the picture. I had an unwelcome fantasy and checked to see if anyone noticed. At the lectern Emilio held his arms wide, encouraging more applause. His teeth were so white. I sighed. He was gorgeous and I *did* feel proud to be sitting with him. But what was I thinking? I wasn't Emilio's girlfriend. I wasn't *anyone's* girl- friend. Not that I needed a man, except to take out the rubbish and get the spiders. I supposed, if I thought about it, putting the rubbish out wasn't so hard.

As Emilio started to speak, a sudden shout from the back of the marquee caused everyone to turn and look. Two men – masked, armed men – came into the room, weapons raised. A woman screamed. The men's masks were stockings pulled over their faces, making them look grotesque. I made a quick note of their body shapes and sizes, as taught by Jack. One man stayed by the entrance – short, skinny. He shuffled from foot to foot, head swivelling. The other man was much taller, with a belly that bulged over his trousers. Short and skinny, tall and fat. Tall and fat shouted, waved his gun and people dived to the floor. I sat statue still. The man moved through the room and I wondered where the security guards were. Maybe they'd been killed, like in the movies. I pulled my phone off the table into my lap. JD and I locked eyes, momentarily. We were probably both thinking the same thing: *Wonder if Jack's nearby?*

Some of the guests were on the floor and under the tables. Most, like me, sat in their chairs.

Emilio said into the microphone, 'What do you want?'

Tall and fat shouted something. I didn't understand what he said. No-one seemed to know what he said.

Emilio said, 'We cannot understand you, my friend.'

The man shouted again. Was it the stocking that made it so hard to know what he was saying? Was he even speaking English? I looked down at my phone and dialled Jack's number. I couldn't hear if it was ringing, but I could tell it had been answered, either by him or his message bank. The man shouted, getting angrier and frustrated because no-one seemed to know what he was saying. He grabbed a woman by the arm and people screamed. I didn't dare bring my phone to my ear. Instead, I dropped my head onto my crossed arms on the table, pretending to cry. 'Siege at Rod Laver.'

Did he hear me? Was he even there?

The man dragged the sobbing woman from her chair and held up her wrist, indicating her watch, then he waved her handbag around. This was a hold-up? Just a robbery? Everyone got the message. He moved quickly through the crowd, collecting valuables, tearing necklaces from women's throats. Shorty stood near the entrance, gun raised. Fatty took JD's wallet and watch. He approached Martin McGann, who made a big fuss. I kicked my handbag out from under my chair and, with my toe, pushed it under the table. No way was I giving up my wallet that easily. Fatty rushed onto the stage, demanding Emilio's watch. Good move on the robber's part – Rolex was one of Emilio's sponsors. Emilio refused to hand it over. The robber shoved him, knocked him down. Emilio tried to stand and the robber put the gun to his head.

'No!' I jumped up.

The robber looked at me.

I sat again, mouth clamped shut. He came at me, pulled at my T-shirt. He put the gun between his legs and shoved his hand down my top. I screamed, gripping his wrist with both hands. I brought my foot up, kicked at the gun, caught his knee. He yelled out, grabbed my hair. He had the amulet in his other hand. I felt the chain break.

The man yanked on my hair and I released his arm to save my wig, but he snatched it right off my head. The pins tore my own hair out by the roots, and he'd pulled so hard he overbalanced and fell backward with a squeal.

Emilio shouted, 'Unhand my Emily!' and ran toward us.

From the floor the man raised his gun.

I screamed, 'Emilio!'

I kicked out at the robber; the gun skittled across the floor. He scrambled for it. JD snatched up the gun and aimed it at the robber, who fled, screaming, from the room with his friend.

And then there were distant sirens, lots of them.

. . .

WHEN THE POLICE rushed into the room, Emilio was sitting on the floor, hugging his knees.

'But Emilio, it's just a thing.'

He glared up at me. 'It is *not*! I cannot play tennis without it!'

'Of course you can. You're the best player in the world!'

Until he'd discovered the loss of his precious, Emilio had been concerned about me and whether I was traumatised, in need of hugging, whatever. I'd confessed, thinking it would mean nothing compared to what could have happened, and secretly pleased that I'd been saved from having to find the real one. 'I'm so sorry, Emilio, he took your lucky charm.'

I'd thought Emilio would brush it off, say something like, 'It does not matter, as long as you are safe.' But instead, he'd collapsed to the floor and hadn't moved, apart from the slight rocking back and forth. Teresa was with him, running a hand over his back in rhythmic circles, murmuring soothing, mother-type noises.

I found my handbag where I'd left it, and sneakily checked my reflection in my hand mirror. Like a jack-in-the-box, my curls had sprung out from their squashed position, celebrating a new-found freedom.

A police officer approached and asked to speak to Emilio. Teresa told him Emilio obviously couldn't speak to anyone right now. I could see Jack at the marquee entrance with JD. I made my way quickly through the tables, overturned chairs, the distressed guests to Jack. He looked me over, spending a moment too long on my hair, and my peeling nose.

'You're okay?'

I nodded. 'I didn't know if you'd answered or if I was leaving a message.'

'I answered.'

'Did you call the police?'

'Yes. And so did others.' He nodded at Emilio. 'Is he okay?'

'No. They stole his lucky charm.' I'd tell Jack about the fake one, but not yet, in case someone overheard. 'Ripped it right off me. They obviously knew what they were after.'

'I'll speak with the police,' JD said, and walked away.

'It's lucky no-one was shot,' I said.

'Gun wasn't loaded,' said Jack.

'What? The robber's gun?'

Jack nodded. 'Empty.'

'Oh.' What did that mean?

We looked at each other. This was familiar territory, us together following some kind of life-endangering event. The aftermath usually, eventually, involved some love-making. He'd probably want to take me somewhere private for a cuddle and debrief. He'd be worried, for sure.

'You were wearing a wig last night,' he said.

'You weren't supposed to notice!'

'It was pretty obvious.'

I fiddled with a rebel curl. 'Did you like it?'

'I like *your* hair.'

'Just as well, because the bandits stole my wig.' I huffed. 'How embarrassing.'

Jack stared at me for a long time.

'What?'

'I have no idea what to say about that.' He looked around at the overturned chairs and crying people. 'Tell me about it.'

I gave him the details and added, 'I couldn't understand a word the guy was saying. I don't think he spoke English. He made everyone hand over their jewellery and wallets.'

Jack said, 'Were you aware the three dead fishermen were Russian?'

I stared at him. 'No. I wasn't. What does that mean?'

He shrugged. 'We don't know. Yet.'

I nodded. I wanted to ask him more about W.A., but now wasn't the time. Across the room, Martin McGann was making a great show of being annoyed about his day being messed up.

'They must have known about the event,' I said.

'Definitely tipped off.'

'I wonder if it was all just about Emilio's lucky charm? Probably worth a bit.'

'They might hold it to ransom.'

'I reckon he'd pay anything to get it back.' I huffed again. 'Don't know what happened to the security guards.'

'There was security here?'

'Yeah. The venue staff plus security at the doors. You didn't find any strangled ones behind some rubbish bins, did you?'

'No, should I?'

I shrugged. 'Just a thought.' Then, 'Speak of the devil.'

The two missing security guards had returned, looking sheepish. Police approached them immediately, led them into the room and separated them. I wondered what they'd been up to.

CHAPTER 26

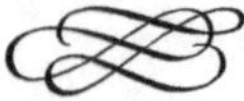

$\mathcal{I}$t was four o'clock by the time I dealt with police questions and got back to work. People were saying the men had Russian accents. Interesting. The security guards had confessed (pretty quickly) that someone had given them money to "disappear" during the lunch. Emilio was so angry and upset about his amulet he wouldn't speak to me. Teresa had said on the phone that I didn't realise the implications of what I'd done. What I'd done? Allowed an armed guy to rob me? I asked if she realised the implications of what might have happened to me at Emilio's charity event? But apart from the near-death experience, losing the amulet, Emilio's distress, Charlotte, Rosalind, my mother, Jack, etc., I was feeling pretty good. God was surely watching over me. He'd sent a robber to take the fake charm, save me from having to 'fess up about losing the real one. And now, all I had to worry about was a legal fight if Emilio decided to cut ties with Dega again. I thought about going to church with Mum this Sunday.

I snuck into the office and sat at my desk. Charlotte was typing. I asked what she was working on.

She didn't look up. 'A new media schedule template.'

'What?' I peered over her shoulder. 'We don't need one.'

'I suggested it to Rosalind and she agreed.'

Hmph. Standing at my desk, I called the supermarket and asked if the lucky charm had turned up. They said it hadn't, and suggested I stop harassing the staff about it. I said that if they didn't find it, I'd harass the staff until they needed group counselling.

'How was the event?' Charlotte looked up at me.

'Eventful.'

She held out a Tupperware container. 'I made scones in the canteen. They were so happy with them they want me to make them every day.'

'But you won't have time.'

'I don't mind. I can make them at home. They'll pay me and they let me take some today.'

'Can I have one?'

'Sure.' She opened the lid. 'I prefer to make date scones but they didn't have any dates,' she said. 'What sort do you like to make?'

'I don't cook.'

'Shame.'

I shrugged. 'I try. Sometimes.' I checked my watch. 'I want to leave by five. It's been a big day.'

'What are you doing tonight?'

'Oh, not much. My parents have fish and chips on Friday night. I might get home in time for that.'

'I *love* fish and chips.' She leaned in, eyes shining.

Without understanding why, I said, 'Would you like to come?'

THERE WAS POSSIBLY a part of me that was fully nice. I really didn't know. Maybe it's there and I was yet to discover it. But I struggled to understand my invitation to Charlotte Johnson to come to my parents' house for dinner. I barely knew the girl. My parents were really embarrassing. I was her *boss*, for God's sake!

Upon acceptance of my invitation, Charlotte asked me where in

Chadstone I lived. She said she lived not far, which at first I thought was a good thing and then I thought might be a bad thing. I didn't know. I told Charlotte I would drive her, but she told me she had her own car and would drive herself.

'I thought you didn't drive,' I said.

'I thought *you* didn't drive,' she said.

We agreed to meet at my parents'. She said she wanted to go home first to change.

On my way, I got a call from *The Saturday Morning Show*, cancelling my appearance the following morning. The appearance I'd forgotten about and therefore wouldn't have shown for anyway. They told me after my "performance" at the charity lunch, during which Emilio's precious amulet was stolen, they thought I'd no longer be a popular guest on their show. That their viewers might change channels if I were to show my evil face.

I called Jack. We hadn't finished our conversation after the lunchtime heist. I wanted to know about WA. I wanted to know when I'd see him. I wanted to know if he was bonking Sharon Stone. My phone rested on my knee, and the tinny ringing sound echoed out of it. I hoped it didn't go to message bank, because if it did, I'd have to assume he and Sharon were having sex.

But he answered. 'Where are you?'

What? He stole my line. It took me a second to find a response. 'Should I be somewhere?'

'Your mother wants to order the fish and chips.'

'My moth — You're at my *parents'*?'

'Uh-huh. Hurry up. I'm starving.'

'Mum called you?'

'She did. This afternoon.' And then a muffled, 'Thanks, Margaret.' She was probably giving him a foot massage. And "Margaret". No-one in my generation calls Mum by her first name. "Mrs J" maybe, like Steve and Lucy, but only if you've known her a very long time. 'Are you on the way?'

I hesitated. My brain told me to put away all confusion and panic and focus on what was important. 'Yes, and I'm bringing a friend. Can you tell Mum to order extra?'

Silence, then in a flat voice, 'Not Mendez, I hope.'

'No!'

'Good.'

'He's not talking to me.'

'Good.'

We hung up. Fifteen seconds later, Mum called.

'Who are you bringing? I haven't dusted the crystal!'

'Just a girl from work. She's new and she lives not far.'

'I don't even know what she likes! Fried flake? Potato cakes? How would I know?'

'Just order the same as me.'

'I don't know how many potato cakes you want.'

'Two.'

'Jack wants four, and you want two, and your father wants three, and two for your friend. That makes —'

'Eleven, Mum. Eleven potato cakes.'

'I'll order ten. They always throw in an extra one.'

'They don't always.'

'When will you be home? Jack is starving. The poor man works so hard.'

'He doesn't work hard.'

'He's exhausted! I think he's had a very traumatic day.'

'*I've* had a traumatic day.'

'Hurry along, dear. You'll need to pick up the order.'

I heard Jack in the background say, 'I can get it, Margaret.'

'Yeah,' I said. 'Jack can get it.'

She hung up.

When I got home, I could hear Mum carrying on, flirting in the kitchen. I approached with caution. Even Dad was out of his chair and offering Jack another beer or whiskey. Jack had brought Mum flowers. Of course he had, the suck. Axle was in his arms. What was missing from this picture? Me. I barged into the happy little group.

'Where's your friend?' said Mum.

'On her way.'

I said hi to Jack and he smiled down at me. His perfect face was clean-shaven; my favourite after his three-day-stubble look. Or his full-beard look. Or any look.

I took Axle and put him down. 'Let's go get the fish and chips.'

'Jack's having a drink with your father,' said Mum, whose daily desperation to be eating by 6pm in order to avert global catastrophe was suddenly on the back burner.

'No hurry,' said Jack.

I crossed my arms, tapped my toe.

'Why don't you have some juice?' said Mum.

Because I'd rather have champagne. Wine. Beer. Don't suppose I could slug down a whiskey in front of my mother.

Dad took Jack outside to show him the vegie garden. Axle and I watched from the back veranda. Jack's got such nice manners, he'd ask Dad all kinds of questions about things he wasn't interested in. Even when Dad bent down to pull a weed and farted, Jack didn't skip a beat in the conversation, or even smirk. Mrs Booth's cat was sitting on the fence, watching us. I shivered, picked up Axle, warned him, 'Don't you go near that spooky one. It might try to take over your body so it can live here with Mum and her roast chicken.' Axle squirmed out of my arms and ran inside.

When Dad and Jack returned, Mum said, 'Show Jack your room, dear.'

Wasn't that a bit risqué for my mother? She'd probably want to chaperone. 'Why?'

Jack said, 'I want to see your room. Where you slept when you were a little girl.' *Now* he was smirking.

I huffed and stomped down the passage and Jack followed. Mum didn't, surprisingly. We stood inside the door of my bedroom and Jack looked at all the pink frills, and the mess on the floor.

'Single bed. Cosy.'

He gave me a look that could have caused me to do something

inappropriate. He leaned in, about to whisper something naughty in my ear, I knew, and I blushed and quivered, but then a voice from the kitchen hollered, 'Erica! Show Jack your brother's room. His train set is in there.'

Time to get the fish and chips.

CHAPTER 27

When Charlotte arrived, everyone was seated at the table. Mum was in the kitchen, singing a tune from *The Sound of Music*. 'Raindrops on whiskers and kettles on kittens …'

I opened the front door. Charlotte had dressed for a formal event – one that required a short skirt and high heels.

'Oh, it's quite casual here.'

She shrugged. 'This is casual.'

Right, whatever. I introduced everyone to Charlotte. I said Jack was my friend. 'And that's my cat.' I pointed at Axle, who was happily draped across Jack's lap.

'I love cats.' She snatched Axle up. But he hissed and swiped at Charlotte's face. She dropped him, pronto, and he ran under the table. Gawd, even *I* wouldn't dare take Axle off Jack's lap. And I'd probably hiss and scratch if someone tried to take me off Jack's lap. I put him outside.

'I'm so sorry!' I inspected Charlotte's face. No dripping blood or claw marks.

'I don't mind.' She settled between Jack and Mum in my usual seat. I sat on the other side of Jack. Mum came in from the kitchen with a tray containing a bottle of tomato sauce, jar of mayo, jar of tartare

126

sauce, salt and pepper and a bottle of fake lemon juice. I introduced her to Charlotte.

'I hope you like fried flake,' Mum said. 'It's not good enough for *some* people.' Her eyes cut to me.

Charlotte smiled. 'I love flake.'

Mum opened the wrapped-up fish and chips and served everyone, counting the chips to make sure Jack got the most. She gave me one potato cake.

'I ordered two.'

'They only gave us ten.'

Jack had four potato cakes. He held out his plate to me. 'Have one of mine.'

'Erica doesn't need it, Jack. She likes to maintain her figure, don't you dear?'

Happily, Dad turned on the telly. *Family Feud* was almost over.

Mum said, 'I love *Family Feud*.'

Charlotte said, 'I love it, too.'

The evening news would be starting soon.

'Can we change channels?' I reached across the table but Dad slapped my hand away. 'Ow!'

I didn't want to see the news, be reminded about the lunch heist, which could cause me to have a delayed reaction to the trauma and which might cause Mum to notice I was no longer wearing her wig.

'There was a massacre at the tennis today,' said Mum. 'I heard it on 3AW. Can you imagine?'

Charlotte looked at me. 'There was a massacre?'

'No. Not a massacre.' I turned to Mum. 'No-one was hurt. It was a robbery.'

'Still, Erica, your company was involved *again*.' She gave me a look, like I was personally responsible for all the bad things my company does.

'I was there. No-one was hurt. Besides, it had nothing to do with Dega.'

'I'm glad you didn't let them steal your watch, Erica.' Mum addressed Jack and Charlotte. 'It was a twenty-first birthday present from Erica's father. He used to be a jeweller, you know. He had a shop at Chadstone!'

The news started. 'Did you hear Myer's having a big sale?' I said. Mum shooshed me.

The lunchtime heist was number one spot. The theft of Emilio's lucky charm was number two. Someone had taken a video on their mobile phone. I watched the tall, fat gunman rip the amulet from around my neck and the wig from my head. At the time, I thought I'd done a pretty good job fending him off, but from the angle the footage was taken, it looked like I readily gave up the amulet to save the wig.

Mum gasped. 'Is that you, dear?'

'No.'

There was footage of Emilio's devastation. Of him on the floor in the foetal position. The report said he may not be able to compete in the tournament.

'Oh, for God's sake,' I muttered.

Mum tsked. 'Blasphemy.'

The news said people had reported that the men spoke Russian. I glanced at Jack, who was watching me. Charlotte stared at the television, eyes shining.

The Dega Oil explosion was the next item. At least it was no longer top story. However, the brilliant journalist noted that the charity lunch, where the heist had taken place, was hosted by the very same company that had "caused" the death of three men and four dugongs, which are apparently endangered.

'They're not endangered,' I mumbled.

The news said that police were investigating a possible connection. They didn't mention the Russian connection, only that Dega Oil was at the centre of both "heinous" events. I hated the news. My mobile buzzed with messages. A Facebook friend commented that I'd single-handedly killed Emilio Mendez's chances of winning the Australian Open. What about the fact that *I* could have been killed?

There was a text from Luce: *Can I have your autograph?*

Helpful.

She messaged a smiley face. I ignored that and she sent another: *No, really, you okay?*

Please, someone talk about something else.

Charlotte said, 'You're wearing a lovely necklace, Mrs Jewell. I love necklaces.'

Oh, perfect. Thanks, Charlotte. Thanks very much. Let's remind everyone of Emilio's missing amulet.

Mum gushed, her fingers fluttering at her throat. 'It was a gift from Erica's father.'

Charlotte said, 'And you've got a lovely home.'

God bless Charlotte.

Mum said, 'I'll give you a tour of it, dear. After tea. You can see Erica's room, if you want.'

That's right. Just show my room to whoever.

'Erica has a wig, you know. I bought it for her and she's had it cut. I don't think she realises how much I paid for it,' Mum said as though referring to someone not in the room. Did she not see the news just then? 'It was long and luscious, like her own hair used to be.'

Jack came to my rescue. 'I like Erica's hair.'

Charlotte's face flushed. 'I love your garden, Mrs Jewell.'

'Oh, Tom works so hard to make it nice, don't you, Tom?' Mum nudged Dad's arm and he grunted.

Mum and Charlotte chatted some more. I could see Mum glancing at me, making comparisons. *Why can't Erica be a nice girl to her mother? I bet Charlotte is nice to her mother.*

'Do you play bridge, Mrs Jewell?'

'Not for a long time. I used to belong to a bridge club, you know.' She gazed wistfully at the wall. 'I loved playing bridge.'

'I love to play bridge.'

'Well, we should have a game!'

Maybe Charlotte would like to move into my bedroom and I could move into Jack's bedroom? While Mum and Charlotte made plans for a happy future together, I took the opportunity to quietly ask Jack about WA. 'How was your ... fishing trip?'

He glanced around the table. Dad was fully focused on adding potato cakes to his salt, Charlotte was flattering Mum, Mum was trying to work out how to give me back and keep Charlotte.

'Reasonably successful.'

'You caught some fish?'

'Not exactly.'

'How can it be successful if you didn't catch any fish?'

Mum tuned in. 'I didn't know you like fishing, Jack. Tom, you should go fishing with Jack in the bay. You could borrow whatsisname's boat.'

Dad grunted. Jack smiled at Mum and gave me a look. *Do we have to do this now?*

The answer was yes, we did. I gave him a big smile.

He said, 'We learned some things about the fish.'

'So that when you go again, you'll know what you need to do to catch them?'

'Not necessarily.'

'So, you'll go fishing in that same spot again?'

'Probably not.' Jack jumped slightly then, and there was a small frown. It was like he'd felt something. Something under the table. I narrowed my eyes at Charlotte. She was intent on soy-saucing her dim sim.

Mum said to Dad, 'Erica's pussy is so naughty, Tom.'

Dad grunted. Charlotte froze. Jack cleared his throat.

I continued. 'What about that … Sharon fish? I've heard it's pretty easy to catch.'

A small smile. 'I wouldn't know.'

Mum said, 'Your pussy went fishing, Erica.'

Jack had a coughing fit.

I watched Charlotte, who didn't look away from her plate. 'Is that so?' I said.

'He came in last night with a goldfish wriggling in his mouth. A goldfish! We don't even have a pond, so I don't know where on earth he found it. The neighbours will probably come knocking, wanting compensation.'

'I'll buy them a new one.' I turned back to Jack, not wanting to let him off the hook, no pun intended. 'Some big fish were killed by that explosion in Western Australia.'

Mum said, 'Oh, those poor dolphins! There, you see? Your company blowing things up again.'

'Dugongs, Mum.'

She shook her head in disgust at the loss of dolphins, dugongs, whatever.

'And those people were killed.' I watched Jack carefully. 'Russian fishermen.'

'Tragic.' Jack took a sip of water. 'I believe there was something about it on the front page of today's *Herald Sun*.' He looked at me pointedly, smirkingly. 'Perhaps there's a copy handy?'

'Well!' squealed Mum, jerking upright, snatching unfinished plates off the table. 'Let's have ice-cream! Come on, dear. You can organise the sweets.' She walked past, giving me a shove with her hip and almost knocking me off my chair, calling over her shoulder, 'Erica's a marvel in the kitchen, Jack!'

AFTER DINNER, Charlotte helped Mum with the dishes. Not something I'd bother doing because I'd get it wrong – if I put something in the dishwasher, Mum would move it. But all I heard from Mum was: 'Oh, you're very good at stacking the dishwasher, Charlotte.' And from Charlotte: 'You've got a lovely kitchen, Mrs Jewell.' Mutual admiration society in the kitchen.

Dad settled in front of the telly in the lounge room. I dragged Jack into the hallway and whispered but it probably sounded like a hiss. 'What was going on under the table?'

'What's going on with Mendez?'

Mum yelled, 'Tom! Just look what pussy brought in this time!'

I opened the hall cupboard and pulled Jack inside. It was pitch-black in there.

'You were playing footsies with Charlotte!'

'She nudged my foot. Actually, it was probably the cat.'

'It wasn't the cat and it was more than a nudge. I could tell by your face.'

'Okay, it was a rub.'

'A rub?'

'It was fleeting.'

'Like, she rubbed your leg with her toe?'

'Something like that.' He chuckled. 'Might have been your mother.'

'Yuck! Don't say that!'

He put his hands on my hips. 'Pretty cosy in here.'

'Maybe you'd rather be in here with Charlotte. Or Sharon.'

'Oh, for God's sake.' He pulled me against him.

I put my hands on his chest. 'What was all that fishing business?' I said.

'I have no idea.'

'You were talking in riddles.'

'Come here.'

He put his arms around my waist and nuzzled my neck; his breath scorched my skin, lips softly tracked the line of my jaw. Which caused me to forget what I was saying, and my body to go off on its own little tangent. My arms threw themselves around his neck and, with my fingers locked in his hair, I kissed him. He tightened his hold and the kiss got deeper. It was pretty sexy, actually, knowing we were at my parents' house, kissing in their cupboard. He gave a little moan and I wrapped a leg around his waist.

And then, there was light. We separated and I blinked at my father. There were a few seconds where no-one said anything, and Dad stood there with a look of slight amusement. Something vaguely interesting had finally happened in his house.

I could hear my mother. 'Goodness gracious groceries!'

'Broom?' said Dad.

I reached behind Jack and plucked the broom off the wall, handed it to Dad. He nodded and closed the cupboard door, and we were in darkness again.

But the moment had, unfortunately, passed.

CHAPTER 28

It was getting late – 8:30 – surely bed time for a woman my age. Jack said he'd go. Charlotte said she'd go. I stood at the door.

'Where's your car?' I asked Charlotte.

She pointed. 'Just up the road a bit.'

I watched Jack get into his car, making sure Charlotte didn't slip into his and do something. Mind you, if she did slip into Jack's car and do something, I was sure he'd kick her out. Very politely, of course.

I said to Mum, 'Thanks for having Charlotte at the last minute.'

'Oh, nothing phrases me.' She was in front of the television, knitting in hand.

Yeah, nothing *fazes* you, Mum, except everything to do with me. 'Okay, well, goodnight.'

'Goodnight, dear.'

'Night, Dad.'

Grunt.

I stopped at the lounge-room door. 'Mum, do you see much of Mrs Booth?'

'A bit.'

'I know you don't like her.'

'Oh, she's perfectly nice! I think she's seen the light.'

'What do you mean?'

'She's been coming to church.'

'You're joking.'

Mum looked at me like she didn't understand what I meant, which she possibly didn't. Mum doesn't make jokes. She doesn't believe in laughing. She thinks it's disrespectful to God or something. But Mrs Booth in a Catholic church?

'I always thought she was a bit creepy.' A pagan. A witch.

'That's not very nice of you, dear.'

No. I suppose it's not. Maybe I should make an effort to be nicer. 'I might come to church with you this Sunday.'

'Confession?' She looked hopeful.

'I don't need to confess.'

I thought for a moment Mum *was* going to laugh. Her mouth curved into the tiniest smile but quickly resumed its usual pursed state.

As I was changing into my pyjamas, my mobile rang. I didn't recognise the number, except that it had the same first digits as my work number. I answered. It was John Degraves, calling from his office. JD had never called me from his office. If it wasn't Team business, for which he used a secret shoe phone or something, he always had his PA call me.

'This is a disaster. I need you to go see Emilio, fix this.'

'What? Now?'

'Yes. Right now. He's threatening to pull out of the tournament.'

'He can't!' But he'd hung up. I called Teresa, who sounded like she'd rather be diving off oil rigs in a cyclone.

'Do you want me to come see Emilio?' Please say no. Please say everything's fine, that he'll get over it.

'I'm not sure it would help. He may never recover from this loss.'

'Loss? But it's just a —'

'You do not understand.'

'Well, if you think my coming won't help —'

'In fact, it is probably a good idea. We must try everything. I will meet you in Emilio's room.'

WHEN I GOT to the hotel, Teresa opened the door to Emilio's darkened suite and ushered me in.

'He is in bed.' She put her finger to her lips.

'Asleep? I can come back tom —'

'No, not sleeping. He just lies there.'

Oh boy.

'Come.' She led the way.

Emilio lay on his side, staring at nothing, with the covers pulled up to his chin. The bedside lamp was on and I could see his face. He'd been crying.

I sat gently, placed a hand on his arm, whispered, 'Emilio? It's me. Eri — Emily.'

He didn't move or acknowledge me.

'Come now, you must be brave.' Oh geez, did I really say that? *Come now.* In fact, I wanted to shake him, slap his face, tell him to get over himself and play the goddam tournament and win the bloody thing so I could get back to my life.

'Emilio, you're the best player in the world. You can win this tournament. You can!'

He turned his head slowly and looked at me, emotionless, which was better than hateful. 'You do not understand.' He looked away.

'I *do* understand. I understand you're very upset by what happened, and I'm truly sorry about that but I couldn't help it! The man had a gun and he was stronger than me.' I played the sympathy card, with a slight whimper. 'I could have been killed, you know.'

'I know. I know it is not your fault.'

'Thank you, Emilio. Thank you for understanding. But now, you and I have a job to do. We have a tournament to win!'

He shook his head.

'I promise you —' What? 'I promise that together we can do it. Emilio and Emily. We're a team!'

He turned and pulled the covers over his head.

Emilio stayed like that for two hours. I sat by his side, gave him a pat, a little shake. I lay next to him, behind him, put my arm around him. 'Please, Emilio.'

Teresa ordered herbal tea. I stared out the window, at the night sky, seeking inspiration from God, the one who'd been so helpful earlier today. I checked the time. I needed sleep!

I took a sip of tea, thinking it might taste better during a crisis. It didn't. 'Maybe he'll be better in the morning.'

'Oh, no, he will not. If anything, he will be worse.' Teresa's lower lip trembled. 'We could pray —'

'Yes! Let's pray.'

'— but I am afraid tomorrow morning we will make the announcement.'

'What announcement?'

'That Emilio Mendez will not play in the Australian Open tennis tournament this year.'

'What?' I gripped Teresa's arm. 'You can't. You can't let this happen!'

'Oh, but it has happened. And it was not *I* who made it happen.' She gave me a long, angry look.

I went into Emilio's bedroom. He hadn't moved, but I knew by the loud sighing that he wasn't asleep. I sat again by his side and leaned over him.

'Emilio.' I gave him a little pat. 'Emilio, guess what?'

From under the covers came his muffled voice. '*Que?*'

'I've spoken with God.' Oh, God help me.

The covers slid down to his chin and he blinked up at me. 'What did he say?'

'He said … he said he's going to help me find your lucky charm.'

'He cannot find it.'

'Yes, he can! Together we can. God and Emily. We can't fail!'

Emilio sat up. I gripped his shoulders. 'Emilio, trust me. Trust that I will do this. For you.'

He stared into my eyes, seeking the truth in the crap I was talking.

I continued with the crap. 'God and Emilio and Emily. Together we are unbeatable, yes?'

'*Si* ...'

'Yes! I will find your lucky charm. I promise. With the Good Lord's help, I will do it.'

'You will find *mi amuleto?*'

'Yes. Yes, I will.'

Yes. Yes, I will go to hell.

*G*ood one, Erica. Brilliant.

After that ridiculous offering, Emilio looked me right in the eye – his face so earnest and beautiful – and I'd nodded enthusiastically, putting a stamp on the deal. The promise.

This was followed by hugging. Emilio had leaped from the bed, wearing only undies, and held me tight against him, whispering Spanish into my ear and following it up with a translation: 'I know now you are completely devoted to me and will do anything to find *mi amuleto* and help me win this tournament. Anything at all, isn't that right?' And he'd held me at arm's length so he could see my face when I'd said, yes, anything. Anything at all. I'd then suggested he focus on his tennis and try not to think about the amulet.

'Ah, but it is always on my mind.'

'But you'll play tennis, won't you? Until I find it? I mean, I might not be able to get it right away. You know, I have to track down … the robbers.'

'*Si*, Emily, but you have made the promise, and until that wonderful moment, when I hold it again in my hand …' Emilio had then turned to Teresa, who was standing by the door, crying quietly, clutching her rosary beads. 'Your precious boy is back, Mother Teresa! Let us celebrate with herbal tea!'

ON THE WAY HOME, I called Jack on his mobile. It was now almost midnight and I didn't care if he was asleep. I didn't care if I woke everyone. I especially didn't care if I woke Sharon Stone, who, if she was in her own bed, shouldn't be anywhere near Jack's mobile phone anyway. He answered, and I could hear the telly in the background.

'Can't sleep?' he said.

'Don't suppose you could help me find Emilio's lucky charm.'

'Where are you?'

'On my way home. JD called me, wanted me to go see Emilio.'

'Why?'

'Because after the bloody thing got stolen, Emilio turned into a baby, thumb-sucking and all. But he's fine now because I promised him the universe. And more.'

'I think there's a word for that, Erica.'

'I didn't promise *that*.' Did I? 'There's something else.'

'Uh-oh.'

I told him about the real lucky charm. The one I left in the supermarket trolley. I told him about going to Chadstone to get another one. 'It cost two hundred dollars.'

He was silent.

'So the guys who stole the lucky charm have got a fake one,' I said. More silence. 'What are you thinking?'

'My mind's empty of anything useful. Never in my life have I had to consider a scenario like this.'

'Well, I was thinking, it's kind of a lucky break for me, isn't it? I mean, I can just pretend the real one got stolen.'

'You're digging a hole for yourself. You do know that.'

'What can possibly go wrong?' I said.

'Why don't you just go back to Chadstone and get another?'

'Oh my God! Why didn't I think of that? But no, that's stupid. Emilio will want to see it and he'll know straight away.'

'That's true.'

'I think his is from some posh Spanish jeweller.'

'No doubt.'

'I need to get the one back from the supermarket trolley.'

'Come to my place.'

'What, now?'

'Yes, you need a good spanking.'

I gave a little shiver. 'Maybe … no, I'm too tired. I've got so much to do. I probably should just go to work right now and stay there all night.' I blew out my breath, thinking about how much I could get done if I was a vampire like Rosalind and didn't need sleep. It would mean I could go to Jack's. 'Do you think the police will try to find Emilio's fake lucky charm?'

'No.'

'Good. Will you help me find the real one?'

'No.'

'Thanks a bunch.'

'You're welcome.'

'Will you at least come to church with me? Help me make amends with God?'

He let out a laugh. 'You're on your own with that one, babe.'

Babe. Funny how a single word uttered by the right person can cause one's heart and stomach to switch places. Mind you, the thought of being put over Jack's knee didn't hurt, either.

CHAPTER 30

Steve called me at nine the next morning, Saturday, waking me up.

'Have you finished my renovation?' I said.

'Have you been appliance shopping?'

'Oh. Um, I'm doing it now.'

'Now?'

'Yep. On the way to The Good Guys. As we speak.'

'I don't believe you.'

'It's true!'

'You're still in bed.'

'I am not!'

'I *know* you're still in bed.'

'*How* do you know, smarty pants?'

'Because I'm sitting in your mother's kitchen.'

'Bloody hell,' I grumbled and hung up. I wandered out in my pyjamas. Mum was dressed, face fully made up, hair perfect. She slid a plate of freshly made scones across the bench to Steve, who sat on a stool, grinning at me.

'Morning.'

'Hi.' I put the kettle on.

Mum huffed, gave me a disapproving glare that translated to: you should have been up hours ago, cooking or sewing, doing things for men.

'I've known you all our lives,' said Steve. 'You wouldn't get out of bed for Santa when we were kids.'

'Is that why you're here? To force me to go buy appliances?'

'Yep. I'm going with you.'

'But I need to go into work.' I shuddered at the thought of everything that needed doing. The tennis was starting on Monday. Emilio's first match was Tuesday. I needed to visit Mrs Booth.

'Let me just say this.' Steve's eyes held mine to make sure I was listening. 'The longer it takes you to buy your appliances, the longer the reno will take, and the longer it'll be before —'

'Okay, okay, I get it.' The longer it'll be before I can move out of my mother's. Suddenly, nothing mattered more than buying my appliances. I wondered if I could just go in my PJs.

Mum said, as she carried Dad's coffee and scones to his throne in the lounge room, 'Remember that poor Stephen is doing you a big favour, Erica.'

I made a face at *poor* Stephen behind Mum's back, just like I used to do twenty years ago, and he gave me a snarky smile, just like he used to do twenty years ago, sitting in the same spot at Mum's kitchen bench.

'It's not a favour, Mum. I'm paying him.' I poked my tongue at Steve.

'Come on,' he said. 'Get dressed.'

'Do you remember Mrs Booth?'

'Of course.'

'Do you think she's still a witch?'

Steve burst out laughing. 'Of course not.'

'I reckon she is.'

'She's probably really nice. Like her daughter. She saw me in Richmond and said hello.'

'Really? You saw Ruth?'

'Yep. She's nice.'

My mobile rang in my bedroom. 'Hold on.' I ran to get it. I didn't know the number so didn't answer, but returned to the kitchen with it. One minute later, the doorbell rang. I heard Dad grunt as he lifted himself from his chair in the lounge room.

'Who on earth could that be?' said Mum, bustling about. 'Maybe the Jehovah's Witnesses. Well, they can just turn right around and visit next door, as far as I'm concerned.' She looked at Steve. 'The good Lord and I are already on excellent terms.'

'You're an angel, Mrs J.'

I heard the front door open, and a loud, familiar voice said, '*Hola, padre de Emily!*'

Oh, Jesus. Emilio appeared at the kitchen door with a huge smile and arms spread wide, looking around the room. He took in the sight of me in my PJs, walked up and wrapped his arms around me in a tight hug. What happened to all the misery? The little boy curled up in bed, crying?

'Goodness gracious groceries!' said Mum.

'This is *madre, si?*' Emilio took Mum's hand and kissed it, bowing low, saying something in Spanish. Mum clutched her other hand to her throat, as if protecting it from a vampire strike.

Emilio turned to Steve, who looked as entertained as I'd ever seen him.

'And, Emily, this must be your brother.'

Yeah, sure, brother. Why not? Steve stood and Emilio shook his hand vigorously.

'You're Emilio Mendez.'

'Yes, my friend! You would like my autograph?'

'Sure.'

While signing one of Mum's pink paper napkins, Emilio told Steve that yes, indeed, he planned on winning the tennis and earning another however-many millions through sponsorship. And just as soon as Emily found his *amuleto*, his life would be perfect. I looked at Mum, hand still at her throat, staring like it was Dracula, not a tennis player, standing in her kitchen. Poor Mum. My phone rang in my hand. It was Jack. I jogged down the passage to my bedroom, answering as I went.

'Hi!' I hoped he couldn't hear the loud Spanish in the kitchen.

'Good morning. Why is there a stretch limo in front of your house?'

What?

'Please don't say it's who I think it is.'

I flicked my pink curtains aside and pulled apart the venetians. Jack's Audi was parked opposite Emilio's limousine, which was as long as my parent's property was wide.

'Is that you sitting out there?'

'Yep.'

'What are you doing here?'

'I … I was passing,' he said. 'Need a few things at Chadstone.'

'You wouldn't be caught dead at Chadstone Shopping Centre.'

'Is the kettle on?'

'Why? You don't want to come in, do you?'

'I've got something for your mother.'

'What is it?'

'Erica —'

'I don't think you should come in.'

'Is someone there I'll want to hurt?' He was getting out of his car.

'Alright, come in, but you'd better leave your gun in the car.'

Too late to change out of my jarmies. I was worried about Mum in the kitchen, having heart failure. I headed for the front door, waving to Dad watching telly in the lounge room. 'Stay there, Dad. It's safer.' Or maybe he should call the police. Just in case. I could hear Emilio talking loudly, telling Mum and Steve about his devastating loss but, fortunately, Emily has vowed to devote her life to helping him in every possible way.

I opened the door as Jack stepped up to it, looking beautiful. About as opposite to the way I looked as anyone possibly could. As Emilio's voice came closer, Jack stopped moving and adopted his the-enemy's-closing-in expression. And then, Emilio was standing behind me.

'Ah, *amigo! Cómo estás?*'

Without smiling, Jack said something in Spanish and Emilio laughed.

'I thought you didn't speak Spanish,' I said.

Jack ignored that and stood there watching Emilio with narrowed eyes while Emilio grinned at him.

Emilio turned to me. 'Come, *querida*, we have things to do.'

'What? Where?'

'Chadstone Shopping Centre. The shopping capital of all Australia.'

'You're going to Chaddy?'

'Yes, *ángel*, with you. I want to see everything!'

'Um, I have to go to church.'

'On Saturday morning? Surely not.'

'It's confession day.'

'It is a good idea to confess about *mi amuleto*. But tomorrow, Emily. Today, Chadstone Shopping Centre.'

'But don't you have to play tennis or something? Do some training?'

'I thought you might like lunch at a winery,' Jack piped up.

My head snapped around and I stared at Jack. 'You want to take me to a winery?'

'I am not interested in visiting a winery,' said Emilio.

And before Jack could inform Emilio that he wasn't invited, Mum arrived. 'Jack! Praise the Lord! Thank goodness you're here.' She ushered him in, pushing past Emilio to make room for her darling. Mum muttered to Jack conspiratorially, as though Emilio and I were out of earshot, 'I just don't know what to make of this business. Italian men coming to the door like that. What on earth he wants with Erica, I'll never know.'

Then Jack and Steve were talking in the kitchen. Mum was probably jamming up some scones for them. There was kettle noise. Laughing. I wanted to be in there, too. In the kitchen with Jack and Steve, laughing, having cups of tea and scones.

'Come, Emily. Go change!'

'Emilio, I'm really sorry but —'

My phone rang. I was still holding it. It was JD. I glanced outside, in case he was sitting in his car.

'Hello?'

'Good morning, Erica.'

'Hi, Mr Degraves.'

Emilio was watching me, smiling his winning smile. *I will get my way with you, no matter what. No matter how much you don't want to go shopping at Chadstone, the greatest shopping centre in the southern hemisphere, you have no choice but to go because I want it. And then you will find my precious amuleto.*

'I had a call from Emilio —'

'I know. He wants me to go shopping.'

'Ah, you're on top of that. Very good, Erica. You know how important this is.'

'I know, Mr Degraves.'

'Good work lifting his spirits, by the way. I don't know how you managed it but … good work.' He hung up.

I managed it by prostituting myself, that's how.

'Emilio, you don't want to go to Chadstone.'

'Yes, I do. I want to go there. I want to see it.'

'But why? You'll hate it.' *I'll* hate it. 'There'll be millions of people all pushing and shoving and long queues —'

'Ah, heaven for me!'

Sigh. How to get out of it? I needed to go to work. I needed to get appliances. I needed time with Jack. I needed to make Emilio happy so he'll win the Australian Open and Rosalind can have her promotion and bugger off and the world will stop hating me. And that was it. My number one.

CHAPTER 31

As the limo pulled out from the kerb, I tried to make myself feel better by remembering that I *do* love Chaddy. But with Lucy, not Emilio. Not even with my mother. And certainly not on Saturday morning. Saturday morning at Chaddy! The only thing worse is pre-Christmas at Chaddy. Or Boxing Day sales.

Jack wasn't happy when I said I had to go shopping with Emilio.

'You're telling me you *have* to go.'

'JD's orders.'

He'd given me a shitty look. 'Well, Sharon's keen to visit some wineries …'

Bastard. Bitch.

Steve reminded me, 'Remember what I told you —'

'I know, I know.'

And they'd all left, except Emilio. Mum took me aside and asked me about the Italian man.

'He's not Italian, Mum. He's Spanish.'

'It's all the same.'

'No, it's not. Actually, he's Australian now.'

Emilio had waited in the car while I had a quick shower, dressed and pushed my hair into some kind of acceptable shape. He was speaking Spanish into his phone when I got in the car, opened for me by the Danny DeVito driver. Emilio stayed on the call as we drove along. The car was several miles long. By the time the back of it passed through the start of an intersection, the front was already through the other side. The driver took his time, sitting there behind a darkly tinted screen. Emilio and I could have done anything in the back and he wouldn't have known. Oh, I shouldn't think those things. Law of attraction, and all that.

Emilio stopped talking and gave me a look. He hung up. Did he hear my thoughts? He moved closer and whispered in my ear.

'Do you know, Emily, even with your unattractive hair, I have the feelings of attraction for you.'

'Really?' Should I feel flattered? I suppose many women would. My hair wasn't that bad, was it? I tried to see my reflection in the window. The car turned onto Poath Road. I pointed. 'Chadstone's over there. We're going the wrong way.'

'But I must not engage in the sexual activity when I play in a tournament.'

'No?' I watched over my shoulder as Chadstone grew further away.

'It will damage my concentration.'

I looked at him. He was smiling at me, very sexily. He moved closer.

'Oh. Um. Emilio —'

He took hold of my hips and I let out a yelp as he pulled me down on the long bench seat. He lay on top of me and kissed my neck.

'Emilio!' I pushed his chest. 'Emilio, stop it!'

'It is alright. I have told the driver to take a detour.' He kissed my face all over. 'We can have some fun, yes?'

'No! Emilio …' I struggled under him.

'It is harmless, Emily. I know how chaste you are.' He blew onto my neck, which tickled and I couldn't help but giggle, scrunching up my shoulders to stop him getting in there. He nuzzled his way in and blurted, and made hungry eating noises like a parent does into a child's neck and I screamed laughing.

'*Stop!*'

Emilio didn't stop but the car did, and I tried to see where we were. I worried someone would be able to see in. Imagine if someone snapped a pic of me lying on the back seat of a stretch limo under Emilio Mendez? And put it on Facebook. My stomach flipped at the thought of it. At least Jack wasn't on Facebook. That's because he'd rather eat his own vomit.

Then I heard the bells of the level crossing. The limo's engine cut out. Something crawled up my spine.

'Emilio, get up.' I shoved him. 'Emilio!'

He sat up, laughing, pushing hair out of his eyes.

I sat up also, looking around, horrified to see that the limo was parked right over the crossing. There were no cars in front of us, and none directly behind. Had the car broken down? Emilio moved to the front and tapped on the glass partition.

I stared up the tracks, watching the train approach. It was coming fast. An express? I tried to the door. It was locked. 'Emilio!'

He looked at me. 'The driver has gone.'

'*What?* Oh, Jesus. The train's coming!'

We tried all the doors. Banged on the windows. People were out there, waving at us, telling us the train was coming.

I kicked the windows.

Emilio yelled in Spanish.

The train's horn sounded in a continuous blast. There was the scream of brakes and wheels on tracks and the screams of people on the streets; all the noises willing the train to stop. I threw myself against the far side of the car, shut my eyes and wrapped my arms around my head. Emilio held me, putting his body between me and the train.

'It will be alright, Emily!'

I could hear the grinding whine of the train's locked brakes, its desperate horn. I squeezed my eyes tighter, tried to press my body through the wall of the car. And then, a dull crunch, and the car rocked gently. There was complete quiet for just a moment before shouts, car horns, the sounds of movement. I looked. Emilio laughed.

The train had nudged the limo and stopped. There it was – the flat front of the train less than two metres from my face, taking up the entire view through the cracked windows. I slid to the floor and sat there.

WE SAT at the outside table of a café adjacent to Hughesdale train station. Someone brought us coffee. I heard sirens. Emilio still wanted to go to Chadstone.

'But Emilio, we've had a very traumatic experience.'

'Yes, Emilita. Shopping will make us calm. Would you rather sit in a police station?'

'I think the police will want to talk to us. That driver abandoned us.' I looked around. 'Where did he go?'

'I do not know.'

'Did you know him? He was the driver who took us to the tennis last week.'

'I do not know.' He shrugged. 'Teresa organises the vehicles.'

Three ambulances, two police cars, a fire truck and two tow trucks turned out. Only one towie was needed, although he stood there gazing at the scene, scratching his head. The train had backed up so the gates could open and let traffic through. The police wanted to talk to us. They asked if we'd been aware of the car breaking down, if the driver had given us warning, who the driver was, *where* he was and what the car company was called. They said someone had seen him running away. Emilio gave them Teresa's phone number and an autograph they didn't ask for. We knew nothing. We went to Chadstone on the bus.

<h1 style="text-align:center">CHAPTER 32</h1>

Emilio hadn't been on a bus in years. He told me he lived in South America for a while with his wealthy father and took the bus just to be rebellious. I used my Myki card to pay but Emilio didn't have one, so he didn't pay. Instead, he gave the driver a fifty-dollar note and as the driver sat there staring at it, Emilio strode down the aisle, saying hello to everyone. The driver and I looked at each other, then he shrugged and drove on, pocketing the money. Emilio chatted to people but no-one talked to him. They stared out the windows. I was worried he might start offering autographs, so I pushed him to the end of the aisle and onto the back seat.

'When you have found *mi amuleto*, life will again be *perfecto*.'

I patted his hand. 'We'll find it. In the meantime, just remember that you're the best tennis player in the world and everyone loves you.'

'*Me amas*, Emily?'

'Sure – what?'

'You love me?'

'Um … look over there, Emilio. That's where my friend Lucy and I used to go for a milkshake after school.'

'I must meet your friend! We will get along well, I am sure.'

I thought about Lucy meeting Emilio and being starstruck, and then I thought about Lucy meeting Sharon Stone and wanting to kill her. Maybe I should organise a dinner party at Mum's and invite them all. And Charlotte Johnson. I smiled at the thought of it. Especially at the thought of Mum having a "foreigner" at her dining table. As a teenager I'd often daydreamed about turning up at Mum's after school with a bunch of friends, all with unpronounceable surnames and "strange" outfits. I giggled.

'What is amusing you, *querida*?'

'Oh, nothing. I'm just … thinking about something funny.'

Emilio took my hand and kissed the back of it. 'You are happy because we are so right together, you and I. Emilio and Emily. We are meant to be. Even though you have made a terrible evil against me.' He tickled under my chin. 'When the tennis is finished, we will have the *amorio*, yes?'

'*Amorio*?'

'There is something about you that tempts me.'

'Me?'

'We will sleep together and I have a happy memory.'

The lady in front of us turned and gave me a dirty look. It was the kind of look my mother would give if she'd overheard such a conversation. Then she'd come home and talk about the hussy on the bus. There'd be no mention of the bloke and his presumptuous behaviour. I pretended to look for something in my bag.

'Emilio, why do you think the driver abandoned us?' I thought I should let Jack know about it, in case. In case what? In case I wanted him to panic about my safety and rush to my side?

Emilio shrugged. 'Who knows? In Peru, this kind of thing happens all the time. A man would kill you for one Australian dollar.'

'Really?'

'*Si*.'

'But the driver didn't steal from us.'

'No. He did not.'

'I was thinking about yesterday, at the charity lunch.'

'Yes, Melbourne is a very violent city. I am pleased to live in Sydney.'

'It's a bit of a coincidence, don't you think? That we'd get robbed by armed gunmen yesterday, then today a chauffeur tries to kill us.' My stomach did another one of those flip things. Is that what really happened? The driver had tried to *kill* us?

'Death today was unlikely. Australian trains do not travel very fast. He was able to stop, you see?'

'But he did run into us. Just.'

'Yes.' Emilio took my hand and kissed it again. 'But we are here, alive, and we are going to the greatest shopping centre in the universe!'

I extracted my hand. 'The universe?'

'*Si.* I hear it is that remarkable.'

'Okay, well, I hope you're not disappointed.'

WE GOT off the bus at the Coles supermarket entrance. Impressive start to our Chadstone Shopping Centre adventure.

'Where shall we go first, *ángel?*' He held my hand and I let him. It was a very European thing to do. It didn't necessarily mean anything, did it? 'I want to buy you a gift.'

A gift! Tiffany's came to mind and I quickly erased it. I didn't want to remind him of the missing amulet. Also, accepting a gift from Tiffany's might give him the wrong idea. I wondered if Emilio was always attracted to much older women. And I wondered how many of his "girlfriends" lasted longer than the duration of a tennis tournament. Probably long enough for them to have the *amorio* before he realised how disappointing they were and moved on. What a poor, confused boy he was. And yet, so charming and brave and handsome. I hoped he'd meet someone special one day. Someone patient and worthy and the same age.

'Have you been to David Jones?' I checked the centre map.

'Yes, in Sydney. But let us go there and see what we find on the way.' He looked around. 'It is annoying we do not have someone to carry the shopping bags.'

Oh, yes. How annoying. I often say to Lucy when we're shopping at Chaddy, you forgot to bring someone to carry the bags. As we walked I could see that people recognised Emilio. Some stared openly, pointing and saying, 'That's Emilio Mendez.' I hoped I looked alright; I didn't want people thinking I wasn't worthy of him. How horrible to be a celebrity. Imagine not being able to go out shopping in tracky dacks and without make-up and with hair looking like mine. Fans aimed their phones at us. Emilio smiled and waved to them. Some came up for an autograph. He laughed and obliged. Someone asked me for an autograph. I signed "Emily" by mistake. Then someone pointed out that I was the reason Emilio might lose the tournament. That I'd been the one charged with safeguarding the famous, precious amulet and instead of protecting it, I'd given it to an armed man.

Emilio had to stop the growing crowd from shouting abuse at me. 'Come now, *mis amigos*, Emily is committed to finding my stolen *amuleto*, and helping me win this tournament.' He gave me a squeeze. 'Besides, she is *muy bonito*, no?'

They murmured their acceptance and took photos of us. I stood with my arm around Emilio's waist, smiling but trying to look shame-faced at the same time. I mean, what else could I do to save myself from a lynching?

BY THE TIME we reached Lululemon, the crowd of people wanting autographs on various things including their skin, or photographs with Emilio, was thick around us. He laughed and posed, lapping up the love. I took the opportunity to step away and phone Jack about the train incident. When I took my phone from my bag, I saw that he'd tried to call me. I dialled, and he answered straight away.

'Are you alright?' He sounded anxious. 'I'm on my way back.'

'Back from where? What have you heard?'

'The news report that said Emilio Mendez and his girlfriend were involved in an accident at Hughesdale train station.'

Bugger, I'd been hoping we could keep Emilio's name out of this. 'That's why I'm calling you.' Jack was in his car, on speaker. Roof down. I could hear the road noise. 'Can you talk?'

'Tell me what happened.'

Was Sharon in the car? Were they on the way to a nice winery for a picnic by the lake? There was part of me – the really childish part – that wanted to launch into a whiny description of the horror, to say how distressed I was and that I thought he should come and get me. But knowing Sharon might be listening, and because it was a ridiculous thing to do anyway, I told him the mechanical details of the event, leaving out the part about Emilio blurting in my neck and making me laugh so hard I nearly wet my pants. 'But I'm fine. You don't need to come back from wherever you are.'

The road noise stopped and the phone was taken off speaker. Had he pulled over? 'Who was the driver of the limousine?'

I shrugged. 'Don't know. Same guy who drove us to Rod Laver the other day. He looked like Danny DeVito. Emilio said his manager organises his cars. He just told the guy where to go and that was it.'

'Who's his manager?'

'Teresa someone.'

'Have you talked to the police?'

'Yeah.'

'Where are you now?'

'Chadstone. Shopping, believe it or not.'

'Emilio's either very brave or very stupid. Does he realise he could be a target?'

'Why would someone want to hurt Emilio?'

'*I* want to hurt him.' Then, 'Why were you travelling south down Poath Road, by the way? Isn't that heading away from Chadstone?'

Oh. 'Um, Emilio wanted to see the sights.'

'The sights of Hughesdale?'

'Yep.' Now I'd lost sight of Emilio. Was he still in there? Two security guards arrived. 'I'd better go. Emilio's being swamped by fans.'

He sighed, loudly. 'I'll call you later. Please be careful, Erica.'

'Okay. See ya.' I nearly said 'Love you' by mistake, like I sometimes say to Lucy.

The security guards had thinned out the crowd and Emilio staggered toward me, laughing, pen still working furiously.

'This is amazing! I love Chadstone Shopping Centre!'

'You see? Everyone still loves you.'

I pulled him away from the last couple of fans and into Lululemon, but not before the security guards got an autograph each. Inside the store I took a deep breath, thinking how much I'd like to be at my desk right now. Or cooking with my mother. What a big, eventful day so far, and it wasn't even midday. Emilio looked around, made his way to the counter to chat with the girls behind it. They got their phones and asked me to take pictures of them with Emilio. No-one asked for a picture of me. I bought a cap for Emilio to wear and told him to put on his sunglasses, telling him I had a peculiar phobia about being crushed to death in a stampeding crowd of tennis fans.

Inside La Joyería jewellery store – where I got the fake charm – was a life-size cardboard cut-out of Emilio Mendez wearing his precious amulet and his Rolex watch across his knuckles. The latest trend in watch-wearing, it seemed, as all posh watch ads with famous people showed them wearing the watches across their knuckles instead of on their wrists. Including Vladimir Vavilov, who was wearing his Patek Philippe on his knuckles and who was not only staring broodily at us from a poster, but who also happened to be in the store, batting off fans and staring broodily at Emilio.

Emilio gazed at the image of himself, at his amulet. Gold replicas were displayed on a navy suede cushion in the window of the store. I stood in front of them so Emilio wouldn't see. Like a mother distracting a sulky child, I said, 'Look, Emilio, there's Vladimir Vavilov!'

'Vladimir, my man!' Emilio pushed through the chattering, excited crowd and took Vlad's hand in one of those blokey, high-five type handshakes. Vlad's expression didn't change from broody. Emilio could take some sulky lessons from him. Russian people never seem very happy, but then in Russia it's pretty cold, and I don't think they have a very good sense of humour. Maybe because of those dictators. Or was it communists? Vlad was probably jealous of Emilio living in Australia now, even though Vlad was still top dog on the tennis circuit. There were also those rumours that Vavilov's family had connections with the Russian mafia, and that wouldn't make you smile much either in case they knocked you on the head with a tyre iron and threw you into the boot of a car. Or was that the Italian mafia that did that? I thought how much the paparazzi would have loved to be lurking at Chaddy right now.

There was a tap on my shoulder and I turned to find Charlotte Johnson standing there.

'Hi!' I said. 'Fancy seeing you here.'

'I love Chadstone.'

'Yeah, it's great, isn't it? But I wouldn't usually come on a Saturday morning.'

'Oh, no, me either.'

'What brings you here today?' I kept an eye on Emilio, who was happy with all the attention.

'What brings *you* here?

'Looking after Dega Oil's charge.' I pointed to Emilio. 'And I suppose I need some more clothes for work. I guess I could get them now.'

'Yes, I need to get new clothes for work.'

'Where do you usually buy your clothes?'

'Where do you usually shop?'

I shrugged. 'Everywhere.'

'Yeah, I'm not fussy either.'

'Oh, I'm pretty fussy once I'm inside a store.'

'Me, too.'

Okay, Madam Robot. Time to move on. I said goodbye, that I had to keep Emilio moving. The crowd around the world's two top tennis players was huge and growing. They'd been forced out of the store by the oozing throng, and more security guards arrived to help keep everyone calm. I pushed through to Emilio, poking and pinching people to force them out of my way. As I got near the front, one girl took particular offence at my poking and shoved me, and if the crowd hadn't been so thick I would've hit the ground. Instead I was pushed into someone else who also gave me a shove, so then I was like a ball in a pinball machine, bouncing off angry people. I heard Emilio shout,

'Hey! That is my Emily!' and he forced his way through the crowd to reach me. Some bloke shoved Emilio for some reason, which caused another guy to shove the shoving bloke and then there were lots of blokes throwing punches at each other. And girls throwing punches at each other. And one at me but I ducked and it landed on Emilio's chin, which he ignored and flung his arms around me, backing out of the crowd using his body as a buffer.

'Emilio.' I watched the mess of bodies, sprawled on the floor, diving and hitting. 'Can we please leave?'

'But, Emilita, I have not bought you a gift.' He rubbed his chin.

I pulled his hand away and inspected it. A small, red mark that would probably bruise. 'Sorry, Emilio.'

He grinned. 'I have saved you.'

I couldn't help but smile back. He was so cute. I kissed his chin. 'Thank you.'

'And now, *ángel*. Let us shop!'

And so we did.

CHAPTER 33

The brawl at Chadstone Shopping Centre made the evening news, with footage that had been taken on mobile phones and posted all over YouTube. It had even taken precedence over the train crash at Hughesdale, and newsreaders discussed the trail of destruction left by Emilio Mendez and his girlfriend, mentioning again the charity lunch heist, and the missing amulet, and throwing in a remark about the oil rig explosion, because that's got everything to do with me, right?

I watched television with Mum and Dad. Can't imagine what else a 33-year-old woman would be doing on a Saturday night. Especially when her charge had "finished" with her for the day and especially as she was too proud to call her friend-with-benefits to see what he was doing.

Mum, resting the knitting on her lap and pointing at the telly, said, 'Is that you, dear?'

'Yeah.' I sighed. On the screen, Emilio was in the process of hoisting me over a couple of women grappling on the floor.

'I knew that foreign man was a troublemaker.'

'He's a famous tennis player, Mum.'

'Still.'

'Actually, I think I might have started it.'

Mum clicked her tongue and resumed interest in her knitting. 'I had a visit from that nice girl this morning. The one who came for fish and chips.'

'Charlotte?'

'That's it. I couldn't for the life of me remember her name.'

'What time did she come?'

'Oh, not long after you left with the dark-skinned man.'

I swear if I ever have children I'm not letting Mum near them until they're at least twenty-one and informed about the world and its prej-udices. 'Emilio, Mum. His name's Emilio.' And his skin's not even dark. It's more … tanned and gorgeous.

She pursed her lips.

'What did Charlotte want?'

'She brought me some roses from her mother's garden. Wasn't that nice? But I don't think her mother's a very nice person.'

And you're so lovely, Mum. 'What makes you say that?'

'Well, she doesn't give her daughter guidance on certain things.'

'Like what?'

'Like choosing appropriate outfits for certain occasions. She was dressed quite scruffily, you know.' Mum's eyes flicked over me, a not very subtle suggestion that I, too, dress quite scruffily. 'She wanted to see your room. She saw it last night but she wanted to see it in daylight.'

How embarrassing. 'Why?'

Mum shrugged. 'That's another reason why I don't think her mother's very nice. I don't think Charlotte has a nice bedroom like yours. She was quite taken with it, you know.'

'It's pretty messy.'

Another look: *Yes, it is messy. You should have tidied it in case someone wanted to see it.*

'I don't really want people going into my room, and I don't want to get too close to Charlotte. She's an employee, remember.'

'I've invited her to come any time she wants, for a game of bridge.'

'I wish you hadn't.'

'The Bible profitised this, you know.'

'Prophesied what?'

'Children being rude to their parents. It's a sign that the end of the world is nigh.'

'You think the world is about to end because I asked you to respect my privacy?'

Pursed lips. End of discussion. Mum focused fully on her knitting, even though she didn't need to look to know what bits went where. She was creating something that looked suspiciously like a baby beanie to add to her collection of knitted baby clothes. I knew better than to ask who it was for, because this was no doubt Mum using the Law of Attraction to get what she wanted. And what she wanted was me, decently married to none other than Jack Jones, spitting out five or six babies like the good Catholic girl I'm supposed to be.

JACK CALLED me as I was getting ready to hop into bed with Axle and read. It was nine o'clock.

'Hope I'm not interrupting anything.' His voice was edgy.

'Oh, yes, you certainly are,' I purred. 'You're interrupting me and Mr Darcy.'

'Mr … you mean —'

'That's right. This is the third time I've read it. I probably should read something different but I can't decide what.'

'Where are you?'

'About to get into bed.'

'Alone? Apart from Darcy?'

'No, Axle's waiting for me. He's keen to know what happens after Elizabeth refuses Mr Darcy's proposal. Mr Darcy makes out he's doing her a huge favour by proposing and she basically tells him to shove it. Elizabeth's my hero.'

'Why doesn't she just say yes? He's got plenty of money.'

'Money's not everything, you know. Besides, she's got her pride.'

'And that awful mother.'

'Yes. That's why Elizabeth and I understand each other.'

He chuckled. 'But Darcy wants her, so doesn't mind the mother.'

'That's right. You've read it?'

'I have. But if you tell anyone —'

'You'll have to kill me.'

'Correct.'

'You'll have to catch me first.'

There was silence for a few seconds during which I imagined a game of chasey around Jack's vast bedroom, and I wondered if he was doing the same. 'I should come and get you,' he muttered. 'Break into your room and kidnap you.'

'Save me from my awful mother?'

'Save you from Elizabeth's bad influence.'

I laughed. 'Actually, I'm really tired. It's been a big day.'

'I know. I saw.'

'Uh-oh. You've been watching the news.'

'What started that brawl?'

'Me.'

'How? No, don't tell me.' He blew out a big breath. 'Erica,' he said, suddenly serious, 'I'm going to talk to Degraves. I don't want you working with Mendez.'

'It's fine, Jack. It's my job.'

'It's *not* your job and no, it's not fine. There was an armed hold-up at his charity lunch on Friday. Today you were nearly cleaned up by a train and crushed in a shopping centre brawl. That's *not* fine.'

'The train just bumped into us. It wasn't a big deal.'

'It could have been worse.'

'At least my life's not boring.'

'I *want* you to have a boring life. I want you to work in a nice, safe office from Monday to Friday and spend your weekends shopping or reading or in my bed, which wouldn't be too dull, I promise.'

What a promise. But for how long? How long would Jack enjoy his weekends with me in his bed before he got bored and wanted another lover? How long would I enjoy it before I wanted to go somewhere? Somewhere like a winery for lunch. Anyway, there was no point arguing with Jack about my work with Emilio, because, well, there was no point. I'd made up my mind. If I didn't get the amulet back and Emilio lost the tournament, my life wouldn't be worth living. At least, I'd never be able to face the crowds at Chaddy again.

'So, what did you do today?' I said, an attempt at distraction.

'What I said I was going to do. I took Sharon to see some of Victoria's finest wineries.'

Stupid, stupid me. Why didn't I stick with the me-being-in-Jack's-bed convo? Now my whole body was flushed with jealousy and I had to bite my lip very hard to stop myself from saying something snarky. But there was a coldness to my tone when I said, 'Did she like them?'

'Yeah. I guess.'

'Did you go to Mornington Peninsula?'

'Yes.'

'Was it nice?'

'Very nice. I bought a case of chardonnay from Montalto. I thought you might like it.'

'Thank you.' I wondered if he bought the wine Sharon liked. I bet she said she liked the same as him. 'Okay, well ...' I was tossing up between my desire to go to Jack's house and save him from Sharon's advances, and my need for sleep. 'If I came to your house now, would you chase me around your bedroom?'

'Sweetheart, if I had you in my bedroom right now ...' He sighed, loudly. 'It could start with a chase, yes.'

I found I was hyperventilating. Not because of his wicked suggestion, but because of "sweetheart". Had he forgotten himself? But anyway, I knew if I went to Jack's house, I wouldn't get any sleep. And then I'd have to come home again because God forbid I actually stay the night, like a hussy. 'I'd better not,' I said. 'I need sleep.' What I really wanted to ask was what he'd do with his evening now that I wasn't available, but I worried he might say something like, 'I'll see if Shazza wants to see a movie.' Except he wouldn't say Shazza.

'Shame,' he said.

'I know.'

'Are you tucked up in that cosy single bed?'

'I am.' I yawned, stretching. 'It feels *so* good to be horizontal.'

'Are you wearing those pink pyjamas?'

'Yes.'

He whispered a curse. 'Tease.'

'I never tease.' Well, not unless there's a likely satisfactory outcome for all concerned.

'I'm coming over,' he said.

'What? You can't!'

'See you in ten.' He hung up.

I got out of bed and paced around, peering out the window. Would he really? Surely not. Yes, he would. I giggled at the mirror. Should I stay in my jarmies? Yes, he'd like that. I turned off the light, got back into bed and waited.

HE WAS SO STEALTHY, I almost didn't hear him come through the window. There was just a vague awareness of another human presence suddenly in the room.

He stood by my bed as I clutched the doona to my chin, tittering quietly.

'Is that you?' I whispered.

Then his mouth was on mine, soft and slow. Against my lips, he murmured, 'Who would you like it to be?'

'Batman.'

'You're in luck.'

He stripped off his clothes, and then he was naked in my single bed. I shuffled over to make room.

'You're still wearing pyjamas.'

'I thought you might like them.'

'I'll like taking them off.'

And so he did.

MY BODY SHUDDERED, almost violently. No-one but Jack Jones could take me to such ecstatic heights, and that's where I was when my bedroom door swung open. Jack went completely still under me. He held his breath and I went from upright to flat out on top of him in a heartbeat, doona pulled high around my shoulders.

'Are you awake?' said Mum. 'I heard moaning.'

'I had a nightmare. Don't turn the light on.'

'Why not?'

'Ah, it'll wake me up. The light'll make my irises go small and I won't be able to sleep.' I could feel Jack's chuckle. 'I'm fine, Mum. Go to bed.'

'Well, I had to wake you, anyway. It's that naughty pussy of yours.'

Jack sucked in a breath. It was almost audible.

'What's he done now?'

'He won't come inside. I've called and called! You'll need to get him.'

'Just ... just leave him out there.'

'I'm most certainly not leaving him outside at night. Goodness knows what he gets up to! He brought a bird home the other day. A budgerigar!'

Oh, crap. Someone's pet. Jack's hands moved over my back and bare bottom. I gave a little shiver. I wondered if he'd wait while I went Axle hunting.

'Okay. Give me a minute and I'll come.'

JACK WAS STILL in my bed when dawn washed my room with pink light. We were spooning – no choice in a single bed – Jack behind me. When I opened my eyes, I knew he was already awake. I could tell by his breathing and the, um, tension in his body.

'Can't hide you if she comes in now.'

He ran a hand over my stomach, pulled me harder against him. 'I can think of a few places to hide.'

Axle was curled up on top of us, exhausted from his midnight garden romp.

'I'm taking them to church this morning.' I flipped onto my back. 'Maybe you should come.'

'Yes, I should come.'

'Really?'

'Not to church.'

He lay on top of me. Axle hit the floor with an angry meow. I prayed my mother wouldn't hear more moaning and come to investigate. I really should get a lock for my door.

CHAPTER 34

*D*ad wanted me to drive them to church.

'Why don't you get your car fixed?'

'We don't need it,' said Mum. 'You can drive us.'

'I can't drive you around forever.'

'Oh, stop fussing, Erica.'

'But you'll want to hang around after the service and have cups of tea,' I said. 'I need to go into work.'

'It's the least you can do. We're providing a roof over your head, food in your mouth —'

'Okay, okay.'

'And you shouldn't work on a Sunday,' said Mum. 'It's blasphemy.'

I drove fast, wanting to get it over with. Dad instructed me like I was on L plates while Mum sat in the back, saying, 'Too fast, missy!' Maybe I could just chuck them out of the car at church and keep driving to Jack's? But no, I needed to make amends with God, just in case. I parked down a side street and we walked slowly through the church gates. Everyone walks slowly into church. No-one ever rushes, running late. Maybe it's not allowed.

St James in Brighton was how I remembered it on my wedding day – the last time I'd been there. It'd been a happy day and everything

167

was perfect, except that my husband took off soon after with some blond woman, all my money in his pocket. Mum likes to go to the Brighton church so she can pretend she lives there. Not because Jack lives in Brighton (which, according to Mum, is good enough reason for me to marry him), but because Brighton has superior snob value. Mum loves the "effluence", as she likes to tell everyone. Chadstone, even with the greatest shopping centre in the universe, just doesn't cut it.

'I remember your wedding day like it was just a few years ago,' she said.

'It *was* just a few years ago.'

'Your dress was so beautiful. Remember Aunty Betty made it for you?'

'Yes, it was lovely. Let's talk about something else.'

'Maybe Jack would like to marry here,' she mused.

I stood in front of her, hands on hips, forcing her to stop talking. 'Don't you ever, *ever* say that in front of Jack.'

She pouted.

'Mum, promise!'

'Hmph.' She scowled at me – a scowl that said we weren't finished with that discussion – and we entered the stately building. The priest was there, greeting his flock. Mum gushed, invited the priest to lunch, which she probably always did and he probably always had an excuse ready. Today's excuse surprised me, though.

'Ah, Mrs Jewell, I'm afraid you're too late. Mrs Booth has already invited me.'

Our Mrs Booth? The witchy weirdo?

'You remember Erica, my daughter?' said Mum. 'She's living with us for free while her friend Stephen renovates her house in Richmond. You remember Stephen? Such a nice lad to do Erica this favour.'

'It's not a *favour*, Mum —'

'There are such unsavoury types in Erica's neighbourhood. I am concerned, Father. She hasn't been to confession in such a long time and I'm in a constant state. I lose sleep, you know, worrying about her forthcoming device.'

The priest welcomed me, hoped that my *demise* could be averted, commented that he hadn't in fact seen much of me since my wedding, and I thought that was very discreet considering he hadn't seen me at all. I told him visiting his church brought back terrible memories of the day my husband abandoned me.

'We have a church in Richmond,' he said. 'Saint Ignatius.'

I hurried inside. I could see Mrs Booth. She was wearing normal clothes: black slacks and jacket with a plain cream blouse. Not a purple dress or anything with mirrors. What was she up to, disguising herself like that?

Mrs Booth stood in a pew near the front, talking to some people. She saw me and gave a surprised look – very suspicious – and a little wave.

'Let's sit over there.' I indicated the row behind Mrs Booth.

'We like to sit here.'

'Well, I want to sit there.'

Mum said to Dad, 'Erica's being difficult, Tom.' Dad headed to where I wanted to sit. Good old Dad. Mum followed, saying, 'You were always difficult when we came to church, Erica. Your father was forever having to take you outside.' She added, loudly, 'And you always dirtied your nappy.'

Mrs Booth said, 'Well, hello, Jewell family! So nice to see you all.'

I bet it's nice to see us all. Probably imagining us in a big pot of soup, ready to serve with crusty bread.

'Erica, you remember Mrs Booth?'

'Hi, Mrs Booth,' I said, feeling twelve. 'I saw you at the supermarket.'

She smiled and nodded. 'Are you still working for that company?'

'Yes.' Why? What do you know?

'I've been having visits from your pussy cat.'

What? Axle going to Mrs Booth's? 'Oh, I don't think it's mine. He doesn't leave the backyard.' But then I remembered the goldfish.

'Oh, yes, he does. He and my Minx are good friends. They're quite alike, in fact. I find it difficult to tell them apart.'

I'd have to do something about that. She might try a switcheroo – keep Axle and give me her voodoo cat.

'So, I'm sorry we couldn't chat at the supermarket the other night.'

'That's alright. You were busy on the phone.'

'And then I saw you in the car park after.'

'You did?' She looked thoughtful, but it was thoughtful like she was pretending to look thoughtful, when she was probably trying to work out how to get around the fact that she stole Emilio's lucky charm. I tried to peer through Mrs Booth's blouse to see if she was wearing the amulet underneath.

'Actually, Mrs Booth, I wondered if you found a token I left in my supermarket trolley?' I watched her, carefully. She looked surprised. It was fake surprise, I could tell.

She gave a little fake laugh. 'Why, no, Erica. I had no reason to look for anything in your trolley! Although, now that you mention it …' I leaned in. Was she going to confess? '… it's a very good idea. One could collect some coins that way!'

Aha!

Mum elbowed me in the ribs and we all sat, ready for the proceedings. Mum wanted me between her and Dad, in case I needed to be corrected, or taken outside, or have my nappy changed. I closed my eyes, tilted my face up, and asked God for help with every aspect of my life. Was that being too greedy? That I wanted him to fix *everything*?

Mum whispered, 'Father will lead us in prayer, Erica. Although it's not a bad idea for you to get in some extra time with the Good Lord.'

We stood. We sat. We knelt. We stood. We sat. We knelt. I watched Mrs Booth's back, her frizzy black hair, which she'd obviously dyed. I wondered if there was a chain around her neck. Perhaps if I just lifted the back of her hair, I could see under —

Mum slapped my wrist.

We did the Sign of Peace. I waited for Mrs Booth to face me but she didn't. I tapped her on the shoulder and she had no choice but to turn, and I gripped her hand.

'Peace be with you,' we said in unison. I held her hand. With a forced smile she tried to shake me free. I released her.

Time for communion, and we all stood and made our way to the aisle. I stood behind Mrs Booth. There was a sharp poke in my back. Mum reminding me to be good.

I took my bread and wine, hoping the good Lord noticed but hoping he didn't notice that I had more wine than I probably should. And that I hadn't been to confession. It occurred to me, as I watched Mrs Booth pretending to be a good Catholic, that she wouldn't tell me if she had the lucky charm. I knew she wouldn't tell. She had one of those I'm-not-telling faces. So, I needed to go to her house and find the lucky charm. I just had to do it when she wasn't home.

'WHEN DO you usually go to the supermarket, Mrs Booth?'

We stood in the church hall, having had tea and Arnott's Family Assorted biscuits and having sucked up to Father in an appropriate manner. Dad stood with some old blokes. Mrs Booth didn't seem to want to hang around. Was she trying to avoid me?

'Oh, it's quite ad hoc, Erica.' Mrs Booth edged away.

'Why do you want to know?' said Mum.

Why? Why? 'Because ... Mrs Booth might be able to do some shopping for you.'

'But we've got you to do the shopping!'

'I'd be happy to help with your shopping, Margaret.'

'Perhaps we could go together one day, Imelda?'

'Great idea!' I said. 'When will you go?'

'Well,' said Mum, 'we've got a full cupboard.'

'Mine's full also,' said Mrs Booth.

'I think you need more prunes, Mum. I only got a small packet the other night.'

'I'm sure it can wait.'

Mrs Booth checked her watch. 'Must dash.' She waved to us all.

And as I watched Mrs Booth hurry away, I saw Jack and Sharon Stone cruise by in his Audi, probably off to lunch at some flash place or more wineries. Maybe this time they'd go to the Yarra Valley. It's pretty romantic there with all those rolling green hills. Hurt stabbed me in the chest. Oh, dear God, weren't you listening?

CHAPTER 35

*J*hurried Mum and Dad into my car and sped away, nearly running over old Mr Bennett and his wheelie walker in the process.

'Heavens!' said Mum.

I could see Jack ahead, ready to turn left down Nepean Highway toward the city. I followed. Dad pointed straight – he wanted me to continue along North Road.

'We can go this way,' I said.

Dad was fully alert to the fact that I was up to something, but didn't comment. From the back seat, Mum told us about the most amazing game of bridge she'd ever played.

'I won that game. It was so satisfying.'

It wasn't until I turned off Nepean Highway onto Hotham Street that Mum had something to say about my driving. 'Which way are you taking us, dear?'

I ignored her and followed the Audi all the way along Hotham to Toorak. I glanced at Dad. He was onto me.

'Erica,' said Mum. 'Where are we going?'

'Sunday drive, Mum. It's such a nice day for it.'

'But I have to get the roast on!'

'Won't be long.'

Dad said, 'Settle, Margaret.'

Mum huffed.

Jack turned right at Toorak Road, left at Lansell, then down a small cul-de-sac. I now knew where he was taking Sharon Stone for lunch. John Degraves's house. I pulled up at the end of the street and watched the Audi park. Jack emerged from his car and jogged down the road. Toward us.

'There's Jack!' said Mum. 'Yoo hoo!'

Jack came to my window and I wound it down.

My face burned so hard I thought it might ignite. 'Fancy seeing you here,' I said.

He smiled at me, looked at Dad and Mum. 'Hi, everyone. What a coincidence.'

'Amazing!' said Mum. 'Would you like to come for lunch? We're having a roast.' Mum's tone changed, suddenly. It dropped from a squawk to quite low. 'You and … your friend.'

I could see Sharon Stone waiting by Jack's car.

'I have lunch plans, thanks, Margaret. Another time?'

'You're welcome any time, Jack. You and … your friend.'

Jack looked at me. 'Everything alright?'

'Yep. All good.' I searched for some secret love signal from our night together. Some sign that he, too, was feeling all mushy about us. Nope. Just amusement in those tell-tale eyes. 'We're going for a Sunday drive after church. Thought we'd check out the big houses in Toorak.'

'I'll let you get on with your tour, then.'

'Okey doke.'

'See you soon.' No secret winks or mouthed sentiments.

'Yep. See ya.'

He jogged away. I wondered what he told Sharon. That Erica was jealous and stupid? I wouldn't mind if he said that because I'd deserve it. Because it's true.

Mum grilled me about Jack's "friend".

'She's a lesbian,' I said, and Mum stopped the interrogation in case I said other rude words.

MUM'S ROAST was the best thing I'd ever eaten. Why didn't I get any of her cooking genes? Maybe because I'd spent my childhood in the garage with Dad and my teenage years avoiding Mum. If I'd spent my teenage years in the garage with Dad, I might have learned something like how to check the oil in my car, which I had to ask Dad to do for me.

After lunch I drove into work and spent the rest of the day there. It was a relief to be able to get things done without phones ringing and people (Rosalind) harassing me. But mostly I found I was thinking about Jack. To say I wasn't seething with hurt and jealousy that Jack had taken Sharon to JD's house would be a big, fat lie. Should I call him? I checked my watch. Three o'clock. Not yet. They were probably having after-lunch drinkies, laughing and chatting with Mr and Mrs Degraves. Sue Degraves probably thought Sharon was a much better girlfriend for Jack. Better in every way.

I heard the lift ping, which meant someone had arrived on my floor. I watched the end of the hallway, waiting to see who it was. Please, God, not Rosalind. Although God might well send me Rosalind to get back at me for being such a liar and a hypocrite. A lying, jealous, stupid hypocrite.

I was surprised to see John Degraves approach. Shouldn't he be pouring after-lunch drinks or doing the dishes?

'Afternoon, Erica. Working hard as always.'

Well, that was something good. JD reckons I work hard. 'Just catching up on a few things. And you, Mr Degraves? Not at lunch?'

'I'm hoping to catch Rosalind. She's often here after hours.' Hanging upside down.

'Not today.' I smiled.

'Yes. Yes, I see that.' He stared thoughtfully at Rosalind's closed office door, then glanced around. 'Anyone else working as hard as you?'

He wanted to know if we were alone. I also looked around for show, even though I knew I was the only one here. 'No, I'm the only hard-working employee at Dega Oil.' I gave him a big smile to show I was joking, and he returned it.

He lowered his voice. 'I've met with our mutual friend.' Code for Jack.

'Yes?'

'He's concerned about your safety while working with Emilio.'

He said that? In front of Sharon? 'Oh?'

'Do you feel threatened, Erica?' JD was looking suddenly serious as he perched his bum on my desk, just like Marcus does. Except Marcus does it with more flair.

'Not really, Mr Degraves.' Apart from nearly being run over by a car, and a train, and assaulted in a shopping centre brawl, and caught in a heist with gunmen, although the guns apparently weren't loaded, so that doesn't count. 'I think Emilio wants me around.'

'Yes, he does. He's come to depend on you.'

'I'm happy to continue working for him.'

He stood, suddenly, gave me another big smile and said, 'Well, let's leave things as they are. I'm sure our mutual friend will come around when he realises you're quite safe.'

Nice that JD felt so confident about that.

'Any more news on Western Australia, Mr Degraves?'

'Only that the Russian men involved are being investigated. As much as one can investigate a deceased suspect.'

'Right. Well, let me know if you need me to do anything.'

'Just concentrate on getting Emilio across the line.' He started to leave, but stopped. 'That new girl seems to have everything else under control.'

I mustered up a small smile.

'Have a good day, Erica.'

'You, too, Mr Degraves.'

I watched JD walk away. After I was sure he'd gone, I mimicked, 'That new girl seems to have everything under control.'

So, I was to keep being Emilio's slave. That's apparently all I'm good for. I thought about Emilio and wondered if he *was* under threat in any way. Jack had said that yesterday, that Emilio could be a target and shouldn't have gone to Chadstone. Pfft. Yesterday. Emilio had talked a security guard into following us around, and the guard seemed pretty happy to do so but had done a lot of texting. The day was a complete waste of time, except that Emilio bought me a whole bunch of new clothes from David Jones. Actually, the clothes Emilio bought me were really nice. Ones I'd never have bought for myself because they were so expensive. He wanted me to buy some nice lingerie for "later" – "later" presumably meaning after the tournament when we would finally be able to consummate our relationship, one that was already several days old (where does the time go?). If the lucky charm re-emerged, as he was so sure it would with my so diligently seeking it. But I'd said no to the lingerie. I shouldn't have let him buy the clothes either, because I supposed it was encouraging him. I justified it by reminding myself that he's got stacks of money and I'm not paid for the time I spend with him out of office hours. I am a hussy, like my mother says. A lying, jealous, stupid, hypocritical hussy.

After finishing our shopping at Chadstone, with the borrowed security guard carrying our bags, a new driver was sent to collect us. Not a stretch limo, this time, and I made sure I wasn't locked in before I agreed to go with him. Then this morning Emilio had called quite early and told me, 'Unfortunately, I will be with my coach all day. But we will have dinner, yes? You will come to my hotel.'

I lied and told him it was my mother's birthday dinner and he wanted to come. So I told him we have a tradition where only people related by blood are allowed to come to family birthday dinners. He wanted to know what that meant for the future husband of my parents' daughter. I said I'd have to cross that bridge when I came to it. '*Si*, one day you must cross that bridge.' So that got me thinking about how much I really cared about Emilio winning the tournament and the potential of a public lynching and getting a promotion and being away from Rosalind. Maybe Emilio would want to marry me, like he has with past girlfriends, except they turned out to be *putas*.

Would I be so mercenary as to take advantage of and marry a famous, gorgeous, rich tennis player with well-filled undies, just because I could? In which case I wouldn't need my job because I'd have access to so much money. But I'd still want to work. And anyway, I reckoned if I slept with Emilio, he'd dump me straight after, as I suspected was his pattern, so I'd have to wait until the wedding night, when it was too late for him to dump me. But what was I doing, having silly thoughts about marrying Emilio Mendez when, really, there was only one man on the planet I'd ever consider marrying?

CHAPTER 36

onday. The start of the Australian Open tennis tournament. Emilio's first match was tomorrow afternoon. I needed to find the amulet. I needed to break into Mrs Booth's house, but when? While the police were supposedly hunting for the perpetrators of the lunch heist, they presumably weren't concerned about the amulet, and that was a good thing. I didn't want them to find a fake lucky charm. But how could I find the real one and do all the other things I needed to do, including being at Emilio's beck and call? I did need to go to the tennis, though. Quite apart from Emilio's demands, my job required that I be there. Tennis Oz would expect to see me. But, problem, what to do with Charlotte? Rosalind fixed that.

'I want you to take Charlotte to the tennis. Show her what you know about sponsorship.'

'It's a bit soon to teach her that stuff, isn't it?'

Rosalind gave me one of her I-can't-believe-you're-questioning-my-direct-order looks and as I backed out of her office, she said, looking at the work on her desk, 'I hope you're close to finding that lucky charm. God help you if you don't.'

God help me this, God help me that. I wish God would just get on with it and help me. When I got back to my desk, Charlotte was holding out my desk phone. With a small smile she mouthed, 'It's the tennis people.'

'Thanks.' But before I took the call, 'You didn't happen to bring a sunhat, by any chance?'

She shook her head.

I spoke into the phone, 'Erica Jewell speaking.'

It was Desi, my contact at Tennis Oz, who didn't bother with any how-are-yous. 'You need to get here. We've got a situation.' And hung up.

I looked at the phone, then at Charlotte. 'Do you have sunscreen?'

As we crossed the river and approached Rod Laver Arena, I could see the "situation". My heart sank. A small group of protesters – about eight people – stood on the corner of Swan Street and Batman Avenue, holding placards with all kinds of awful, badly spelled messages about how horrible and unethical Dega Oil was and, by association, Emilio Mendez. I drove slowly by, parked illegally and called Rosalind.

'You'll just have to fix it.' She hung up.

Perfect. Maybe I could send Charlotte to fix it. She could beg them to go away or invite them all to my mother's for a game of bridge.

I drove into the Rod Laver Arena players' and officials' parking area. Teresa was waiting by the entrance for me. I wondered what she'd told the police about the disappearing limo driver.

Charlotte and I got out of the car. Teresa spotted me and headed my way, frowning at Charlotte.

I introduced them. 'Charlotte works with me.'

Teresa walked away, expecting us to follow.

I said, 'Any news on that limo driver?'

Teresa was apparently deaf. She walked on without response. I stopped, touching Charlotte on the arm to indicate she should also stop.

Teresa said, 'Please come this way.'

'I have to see the tennis people first.'

'About the protesters?'

Shit, she knew. 'Yeah.'

'I hope you can do something about them. Emilio will not wear your logo.'

'What? But he has to!'

She looked at me as though I was crazy and said, 'Hurry back to us. There is something else.'

Teresa said she'd meet me in the players' café. I indicated for Charlotte to follow Teresa while I made my way to the Tennis Oz office.

'You're causing us a giant headache, Erica,' said Desi. 'The lunch heist was bad enough and now this.' She waved her hand out the window of her office.

'The heist wasn't our fault.'

'Indirectly, it was. Dega is Emilio's sponsor and it was Emilio's event.'

'But —'

'I'll tell you what the protesters want, and we can talk about what to do.'

I walked, my head full of worry, to the players' café, thinking about what Desi had told me. What the protesters wanted was Emilio Mendez off the tournament. As if. And it was certainly not a solution Tennis Oz would consider. Emilio was a huge drawcard.

The players' café was buzzing, not so much with people as with vibe. The Australian Open tennis is such a big deal in Melbourne and people come from all over the world to watch and participate in it. I found Charlotte, sitting by the window, and joined her. There were a few other familiar faces there, including Vladimir Vavilov with his coach. Vlad was still looking sad or angry or something. Maybe he just always looked like that. Maybe he was nervous about his first match, which was today. Not that he had much to worry about because he was number one, and he was probably facing some poor no-seed.

'I'm having coffee,' I said to Charlotte. 'You want one?'

'But we've already had one coffee today.'

'Well, I need something, and it's too early for whiskey.'

She blinked at me.

'Just kidding. Coffee?'

She nodded. 'Okay.'

I returned with our drinks, but before I sat, I saw Teresa at the doorway across the room. She held up a hand, waving for me to come. I told Charlotte to wait. Teresa and Emilio were in the corridor. They were arguing quietly – hands waving.

Teresa said to me, 'We must not call the police.'

'What about?'

'This peoples,' said Emilio. 'They cannot get away with it!'

'The protestors?' I said.

Teresa pushed a folded note into my hand and I opened it. In rough newspaper cut-outs it read: DEGA = Dead Emilio Game Over.

I almost laughed. 'They made a typo.'

Teresa said, 'What is typo?'

I pointed. 'The acronym doesn't work. See? The last word should have started with A.'

Emilio said, 'You see, Mother Teresa? *Es estupido*. The police will find them and put them in jail for stupidness.'

Teresa said, 'This is important, this typo?'

'No, not important. Why won't you tell the police?'

'Emilio does not want this attention. With the loss of his *amuleto* it is difficult for him to concentrate on his game without the police making more questions.'

Emilio said, 'Because, remember, Emily, you lost *mi amuleto*. That makes it so much harder for me.'

'Anyway, I think we need to take this note seriously.' I gave it a flick with my fingers. 'Where did you find it?'

'It was left at the reception desk of the hotel.'

Which meant whoever left it knew where Emilio was staying. Not that this was a clue – Emilio's hotel was no secret as they, too, were sponsors of the tennis. But this was certainly a problem.

I addressed Emilio. 'You remember Jack?'

'Your friend with the beautiful blond girlfriend?'

'That's the one,' I said through clenched teeth. 'He's kind of a … security guy. And he's got friends in the police force. He could do something quietly. Do you want me to call him?'

Teresa said to Emilio, 'I do not think we need a private investigation, my darling.'

I kept my eyes on Emilio. For some reason, I wanted him to trust me, not her. 'I think you do, Teresa.'

'I am concerned for Emilio's attention to his game.'

Emilio held my gaze. '*Si*, Emily. I think that would be an acceptable option.'

Jack answered straight away. 'Hey.'

'I've got a problem.'

'I've been trying to tell you that. His name's Emilio Mendez.'

'Well, it's gotten bigger.'

'How?'

I told him about the protesters and the threatening note.

'Are you thinking the protesters had something to do with the note?'

'I suppose. They say they want Emilio off the tournament.'

'How many protesters?'

'Seven or eight.'

'Interesting.'

'Why?'

'A serious protest by environmentalists would attract thousands,' he said.

'What are you saying?'

'I'll handle the protesters.'

'What does that mean?'

'Don't worry about it.'

'What will you do?'

'Has Emilio had any other direct threat? Apart from the lunch heist and train incident.'

'I don't think so.'

'Tell him we'll meet this afternoon.'

We hung up and I wondered what Jack planned to do with the protesters. A part of what Jack's secret team does involves sneaking around at night and dealing with bad people in a way that ensures the bad people never get a chance to do what they'd planned to do, maybe like blowing up something that involves lots of innocent lives. Surely Jack wouldn't just go and, you know, "deal with" those protesters?

I found Emilio and Teresa in the players' café, sitting at a table near Charlotte, who was staring at Emilio. I told Emilio that Jack would come to see them this afternoon, that they could trust him, and that he would fix everything. I didn't know if he *could* fix everything, but Teresa still looked worried.

Emilio stood. 'And now we must eat!'

I indicated for Charlotte to join us, and she was by my side in a flash, gazing at Emilio, smiling hungrily.

'Who is this?' said Emilio.

'This is Charlotte. She works with me.'

Emilio went to kiss her and I hoped it would be on the cheek, but Charlotte threw an arm around his neck and kissed him full on the mouth.

I gasped, 'Charlotte!'

Emilio laughed. 'I wish you were so passionate with me, Emily.'

Charlotte looked for all the world like a love-sick puppy.

Emilio looked at her, amused, as though she *were* just a puppy. 'She will watch the tennis, yes?'

'Er, yes. Wherever I am, Charlotte will be with me.'

He gave me a horrified look. '*All* of the time?'

'Between nine and five, yes.'

Teresa said something in Spanish.

'We must eat!' Emilio said and sent Teresa to fetch food for us all.

CHAPTER 37

J hadn't wanted to be at the meeting between Jack and Emilio, but they both insisted. Jack said *he* might carry out the death threat if I wasn't there to act as a buffer (Emilio wasn't *that* annoying, was he?) and Emilio just because he wanted me to be wherever he was. The meeting was to take place in Emilio's hotel suite with Teresa there, too. Emilio had given Charlotte two tickets for Vavilov's match, which she was now enjoying with whomever she found to go with her at the last minute.

And something else happened. The limousine company contacted us to say they had the runaway driver and they wanted him to meet us, explain why he'd abandoned us on the train line. The limo company said it was up to us if he still had a job.

I called Jack and told him.

'Tell them I want the driver in Emilio's room when I get there.'

'What will you do?'

'Talk to him.'

'You won't be mean to him, will you?'

'Erica, the guy left you on a train line with a train coming. You could've been killed.'

'So you're saying you *are* going to be mean to him.'

I heard his sigh. 'You need to know something about this limousine company.'

'What?'

'It's owned by mafia. Russian mafia.'

I didn't say anything for a minute. What did that mean? 'You think Teresa knew that when she booked the driver?'

'I don't know. It's a legitimate business, but I happen to know who owns it, and it might have something to do with what happened to you.'

'More Russians.'

'Uh-huh.'

'Any thoughts?' I said.

'Yes, but just so you know, Vavilov's team is helping the police with their enquiries.'

'Enquiries about …'

'All the shit that keeps happening to you.'

'Right. Vavilov is Russian.'

'That's right.'

'And I suppose Russian people want him to win.'

'I suppose.'

'So you think maybe Vavilov's mates are trying to get Emilio off the tournament.'

'I don't know. But I've got a list of favourite theories and it's right up there.'

EMILIO, Teresa and I waited in Emilio's hotel suite. The limousine driver – the Danny DeVito lookalike – was there, too, sitting on the edge of a chair, fidgeting, checking the time, watching the door. I thought about the movie *Romancing the Stone*. Danny DeVito was a baddie in that, but a funny one. The driver hadn't said much but I noticed he did have an accent, and I assumed it was Russian.

Emilio yabbered Spanish into his phone, Teresa was at the dining-table, reading her romance novel, and I paced by the window: back and forth, back and forth, like a caged lion, chewing my nails. Not that lions chew their nails. Maybe they do. But my anxiety had nothing to do with death threats and protesters, not even about the driver, and everything to do with the meeting that was about to take place. Actually, not the meeting per se, but more about Jack and Emilio being in the same room, Emilio with romance on his mind, Jack with murder.

There were two sharp raps on the door.

'I'll get it.' I ran to open the door. And caught my breath. Wearing a super serious tough-guy face was Jack, sexiest man on the planet in perfect-fitting jeans and plain white, untucked shirt with sleeves rolled up, unruly hair, perfect body, perfect face, etc, etc. And Joe, a fraction shorter than Jack but still about six foot three, brick shit-house, army hair, Ray-Bans, black tee with army camouflage pants and full-sleeve tattoo on the right arm, barbed-wire tattoo on the other, circling his massive biceps. My boys.

Someone else stepped up behind them, having been delayed perhaps by the weight of her boots. Sharon Stone was wearing a tight black sleeveless leather bodysuit. She carried a full-faced black motorbike helmet under her arm and a leather jacket (black) slung over her shoulder.

'Hey,' she said.

It took me a full five seconds to stop gawping at her. 'Hi.'

I turned and they followed me into the room. Before I could make any introductions, Jack approached the driver, fisted his shirt and lifted him off the chair so his feet were swinging. Teresa and Emilio both shouted, I let out a squeal and Joe and Sharon flanked Jack.

The driver clung to Jack's wrists, yelling in Russian.

'Who ordered the hit?' said Jack, his voice quiet but hard.

'No hit! There is no hit!'

Jack shook him.

'I scared! I so scared!'

Jack dropped the driver, who fell back on the sofa. He talked rapidly in Russian, wiped his hands over his face. Jack gave him a smack across the head.

The driver's hands were up. 'Okay, okay. The limousine stop. It not go. I so scared and I run.'

'Why were you scared?'

The driver pointed at Emilio. 'Much trouble for me.'

I said, 'You locked us in!'

'No! No, I not. The door, it no open inside. I run.'

'You had time to open the door for us.'

'No time. You busy in back.'

The blush started at my toes and flooded my body. I avoided looking at Jack, and mumbled, 'You're just a big coward.'

'*Da.*' He nodded.

Jack had been watching me, letting me have my say, and he was now probably contemplating the "you busy in back" comment. Emilio and Teresa sat at the dining table, wide-eyed and silenced by Jack's brutish interrogation methods.

'And now I have to decide what to do with you,' Jack said.

'I know about men at heist. Men with guns.'

'The charity lunch?'

'*Da.*' He nodded. 'They no Russian. They pretend Russian.'

Jack, Joe and Sharon glanced at each other.

'How do you know?' said Jack.

'I watch the television. I hear. They pretend Russian but they no Russian.'

'Where are they from?'

He shrugged.

'What about it?'

The driver shrugged again. 'I help so you know I am not bad person.'

WE ALL WATCHED the door close after the driver. I said to Jack, 'Do you believe him?'

'We'll see.'

He turned his attention to Teresa, no friendlier than he'd been with the driver. 'Why did you book that limousine company?'

Teresa opened her mouth and closed it again. 'I think … it is one of the recommended companies for the players.'

'No, it's not.' Jack pinned her with his glare.

She shrugged. 'Then, I cannot remember where I got the name.'

'*Conveniente.*'

Open-mouthed and infuriated, Teresa turned to Emilio. '*Estas personas se atreven —*' she spat.

Emilio stood, smiling broadly. 'Teresa has told the police the information.' He walked quickly across the room. 'Come now, let us be friends!' He caught Jack, Joe and Sharon in a group hug. An embrace Jack quickly removed himself from but poor Joe seemed frozen with shock. Only his expression – what I could see of it under the glasses – changed very slightly. Sharon hugged back.

Emilio chatted nonsensically, hands waving. Jack didn't say much. He stood very tall and aloof, chin high, regarding Emilio down the length of his perfect, straight nose. Mr Cool. He was taller than Emilio, probably by four inches. Joe and Sharon checked out the room, walking slowly around it, lifting things and inspecting under them.

'This room been checked for devices?' Joe asked me.

I shrugged.

Jack said, 'Let's get on with it,' and indicated the dining table.

Teresa rang for tea and coffee. Her hand shook as she held the phone. I didn't believe she'd have anything to do with the threats against Emilio. She adored him like a son.

Joe and Sharon stood like sentries on either side of the dining table. They looked like secret service people or something, all serious and scary. Was it deliberate, I wondered? That they looked so intimidating? Probably.

I tried to sit at the end of the table – away from everyone – but Emilio wanted me next to him, with Teresa on his other side. Jack sat opposite. Sharon was behind Emilio. Joe stood behind Jack. Emilio put an arm along the back of my chair and I jumped up.

'Goodness! Is it hot in here?' I looked for a way to open the windows.

'They do not open, *querida*. Come. Sit.' Emilio patted the chair next to him.

I glanced at Jack. His eyes were on me, serious. But I knew those tell-tale eyes, and part of him was enjoying watching me squirm.

'Please,' said Emilio to Jack with a wave of his hand. 'Tell me what you need.'

'Show me the note you received. The threat.'

Emilio pushed the note across the table. Jack read it – I could see from the look on his face, the slight twitch of his mouth, that he saw the typo – and Emilio leaned toward me so our shoulders were touching.

I jumped up again. 'I think that was room service at the door.'

'No, it is not,' said Teresa. 'I will answer when they come.'

I sat. Emilio shuffled his chair closer so he didn't have to lean to touch me. He addressed Jack. 'Please, continue.'

I couldn't look at Joe. I was worried he'd pull a gun on Emilio and shoot him, right there and then. The whole business was making me sweat and fidget. I shuffled around on the chair.

'What is wrong, Emilita?'

'Um, I've got a sore back.' I stood. 'I'll just stand for a while.'

Emilio took my hand, tugged it. 'Here, sit on my knee and I will rub your back.'

I snatched my hand away. 'It's fine. Really.' I moved away.

'Why don't you lie on my bed? I will give you a massage later.'

I gave a high-pitched, hysterical-sounding laugh, stepping sideways so fast I nearly fell over. 'No, I don't need a massage!'

Jack cleared his throat.

'Actually, I feel a bit faint,' I said. 'I think I'll just go lie down.' I pointed at the sofa.

Emilio stood, taking my elbow, supporting me. 'But no! My Emily is unwell? Come. You will lie on my bed. I think you must be very frightened and worried about me.'

Jack's face was in his hands and he rubbed his eyes. I tried to move away from Emilio.

Jack looked up at me. 'Will you be alright, Emily?'

'I'll be fine. Thanks for asking. I'll just go over here.' I shuffled away from the table. 'Don't mind me. Carry on with the meeting.'

I flopped onto the sofa with relief, and threw an arm across my forehead. Actually, it felt pretty good to lie down. I gave a big sigh, and closed my eyes.

I was woken by a gentle shaking and soft calling, 'Emily … Emilita … it is I, Emilio. Wake now. Come. We must return to the tennis.'

I opened my eyes. Emilio was sitting next to me on the sofa. He leaned in and lightly kissed my lips.

'Oh!' I scrambled back, as far as I could go, glancing around the room, looking for Jack. Had he seen that? Emilio kissing me? Where was everyone?

'Are you well now? You were sleeping. There was a little bit of snoring.' He stroked my face. '*Usted es tan irresistible!* I cannot wait until the tournament is finished, and we can finally —'

'Where's Jack?'

'They have left.'

I checked my watch. 'How long did I sleep?'

'Maybe one hour.'

I swung my legs off the sofa and stretched my back, which was now aching, whereas before, when I said it was, it wasn't. 'Where's Teresa?'

'In her room, having the rest. She is overwhelmed with anxiety about me, I think.'

Overwhelmed with anxiety about Jack's accusation, I think.

Emilio tried to kiss me again. 'Ah, *mi amor*, how tempting you are. I have you here in my hotel room, and we are alone – but no! For the sake of my tennis, we must be strong.'

'Yes, we must.' I pushed him back. 'What did you all decide at the meeting?' How loud did I snore?

'Your friends are very knowledgeable about criminals.'

'Yep, that they are.'

'Your friend, *Yack*, said he will speak with the tennis security people. He wants some of his own people there to keep an eye on me.'

Emilio cocked his head. 'You know, Emily, I am surprised that you are not attracted to *Yack*. He is very good-looking, *si?*'

I yawned. 'I hadn't noticed.'

'I think he is almost as handsome as myself.'

'No-one is as handsome as you, Emilio.' I patted his cheek. Where was my bag?

'Yes, I know, but sometimes I meet someone like your friend and I do wonder. It does not happen very often.' He looked thoughtful for a second. 'Emily, if she were not the lover of *Yack*, I would be tempted by Sharon Stone.'

'Really? I can get her number for you.' An opportunity to kill two birds! Although it was annoying he had no problem remembering her name.

He laughed. 'You are so funny.'

'Come to think of it, I do quite fancy Yack, after all.'

'Ha ha! My cheeky monkey. Let us go now. My coach, he wants to do the training!'

Sigh. 'Alright.'

CHAPTER 38

t the tennis, I looked for Charlotte. Emilio went to his dressing room, where I wasn't allowed, thank God. He wanted me to meet him at the practice courts so I could watch him train, but I wanted to find Charlotte, see if she'd found someone to go with her to Vlad's game, and if not, I wanted to go. The match had already started. I had a sudden brainwave – maybe I could offer Mrs Booth tickets to the tennis and go into her house while she was away!

I'd tried calling Charlotte, and I'd sent her a couple of texts asking her to meet me in the café, but I hadn't heard back. I went there, anyway, and looked around. No Charlotte. It was almost empty, understandably, but there were a couple of television screens, so I got a coffee, sat and watched for a while. The Vavilov match was between sets. Vlad had easily won the first. The camera shots flashed from Vlad to the poor young Aussie he was thrashing, and to people in the crowd. I knew roughly where Charlotte would be sitting, so I looked for her, trying to remember what she was wearing. The camera zoomed in on some famous person. I leaned in, squinting at the screen. It was an Australian actress, and right behind her was Charlotte. The person sitting next to Charlotte was wearing a large sunhat. Her head was down, concentrating on something in her lap. She looked up suddenly and bent toward Charlotte, whispering in her ear, hand up so no-one could hear her gossip. The woman was my mother.

I shot out of the chair and fumbled in my bag for my mobile phone. I dialled Charlotte's number, watching the television, waiting for the camera to swing back to the actress. There. I saw Charlotte reach down, and my call went to message bank. Bloody hell. Charlotte Johnson was sitting in *my* seat at *my* tennis with *my* mother! I sat again, arms crossed, and huffed. It hadn't occurred to me to offer Mum and Dad tickets to the tennis. I didn't even know Mum liked it. Had I ever asked? No, I hadn't. Did she and Dad watch it on telly? I didn't know.

I realised I had my Access All Areas pass around my neck, which meant I could enter the arena without a ticket. I waited at the gate for the end of the game, when ushers released the ropes and let the crowds move in and out of the stadium.

As I headed down the steps, Mum and Charlotte were on their way up.

'Hello, dear. Look out, we're going for a cuppa.'

I stood aside and they walked by. Charlotte said, with that annoying small smile of hers, 'I was just going to call you.'

Yeah, sure you were. I followed them out of the stadium into the concourse.

Mum looked around. 'Now, where is the lavatory?' She started waving excitedly. 'Yoo hoo, Jack!' She elbowed me. 'Look, dear, there's Jack.'

Sure enough, there he was, sauntering toward us. Women's heads swivelled, tracking his movement as he passed them. Not that he was wearing anything special, but it was good enough to make me swoon. I looked for somewhere to sit among the seats against the wall, but all were taken. I took Mum's arm.

'What's the matter, dear? Feeling faint from the heat?'

'Uh-huh.' I fanned my face.

'You should drink some water.' She patted my hand in a rare display of affection.

Jack arrived, gave Mum a kiss on the cheek. 'How are you, Margaret?'

'Fancy seeing you here!' Mum threw me off. 'Isn't the tennis marvellous? I love watching that Russian man, Volvo Voldemort.'

Jack said hello to Charlotte. She stood on tiptoes and kissed his cheek, cheeky thing. He was yet to acknowledge me.

Mum said, 'Now, I really do need to go *you know where.*'

'Charlotte,' I said, 'why don't you help Mum find the ladies'?' Seeing you brought her here and I don't trust you alone with Jack.

'Sure.' She took Mum's arm and they left.

I looked up at Jack, gave him a smile. 'Hello.'

He didn't smile back. 'Hi.'

'Something wrong?'

His mouth pursed and he put his hands on his hips.

I said, 'Were you happy with how the meeting went with Emilio?'

'Yes and no.'

'What does that mean?'

He leaned in, eyes narrow, voice low. 'You do realise that Mendez is completely deluded.'

'Um, about something in particular?'

'Something in particular?' His voice was slightly raised now and a few people glanced at us. This was a Jack I'd never seen. I'd seen him out-of-control angry, but I'd never seen him slightly-not-in-control angry. 'Mendez thinks you're his girlfriend.' He waited for a response, which I didn't give him. 'Maybe you are.'

'Of course I'm not.'

'Then why are you leading him on?'

'Hold on a minute. I think Sharon thinks she has a chance with you. Maybe you're leading her on.'

'Don't change the subject.'

'It doesn't suit you to change the subject?'

I heard someone say, 'That's *her.*'

People were watching us now. One, because I'm the most vile person on the planet for losing Emilio's precious, and two, because they were already watching Jack because he's so hot. Jack took my elbow and we went outside, stood in the sun and I shaded my face, which really didn't need another dose of skin cancer.

'You're letting Mendez think he has a chance with you.'

'He's like that with everyone. He's just … passionate. He even hugs and kisses you.'

'He's different with you. I'm a man. I know what he wants.'

'Look. I didn't ask for this —'

'Maybe that's how you operate with men.' He folded his arms across his chest.

My jaw fell. *Operate?* I wondered if anyone would notice if I slapped his face. Instead, I said, quietly, 'No, it's not. You know it's not.'

'How would I know that?'

'Because you know me quite well and I'm telling you and I'm not a liar.' Except to my mother. And Rosalind. And Emilio. And God.

'So, why?' His tightly crossed arms dropped, along with Mr Tough Guy. This was a *totally* different Jack. He seemed almost vulnerable now. Maybe the heat was getting to him. Maybe he was tired and grumpy.

I took a big breath and blew it out. 'It … it just sort of happened. JD wants me to look after Emilio, make sure he has everything he needs to win this tournament. Then the whole business with the lucky charm —'

'I'm sure John didn't mean *everything*.'

'I know, but Emilio …' Another breath. 'Actually, I feel a bit sorry for him. He lives in fantasy land. I don't think he's got very good parents. I … I don't want to spoil it for him. Not yet.' I gave him a small smile. 'Once it's over I'll never see him again.'

He nodded, hands back on hips, eyes focused on the ground.

I nudged his arm. 'It would be pretty good if he won the Open, wouldn't it?'

He looked at me over the top of his sunglasses. 'How far will you take it?'

'How far will I *take it*?' He watched me, waited for a response. What to say? Well, I'm thinking about marrying him but not having sex until our wedding night so if he dumps me after I can make a claim on his millions. Is that too far? 'Emilio has a new girlfriend every month. I'm keeping him at arm's length, don't worry.' Why would Jack worry, anyway? What was his problem? He's made it perfectly clear he doesn't do relationships. But look at him and Sharon Stone. Why did he invite her to live with him? Maybe he didn't invite her. Maybe she asked to stay. 'Anyway, you've got Sharon to amuse you.'

'Is that what you think? That you *amuse* me?'

'And annoy you.'

He laughed. His whole body changed, relaxing. 'Alright.' His tone was much friendlier. 'I guess you know what you're doing.'

And then *I* was laughing. Yeah, right.

'You fill me with such confidence.' He gazed at me with some warmth, and put a hand on my cheek. His face came closer.

I whispered, 'Are you going to kiss me?'

'I thought I might.'

'In public?'

'I'm sure no-one's looking.'

I heard the unmistakable click of an old-fashioned camera shutter, a popular sound effect for the cameras in most mobile phones. When I looked, a girl was snapping a second – or was it a third? – shot of Jack and me together. Me, Emilio Mendez's girlfriend. The girlfriend who could cause the demise of Emilio's career because of the lost amulet. The girlfriend who had just been photographed almost kissing another man. The photographer put her head down and hurried away.

Jack and I looked at each other. He shrugged. I shrugged.

'You could shoot her,' I suggested.

He smiled, not realising I was serious.

As we walked back inside, I said, 'Do you really think Teresa's involved in this? The threat against Emilio?'

'It's a possibility. Anything's a possibility. She has no reasonable excuse for choosing the driver she chose.'

'But she loves Emilio like a son.'

'Police won't rule her out for that alone.'

This was true. I remembered the movie *The Bodyguard*, where the baddie turned out to be Whitney Houston's jealous sister. But why would Teresa want to hurt Emilio? I didn't believe it.

Jack and I said a polite, no-touching goodbye, and he went off to do whatever tough-guy stuff he was doing for Emilio, and I went looking for Mum and Charlotte, only to realise they were back watching Volvo whatsisface beat the pants off our poor young Aussie, who wouldn't have known what hit him.

I went to watch Emilio train, much to his pleasure, and much to the disgust of his coach.

CHAPTER 39

I made it to the media room in time to watch Vavilov's interview. I slipped into the back seat and gazed across the heads of journalists. Booms were raised, camcorders positioned on tripods. The room was packed. There was a table set up on the low stage and the wall behind was covered with sponsor logos. Vavilov arrived and sat at the table with hands clasped in front of him. Some of the media applauded, not everyone. He gave a brief nod and the questions began. There were the usual comments about his brilliance and questions about the match. Someone asked if he thought Emilio Mendez had a chance against him.

'Everybody has chance,' he said.

'Are you worried about Mendez?'

'He is good player. I am better.' Vavilov gave a brief, rare smile to show he was teasing.

'What do you think about the threats against Mendez? We know the police interviewed you about it.'

A murmur started up in the room. Vavilov scowled and turned to his coach. The coach's hands were up. *Don't go there.*

'Please,' said Vavilov. 'Talking about tennis.'

'Are the Russians trying to sabotage Mendez?'

Vavilov slapped his hands on the desk, sat back, crossed his arms. Desi from Tennis Oz approached, leaned across Vavilov and spoke into the mic.

'Only questions about the tennis, please. Mr Vavilov is happy to talk to you about his game.' Desi stood to the side.

Vavilov moved to the mic again. His voice shook slightly. 'I am professional person. I think Mr Mendez my friend. I am look forward to match with him.' He stood and left.

Security guards watched the offending journo leave. As I left the room, I said to the security guy, 'Don't suppose he'll be allowed back.'

The guy scowled down at me. 'I not know.'

I wasn't a hundred per cent sure, but I reckoned the guy's accent was Russian.

CHAPTER 40

$\mathcal{E}$milio's first match was on Tuesday afternoon and he wanted to meet me at eleven o'clock in the players' café. I was there on time but he wasn't. I sat at a table and called Jack.

'I'm at the tennis but didn't see the protesters. You didn't, you know, sort them out, did you?'

'Sort them out?'

'You know what I'm saying.'

'I have no idea.'

'Did you, you know … send someone to pay them a visit in the night?' I hoped he didn't do it himself. That would have been awfully hard for me to live with. For a while, anyway.

'Erica, are you asking me if I had half-a-dozen innocent young people murdered in their sleep?'

'Um. No.'

'Yes, you are.'

'I didn't mean it.'

He sighed. 'I spoke to them.'

'Really? What did they say?'

'They had no idea what they were protesting about.'

I sat up straighter. 'How could they not know?'

'Because someone paid them to stand there. One of them was approached at Centrelink and asked if he had a few friends who wanted to earn some easy money.'

'Who approached them?'

'They didn't know. The guy didn't give a name, but he had an accent.'

'Like fifty per cent of Melbourne's population.'

'That's right. The kid had no idea what kind of accent it was, and couldn't give me a description beyond male, overweight, about one hundred and eighty centimetres, with brown hair.'

'Like fifty per cent of Melbourne's population.'

'Exactly.'

'Do you think the accent was Russian?'

'Of course.'

I considered all that. 'How did you get them to leave?' I said, eventually.

'I paid them more than the other guy and suggested it wouldn't be a good idea if they came back. Joe was with me.'

'Scared the shit out of them.'

'Certainly did.'

At 11:30, Emilio walked in with his head bowed and hands stuck in his pockets, Teresa by his side. I stood to greet him, and he gripped me in a fierce hug.

'Oh, Emily, I would not cope if you were not here.' He pulled back and took my face in his hands. 'You have found —'

'No, Emilio. Not yet.'

His shoulders sagged.

I said with a bright smile, 'But today you will be brilliant and win this match!'

He nodded, sighed. 'Perhaps. Perhaps today it will end for me. My tennis career.'

'Oh, come now. Together, we can help you win. Isn't that right, Teresa?'

She gave me a mournful face and I wanted to slap it.

'Cheer up, you two! Emilio, I'm here for you. What do you want me to do?'

'You will watch me play, yes?' He looked past me. 'Where is your little friend, Charlotte?'

Why doesn't he have trouble remembering Charlotte's name? And Sharon Stone's? And Yack's?

'At work,' I said. 'The protesters have gone, by the way.'

'A miracle!'

'No, Jack got rid of them. Someone paid them, Emilio. They weren't real protesters.'

'Who would do this?'

'Someone who wants you off the tournament, I suppose.' I glanced past Emilio to where Vladimir Vavilov and co were sitting at a table. 'Because you're the favourite to win,' I thought to add. 'Because you're the best player in the world. Number one. No-one can beat you, Emilio. You're awesome. And so handsome —'

'Enough now!' said Teresa, laughing. 'Emilio already has … how you say … big head.'

'You were saying, Emily?' said Emilio.

'Anyway,' I said, 'let's go do whatever it is you need to do.'

'Do you know, today I think will be *muy buena*. A very good day.'

'That's the spirit!'

Teresa said, 'Just look how much happier you are, my darling. Five minutes ago you were a mess.'

Emilio put his arms around me. 'It is Emily. She calms me.' He waved his hand. 'Now, let us eat!

CHAPTER 41

Part of the reason why Emilio Mendez has so many fans is because women and gay men across the planet want him to spend as much time as possible on the court for their viewing pleasure. All the girls in the crowd went nuts when Emilio walked onto centre court. He pretended to be embarrassed but I knew he wasn't – he loved the adoration. Emilio was tanned and had a gorgeous body – almost as good as Jack's – and with his black hair and sparkling white smile, he won every female heart in the stadium. Even the blokes loved him. A group of four guys with green-and-gold-painted faces yelled from the back stalls, 'Aussie, Aussie, Aussie!' and the crowd responded with 'Oi, Oi, Oi!' Emilio laughed and waved to them.

Emilio's first match was against an unseeded Hungarian player. Teresa showed me where to sit, then left. Emilio's team's seats were right on the corner, near where the players walked out. I got a dirty look from the misogynist – I mean, John the coach – then he ignored me. I wondered why Teresa didn't stay. Probably resting from the exhaustion of being with Emilio. Part of me – a really big part – hoped Emilio would lose this first match and put us all out of our misery.

I watched them warm up, hitting the ball back and forth, practising serves, lobbing the ball to each other. They sat to prepare for the match. Emilio and the Hungarian drank from their water bottles, fiddled with their racquets, checked shoe laces. Emilio pulled his hair into a ponytail. They were ready to play. The ump called for silence and the Hungarian served to Emilio's forehand. Emilio slammed the ball down the sideline. The crowd screamed.

I watched Emilio win the first set, six-love. He was so elegant and calm, his strokes long and sure; the way he confidently placed each ball made him look like he'd been born for this game. He would win this match and maybe even the tournament. This would be my life until the end of next week. I felt sorry for the poor Hungarian, who'd come all the way across the planet for this annihilation. He sat there with his head bowed. Emilio took off his shirt. Women screamed, whistled, cheered. He stood and took a bow. As he pulled the fresh shirt over his head, all the women booed.

Watching Emilio's glistening, tanned, muscled torso reminded me not only that I'd like to see more of Jack, but that it was so hot. Thirty-five degrees outside the stadium; probably forty-five within. As I stood I saw a familiar head, just under where I was sitting. I peered over the railing. It was Joe, who'd popped out from backstage to check the crowd, keep an eye on Emilio. I wondered where Jack was. Was he here, or with Sharon somewhere? I left the arena and entered the cool concourse, with relief. I stood in line for the toilet, bought a bottle of water, and took a seat, waiting for my body temperature to lower. I checked my phone. A few messages. Text from Steve about my appliances. Nothing from Jack. I wandered outside and toward the merchandise tents, texting as I walked. My head was down, pressing out the letters, and I nearly got knocked over. I turned to the man who stood there, glaring at me.

'I'm sorry,' I said.

He walked away but there was something about him, the look in his eye, that made me watch him. He was a very fat man, wearing shorts and a T-shirt with socks and sandals. His round, hairy belly hung out over his shorts and from under his T-shirt. He was unshaven and dirty-looking, and as he walked he turned his head and looked at me. I shuddered. He bowled over a small kid but didn't stop as the child's mother shouted something at him. I walked on, checking over my shoulder every few seconds.

Another of Emilio's sponsors, Gleam toothpaste, had their own marquee offering free dental check-ups and show bags, and I remembered Emilio telling me I should go there and "have fun". But there was a better tent, for *Jolie* skin care. They were giving free pedicures and had really fab things in their showbags. I grabbed myself a Pee Wee pie and stood in the line.

I heard the crowd going crazy in Rod Laver Arena. I figured Emilio would be close to putting away the second set and thought I probably should get back to watch him win the third set, and match. I hesitated, torn. Pedicure. Emilio. Pedicure. Emilio.

Emilio. With a sigh I left the line and headed back to the stadium, taking my time, looking around for the creepy man. I had to wait for a break to get back in. As I made my way down the steps, I glanced at the players in their seats. Emilio's face was in his hands. What was wrong? I looked at the scoreboard. Oh, shit! The Hungarian had won the second set! I sprinted down the stairs and found Emilio's coach and the rest of his crew, also with heads in hands. Teresa was there now, looking tired and anxious.

'What happened?' I said to anyone who might have the answer.

Teresa said, wearily, 'We do not know. He just went to pieces. He is thinking about *el amuleto*.'

EMILIO WON that match but it was exhausting. It went to five sets. After, he wanted to have dinner with me, tell me something, he said. Something good. But something bad happened between his match and our dinner. Teresa showed him the photo of Jack and me – of Jack almost kissing me – which had gone viral on Twitter, Facebook, Instagram, whatever. The photo was tagged: *#Mendez #legend #hottie #unworthybitchgf #randomhottie*. I hated that girl's guts.

At dinner Emilio challenged me about it, showing me the photo on his phone.

'What is this? You tell me *Yack* is your friend, and now I am ... how you say ... laughing stock. First *mi amuleto* and now this. What are you doing to me? Please tell me this isn't true. Tell me this photograph is telling a lie.'

Well, I *was* going to tell Emilio that Yack is, in fact, a bit more than a friend. I *was* going to tell him that I'd work for him, cheer him on, organise his dry cleaning and help him find a new girlfriend if he wanted – offer up Sharon Stone, for example – but that he'd have to understand I was not his girlfriend. And that I'd try very hard to find his lucky charm. I didn't say any of that, though, because Emilio was shattered. He sat there like little boy lost.

'It's telling a lie.'

'So, it is not true? You and *Yack* are not seeing each other behind my back?'

'Er ... that's right. We're not. It's all a lie.'

'But this photograph ... I feel very foolish, Emily.'

I looked at it again. Jack's hand on my face, leaning close, about to kiss me. My argument that Jack and I were just bed pals wouldn't hold much water using this as evidence. We looked like a couple. In love.

'Sorry, Emilio, what were you saying?'

'This photograph makes it very clear that something is taking place between you.'

'Well ... I was meeting Jack to find out what he'd done about your security issues, you see. And then –' I pointed '– Jack noticed something on my face. You can see it there. He's just wiping it off.'

'I cannot see anything.'

'It's there. You need to squint. It's a bad photo.'

'I think it is quite a clear photograph. But Emily, he is leaning close to you. It looks like he might kiss you!'

'Oh, no, it's just ... he's got bad eyesight. He had to lean in to see the thing on my face.'

'But if he has bad eyesight, how did he see the thing was there?'

'Um, actually, he didn't notice it at first, but I felt it there. I said to him, "Is there something on my face"? And he leaned close and saw there was something there. See?' I gave Emilio a big, bright smile.

But the poor thing looked so miserable. I patted his hand, saying, 'There, there. Soon you'll win the Australian Open and you'll be the greatest tennis player in the world. And just think how much money you'll have!'

'Emily. There is something I wish to tell you. It is important.'

'Oh?'

'Today, I nearly lose the match.'

'But you didn't. You won.'

'*Si, si*. But do you know when I play bad today?'

'You were thinking about your amulet?'

'No, it is when you go. I cannot play because you are not there.'

'Really?' I had a warm fuzzy. How nice!

'*Si*. I realise something. I have never felt this way. No other woman – even woman so much more beautiful – has made me feel I cannot win without her. But today I know, it is not *mi amuleto* I am needing. It is you.'

Oh. Shit. I sat there, blinking at him.

Rather than ask if I felt the same, Emilio gripped my hand and kissed my palm, sighing loudly, eyes closed. 'Ah, my Emily, *mi amor*, my most beautiful flower. I wish we do not have to wait to consummate our love.' He kissed along the soft inside of my arm. 'Perhaps tonight?' He looked at me from under luscious black lashes, all dewy-eyed and hopeful, wanting my permission to break his own rule about no bonking during a tournament.

I shook my head, breaking the trance, and took my arm back. 'I think you need your lucky charm, Emilio. I'll find it for you, don't you worry.'

'No, I do not need it. It is special, *si*, a gift from *mi abuela*. But it will not be the end of my life if you do not find it. I know now, Emilita, all I have ever needed is you. This is why there is an explosion! To bring us together, you see?'

I cleared my throat, picked up the menu. 'Let's order, shall we?'

· · ·

AFTER DINNER, Emilio wanted me to go to his room for herbal tea.

'I don't think that's a good idea, do you?'

He sighed. 'Perhaps not. I may be tempted, and then I will surely regret it.'

I wasn't sure what to feel more offended by; the fact that I didn't seem to be included in the decision about whether or not there was to be any sex, or that he'd regret it later, which I was pretty sure he would, judging by what I'd read about him. He'd regret it so much he'd be suddenly repulsed by me, which, in a strange way, I found tempting. If I was suddenly repulsive to Emilio, then he'd leave me alone and have to find someone else to be his muse. But no, I wouldn't do it, as beautiful as he was and as much as I believed that Jack and I had no claim on each other and as much as I worried Jack and Sharon might be doing the very same thing, right now…

As I walked to my car, I wrote Jack a text: *Miss you.* I hesitated before sending. It just came out – not what I'd intended writing (what did I intend writing?) – and it was a message full of a not-so-hidden other meaning. One that suggested I had actual feelings for him. It was a gutsy decision on my part, but I did miss him. I missed him, desperately. All I wanted was to be in his arms for a while. In his bed or in front of the telly, or – anywhere, I didn't care. I just wanted to *touch* him and be in his space. And I wanted him to know that, even though I'd been with Emilio, he was on my mind. I hit send, and as I sat in my car, his reply came through: *Where are you?*

About to drive home. Can I come over?

It was only nine o'clock, so I thought Jack wouldn't mind if I called in for a coffee, nightcap, shower … There was a full minute before he responded, and I wondered why.

I'm not home.

Oh. *Where?*

Out for dinner.

My turn to hesitate. I didn't want to know what I suspected to be true. But I couldn't stand not knowing.

With S?

Yes.
There it was. So be it.
I messaged: *Enjoy your evening. Night.*
Goodnight.

CHAPTER 42

 drove home in misery via Jack's house in Brighton, which wasn't on the way to Mum's. His house was in darkness and I wondered where he went for dinner. Was Joe at dinner, too? Or tucked up in bed? Did they go to that nice restaurant in Southbank? I thought I'd drive to Church Street in Brighton and see if I could find him. But then, if he saw me lurking outside a restaurant, what would he think? I headed for Chadstone, drove past Mum's and around the block to Mrs Booth's. I needed to focus on the amulet, finding it, getting it back to Emilio, so he'd stop obsessing about me.

I parked a few houses up the road and snuck back. Crept up the driveway, past the double garage, and down the side of the house. At the back was the kitchen window, the laundry door, the large living room windows and the outside basement door, which was overgrown with weeds. I think it used to be access for the wood or coal delivery guy or something. Mr and Mrs Booth were Americans who moved here in the '50s, which is why they built an American-style house. Part of the reason as kids we were spooked by it was because it was so different to the single-storey, cream-brick creations of the Australian 'burbs. I went into the garden so I could watch without being seen.

Lights were on. Blinds were drawn. I saw a shadow moving around and my heart started racing.

'Don't be a sook, Erica,' I muttered. 'It's Mrs Booth.'

A second shadow appeared in the kitchen. Who? The living room lights went out, and a few seconds later an upstairs light came on. Someone still in the kitchen. The shadow moved out of the kitchen and then a second light came on upstairs. Ruth's old bedroom. The trellis was still against the wall under Ruth's bedroom window, the vine covering it long dead. Ruth used to climb in and out of her bedroom via the window and trellis. She told Steve and me that she snuck out in the night with her mother's cigarettes. She was only nine at the time – we would have been twelve – and we didn't believe her, so she stole cigarettes from her mother and showed us. While Ruth stood there, smoking sophisticatedly, I had one puff and vomited.

I watched a while longer. The two bedroom lights were still on, but so was the kitchen light. I saw movement in both upstairs rooms, so I crept to the kitchen window. If Mrs Booth had taken the amulet, where would she keep it? I could start with the kitchen. The blind was down but there was a one-inch gap at the bottom. I peered in. I could see through the kitchen to the living room. There was a fish tank. Is that where Axle got his goldfish? How on earth did he pluck it out of there? The blind moved suddenly. I ducked down, hand over my mouth, neck craning to see if someone was there. Maybe a breeze caused it? Slowly, I came up, eyes level with the gap; the blind moved again and the black cat stared out at me. I squealed, backed away and ran down the driveway as fast as I could, not stopping until I got into my car. I screeched off down the road, around the corner and parked outside Mum's.

I sat there for a while, calming myself from the terrifying ordeal of having a cat look at me through a window. Inside, Mum and Dad were watching television.

'Oh, good,' said Mum. 'You're home.' She stood and headed for the kitchen. 'I was just going to make a cuppa.'

I sat opposite Mum at the kitchen counter, hanging on to stop the stool from swivelling to the right.

'Mum, do you remember Mr Booth?'

'Yes, dear. Not well, though.'

'What do you think happened to him?'

Mum put down the kettle and gave me a considered look, like she was trying to decide something. 'I suppose you're old enough to know.'

'Know what?' That he was murdered and buried in the basement? If Mum knew that, why didn't she tell the police?

'That he ran off with Mrs Smith.'

'Their next-door neighbour?'

'That's right.'

'Do you know that for sure?'

'Rumour has it that's why Mr Smith sold up and left.' She put a mug of tea in front of me. 'Why do you ask?'

'I just drove by the Booth house. I think someone else is living there.'

'Really? Imelda's been on her own since Ruth moved away.' Mum put a finger to her chin, looked up. 'That was probably fifteen years ago.'

'Where did Ruth go? I never knew.'

'Imelda wouldn't say. With her father, presumably. Poor thing didn't see much of her daughter after that. But since then, I've heard Mr Booth left Mrs Smith and returned to America.'

'With Ruth?'

'I'm not sure, dear.'

'I wonder if she's moved back home to her mother's?'

'I don't know.' Mum looked at the clock. 'Now, Erica, it's bed time! Before you know it, you'll be up and off to work again.' And she left the kitchen with a mug of tea, and Tim Tam biscuits for Dad.

CHAPTER 43

'My stapler's been missing for days!' Rosalind gave me a look. 'Did you take it?'

Where? Where would I take it? To the tennis? Surely, dear boss, there are better, more important things for you to worry about than whether or not your stapler is missing? Like dealing with the company's plummeting share price, the angry public, delegating my workload or doing it yourself, for example.

Emilio had called me first thing. 'Today is rest for me. You will come? We can do the sightseeing?'

Teresa called me five minutes later, saying I needed to stop harassing Emilio to spend time with me. He needed rest. 'He will see you for tomorrow's match.'

Fine by me. That meant I got to stay at work and actually get things done. It meant I could spend all day with Rosalind and Charlotte. Joy!

Emilio called me again. 'When are you coming, Emily?'

What? 'Teresa said I shouldn't come because you need to rest.'

'Teresa is not the boss of me. I think Mr John Degraves would like you to make me happy, *si?*'

Nice backhand, Emilio. 'Alright. I'll come and visit you. But not in your room, okay? Let's have lunch or something.'

I told him I'd be there at lunchtime. But Rosalind stood in front of my desk and tapped her toe, arms crossed. 'What are you doing?'

I looked up from my computer. 'Work.'

'My dry cleaning's ready to be collected.'

I checked my watch. 'Actually, Mr Degraves wants me to meet Emilio. I have to go now.'

'How am I supposed to get my dry cleaning?' she shouted to the general office.

I stood and looked over the partition to where Charlotte was doing Marcus's filing. 'Charlotte, can you please pick up Rosalind's dry cleaning?'

'Sure!' She jumped up. 'I'd love to.'

Of course you would, you suck. I left too early to go to Emilio. I thought maybe I could sit in the bar and drink Bloody Marys, but as I pulled into the hotel driveway, I saw Teresa leave the building and get into a taxi. I don't know why I felt the need to do so, but I followed her.

TERESA DIDN'T GO FAR, just to the top end of the city. The taxi pulled into the Sofitel. I parked in a no-standing zone and trotted up the hotel's driveway. Inside, I saw Teresa at the reception desk. I sat on a sofa and picked up a magazine, holding it in front of my face like they do in detective stories. Teresa signed something, collected something from the receptionist, and headed for the lifts. I checked my watch and waited, I didn't know what for.

I ordered a Bloody Mary and read *Storage Superstars* magazine. I got some good ideas for my renovation. I called Steve to tell him about an idea, but just as he answered, I saw Martin McGann walk into the hotel.

'Sorry, can't talk.' I hung up before Steve could say anything.

I held the magazine high, peeking over the top of it. Martin

McGann didn't approach the reception desk, but headed straight for the lifts, reading his phone as he walked.

I sipped my Bloody Mary, staring at the lifts with narrowed eyes. Was this just a coincidence? That these two people had arrived at the same five-star hotel within ten minutes of each other? I wasn't sure, but as I left the hotel to deal with my parking fine, I mentally referred to some tips from *Storage Superstars* to store this particular piece of information.

'Come,' said Emilio in his undies. 'Lie on the bed and cuddle.' He took my hand and towed me toward the bedroom.

I stopped, took my hand back. 'Emilio, I have to tell you something.'

'*Si?*'

'I don't feel the same as you …'

Both hands clutched his heart. His face crumpled.

'… about tennis.'

He perked up. '*Qué?*'

'I don't love tennis as much as you do.'

He laughed. 'That is okay, Emilita. But you like to watch, yes?'

'Well, yes.' Geez.

He came at me again and, gripping my waist, pulled me against him. I put my hands on his chest. His crotch was pressed against my lower belly. He gazed at me with smouldering eyes. It was the first time I'd seen eyes that smouldered. Emilio's were usually blue, but right now they were dark grey. Warmth flooded my body, pooled in one particular spot. I shook my head, patted his shoulder, tried to speak. My heart thumped. Could he hear it?

'*Prontito*, Emily. Soon.'

He bent his head to kiss me. I gave him a half-hearted push that had no effect on the space between us. His face came closer. Mine tilted up. It was going to be a proper, full-on pash, I could tell by the look in his eyes. I was transfixed by their intensity. They burned into me. My breath mingled with his. His lips touched mine, which parted.

I shoved him away and took three quick steps back.

'What is wrong, *mi amor?*'

'God, Emilio, I'm … um …'

'You find me irresistible, no?'

'No. I mean, yes. I mean —'

'We will go to lunch, yes?'

'Yes. Alright. Get dressed now, okay?'

He grinned and watched me trying to avoid looking at him. A specific part of him. I stood at the window and fixed my eyes on the river. The still, dull, cold-looking river.

CHAPTER 44

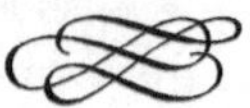

$\mathcal{E}$milio annihilated his round two opponent. We had dinner together that night.

'You see? It is you, Emily. You make me play so well. I win because of you!'

'I think you win because you're a fabulous tennis player.'

'No.' He forked a piece of lobster. 'It is you.'

I needed to get that amulet. Convince him he needs it, not me, even though he didn't need either. Maybe counselling?

'Emilio, how do you know Teresa?'

'She was my father's lover.'

'Really? But doesn't that make it difficult for you to be with her? Doesn't it remind you of him?'

'No, *querida*. We are … how you say …' He muttered in Spanish. 'We have both been wronged by him, so together, this makes us stronger.'

'You're kindred spirits.'

'*Si*. Kindred spirits.'

'Do you pay her? I mean, I know it's not my business —'

'Pay? How do you mean?'

'Like, a salary. She's your manager, right? Does she get a salary?'

He looked thoughtful. 'I pay for everything. If she needs something, I buy it. She lives in a house I own. Her car is one I bought. If she wants clothes, I take her shopping.'

'Wow. Maybe I should be a tennis player's manager.' I smiled to show I was joking, but couldn't help wondering why the loyal, well-kept Teresa might be meeting up with Martin McGann.

Emilio took my hand. 'Ah, Emilita, I am the only tennis player you will ever know. And soon, you will need no money.'

CHAPTER 45

When I arrived at work on Friday, Charlotte was at my desk.

'Um, can I have my desk back?'

'You don't need it. I've done everything.'

'What do you mean?'

'I've done all the work.'

'*All* of it?'

She looked around at the super-neat space. 'I think so, yes.'

'What about the media release about the oil spill?'

'Mr Degraves has it for approval.'

'What? Who wrote it?'

'Me.'

'You?'

Charlotte checked her watch. 'Here, you can sit here for a while. I need to get my scones out of the oven.'

As she headed for the canteen, I called out, 'Can you bring me one?'

'You'll have to pay for it.'

While Charlotte was gone, I Google-Earthed Mrs Booth's house and zoomed right in. Yes, I could see all the things I already knew she had. A house, a driveway, a backyard. I looked at Mum and Dad's house, squinting at the screen. I think Dad was in the vegie patch.

Charlotte arrived and stood behind me. 'What are you doing?'

I shut down Google Earth.

'Can I have my chair back? I need to finish something for Marcus.'

I stood and we faced each other. 'Just to be clear, Charlotte, this is *my* chair. We'll find you a desk soon, I promise.'

Without responding, she slipped into *my* chair, head down, and resumed the work she'd been doing.

EMILIO CALLED me in the afternoon and told me that tomorrow evening – Saturday – was his next match.

'I do not want to think about the tennis, *querida*. What shall we do together in the daytime?'

'Well, I have to shop for appliances in the morning. And then I have to go to the office. But I'll see you before the match, okay?' I didn't *need* to go to the office because, apparently, Charlotte had done everything, but I wanted to go there when she wasn't so I could find out exactly what she'd been up to.

'What is this appliance shopping?'

'My house is being renovated. I need appliances for my new kitchen.' Actually, saying those words – new kitchen – gave me a buzz. Wouldn't be long before I'd be cooking in it. And putting all the dirty dishes in my new dishwasher – something I'd never had before. Well, not too much cooking. Preferably no cooking, in fact. But how else would I make dirty dishes to put in my new dishwasher? Take-away containers. Instead of throwing them out, I'll put all the take-away containers in my new dishwasher and keep them.

'Emilita?'

'Huh?'

'You will move to Sydney to be with me, no?'

'Er ...' No.

'Otherwise, how will we be together?'

'I really like Melbourne, Emilio. And my house. I really like my house.'

'You can rent it. That will give you spending money of your own. And, Emily, it is important to put quality appliances in your house for your tenants.'

'Right.'

'I will come appliance shopping with you!'

'What?'

'I will pick you up in the limousine.'

'Oh, no. No more limos, Emilio.'

'Well, you will pick me up, yes? Is it popular, this appliance place?'

'Very popular. There'll be huge crowds there, probably.' I thought of our Chadstone shopping expedition and felt suddenly faint.

'That means there will be many of my fans there?'

'Probably.'

'*Estupendo*!'

'Is that good?'

'*Si*, Emilita. You will pick me up?'

'Ah …'

CHAPTER 46

On Saturday morning I arrived at Emilio's hotel to pick him up in my crappy old Mazda. The valet-parking guy didn't believe I was who I said I was. He had to call Emilio to confirm it, but still he gave me a suspicious look.

Emilio wasn't ready, so I went up to his room. He was alone.

'Aren't you supposed to have a body guard?'

'It is okay. They think I am spending today in my room. Besides, there have been no attempts on my life or threats.'

'No *further* threats. Emilio, I don't think you're supposed to go out without protection.' I didn't actually *know* this. I hadn't had that convo with Jack but I assumed Emilio shouldn't.

'Look, I will wear a disguise!' He put on his Dega Oil cap and grinned at me.

I couldn't help smiling back. 'You look like Emilio Mendez.'

He laughed. 'Let us go!'

As we left his room, I said, 'Where's Teresa?'

'Ah, she has a boyfriend, I think.'

I stopped walking. 'Really? Do you know who it is?'

'I think she does not want me to know, but it is nice for her, yes?'

I didn't respond, thinking about that. Was it Martin McGann? The *married* Martin McGann? Where did they meet? The charity lunch, maybe. Before or after the heist?

'Come, Emily.'

Emilio hesitated about getting into my car. Finally, he sat, quickly pulled the door closed. 'No-one would suspect me of travelling in a vehicle such as this, so I think I am safe.' He looked up at the torn roof lining. 'You must get a new car, Emilita. This one is not good. When you live with me in Sydney, I will buy you a car that is … how you say … appropriate.'

Goody gumdrops. An appropriate car for the prostitute of a famous tennis player. Surely that would be something good? A convertible?

Emilio sat lower in the seat and adjusted his sunglasses and cap. 'I hope I am not recognised in this car.'

We drove to Nepean Highway, Brighton. I parked in The Good Guys car park and we went inside. The whispers started straight away: *That's Emilio Mendez.* Probably because he walked in the door and said, loudly, '*Hola, amigos!*'

Emilio followed me around, signing autographs as we went. There was a fridge and I fell in love. It made ice and had a thing for pouring yourself a glass of cold water. It stored meat forever, had a special spot for wine, cleaned itself, and cooked the dinner. It was a metre wide, required its own power plant, and cost five thousand dollars. 'I love this fridge, Emilio.'

He looked up from his signing. 'It is a beautiful refrigerator.'

I called Steve.

'I'm at The Good Guys.'

'Great. Know what you need?'

'How much room have I got for a fridge?'

'You don't need a new fridge.'

'I know but you should see it. It's gorgeous.'

'You need to get —'

'I know, I know. The fridge?'

'As much room as you want.' He sighed. 'Stan'll design the kitchen around it.'

I hung up and took a photo of the fridge. We stood in front of the Australian brand dishwashers. I knew they weren't the best quality. Jack would tell me to buy European. Emilio wanted me to buy Emilia appliances.

'Is it a good brand?'

'I am sure it is.'

I opened and closed doors, inspecting the insides, and eventually became aware of excited chatter around me. Emilio's crowd of fans was growing. Good, I thought. I'll go shopping while he's occupied. But he called me, beckoning.

'Come, Emily. *Aquí.* My fans want a photograph with us!'

'Oh, no, really, you don't want —' Phone cameras went off. I stopped talking and smiled, teeth jammed together, mouth stretched wide.

Emilio stood next to me, arm around my shoulders.

I pushed gently away, still smiling. 'I really need to buy these appliances, Emilio.'

Someone in the crowd squealed, 'Are you setting up home together?'

'Ha, ha! We will all shop with you, *ángel!*'

The fans followed us to the Smeg department. Emilio said to the crowd, which was yet to include a salesperson, 'I think Emily should buy Emilia products, what do you all think?'

General murmurs of agreement. Applause even. Bloody hell.

We left. There was no point. I'd just have to come back later while Emilio was resting at the hotel. As we went to get into my car, someone shot at us. I wasn't sure at first – too stunned to think straight. But Emilio casually said it was indeed a gunshot – he knew because when he lived in South America people were always shooting each other on the streets, so he knew that sound. Also, my windscreen was now all over the front seat. Several images flew through my mind, mostly of me or Emilio lying dead in a pool of blood. Who was the bullet intended for? Or was it some kind of freak accident?

It seemed ages – but was probably only seconds – before I thought to see if there was a gunman still standing there, taking aim, ready for another go. I had a frantic look around.

Emilio took my hand. 'We really should not stand here.'

We ran back into the store. I stood at the window, staring out, and Emilio wandered off. I looked up and down the road, across Nepean Highway. Hold on, there was a black BMW speeding away. The tyres even screeched, it was in such a hurry. Shane McGann had black BMWs. I rushed outside but couldn't make out the plate. I called Jack.

'Good morning,' he said.

'It's me.'

'I know.'

'Someone just shot at me … us.'

'*What?*'

'It might have been an accident. I don't know. But my windscreen's not where it should be.'

'Where are you?'

'I'm fine. We're safe. At The Good Guys in Brighton.'

'When you say we —'

'Emilio.'

Silence. Then, 'Have you called the police?'

'Not yet. Just you.'

'I'll make the call. Wait inside. Stay with people but *not* Emilio. I'll be there in five.'

When Jack arrived, I was standing in the window, staring out. I could hear police sirens as I watched him park on the street and get out of his car. He looked around, saw me and frowned. He walked into the store. 'Being a target in the window isn't exactly what I had in mind when I said wait inside.'

I pointed. 'I saw a black BMW.'

'What about it?'

'Well, it was speeding away. Shane McGann has black BMWs.'

'Shane McGann's in jail, Erica.'

'But his friends might have his car.'

'Don't you think it makes sense that the bullet was intended for Mendez? His life's already been threatened.' We looked around, spotted Emilio in the Bosch department with fans. 'He wasn't supposed to leave the hotel today.' Jack cursed quietly and mumbled, 'Making my life difficult.'

'But it's not totally improbable. The BMW, I mean.'

He stared across the highway, considering it. 'Where did you see the car?'

I pointed.

'Going which direction?'

'Toward the city. It was speeding.'

Police cars arrived. Lots. Jack looked at me. 'Why are you here, anyway?'

'Shopping for appliances.' I pointed to the gorgeous fridge. 'I'm getting that one. It's better than yours.'

'You can't go shopping without a tennis player tagging along?' The way he said *tennis player* made it sound like some low form of life.

'It's not – he just wants to hang out with me. I don't know why.'

'I think I know why.'

'*Hola, Yack*! Where is your beautiful lady?' Emilio rushed up and hugged Jack.

Jack's expression changed from scowly to fully annoyed as he unhooked Emilio's arms.

I jumped on the opportunity to change the subject. 'Yeah, where's Shags?'

Emilio was distracted by a fan with a camera. Lots of police came into the store. Jack told me to wait and approached a plainclothes policeman, one I'd met before on another case with Jack: Bill Lucas. The police taped off the car park, which was soon crawling with cops – uniformed and not uniformed, guy with a camera, whoever else turns up at these things. There were people all around my car. Jack and Bill Lucas were checking out a plastic bag with something inside it.

Emilio was bored and wanted to leave.

'We have to answer questions for the police first.'

'Let us shop while we wait!'

I pointed at the washing machines and suggested he choose a nice one for me, even though I didn't need a new washing machine, but Bill Lucas intercepted him and took him to one side.

Jack approached, looking worried. He took my arm and pulled me away from prying ears.

'Did you see anyone hanging around you might have recognised? Anyone at all?' He looked *really* worried as he stared into my eyes, waiting for my response.

'Why? What —'

'Just think about it.'

I looked outside, giving it some thought. 'No, no-one. Just the BMW.'

He glanced around, lowered his voice even more so I had to lean close to hear him. 'We found the bullet embedded in the driver's seat of your car.'

'Right.' Shudder.

'It's one of mine.'

I had to pull back a bit so I could look right into his face. What was he telling me? That a bullet from a gun Jack owns was fired at Emilio? Or me?

'How do you know?'

'My bullets are marked. It's mine. No doubt.'

'Jesus.'

He nodded. 'Think again about whether you saw anyone you might have recognised.'

'Like, someone who works for you?'

'Exactly like that.'

Nausea swept through me and I had to take a few quick, deep breaths while I processed that. 'You think one of your guys is working for Shane McGann?'

Jack looked at me for a long time. 'No, actually, that's not what I was thinking.'

'What are you thinking?'

'That someone who uses one of my guns shot at Emilio Mendez.'

'Why would they?'

He shook his head. His face was pale.

'It might have been meant for me. You have to consider the possibility, at least.'

'Maybe.' He stared out the window. 'I'll pay McGann a visit.'

'You mean, visit him in jail?'

He nodded.

'I'm coming with you.'

He almost laughed. 'No, you're not.'

Emilio returned, grinning, happy with all the fuss.

'This is better than my boring hotel, *querida!*' He went to sling an arm around me but I ducked out of the way.

Bill Lucas saved me. He asked me the same things Jack did: whether or not I saw anything suspicious, anyone I recognised who might want me or Emilio dead? By the time he'd finished interviewing me, most of the police had left and the crowd had dissipated, finally bored with the proceedings and Emilio.

I found Jack and Emilio standing together, speaking Spanish.

'When did you learn Spanish?' I said to Jack.

'*Yack*, you must convince Emily to buy Emilia products.'

Jack stood a bit taller. 'She'll buy Gaggenau.'

'I will buy your Emilia products for you, *querida!*'

Jack said, 'I'll buy your appliances. Just email me a list.'

I said, 'My electricity bill is due, if either of you is interested.'

'But Emily,' said Emilio, 'we agreed on Emilia!'

'We didn't *agree* on anything...'

Jack faced me, his back to Emilio. 'I need to leave before someone gets hurt.'

'Okay.'

A staff member asked Emilio for photos with the rest of the staff. Emilio went to have the photos taken.

Jack said, 'I'll buy your appliances.'

I shrugged. 'Okay.'

'Sharon's coming to get Emilio. She'll stay with him. Joe's coming to get you and take you home. He'll sort your car.'

'I don't want to go home.'

'You're going home.'

Sigh.

CHAPTER 47

*S*haron came to take Emilio back to the hotel and, annoyingly, he seemed quite happy to go trotting off with her in Jack's Merc. What about her car? Doesn't she have one? Joe took me home and on the way I sulked, staring out the window.

'Joe, does Sharon have a car?'

'Yes, but the Merc was last in the garage. If that's why you're asking.'

'Yeah, that's why.'

I sulked some more. 'Why couldn't Jack bring me home? Not that I mind being with you, but ... you know.'

'Yes, I know. Time management.'

'What do you mean?'

'The reason Jack sent me. Jack's managing his time. He had other things to do.'

'Time management,' I said in a shitty, mimicky voice. Jack's reason for abandoning me after a traumatic experience.

When I got home, I told Mum and Dad a tree had fallen on my car, and so they'd have to order stuff online from the supermarket. 'Or you could get your car fixed.'

Mum suggested I do some baking. Emilio called to say a driver would pick me up to bring me to his match at the tennis. Jack called me almost immediately after to say not to even consider leaving my mother's house, not even to attend the tennis. That my life would not be worth living if I made such a stupid, life-risking decision. That, if I went out and got killed, Jack would kill me. I got the message.

I sat on my bed and Axle climbed onto my lap, purring. I scratched his ear; he rolled onto his back and attacked my hand, causing me to swear. He ran out the door and my mother appeared.

'I hope that wasn't you using such bad language, Erica.'

'Nope, not me.'

She left, probably to offer Axle something delicious to make up for his mother's neglect. Maybe Axle had hired a hit man to get rid of me so he could live with my mother and her roast chicken.

I blew out a sigh and checked my watch. Midday. I most definitely had to go to the tennis tonight – that was not negotiable. If Emilio lost because I wasn't there, well, the thought of it made me feel sick. But for now, as I stared through the pale pink curtains on my window, I considered the shooting. There were several possibilities. My favourite was the Shane McGann payback theory and that one of Jack's guys was working for him, like a double agent. The only thing about that theory, is that Shane McGann would want to make me pay. I mean, really *pay*. Not just a simple gunshot to the head, that wouldn't be horrible or terrifying enough. So, maybe not Shane McGann.

What about the train incident? Did the car really break down and was Danny DeVito really just afraid? Or maybe Emilio was the target. If so, why would one of Jack's men want to kill him? And, what about the charity lunch?

A car turned up and parked out the front of Mum's. I recognised the driver: Andrew, one of Jack's guys, sent to mind me. I called Jack. No answer. I called Joe. No answer. I wished I had Sharon's number. Maybe she and Jack were together. In his bedroom. So much for sneaking out. I went into the backyard, stood on the fence railing and looked into Mrs Booth's. As I did, I heard what sounded like a car backing out of her driveway. I went inside.

'Mum, have you got Mrs Booth's phone number?'

'Yes, I think I do.'

She found an old thing she called her "teledex" and flipped through it. 'Why do you want it?'

'Um, I want to arrange a play date for Axle with her cat.'

'Silly girl.' Mum read out the number to me.

I dialled. It rang out. I waited until Mum was settled in front of the television before I snuck out the back door and over the fence. I didn't hesitate about jumping the fence because I knew if I did hesitate, I'd chicken out. To be on the safe side, I rounded the house and knocked on the front door. I rang the doorbell. Knocked a few times more. Called from my mobile. I could hear the phone ringing inside the house.

'Right,' I said to the door. 'No-one home.'

I went to the back of the house again and looked through all the windows. No lucky charm that I could see. And then, like the no-hesitation-at-the-fence, I started up the trellis before I could think too much about it and change my mind. First, I stepped up onto the old basement doors, now covered in vine. The doors creaked under my weight. I supposed they were pretty old. I climbed a few feet, and glanced down to see where I'd land if I fell. Onto the basement doors, that's where. Or the ground, if I jumped away from the house. Surely I wouldn't hurt myself too badly. I'd have to bend my knees and roll, like they do in the movies. Or I could just get on with it and stop thinking about falling. I climbed, reaching Ruth's old bedroom window. I hesitantly peered inside, cupping my hand around my face to get a clearer look. The window was open a tiny crack. Inside, the bedroom had changed since the last time I was in there, well over fifteen years ago. Ruth's bedroom had been like her mother's, all dark and velvety. Purples and crimsons, mirrors and crystals hanging from the ceiling. I didn't know if Mrs Booth's was still like that, but Ruth's certainly wasn't. Now, Ruth's bedroom walls were painted a pale pink. There was a framed Emilio Mendez poster above the single bed.

I could see evidence that someone was living there now. A hairbrush on the dressing table. A pair of high heels set neatly on the floor. Hold on. I pressed my face against the glass, tried to lift myself higher. Those high heels looked suspiciously like the ones I was missing.

'Erica Jewell!'

I squealed and jumped; my feet slipped and I hung there, clinging to the trellis, scrabbling for a foothold again. As I climbed down, I looked over my shoulder at Mum, who was peering over the fence at me.

'What on earth!'

I ran across Mrs Booth's backyard and hoisted myself up the fence and back into Mum's yard while she stood there gaping at me.

'I think someone's living there with Mrs Booth. You won't tell her, will you? That I was snooping?'

'I just don't know what to make of you sometimes, Erica. I really don't.'

'Don't worry, Mum. I'm usually pretty normal.'

CHAPTER 48

I went out and spoke to Andrew the bodyguard, who was mid-yawn and back stretch.

'Are you here to babysit or kill me?'

He laughed. 'Babysit.'

'You didn't take a shot at me earlier, did you?'

'Not me.'

I checked the time again. Fifteen minutes later than the last time I looked. I really wanted to go into work to see what Charlotte had been doing. Andrew could take me, I thought. Hopefully, Rosalind wouldn't be there, upside down in her office. What if she was? What if I arrived and discovered her true identity, what would she do? Would Andrew the bodyguard protect me from her? Or help her kill me?

'I'm going to Jack's.'

'You're not allowed to leave the house.'

'Well, I could walk to Dandenong Road and hitchhike while you wait here with my mother. She'll make you scones. Or you could take me.'

He sighed, exactly like Jack often does. 'Alright. Get in.'

'I'll be right back.'

Inside, I told Mum that Jack had sent me a chauffeur to use until my car was fixed, and that I was heading out for the day. I neglected to mention that my chauffeur packs a weapon. Probably more than one. Maybe even a rocket launcher in the boot.

At Jack's, Joe greeted me at the front door with, 'You're not supposed to leave your house.'

'My mother's there.'

'That's not a good enough reason to risk your life.'

'Yes, it is. I tried calling you all. No-one answered.'

We walked through to the kitchen. There were cupcakes cooling on the bench.

'Jack's just back from a run,' said Joe.

'Is he in the shower?'

'Yeah.'

'Alone?'

Joe laughed, went to speak but shook his head instead.

'Where's Sharon?'

'Not in the shower with Jack.'

I shrugged and helped myself to a cake. 'Are you going to ice these?'

'Not yet. They're still hot.'

'What flavour will you do?'

'Passionfruit,' he said. 'Or lemon.'

'Maybe some passionfruit and some lemon?'

'Maybe.'

'Nice.'

I heard Jack's bedroom door open and close and then his footsteps on the stairs. He looked delicious with his hair all wet and combed back. But then, he always looked delicious, even when he scowled at me, as he did now. 'Damnit, Erica —'

I shoved the plate of cakes in his face. 'Have a cupcake.'

He took one, still frowning, said to Joe, 'You going to ice these?'

Joe made a hissing sound and turned to the coffee machine.

'Andrew drove me,' I said. 'I didn't give him a choice, so don't be mad with him.'

Jack sat on the stool next to me. He was still looking all grumpy and concerned but his tell-tale eyes softened a little. 'I don't want you running around everywhere.'

'I'm not running; I'm being driven by a tough guy with guns. You don't think he's the one who shot at me, do you?'

'No.'

'I asked him.'

Joe laughed. 'What did he say?'

'He said no.' Jack's eyes smiled. I continued, 'Do you think he's got a rocket launcher in the boot? He looks the type.'

'Maybe,' Jack's smile was now fully fledged.

'And besides. I need to give you my list of appliances.' I asked Joe for a pen and paper.

Joe handed me both, plus a cup of tea, and Jack a coffee.

I scribbled my list. 'Why do you want to buy appliances for me? Not that I don't appreciate it.'

He hesitated. 'Late birthday present.'

'You gave me one.'

'Next birthday present.'

'Okay, well, thank you. It's gonna cost a bucket.'

'I'm sure you'll make it up to me. Cook me a nice meal in your new oven.'

I slammed the pen down. 'Oh, no. You're not using blackmail to force me to cook. Forget it. I'll buy my own appliances.' But I picked the pen up and kept writing. 'I'll still expect a birthday present on the day, you know.'

He laughed, finally, and shuffled his stool closer, nudging my knee with his. A bolt of heat shot through my leg.

'Are you alright?' He hooked a curl behind my ear.

'I'm a bit hot.'

'Yes, you are, but apart from that, I mean.'

'I'm fine. Why wouldn't I be?'

'Someone shot at you this morning.'

'Oh, that.' I waved a hand. 'I'm used to it.'

Jack shook his head, looking all worried again. Joe's phone buzzed in the distance and he left the room. I should go to work, I thought. Instead, I hopped off the stool and stood between Jack's legs, put my arms around him. What time was it? Maybe I had time for a quick visit upstairs. He pulled me close and pressed his face in my neck, taking a deep breath.

'You smell nice.'

I wondered if Andrew would want to come up to the office, or wait in the car for me. Jack kissed my ear, my jaw, the corner of my mouth. There might be someone waiting to ambush me in the lift. He pressed his lips very softly onto mine. Rosalind and her vampire teeth.

'Jack.'

'Mmm?'

'Who do you think shot at us?' I pulled back. 'Really, the truth.'

'Can we brainstorm that later?'

All the blood had left my head, and that had little to do with being shot at. 'I need to lie down.' I staggered across the room to the sofa and flopped onto it, lying on my back.

'Great idea.' He followed and lay on top of me, and kissed my face, my neck, supporting his weight but I could still feel his body. It was a nice, hard body. *Really* nice. Especially when it was naked. But I shouldn't be thinking about naked Jack when there was so much to do, and when someone wanted to kill me. Or Emilio. Maybe I wasn't the target. Maybe I was being selfish, wanting all the murderers to focus on me.

I heard Joe walk into the room. And out again.

'Jack.'

He pushed up on his hands. 'You want to talk about the shooting.'

'Yes.'

'Fair enough.' We both sat up. 'Then I'm taking you upstairs.'

'I have to go to work.'

'No work today.'

'Really. I do. Emilio's been taking all my time.'

Well, that threw a bucket of ice on the situation. Jack went all stiff and moved a bit further along the sofa.

'Do you think Shane McGann will talk to us?' I said.

'Not us. Me.'

'I'm coming with you.'

'The idea of you coming with me to visit McGann in jail is the most ludicrous —'

I heard the front door open, and those annoying, light footsteps tapped their way across the foyer and into the living room.

'Hey, y'all.' What an annoying accent. *Hey y'all.* She always said that. Couldn't she think of something else?

'Hey,' said Jack.

She helped herself to a cake – didn't bother asking – which she cut into eighths, eating one at a time, delicately, unlike someone else, who tried to shove the whole thing in her gob.

'Hi!' I said as though I couldn't have been happier to see anyone. She didn't believe me. I could tell by the subtle eye roll. She seemed disappointed to see me sitting there.

Sharon ate three-eighths of the cake and didn't complain they weren't iced.

Jack stood. 'How'd you go?'

'Good.' She popped another tiny piece of cake in her mouth.

'Anything to report?'

Her eyes cut briefly to me. 'Sure. Later.'

'You can speak freely in front of Erica.'

I wanted to poke my tongue at her but being the mature, secure and confident gal that I was, I refrained. Although I did wish we'd still been lying on the couch together when she walked in, Jack on top of me.

Sharon checked her watch. 'Gotta run. I'll call you with the info.' She picked up another piece of cake – that made five-eighths – and left without eating the rest, which I thought was very rude, considering all the effort Joe had gone to. I heard the front door slam.

Hands on hips, staring after Shaz, Jack clicked his tongue, annoyed that she hadn't coughed up with whatever info. His romantic mood was now smashed to smithereens, thanks to Sharon barging in. Sharon Bloody Stone, who was probably cursing that the shooter missed me and who was probably wondering how to get me alone in the closet with a length of piano wire.

Oh.

CHAPTER 49

Before I left Jack's, standing at his front door, I told him I needed to go to the tennis.

'You don't *need* to go.' With hands on my hips, he pulled me close. 'Spend the evening with me. I'll chase you around my bedroom.'

'Really? You'll chase me?'

'Uh-huh.'

'All around the house?'

'If you want. I'll send Joe and Sharon to the tennis,' he said into my ear, closing in even further, arms around me. 'We'll be all alone. Just you and me and my bed.' He kissed me then, tongue probing gently.

I moaned, clutching him. The kiss got deeper. We side-stepped away from the wide open door and he kicked it shut. But wait! What was I doing? I couldn't *not* go to Emilio's match. What if he lost because I wasn't there? I pulled away, stepping back to get some distance so I could think straight. I shook my head to kick-start my brain.

'I have to go to the tennis. If Emilio loses the match because of me, I'll never forgive myself.'

Jack groaned and sat on the stairs, put his face in his hands. I sat next to him, but not too close.

'Did I tell you what happened at his first match?' I said.

'No, but I heard.'

'He says he can't play without me there watching. He thinks I'm his muse or something.'

'This is getting out of control.' He shook his head. 'This whole thing with you and Mendez.'

'It's fine, really. I'll manage it. But I need to go to his games.'

'Alright.' He sighed. 'I'll come and get you later, take you in. Joe will get Mendez.'

We stood and I held out my hand.

He looked at it. 'You want to shake my hand.'

'It's safer than kissing.'

He took my hand and hauled me in, kissed me passionately, sent me on my way with a smack on the bum.

Back in Andrew's car, I asked him to take me to work. As we neared my office, I said, 'Will you come in?'

'Of course.'

'Do you know Shane McGann?'

He gave me a quick look. 'Why? Is he in your office?'

'No. I think he's behind the shooting this morning.'

'How?'

I shrugged. 'He's got nasty friends. And good reason to want payback. You know about what he did to me in Sydney?'

'Yeah.'

'I reckon Sharon would know him.'

Andrew didn't respond, concentrating on parking the car.

'Do you know if Sharon knows him?'

'She would.' The look he then gave me said: Where are you going with this? 'McGann and Sharon were both under Jack in Iraq.'

'Can you rephrase that, please?'

He laughed. 'Sharon *reported* to Jack in Iraq.'

Andrew came with me to my desk, looked all around and under it, then found a comfy spot to read his crime novel. I stole occasional glances at him, wondering if, in fact, it was Andrew, not Sharon, with the contract on me, even though Jack says he trusts him like he trusts

Joe. He certainly had his chance on the deserted floor of my office. Mind you, if Andrew strangled me in my office and left me there, Jack would have a pretty good idea who'd done it. Unless he somehow made it look like a vampire attack – maybe with a staple remover – in which case, we'd all know who the prime suspect would be.

I searched all my drawers, went through files, inbox, outbox, trying to find evidence that Charlotte hadn't done all the work she'd said. I did find some, actually. A pile of my filing that she said she'd done was shoved into the bottom drawer of my filing cabinet. Exactly the sort of thing I'd do. I checked out the documents she'd created. Read the media release she'd written. I opened one I'd written earlier on the same subject. Yep. She'd pretty much plagiarised mine. Oh well. No harm done, I supposed, except that Rosalind was possibly thinking of replacing me with her new favourite person. But not if "all goes well with the tennis" and Rosalind gets transferred outta here. An evil cackle sounded in my head.

Before I left work, I called Emilio and told him the plans for the evening. He wanted me to come straight away, and for the first time since meeting Jack and being under what seemed like constant house arrest, I was pleased about needing a bodyguard. 'You and I both need protection now, Emilio. I'll see you in the café before your match.'

Andrew took me home in time for me to change for the tennis.

Jack picked me up and, on the way, I said, 'What are your plans for when we get there?'

'I'll deliver you to Mendez and stay with you until his match starts.'

Oh, shit. What if Emilio is feeling all sooky and wants to be all touchy and feely with hugs and the like? 'Er, you might not want to come into the players' café. It's pretty … noisy and … annoying. You know.'

'No, I don't know.'

'Um, it's full of … tennis players.'

'And?'

'And Emilio.'

'Who'll be all over you and you don't want me to see that.'

'Yeah.'

He drove a bit faster. 'I'll handle it.'

JACK and I both had All Access passes, so we were able to walk straight into the players' café. Mind you, I reckon Jack could just turn up anywhere and be allowed in. We got something to eat, and waited. I called Teresa from my mobile and told her we were there. She said that Joe was at the hotel, and he would bring her and Emilio, and that Emilio was feeling very happy. 'The shopping expedition and the shooting have made him feel so alive, *chica*. He is, how you say, buzzing with energy.'

I wondered again about Teresa. She seemed to sincerely care for Emilio, but then the sister in *The Bodyguard* had really seemed to care about whatsername. Did Teresa organise the shooting? But if she did, how did she get one of Jack's guns? Maybe she got Martin McGann to pay Sharon.

'Apparently, the assassination attempt has had a positive effect on Emilio's state of mind,' I told Jack.

'Interesting.'

'Maybe we could organise another heist before the finals.'

Jack chuckled.

'Let's plan something really big for the grand final,' I said.

'Careful what you wish for.'

We waited, seated next to each other but not too close. I looked around the room. Not many people, no-one near us to listen in on our convo.

I whispered, 'Are you still considering Teresa?'

'Regarding the train incident?'

'All of it. There's something I haven't told you yet.'

He looked at me.

'I saw Teresa and Martin McGann arrive at the Sofitel within ten minutes of each other.'

'What were you doing there?'

'Following her.'

He nodded, looked away, stared at the television for a long

moment. Finally, he shrugged. 'It doesn't necessarily mean anything. Could be a coincidence. Maybe they're having an affair.'

'I think she might be trying to get rid of Emilio.'

Jack gave me a long look. 'I don't know how either Martin or Teresa would acquire one of my weapons.'

'Maybe she's paying someone.' Should I go there? Okay, I will. 'What about Sharon?'

He stiffened, eyes on the television. 'What about her?'

'She has access to your weapons. And she knows Shane McGann, if you'd prefer to think along those lines.'

He held up a hand. 'No.'

'But —'

'No.' He looked at me. 'I've known Sharon a long time. We saw active duty together, for God's sake.' His voice was hard. He meant it. *Don't take this further, Erica.*

'I think she wants you.'

He leaned close. 'Even if that were true, and she was prepared to kill for it —' He gave me a stern look, one that demanded we drop the subject, pronto, '— if Sharon had made that shot, you wouldn't be sitting here now.'

End of subject. Hmph. I bowed my head, duly chastised, reminding myself to go practise at the shooting range some time. I wasn't such a bad shot myself. And that reminded me, I still hadn't moved my gun.

We sat in silence, watching the television. I let five minutes pass before I dared speak. In fact, I didn't speak, just leaned in and nudged him with my shoulder, testing the water. He looked at me and I gave him a smile. After a few seconds he returned it. There was lengthy eye contact – I gazed into his beautiful, smiling eyes, and then they weren't smiling. Uh-oh. He turned back to the television. I didn't say anything, not wanting to know if he was thinking angry thoughts about me and my accusation. But he surprised me when he said, 'Does he … do you let him …'

'Who?'

'You know who.'

'Emilio?'

'Do you let him kiss you?'

'No, of course not.' Sort of.

'Does he try?'

'Yes.'

'How do you get around it?'

'I managed to side-step you earlier.' I gave him another nudge.

'That's true. You're good at it.' He frowned. 'Mendez ... he must want to sleep with you.' Jack's voice had tightened, and he was now scowling, searching my face, seeking the truth or reassurance, I wasn't sure. Jack clearly doesn't like to share. 'He's completely in love with you.' Unlike someone else, who I'd like to be in love with me.

'He *thinks* he is. Like every other girl he's with. But anyway, he believes if he sleeps with me, it'll upset his game. It's not a problem.'

'So, he's planning to wait until after the tournament.'

'That's right.'

'By which time you'll —'

'Be in your bed.'

He sat back, shook his head. 'It's a wonder I'm not a nervous wreck. Since the day I met you, I don't think I've had a good night's sleep, except when you're with me.'

'And when I'm with you, neither of us gets much sleep.'

He smiled. 'True.'

Emilio, Teresa and Joe arrived and joined our table. As predicted, Emilio wanted to hug me, but it was quick, not too intimate, because he was feeling so buoyant. He also wanted to hug Jack, and somehow, I think that made Jack happy.

Emilio sat beside Jack and put a brotherly hand on his shoulder. 'You know, *Yack*, I thought that photograph of you and my Emilita ...' He laughed. 'Well, you can imagine what I thought.'

Jack nodded. 'Yes, I can imagine.'

'But you have a magnificent lover in Sharon Stone.'

Jack smiled and looked at me. 'Yes, magnificent.'

Joe groaned, Lurch style.

My mouth pursed, mother style.

· · ·

JACK DELIVERED me to centre court. We stood at the top of the steps, looking down at the growing crowd.

'What are you doing now? Looking for baddies?' I glanced around. Couldn't see any.

'No, I need to leave. Joe will take you home.'

'Where are you going?'

He could have made something up and I would've believed him, but it was his hesitation and the way he looked away before saying, 'Need to pay someone a visit,' that made me press further. Jack occasionally "pays someone a visit", which could sometimes mean that that someone, as a result of Jack's visit, will change their behaviour or leave town, never to return.

'Who? Where are you going?'

'Never mind.' He lifted his hand to touch me, thought better of it.

'Tell me. You're being all funny.'

'I'm hilarious.' He smiled.

'You know what I mean. Where are you going?'

He took a breath. 'I've lined up a visit with McGann.'

'But I want to come.'

He huffed a laugh, shook his head. 'Just stay here, and I'll let you know how I go.'

We didn't speak for a minute, but then I was worried about being photographed. I took a small step back. 'Okay. You'll call me?'

'I will.'

'See ya.'

'Bye.'

He watched me walk down the steps to my seat. I kept looking over my shoulder, not wanting to lose sight of him. If I could arrange it, I'd walk around everywhere with Jack Jones in my sight, just for the pleasure of looking at him and knowing he was near. John the coach hadn't arrived yet – still with Emilio backstage – but someone else I knew was happily waiting for the match to start, sitting with the friends of Emilio Mendez. It was me. Rather, someone who looked like me, wearing a large sunhat, even though evening was approaching.

'Charlotte?'

'Hi.'

'What are you doing? Is that a wig?'

'Yes. Your mother told me where she got yours.'

I looked around, checked that I hadn't fallen down a rabbit hole. 'You don't have to come to the tennis out of hours, you know.'

'I can help you.'

'In what way?'

'You can take a break and Emilio will think I'm you.'

I laughed, assuming she was joking. But those dark sunglasses gazed steadily at me. 'I don't think so.'

'You can go and have fun somewhere.'

'It's fine, Charlotte. I'm happy to stay and watch Emilio.'

'But —'

'I'm not leaving just because you want me to, okay?'

Charlotte sat there with a stony expression. She stood suddenly, pushed past me and left.

As I checked the crowd, a few people looked quickly away. 'That was weird,' I muttered to whoever was interested. No-one seemed interested.

Jack sent me a text while I was watching Emilio's match. I'd been keeping a close eye on my phone – trying not to let Emilio notice that my eyes weren't glued to his every move – but the match was so thrilling I didn't check my phone for almost half an hour. It went to five sets, and I was busting for the toilet. And I was tired. It was nearly 11pm.

Visit waste of time, said Jack's text.

What happened?

Wouldn't talk.

Bugger.

Andrew will take you home.

EMILIO WON THE MATCH, which meant both he and Vavilov were through to the fourth round. I called Jack.

'Did you ask McGann if his mates are stalking me?'

'No, I didn't mention you.'

'Why not?'

'If it's not him, I don't want to put ideas in his head.'

'So, how will we know?'

'I'm working on it.'

'What does that mean?'

'Erica, please.'

'What are you doing now?'

'Going to bed.'

'I thought you might want me to come over for a game of chasey.'

'I'm buggered.'

'You could have at least thought about it for a second or two.'

I could hear his smile. 'Soon. I promise.'

'Okay. Well, goodnight.'

CHAPTER 50

I decided to visit Shane McGann.

When I got home from the tennis, sneaking in so I wouldn't wake Mum, I sat in my room and studied the Northern Star Prison website. Quite apart from all the rules and regulations and visitor procedures, it told me I needed to be on the prisoner's approved list. So first thing in the morning, I rang them. It was Sunday, but that didn't seem to matter. They said it could take some time to get the approval or maybe never – it was up to the prisoner. They needed my full name, date of birth and address before seeking McGann's approval. Every cell in my brain was telling me not to give Shane McGann any information about me, but I reminded myself that it didn't really matter if he knew when I was born (did it?), and he already knew my address, so I probably needed to not panic if I really wanted to see him (did I?). I gave them my details, and they emailed me within the hour to say he'd approved my visit. I rang and asked them if I could have a non-contact visit that afternoon. They said it was up to him if he wanted to see me.

He wanted to see me.

. . .

I HAD no way of getting to the prison unless Andrew took me, and I didn't think there was a bribe or threat invented I could use to get him to do that. The prison was over an hour from Melbourne, so I couldn't sneak off and take the train.

Lucy answered on the first ring. 'Hey, hon.'

'Are you working?'

'Nah. Got the whole day off. Steve's taking me to see a movie.'

'Can you take me to visit Shane McGann in jail? I haven't got a car.'

'Can't you borrow your dad's? Hold on – why are you visiting that bastard?'

'Kind of a long story.'

'If I take you can I come in?'

'You need advanced permission. But will you take me? Go to the movies tonight instead?'

I called Emilio and told him I had "extremely important business".

'What is the business?'

'I'm, um, looking for your amulet.'

'*Si?* I hope you can find it, Emily.'

I told Mum and Dad I was going to see a movie in Brighton with Lucy, and that she was picking me up, and that I had to meet her in the street behind us because she had bad childhood memories coming to our street. Mum didn't seem to believe me, nor did she seem to care, rolling her eyes and resuming interest in her magazine.

To avoid Andrew, I hurdled the fence into Mrs Booth's, having peered at the house for ten minutes first to make sure no-one was watching. I snuck up the side and onto the street. Lucy was there in her car. We headed for the Monash Freeway, which would take us onto the Bolte Bridge and ultimately the Western Ring Road.

'I'll give you petrol money,' I said.

'You'll notice I'm not asking why you were sneaking around Mrs Booth's house, but I assume it has something to do with the missing thing.'

'Not this time. I just can't go out the front of Mum's because the bodyguard'll see me and tell Jack.'

'Okaaaay.'

'Do you want to know why I've got a bodyguard?'

'No.'

'Good. Because you wouldn't like the answer.'

'Alright. So, tell – why are we visiting Shane … God, I feel sick just saying his name.'

'I know.' And even though I wasn't going to mention the shooting at The Good Guys, I said that I thought McGann was somehow involved in the shooting at The Good Guys.

'Hold on. That was *you* being shot at yesterday? It was all over the news! Someone shot at Emilio Mendez.'

'I think someone actually shot at me.'

Lucy slammed her palm on the steering wheel. 'See? Life in danger. Status quo in Erica Jewell's life since Jack bloody Jones came along.'

'I know, Luce.' I patted her knee. 'I know.'

THE PRISON PEOPLE had told me to be prepared to enter with nothing but the clothes I was wearing (which should not be provocative or advertise my love of outlawed bikie gangs), and prepared also to be searched and sniffed all over by a dog. Bad luck if I'd wanted to bake a cake with a file in it. Or slip him a shovel. Or pass some dynamite through the bars. They also reminded me they couldn't make Shane McGann see me if he didn't want to. (Unlike Jack's visit, which he was probably forced to entertain.)

We arrived an hour earlier than the appointed time, and I waited with Lucy for half an hour under one of the few trees in the visitor car park. When I was ready to go, I asked Luce if she'd be alright. She reached into the back seat for her novel and a pair of binoculars.

'What are the binocs for?'

'So I can check out the prison guards. Love a man in uniform.'

In the prison, I handed over my ID for the 100-point check against the name they had on their approved visitors list. I stuck my stuff in a locker, asking if I could take some tissues. No, they said. I might need to blow my nose, I told them. They told me to take a seat. After a short while, I was shown the way along a corridor, was buzzed through a solid door by someone who gave me a suspicious look, then sent through an X-ray machine thingy like they have at the airport and I hoped they couldn't see through my clothes. A gloved woman who clearly hated me told me to bend forward, which I did, and she ran her fingers through my hair, catching knots. 'Ow!' Next I was told to line up with other visitors – unsavoury-looking children with their tattooed mothers – which I did, and a dog stuck its nose in my crotch. I wasn't allowed to move or complain, and the guards watched the dog carefully to see how it reacted to what it found there. Happily, it moved on, seemingly uninterested.

I wondered what Jack had had to go through to visit McGann. The police probably delivered McGann to a special place that suited Jack's purposes. He wouldn't have had to put up with all this business, being treated like a criminal, surely. Even though officially he was a criminal, but they didn't know that. Actually, they probably did.

I was given a number, a door opened and, as a group, we walked single file past a security guard into … an open area. An open area with tables and chairs. What? I spun, walked against the crowd back to the security guard, who scowled, stood taller and moved toward me, threatened, it seemed, by my unruly behaviour. I held up my number.

'I'm supposed to be in the non-contact area.' The desperation made my voice squeak.

She took my number. 'Follow me.' We walked across the open area to table number 13. 'Sit here.'

'But I don't want to be in the same room as him.'

She walked away. A male voice came over the loudspeaker. 'Table 13, sit.'

I sat. Sweat poured from my armpits. I tried to make myself feel better by imagining Jack's horror if he could see me now. Normally, I'd find it funny – the thought of the look on his face. It wasn't funny.

Prisoners walked into the room, looked around for their visitors. McGann was at the back – tall, blond, not bad-looking, apart from his beady eyes and the fact that he was a scumbag. Last time I saw him was in the court room. Before that, it was when he'd stood over me with a gun in one hand while the other pulled the belt from his jeans. McGann smirked when he saw me. I glanced at the security guards who were armed and hovering, but not looking like they expected a rape. Or murder.

McGann stood before me. I stared at his knees.

'You're in my seat.'

'What?' I looked up.

'The blue one. It's mine.'

I stood. Yes, one blue seat, three white. I moved to the opposite side of the table, as far from him as I could get and still be where I was meant to be. I stared at my lap.

'I'll talk to you if you look at me.'

I looked up. And down again. My hands gripped each other to stop the shaking. Damn you, traitorous hands!

McGann leaned in. I could sense it rather than see it, because my vision was now blurred.

'What do you want?'

'To ask ...' My voice quavered and I cleared my throat. 'To ask if you have any further plans for me.'

He laughed softly. 'The mind boggles. Oh, yes, the plans.' In my peripheral vision, I saw him rub his hands over his face. 'I don't think your new boyfriend would like it, though, do you?'

Don't say anything to encourage him. Just stick with the facts. I looked at him. 'Someone tried to kill me.'

'You?' He smiled. 'Or Mendez?'

'You're trying to kill Emilio?' My shaking stopped. I was now far more interested in the conversation than the fear for my life and horrible memories of being near him. Shane McGann was having fun. I checked the security guards. There was one close, and they all looked pretty alert.

'You think I organised the shooting yesterday? And the train wreck?' He was leaning right in, elbows on the table. 'What about the heist at your lunch – you think that was me?'

I tilted back as far as I could on the cold, fixed chair. I supposed if he knew about Emilio and me, he would know about those things, too. I imagined he had a television.

'And someone tried to run me over.'

There it was. Genuine surprise. Just a flash of it.

'Run you over?' He laughed out loud. 'Yeah, sure, why not?'

I stood.

'Don't leave.'

I walked away.

He called after me, 'Come again, *Emilita*.'

I kept walking, didn't look back. I pushed the buzzer and waited to be released from prison. And made a deal with myself that I would never come here again, and I would never again lay eyes on Shane McGann, as long as I lived. I didn't believe McGann was responsible for the threats against Emilio's and/or my life, but he knew something. He knew that Emilio sometimes called me Emilita, which means someone told him that. Who? Who would have been in touch with Shane McGann who knew that? The same person who had access to Jack's guns? His good friend, Sharon? Or his father, who was possibly bonking Teresa? I didn't know, but was pretty sure I'd be finding out soon enough.

CHAPTER 51

I sat in Lucy's car, put my head back and shut my eyes.

'Are you alright?' she said.

I nodded, started to cry.

'Aw, sweetie.' She hugged me.

I pushed her back. 'I'm fine. It's okay.'

'What happened?'

'Let's get away from here and I'll tell you.' I pointed at the exit, which I couldn't wait to drive through. Lucy started her car and drove. We headed for the highway. 'I think it's Sharon Stone who's trying to kill me.'

'Who?'

'She's Jack's new recruit. Staying at his house.' But what about the Russians? Did she have Russian contacts? I shook my head. Couldn't think about that now.

'And I think Jack's having an affair.'

'He is. With you.'

'No. With her.'

'Well, just have an affair with Emilio to get back at him.'

'No!'

'Emilio's gorgeous.'

'Yes, but he's not …' What? He's not Jack?

'What's she like?' said Lucy.

'Gorgeous. Accomplished.'

'Shit.'

'Yeah.'

I stared out the window and Lucy was silent, giving me time to do whatever she thought I needed to do in my head. She turned on the radio. The Melbourne skyline approached. She looked at me. 'What next?'

I shrugged. 'Jack won't believe it's Sharon. I've already made the accusation. He got really mad.'

'He likes her.'

'Yeah. They went to war together.'

'Really?'

'She was a fighter pilot.' My voice broke on the last word. I didn't know what to do.

Lucy pulled over so she could look me right in the eye without risking our lives. 'Hon, you are totally in love with Jack.'

'I am not.' I am so.

'You are so.'

'It's just – we're friends. With benefits.'

'I think he loves you, too.'

'Pfft. As if.' I crossed my arms and glared out the window. 'He's not capable of that much emotion, Luce.'

Lucy kept driving. And my mobile rang. It was Jack. Before I answered I needed to compose myself. Where would I say I was? Who with?

'Turn off the radio. And shut all the windows. It's Jack, and I'm supposed to be at home with a bodyguard.'

I answered. 'Hey.'

There was silence at the other end.

'Hello?' I said.

Finally, Jack spoke, his voice sounding so tight and tired. 'I'm struggling to know what to say.' Uh-oh. 'I can't believe you did what you just did.'

'How did you know?'

'What were you thinking? A *contact* visit, for fuck's sake!'

'It wasn't supposed to be a contact visit.'

'I ...'

'Yes?'

'I don't know, but Andrew's done his dash. He let you slip away.'

'Don't you dare blame Andrew!'

'What else can I do? You need protection by someone who can give it. Do you even understand the concept?'

'Jack, I went over the back fence. Andrew probably thinks I'm sitting in my bedroom reading.'

'He doesn't, because I told him. He's waiting to hear back from me about a future with my team.'

'Please don't blame or punish Andrew for this.'

More silence. I waited. Finally, he said, 'You're with Lucy.' It wasn't a question.

'How did you know?'

'You're heading home now?'

'Yes.'

'Alright. Andrew's there.'

'I like Andrew. He's nice.'

'He's a good guy.'

'So,' said Lucy after we hung up, 'I need to take you straight home.'

'First, Jack's. I want to see what's going on in there. I mean, there are so many times he could suggest we catch up – like tonight – but he doesn't and he's always with Sharon when I suggest it.'

'You want to spy on him?'

'Yeah, I guess.'

'What about Andrew?'

'We'll just be a few minutes. It's fine.' I checked my watch. 'What time's your movie?'

'Later. It's okay.'

'Thanks, Luce.' I gave her hand a squeeze.

. . .

WE PARKED RIGHT in front of Jack's and I hoped, if he looked out the window, he wouldn't remember what kind of car Lucy drove. Her windows were tinted so we had a bit of cover, and there were lots of bushes and trees in front of Jack's house, so we weren't too obvious. We had to park in just the right spot so we could see through the bushes and into the front windows of the house. It was now just after 5pm, so Joe would probably be thinking about getting dinner organised.

'We should be doing this in the dark,' said Luce.

'*Everyone* does it in the dark. We're being original.' I took the binoculars off her lap.

Lucy checked her Facebook page.

I said, 'You're supposed to be spying.'

'Only one set of binocs, hon. Knock yourself out. Hey! Check out the photo Steve posted.'

I trained the binoculars on the gym window. Empty. I swept across the front of the house, trying to find a gap in the bushes, trees and blurry things, and just as Lucy said, 'Oops,' I realised the blurry thing was a face.

I dropped the binoculars like they'd burned me. The heat started at my ears and worked its way forward. I reluctantly slid the window down.

'Wait one minute,' said Joe. 'I'll follow you home.' He looked super worried. And annoyed.

But one minute was too long because Jack was now standing there. His face replaced Joe's at the window. He glowered at me. 'This is not home.'

'It's your home. I thought that's what you meant.' Good one. Jack stared at me, seeking a proper response, knowing I was bullshitting but not knowing how to combat it. I jumped on the opportunity to say, 'You're being rude to Lucy.'

Jack looked past me. 'My apologies, Lucy. It's not personal.'

'No worries, Jack,' she said.

He opened my door. 'Come inside, tell me about it.'

I didn't want to go in. I didn't want Jack to tell me off in front of Sharon Stone. 'Lucy has to get going.'

'Then Lucy can go and Andrew will come get you.'

Why couldn't Jack take me home? Because he didn't want to be away from Sharon for too long? I turned to Luce, but she was already out of the car and marching up the path to Jack's front door.

I called after her, 'What about your movie?'

'There's another session later.' She disappeared inside.

SHARON STONE WAS COOKING. By the time I arrived in the kitchen, Lucy had introduced herself. Joe was wisely absent. Jack asked what we wanted to drink.

'Whiskey,' I said.

He nodded. I only drank whiskey when I was stressed, and he knew it.

Lucy and Sharon both said, 'Beer.' And smiled at each other.

'So,' I said to Sharon, 'Jack's making you cook.'

'Oh, no, I lerrrrve cookin'. Nothin' better than good ol' Cajun stew. Ain't that right, Black Jack?'

'You do good Cajun, Sexy,' said Black Jack and gave me a look that said: I know you hate me calling her Sexy but this is part of your punishment.

I pretended not to notice or care.

Lucy said, 'Did you just call her Sexy?'

Sharon said, 'It's a military call sign. Mine was Sexy Texan.'

'Oh, right,' said Luce. 'Good call sign.'

'I always liked it.'

Of course you'd like it if you're vain. I tried not to sound bitchy when I said, 'Strange call sign to give yourself.' I sounded bitchy.

'Your buddies give you your call sign. You don't choose your own.'

So now I was glaring at Lucy, because I knew she'd want to know who'd named her Sexy Texan, and I didn't want to know if it was Jack. She got the message.

Instead, Lucy said to me, 'I wonder what yours would be?'

'Red Ruby or somethin' like that,' said Sharon as she deftly stirred the pot on the stove. 'Given your name an' all.'

Red Ruby was an ugly name, and she knew it.

Jack jumped in before I could take the very large kitchen knife off the bench and put it through Sharon's heart. 'Come with me.' He handed me a glass of whiskey and indicated the formal living area at the front of the house. 'Let's talk.'

I said to Luce, 'Get going if you need to.'

'That's okay.' She glanced at Sharon. 'I've got time to stick around a bit longer.'

I followed Jack and he sat on one of two luxurious sofas, facing each other and set against the magnificent backdrop of gorgeous old fireplace under an ornate mantle and giant antique mirror. Jack patted the seat next to him.

'I'll sit here.' I indicated the sofa opposite.

'Don't make me come over there.'

I sighed, checking my rear end for dirt before I sat next to him on the gold fabric. But I sat right at the end, as far from him as I could.

'Jesus, Erica, I'm not going to hurt you.' He raised his hands and let them flop onto his knees, raising his voice, slightly. 'Why do you always think I could do that?' He wiped a hand over his face. 'Don't answer that. Tell me what happened with McGann.'

'He knows something.'

That surprised Jack. 'He talked to you?'

'Oh, yeah.'

'What did he say to make you think he knows something?'

'Well, he knew about the train thing and the shooting yesterday.'

'He has a television.'

'And he referred to Emilio as my new boyfriend.'

'Again, he has a television.' He added, unnecessarily, 'You and your boyfriend aren't very discreet.'

I opened my mouth and snapped it shut. Now wasn't the time for bitchy retorts.

'He also knows that Emilio calls me Emilita.'

That silenced Jack, and he stared at me as he processed the information.

I said, as a joke, 'You didn't happen to mention that to him, did you?'

He ignored that. 'Has Mendez used that name in public? Could the media have heard it?'

I shook my head. 'I really don't think so. Only in private. You would have heard him say that.'

Jack nodded. 'I think so. Mostly, I ignore the shit he says.'

'So, who do we know who might want to get rid of me and who knows Shane McGann and has access to your guns?' I gave him a smug look.

'And who has Russian contacts.' He looked right into my eyes. 'Don't go there.'

I sat back on the sofa, crossed my arms. 'Were you surprised he agreed to see me?'

'Of course not.'

'Why?'

'Why do you think?'

Because he thinks he can get at Jack through me. Maybe I should be flattered.

WHEN WE LEFT JACK'S, Andrew was leaning on his car, arms crossed and wearing a poker face.

'Sorry, Andrew.'

He nodded and held the door for me.

'Do you mind if Lucy drives me home? I need to talk to her about something.'

'I'll follow.'

Back in Lucy's car – with Andrew in his car behind us – I turned on Lucy, ready to yell at her for being so friendly to Sharon Stone. But before I could speak, she said, 'She *so* wants him.'

'What?'

'Just like you said, she wants him.'

'How can you tell?'

'Hon, you know as well as I do what men want.'

I blinked at her, confused.

She continued, 'Men want to be loved and fed. That's all. Love them and feed them. God, did your mother teach you anything?'

'No.'

'Well, I don't think there's anything going on, but let me tell you, all Jack has to do is open his bedroom door and Shaz'll dish out all the lovin' as he wants.'

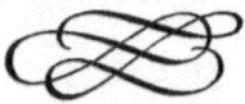

Steve called me at seven on Monday morning to say he needed to see me, briefly, and asked if I could call in at my house on the way to work. My night-shift bodyguard changed with Andrew on the way there. When I sat next to Andrew in his car, he said a quiet, 'Good morning,' and that was all.

'I'm really sorry, Andrew.'

He didn't respond.

'I didn't mean for you to get in trouble. It's the last thing I wanted. I hope you know that.'

He nodded, slightly, and we carried on. We arrived at my house just after eight and I asked Andrew to wait in his car so Steve wouldn't worry about why I needed a bodyguard. I couldn't say Andrew was my "driver" because then Steve would think I was a wanker.

Steve and some other blokes were working on and among the criss-cross of beams that now sat on the stumps. I waved from the back gate, and Steve introduced me to Ian the electrician, who asked where I wanted power points (how the hell would I know – one for the hairdryer?) and Phil the plumber, who told me loudly that I had a serious problem caused by a "surfboard" someone had stuck down the "shitter" and which was now tangled in tree roots and with that and all the "brown growlers" and "white mice" the whole thing had caused a "shitload of mess". He laughed raucously. 'Shitload! Get it? Was probably okay for a while,' he shouted, 'till someone took a dump the size of a footy and that was like the icing on the cake, ya know?' He gave me a nudge with his elbow, almost knocking me over. 'Ya'll never have chocolate icing on ya cake again, will ya.'

'How could a surfboard fit down there?'

'Ya know. Pussy hammock.'

My face remained blank.

'Ya know. Sanitary pad.'

'Why don't you just say sanitary pad?'

'Gotta get kitten on the job.'

'Kitten?'

'Yeah.' He pointed to a machine on the ground that looked like it had metal jaws and sharp teeth. 'Gonna cost a bit extra.'

Thankfully, Steve stepped in and explained what extra work Phil needed to do to fix the problem. Steve didn't say "pussy hammock". I said I didn't care what it cost just as long as no-one ever mentioned pussy hammocks again. Steve headed for the house, striding across the joists.

I followed, tottering in my heels. 'I can get the appliance info to you —'

'Got it.'

'What?'

'Got it this morning. Jack emailed me the specs and I've sent them to Stan.'

'What do you mean?'

'I assume Jack's buying your appliances?' He said it, slowly, like I might have forgotten how to speak English.

'Well, yes —'

Steve jumped to the ground and turned, holding out his hand to help me. 'He sent the info this morning.'

'Already?'

'You should be nice to Jack. The induction cooktop would've cost six grand.'

'Six thousand! Just for the cooktop?'

'Yep.'

Bloody hell. I supposed I'd have to cook him a meal or two. 'He's just chesting up to Emilio.'

I asked Ian the electrician about ceiling fans.

'You don't want ceiling fans.' He walked away, back across the joists, and stood at a spot where power points would presumably go.

'Do I have to come over there?' The joists weren't easy to navigate. I pointed instead. 'That's where the telly will go.'

'You don't want the TV there. You want it here so you can watch while you're cooking for the man.'

Oh, how nice to be allowed to watch television while cooking for a man. But perhaps I should be banished to an underground room or somewhere with the ironing so I don't disturb him. I went back to Steve, found him in the spare bedroom. He put the kettle on.

'Cuppa?'

'Nah.' I checked my watch. 'I'll sort the power points, then I gotta go.'

'You got shot at on Saturday.' Steve was busy adding a tea bag and sugar to his mug.

'Yeah.' I watched him jiggle the bag. 'You seem so worried.'

He looked at me, not with his usual smiley face, but with concern and ... was that annoyance? 'Not much point trying to get you to be safe. You ignore anyone who suggests it.'

That stung. But it was probably fair enough. I didn't know what to do but give him a shrug.

'What's going on with Emilio?' he said.

I went to explain, but it was all too hard. And then, thinking about Emilio and appliances, good guys like Steve and Jack – who deserved delicious meals cooked for them and served in front of the telly – and the shooting on Saturday morning at The Good Guys, reminded me that I still hadn't moved my gun.

'I need to get something from my room.' I headed through the dusty piles of crap in the passageway.

I rifled through the dirty laundry in the hamper, thinking I really needed to take it to Mum's and wash it. I felt around for my gun in the purple sock, seeking its hardness, but could feel nothing but soft things. I peered into the hamper and rifled some more. Nothing. I upended the hamper on my bed. Purple socks – two of them. No gun. Had I moved it and not remembered because I'd been so stressed? Probably. I found the secret drawer key and lay on my back under the bed and unlocked the drawer, which was empty – its usual state of affairs. But where was the gun? Had I taken it to Mum's and not remembered? If I'd taken it to Mum's, where would I have put it? In her laundry hamper? I shuddered at the thought of it and stood, scratching my head.

Steve knocked at the door. 'Ian still needs the power point info. Can you come?'

I opened the door. 'Have you been in here?'

'No. Why?'

'Has anyone been in here?'

'Not a chance. The guys don't need to come to this part of the house.'

'But someone *might* have come in here when you weren't looking.'

Steve frowned. 'I know these guys. They wouldn't. What's wrong?'

I sat on the bed. 'Jesus.'

'What's wrong, buddy?'

'I keep a gun in here.'

'*What?*'

'And it's gone.'

ANDREW DROVE ME TO WORK, or rather, we sat in unmoving traffic for half an hour and I tried to think of a simple, harmless answer to the missing gun problem. Where had it gone? The answer that I avoided was, of course, the most obvious one. Someone had come into my house, gone to my laundry hamper, and taken my gun. I thought again about the footprints I'd seen.

I wasn't sure what to do about Sharon Stone. Would she really feel so threatened by me to want me dead? I mean, she's probably killed people before. Not good ones, like me, but bad, enemy-type people. Maybe good ones, too. I suppose once you've killed a couple of people, you get a taste for it and even become a bit blasé about it. I shot a man once. I didn't kill him, but he didn't seem very happy about it.

Yesterday, I'd called Joe and asked, 'What sort of car has Sharon got?'

'BMW. Why?'

'Black one?'

'White and I know what you're thinking. Stop it.'

'Geez, I was just wondering what kind of car a girl like her would drive.' (A wanky car, that's what kind.)

And now, with my own gun missing, and knowing that Sharon would know where I lived and had a car to get there and, I supposed, could easily break into a house, I was more sure than ever it was her.

We pulled up at the Swan Street/Punt Road intersection.

I glanced at Andrew, sussing his mood. 'Sorry again about yesterday.'

'Makes my life hard.' But he was almost smiling. 'Actually, I was impressed. Didn't think you were that sneaky.'

'It's Lucy's bad influence.'

He nodded, smiling.

'Did Jack tell you the details of the shooting on Saturday?'

'You mean, like, that one of Jack's bullets was used?'

'Yeah. There's something else but I don't know how much I'm allowed to tell you.'

'Spill it. Jack won't care.'

'My gun's missing from my house.'

He whistled long and low but didn't look at me. He shook his head slowly, said nothing.

'I need to tell Jack,' I said.

'I don't envy you.'

I dialled Jack's number, hung up, shut my eyes and turned my face to the ceiling of the car, asking it privately if it could guide me through this mess. Then I dialled again.

He answered. 'Hey.'

'Hi. Where are you?'

'Home. Where are you?'

'On my way to work,' I said. 'You're having a late start.'

'Just back from a run.'

I took a huge breath because I didn't want to tell him what I knew I had to tell him. It would be completely irresponsible of me *not* to tell him my gun was missing, even though not telling him was my preference.

'Are you with Andrew?' he said.

'Yeah. He's driving me.'

'Good.'

'Are you sitting or standing?'

'Sitting in front of poached eggs,' he said. Hint, hint. Hurry up, Erica.

'Maybe I should call you later.'

'No, go ahead.'

I could hear him take a mouthful.

'Something's happened.' I hesitated before adding, 'Something bad.'

Slight pause. 'What?'

'You remember I left my gun at my house?' Silence. Everything was silent. Andrew held his breath. There was even a weird pause in the traffic noise between light changes, like the whole of Melbourne was holding its breath, waiting for me to continue. 'And I told you it was in the secret drawer?'

'Go on.'

'It was never in the drawer. It was at the bottom of my laundry hamper.'

Long pause. 'And?'

'It's gone.'

'Oh, Jesus fucking Christ, Erica!'

He was up now. I heard the loud scrape of his chair as he pushed back from the table. I cringed, picturing him pacing the room, looking for a wall to punch. Next thing I heard was a loud crash – loud enough to cause me to jump – and the line went dead.

Andrew looked at me with sympathy. And like he wouldn't want to be me, not for all the guns in America.

CHAPTER 53

So there was now not only a murderer who owned a bullet with my name on it, but Jack Jones also wanted to kill me. I'd have to avoid him for a while. There wasn't much I could do about it – the missing gun – and he was so scary when he was angry. So when I got a call at my desk to say that Mr Jones was downstairs and wanted to see me, urgently, of course I hesitated.

As the lift doors opened, I saw him across the lobby, his back to me, arms crossed as he gazed through the window at whatever. I wondered what he was thinking. He must have heard me sneaking up on him because he turned, and I had a pretty good idea what he was thinking.

'Let's go for a drive.' He headed for the exit.

'No way!'

He stared at me, incredulous.

'I'm scared of you when you're angry.'

He took a breath, glanced heavenward, looked around. 'We'll walk.'

So we left my office building and he strode toward the river. I had to trot to keep up. When he reached the river, he stuck his hands in his pockets and continued at a stroll, away from the bulk of the crowds. The stroll was for appearance's sake rather than mine, so we wouldn't attract unwanted attention; Jack's standard modus operandi, even though he always attracts attention because he's so hot. And I always attract attention because I do stupid things.

I fell in step beside him, looking around, hoping no-one would recognise me as the evil lost-lucky-charm lady. I shaded my face from the sun, but really, it was a weak attempt at disguise.

Jack said, looking at the ground, 'I can't tell you how offended I am that you think I could hurt you.'

What to say? I'd never really been sure the job didn't come first. That I wasn't expendable if it mattered enough. Or if I messed up enough to create a big problem for the Team. 'You're a violent man, Jack.' He looked at me and I shrugged. 'The Team comes first.'

'Not always,' he said, quickly.

His mood had faltered. I said nothing more.

'Tell me what you know,' he said, softly, recovering.

I mentioned again the footprints in my house.

'Anything else?'

'Yes.' I hesitated. 'There was someone outside my bedroom window. The night of the storm.'

Jack stopped walking. 'What did you see?'

'A human shape through the blind. By the time I checked, they'd gone. I reckon it was a homeless person or something. Someone looking for shelter.'

'Why didn't you tell me?'

Again, I shrugged. I hadn't wanted to be forced out of my home before absolutely necessary. That seemed so stupid now. 'I nearly got run over last week.'

'Where? What happened?'

I told him, without mentioning the fact that it was him being in WA with Sharon Stone that had distracted me. 'But it might have been an accident. I wasn't looking where I was going.'

He turned and kept walking, shaking his head. 'When did you last see it?'

I walked beside him. 'The gun? I don't really remember. I hadn't checked it for months.'

'So it could have been missing for months.'

'I … I suppose.'

'What about Steve?'

'I asked him. He said no-one's been in my room and I believe him.'

Jack stopped again. 'This is disastrous, but I don't blame you. You didn't ask for any of this.' He looked at his feet. 'This is my fault. I should —'

'Oh, no, you don't.' I stood in front of him and waved a finger in his face. But I really wanted to grip his shoulders and shake him. We'd been here before, last year, when Jack tried to end our friendship for the sake of my safety. 'Don't you go giving me that "you'd be better off without me in your life" crap!'

'I wasn't.'

I sniffed. 'You weren't?'

'I was just going to say I shouldn't have forced you to keep a weapon in your house. I did it to make myself feel better, thinking you'd be safer. That's all.'

'Oh.'

'I'm tempted to ask why it was in your laundry hamper, but I know better.'

'I was scared to touch it.' And then, as if it might make it seem somehow more secure, 'It was in a sock.'

He went to say something, drew in a deep breath and blew it out. 'I'll walk you back to work.'

'What will happen now?'

'I'll report it to the police. There could be some kid running around Melbourne with a handgun.' He shuddered, slightly. 'I'll tell Bill. He might be able to keep it quiet for the time being.'

'You'll be in trouble?'

He hesitated before saying, 'Yes.'

'I'm sorry, Jack. You trusted me and I let you down.'

He gave my elbow a quick squeeze.

<h1 style="text-align:center">CHAPTER 54</h1>

When I got back to work, Emilio had left several messages on my office and mobile phones. Charlotte told me he called Rosalind.

'What? Why?'

'He couldn't find you. He complained that he hasn't seen you since Saturday.'

'Oh, for God's sake.'

Rosalind called me in. 'Where were you? Everyone's looking for you.'

'Actually, Rosalind —'

'Sit down, Erica.'

I hesitated then sat.

'The tennis player has complained. He was about to call John and I asked him not to, which I hope you appreciate.'

'Of course, thank —'

'Sounds to me like you're slacking off. Not doing your job.'

My mouth fell open.

'Running here, running there, disappearing from your desk,' she snapped. 'You're supposed to be at the tennis, helping the tennis player. I've been very patient with you, given you guidance, and this is the thanks I get.'

The thanks *you* get? 'I've been working so hard!'

'Working hard? Watching tennis? Out to dinner every night?'

'I've been with Emilio and it's not like I —'

She slapped her pen down and sat back in her chair, looked at me squarely. This was serious shit. Rosalind rarely devoted this much oxygen to me.

'Things need to improve. It's imperative for Dega that the tennis goes well. Having the tennis player call here because you're not doing your job is not my idea of *going well*.' She leaned in. 'Do you understand what the signs of *going well* are?'

Enlighten me, vampire. 'I'm pretty sure —'

'The *tennis*, Erica. The *tennis*. Do we want our tennis player to win? Hmm? Do we?'

'Yes, Rosalind.'

'So, why are you here, swanning around and chatting with people and doing God knows what while he's unable to play because you're not there!'

I stood, sighed, wishing I had a stake handy. Or a silver bullet. Or was it gold? 'Okay, I'll go now.'

She looked at her desk again, waved her hand, shooing me away. 'And send Charlotte in. She's doing a wonderful job in your absence.'

ROSALIND WANTED to reward Charlotte for all her fabulous hard work; she sent her with me so she could enjoy the tennis. I dropped Charlotte off at Rod Laver Arena and gave her the fifty dollars Rosalind had ordered I give her. I told her to have fun, knock herself out, whatever. Then I'd called Teresa. She told me Emilio was still at his hotel and he wanted me to go there. His round-four match was later this afternoon, and he was struggling.

Teresa opened the door when I knocked and I walked into Emilio's suite. He was pacing, hands in his hair. Teresa tried to calm him.

'Finally, she is here.'

He came at me, eyes blazing. 'Where have you been? What is going on?'

I held up my hands. 'I've got a lot on my plate.'

He stood close, waved his arms around, shouting in Spanish.

'I don't understand what you're saying.' I kept my voice calm.

He spun, looking for Teresa who, unlike me, was right there for him, arms open. He fell into them; she clutched him and he wept on her shoulder. I tried to feel the compassion the moment surely deserved, but could drum up only resentment. And some pity. For me.

I stepped forward. 'Emilio —'

Teresa held up a hand to stop me. With the other she stroked his hair. She whispered something, he nodded, and let her lead him to the bedroom. To me she said, 'Please wait. I will tell you when he is ready for you.'

I took a seat at the dining table, where a pot of stinking camomile tea sat, freshly brewed. After a few minutes, Teresa emerged from Emilio's bedroom and held a finger to her lips, like a mother who's finally gotten her baby to sleep. 'He will sleep for one hour and then you can go with him to the tennis.'

'Is Joe coming? The bodyguard?'

'Yes, in one hour someone is coming, I am told.'

For one hour I stared out Emilio's hotel window, reminding myself of these things: First, I like my job. And I'd like it even more if Rosalind moved to Sydney and I got a promotion. Second, I didn't want to be the subject of a public lynching. Third, a small part of me didn't want to face Jack when he said, 'I told you so.' And fourth, for a tiny and very secret reason, my ego quite liked the idea of being in such a powerful position with Emilio Mendez. At the end of that hour, I could hear Emilio in the shower. He yelled something in Spanish, but Teresa had gone back to her room.

I cracked open the bedroom door. Steam swirled from the open bathroom door. I called out, 'Teresa's not here, Emilio. Just me.'

'Ah, *mi amor*, bring me a new soap.'

'Um ... I don't really think ... I shouldn't ...'

'You have seen a naked man, no?'

'Um …'

'Maybe you have not!' He laughed. 'Come, Emily, I do not have time for the games.'

I walked across the bedroom and stood at the bathroom door, face angled to the ceiling, trying to see in my peripheral vision where the soap might be. Emilio sang in Spanish. He had quite a good voice. The vanity was to my left – there'd be soap somewhere there, for sure. But, of course, behind the vanity was a mirror, mostly steamed over, except for one small patch around the power point, and in that patch I could see Emilio's gorgeous bottom. I stared at it, watching the muscles flex with his hair-washing action. It was mesmerising, and I was so fixed on the vision that, when he turned suddenly, I kept staring into the mirror.

'Ah, *querida*, you have found the soap, yes?'

Still it took me a few moments to divert my stare and continue the search for soap. The search that had not yet begun. A spare soap was there and I picked it up. I turned, keeping my gaze at eye level. Emilio smiled at me through the glass – he opened the shower door and leaned out of it. I held his eyes, and fixed a small smile on my face.

'Here you are.'

'Can you unwrap? It has paper.'

'Oh, yes.' I looked down at the soap in my hand, and beyond that … My eyes snapped up and I unwrapped the soap without looking.

Emilio reached out and stroked my cheek with a wet finger. 'I think we would both fit in this shower.' He gave me a wink.

I gritted my teeth, stretched my smile a little wider. 'Here's the soap.' I handed it to him.

'As you can see, I am very forgiving. Especially with you, my darling Emilita.' He opened the door wider.

Eyes north, Erica. Eyes north. 'I'd better let you get ready.' I looked down at my watch. Whoops! Looked down. I turned, walked quickly from the bathroom and bedroom, fanning my face, and there, waiting with Teresa by the window, was Sharon Stone.

'Oh! Hi!' I fanned more quickly.

Sharon nodded. 'Hey.'

Teresa said, '*Bueno*, you are helping Emilio with his shower.'

'Oh, no! No, I'm not.' I stopped fanning. 'I just … ah… he needed a new soap.'

'You gave him a new soap?'

'Oh, no … no, I threw it to him. I closed my eyes and threw it. He caught it. I think. I wouldn't know.' I laughed. 'I wasn't looking.'

Teresa moved to the bedroom door. 'I will check.' She walked through to the bathroom and I heard her say, 'Did you get the new soap, *mi precioso*?'

I stood there, facing off with Sharon Stone in an unspoken, motionless duel, as Emilio said, in loud, clear English, 'Yes, my devoted Emily, she brought me one. She found it on the vanity and brought it to me in the shower. I think she wanted to come into the shower with me!' They laughed. 'I tell her she must wait!' More laughing.

Sharon Stone smirked. I wanted to ask if she planned to kill me, but I was pretty sure I knew the answer to that. Instead, I said, 'Did you know that Emilio sometimes calls me Emilita?'

At the tennis I'd spotted Jack, who, with Joe and Sharon, walked onto the court between games and sets and scanned the crowd. I was sure he spotted me – he knew where I was sitting – but he didn't show any sign of it. I'd sent him a text to ask what he was doing after the match, but I hadn't heard back. I wondered if Sharon had told him about me and Emilio in the shower. Of course she had.

Emilio won his round-four match, wooed the crowd even more with spouts about Australia Day, how proud and joyful he was to be an Australian and how, hopefully, he said with a wink, he'd be adding to the Australian population in the future with an Australian wife. A television camera zoomed in on my face, which meant I needed to adopt the appropriate expression. What would that expression be? Coy smiles and finger waves? Kisses blown across the space? Fingers stuck down my throat?

Charlotte had had a terrific, relaxing time at the tennis, joining me for some of it, wandering the grounds, having a free pedicure. I sent her home in a taxi and had to wait while Emilio was interviewed in the media room, then some more while he showered and changed in his dressing room. He wanted me to have a late supper with him. In the players' café I sat at a table, put my head down on my crossed arms, and a minute later, my snoring woke me. I looked around, but the room was mostly empty. Andrew had returned to his car, waiting for Emilio and me. I snuck off for a walk to get some air, trying to wake myself up. But the warm evening air was so caressing, and so ... warm, I just wanted to lie on the grass and sleep. I circled the stadium, taking in deep breaths. I strolled toward the river, crossing Batman Avenue, drawn to the idea of a picnic with Jack there on the sloping grass.

A boat was docked at the small pontoon; a twin-hulled cabin cruiser. I walked closer to it, and wouldn't have taken much notice, but I could see that its name was *Iodka*, which looked to me like a Russian word. Under that was written *St Kilda Australia*. A man emerged from inside and I turned and walked away, watching over my shoulder. He disembarked with some effort and headed up the grass to the road. He was quite a fat man, and familiar. I stopped and watched him cross the road, walk around the front of Rod Laver Arena and then, perhaps because I felt I knew him, because he looked like the man who'd nearly knocked me down that day at the tennis, the angry-looking fat man who'd bowled over a child, I followed him.

The man passed by Rod Laver Arena and headed up the stairs to the pedestrian overpass, which led to the MCG and surrounding parkland, where parking was available during the Australian Open. I followed at a distance, keeping the thin crowd of departing tennis fans between us, ducking out of sight when he checked over his shoulder. Why was he checking? Did he expect to be followed?

Apart from the moon and soft lighting along the pedestrian walkway, the MCG was in darkness. As its soaring, dormant light towers loomed, most people veered off to the left to find their cars, but the man kept walking to the right, around the Brunton Avenue side of the stadium. I dropped back, now with fewer people to use as a shield. My phone buzzed and I looked at it. Andrew. I considered not answering, but knew that would throw him, Emilio and probably all of Jack's team into a panic.

I stopped walking and stepped behind a light tower, whispering, 'Hello?'

'Can't find you.'

'I'm, um, in the loo.'

'No, you're not.'

'Is Emilio with you?'

'He's looking for you. Where, Erica?'

'I'm, um —'

'No bullshit.'

I took a breath. 'I'm following someone suspicious.'

'Where?' His voice was tight.

'The MCG. Brunton Avenue side.'

'I'm coming. Start walking back.' He hung up.

Of course I kept following the man. I figured, once I knew what he was up to, I'd message Andrew and let him know where I was. At light tower number three, the man stopped. He looked like he was talking to someone behind the tower. I crept forward, keeping to the shadows of the stadium walls. A person stepped out from behind the tower. A man wearing a baseball cap. I moved forward. The baseball cap man gave the fat man something. I squinted. A departing car went by, its high-beam lights sweeping the stadium. Baseball cap man looked up, startled by the light, and I got to see his face. It was a face I knew but not usually with a baseball cap, so I couldn't be one hundred percent sure. But I was pretty sure the man was Martin McGann.

I'D WALKED BARELY a hundred metres back when I saw Andrew running toward me.

'You're a slow walker,' he puffed.

I shushed him and walked faster, glancing over my shoulder, but the two men were now out of view. 'Wait till I tell you what I saw.'

'I'm not interested. I've got one job to do, and you're making it hard for me.'

'Did you tell Jack?'

'Not yet.'

'Thanks.'

'But I will.'

'Please don't.'

He didn't respond, and I told him what I saw. He shrugged. 'Even if it was McGann, so what?'

'It looked pretty shady. They exchanged something.'

'What's it got to do with anything?'

'I don't know, but I'm guessing Martin would be one of Shane's regular visitors, and I'm still wondering how Shane knows a certain fact about me.'

'Which is?'

'That Emilio calls me Emilita.'

'How would he know?'

'I saw Martin McGann and Emilio's manager Teresa in the Sofitel. I think they're having an affair.'

Andrew seemed to consider all that. 'Even if you're right, McGann and Teresa together might be nothing more than a harmless affair.'

'Harmless? He's married.'

'You know what I mean.'

Yeah, I knew what he meant.

ANDREW DECIDED to join Emilio and me for dinner, rather than wait in the car. He said he didn't trust me not to run off and so took a table near the restaurant entrance, perhaps in case he needed to rugby tackle me as I headed out the door, unable to resist the idea of risking my life and annoying others with some dangerous yet appealing adventure.

Our table wasn't far from Andrew, and as he sat there reading a book, I wondered if he had a long-distance microphone so he could hear our conversation and report back to Jack.

'In the shower today,' said Emilio, loudly, 'I was so tempted by you.'

'I wasn't *in* the shower, Emilio. Remember? I just brought you soap because you didn't have any and there was no-one else to bring it.' I glanced at Andrew, who appeared to be intent on his novel. But there was a smirk. Definitely a smirk.

'I think you wanted to join me in the shower, yes?'

'No! No, of course not.' I laughed. It was very high-pitched and way too loud.

'Ah, so chaste, *ángel*. But in the future, perhaps we will have many showers together, *si?*'

'Let's order.'

'We have ordered already.'

'I forgot to order … bread.'

'They will bring the bread. You see! Here it is.'

Emilio took my hand and I snatched it back. His face was so hurt and shocked by my abrupt action, I explained, 'Um, I think I have a fungal infection. I don't want you to catch it.'

'So caring, my sweet Emily.'

I put my hands in my lap.

'I cannot believe how well I am playing.'

'You're a very good tennis player.'

'I am brilliant!'

'Yes. Yes, you are.'

'And a brilliant lover, also, you will see.' He sat back in his chair.

I took a breath. 'Emilio —'

'Please, call me *amante*.'

'*Amante?*'

'*Si.*'

'What does it mean?'

'Lover.'

'Oh. Um. Emilio —'

'Practise saying it.'

'I really don't think —'

'Say it with feeling, with sex. Like this: *Amante*.'

Sigh.

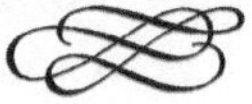

CHAPTER 56

On Tuesday, Emilio rested up for his quarter-finals match, which was to be played the next day. He told me he'd be staying in his hotel all day – apart from some brief training time with his coach – and he thought it *wouldn't* be a good idea if I went there to spend the day with him, sitting around while he slept, read, watched TV. Me twiddling my thumbs, just being there in case he wanted to look at me or ask me to do a little pirouette or tell him how magnificent he was. Because, after all, I have *nothing* else to do. Anyway, the reason he didn't want me there, Teresa said, was because 'he might be tempted by you'. Tempted by the evil hussy who apparently had no say whatsoever in whether or not there was to be any sex. But I didn't complain because I was so happy to have the whole day away from Emilio – spending it instead with Rosalind (yay!) – and then the evening to myself. Which meant I could see Jack and report what I'd seen at the MCG. And, hopefully, other things. I sent him a text: *Can I see you tonight?*

It took him ages to respond and when he did: *I have plans tonight.*

Bloody hell! What plans? Who with? I sat at my desk, brooding for a while.

He sent another text before I could respond: *You're not with your amante tonight? In the shower perhaps?*

Geez Louise, talk about childish. *I don't know what amante is.*

Yes, you do.

Ok I do. Is Andrew carrying a listening device? Are you eavesdropping?

You and your amante have very loud voices.

He's not my amante.

He seems to think he is.

I rang Jack. I thought he might laugh, having had fun with our convo, but he most certainly didn't. He took a while to answer, and his voice was cold when he said, 'Hi.'

'Who's reporting back? Sharon or Andrew or both?'

'No-one's *reporting* back about your affairs, Erica.'

'Affairs? With an "s"?'

'Your day-to-day activities. You know what I mean.'

'No, I don't know.'

'Maybe you've got a guilty conscience.'

I sighed. 'I'm not looking for an argument.' Oh my God! That's such a couples thing to say. 'I just wanted to know if I could see you tonight. I've got something to tell you. Something I saw.'

'I already know. Andrew told me.'

'And? What do you think?'

'I think you should stop running away from Andrew. It's pissing us both off.'

'But what about what I saw?' I said. 'What do you think?'

'I don't know. Yes, it's suspicious, but there's no law against two men meeting in a public place and exchanging something.'

'Martin McGann might have passed on to Shane that Emilio calls me Emilita. I think Martin McGann and Teresa are having an affair.'

'Okay. So what if Teresa has told Martin?' he said. 'It doesn't mean anything.'

We were silent for a while. There was some huffing from both ends.

'Anyway,' I said, 'I think that fat man is suspicious and Martin McGann is paying him for something.'

'You don't even know for sure it was McGann.'

'I'm *pretty* sure.' More silence and huffing. I said, 'It'd be nice to … catch up.'

There was a long pause. 'It would.' Ah, better. His voice was gentler.

'So? Tonight?'

'I'm out tonight.'

In a flat voice, I said, 'With Sharon.'

'Actually,' he said, 'I'm visiting a Russian club.'

'Sussing out the Russians? The boat I saw is called *Iodka*.' I spelled it.

No response. He was thinking about that.

'Can I come?' I dared.

'It's not really – I'm not sure it's safe for you.'

'Is Shags going?'

There was a very slight smile in his voice when he said, 'Yes.'

'I want to come. Please?'

He lowered his voice. 'Sharon is armed and capable. You're not, remember?'

'I'm not capable?'

'Armed.'

'Oh.'

'Not that I want you carrying a weapon, anyway.'

'I don't need a weapon. I've got you.'

'You do.'

'So …'

'I'll pick you up at ten.'

WHILE I WAITED for Jack to pick me up, Emilio called. 'You miss me, yes?'

'Um —'

'So bored, my poor Emilita.'

'Oh, not really —'

'But today I am feeling, how you say, tempted for the sexual activity.'

'Emilio, do many people know you call me that? Emilita?'

'No, just you.'

'I don't think so. I'm sure you've said it in front of others. Teresa, your coach, a few others.' Sharon.

'Hmm. Perhaps. Is this important? Do you want me to call you by another name?'

Yes, actually. How about Erica? 'No. It's fine. I was just wondering.'

'Do you miss me?' he said.

'Well, I've been so busy —'

'Tomorrow you will see me.'

'Ah, yes —'

'And all will be well.'

'All will be well.'

By the time Jack came to get me from Mum's I was wishing I hadn't insisted on going. Sneaking around at night in dangerous places wasn't what I'd had in mind when I'd asked Jack about catching up tonight. What I *did* have in mind was something more along the lines of pizza and beer in his bed. Or pizza and beer *then* bed. And home by ten so I could get a decent night's sleep. Actually, pizza, beer, bed, then the Russian club would have been a preferred option, too, but he hadn't offered an earlier catch-up, so I didn't suggest it in case he said no.

Mum was in her dressing gown. 'Why are you going out so late?'

'Um, it's what young people do these days.'

'But it's a work night!'

I yawned. 'I like going out late.'

Jack arrived. I wanted to run out to his car but there were two reasons I didn't: One, Mum had waited up to see him and two, Jack had such impeccable manners he wouldn't have liked not collecting me from the door. Actually, three: someone might have taken a shot at me as I ran from the house to his car. Maybe Sharon.

'Where's Sharon?' I said as we walked down the driveway. I could see she wasn't in his car. He opened the door for me.

'Gave her the night off.'

'Oh.'

'I don't need her if I've got you,' he said.

'But I'm not armed and dangerous.'

'You most certainly are.' He gave me a lingering look. Goody. Admittedly, I'd made a special effort. Straightened my hair – cursing the theft of my wig – worn my sexy little black dress, although I still hadn't found my favourite heels, which I reckoned might be in Mrs Booth's house along with Emilio's amulet.

'Where's the club?' I said as we drove.

'Brunswick.'

'Are we going in disguise? I mean, who do we say we are? Natasha and Boris?'

'Not unless you speak fluent Russian, with the right accent.'

'Do you speak Russian?'

'No.'

'Why not?'

He laughed, but I thought it was a reasonable question. Jack speaks six languages, plus some Spanish, apparently. I loved when he whispered French nothings in my ear. With that in mind, I gave him a nudge. 'You know, when we finally catch up in your bedroom, I want you to say naughty things to me in French.'

He gave me another look, but this time not lingering or sexy or wanting in any way. 'I would have thought you'd heard enough sexual Latin language to last a lifetime.'

I crossed my arms and stared out the window.

CHAPTER 57

The Vodka Club was in a 1970s building above a row of ugly shops. As we climbed the stairs, Jack handed me a fake driver's licence – with my photo and the name Susan Smith on it – gripped my hand and said, 'We've been out for dinner, had a few drinks, okay?'

'Okay. What's your name tonight?'

'My real one.'

'Your real … oh.' I remembered that Jack's real name was "Jacques", changed to "Jack" when he moved from Switzerland to Melbourne so he wouldn't get beaten up at his posh new private school. I practised. 'Jacques.'

'Like this. *Jacques*.' His version sounded better.

We approached the man at the front desk, and Jack said in English but with a French accent and a beaming, drunken smile, 'How are you, my friend?'

He was a big man, wearing a tux and no smile. 'You are member?'

'We are meeting Vladimir. *Est-il ici?*' Jack peered beyond the man into the darkened room, where people played cards and drank vodka.

'Many Vladimir.' The man waved his arm at the room.

'Vladimir Vavilov. You are familiar with the tennis player?'

His eyes lit up. 'Vladimir Vavilov coming here?'

'*Oui*. We have been for dinner.' Jack checked his watch. 'He is late.'

The man pointed to a sofa. 'Please wait.'

Jack swayed a little, just like a pissed person, and hooked an arm around my neck. I had no choice but to sway with him, and it was annoying. I thought it must be horrible to live with someone who behaves like this, going out and getting drunk all the time. I bet if Sharon Stone were here instead of me, she'd love it. He'd have his arm around her and she'd have her arm around him. I threw him off. He let out a surprised laugh, said something in French. Too late for French, I thought.

'Look,' I said to the big man in the tux, but he was focused on someone behind us. I turned to find the Danny DeVito limo driver standing there, waiting for us to get out of his way so he could enter the club. He got a big shock when he saw our faces, and took a step back.

Jack said, 'Ah, here is our friend!' and gave Danny DeVito a look that suggested we knew where he lived.

'Oh, yes,' I said, 'our friend!' Our dear friend whose name escaped me.

'This not Vladimir,' said big tux guy.

Jack put an arm around Danny, giving him a big squeeze. 'This is our very, very good friend.'

The terrified Danny looked from Jack to me and back again. I held what I thought was a tough-guy face, and whether or not he thought I was scary, I wouldn't know, but he finally said, 'They friend.'

Tux guy asked for our IDs, recorded the false names we gave him, and let us in.

WE SAT IN A BOOTH, Danny trapped next to me, Jack opposite so he could see Danny's face as he questioned him. Jack, now without a French accent, told Danny that if he answered a few questions for us, we'd leave quickly and quietly and never bother him again. Before Jack left for the bar to buy drinks, he said to me, 'Shoot him if he tries to leave.' I plonked my handbag on the table in front of me and patted it.

Jack returned with three glasses of vodka and Danny stared at them like they might contain poison. 'I not know nothing.'

I took a sip of mine. Yuck. Maybe they did.

'Tell me about the company you work for,' said Jack. 'We know who owns it.'

'They not involved bad things. It is legitimate business.'

Jack nodded. 'The Federal Police are looking into the train incident.'

'No! There is no more about that!'

'There will be. And the matter of the drugs found in the boot of your vehicle.' Jack addressed me. 'Ice, I think we decided?'

'Yep.' I gave Danny a serious look. 'Not the kind you keep in the freezer, either.'

Danny DeVito's eyes grew so wide I thought they might pop. 'You,' he spluttered. 'You …'

Jack munched on salt and vinegar chips. I made a mental note that he liked that flavour. 'You've got something to say?'

Danny fell back, defeat on his face. 'I make new life in this country.' He looked at me. 'My family. I not want trouble.' And I felt sorry for him.

'Neither do I,' said Jack. 'Tell me about the company you work for.'

'I am honest.' He gave me another look. 'Coward, *da*, but not liar. There is no thing to tell.'

Jack went to speak but Danny held up a hand. 'I tell about heist.'

Jack's face went serious. 'The tennis lunch?'

Danny nodded.

'You indicated you'd said everything you knew about that.'

Danny shrugged.

'Talk.'

Danny leaned in. 'The two men, they come, want be member Russian club.'

I piped up. 'So you *do* know the men involved.'

'Not know. But know who.'

'You told us they're not Russian.'

'Not Russia. Ukraine. They want make friend here.' He nodded at the room. 'They looking cash work.'

'They're here illegally?'

'*Da.*' Danny looked up at the ceiling, reminding me of myself in church, praying quietly to God who, just by the way, hadn't been too helpful since. 'Here, much work possible. Many trade people, but not work for Ukraine person.'

Right. Tradies who looked after their own.

Jack said, 'Get to the point.'

'A man, he come, want pay cash for work. Ukraine men take work.' I stopped breathing and I suspected Jack had also. 'Then I see the television and I know what work they find.'

Jack said, 'Who was the man who employed them?'

Danny shrugged. 'I not know.' He gave Jack a pleading look. 'I not know more.'

Jack and I exchanged a look. 'What'd he look like?'

Danny sighed and looked around the room, as though seeking inspiration. 'Average man. Hair dark. Maybe forty.'

'Australian accent?'

Danny nodded.

'When did he come here? What date?'

I knew what Jack was thinking. He could have the club's register checked, the one that recorded people's IDs.

Danny shook his head, closed his eyes. 'I not remember.'

Jack reached across the table, took a handful of Danny's hair, yanked him forward. 'Try.'

'I not remember! I will find!'

Jack released him, flicked him a business card with nothing but a gold embossed number on it. 'If you never want to see me again, you'll remember.'

Danny looked hopeful. 'I can go?'

'No, you can stay.' Jack gave me a nod and I stood. He took my hand and we left the building without looking back. And I thought I'd like to go undercover with Jack more often. It seems to be the only time he holds my hand in public.

IN HIS CAR outside my mother's neighbour's house, with the seat laid back and his hands all over me, Jack kissed me so lusciously I had an orgasm. He pulled back and gazed into my eyes.

'Did you —'

'Yes,' I panted.

'God,' he whispered and kissed me again, and when I snuck into my bed ten minutes later, having left Jack with glazed eyes and his face kind of pained looking, I found sleep arrived very quickly. When I woke the next morning, I was still smiling.

CHAPTER 58

On Wednesday I watched Emilio play very badly in the quarter finals. I sat through the first four sets chewing my fingernails. The other guy won the first set, Emilio won the second and third, the other guy the fourth. John the coach swore every time Emilio lost a point. Emilio glanced up at us occasionally – at me or John or Teresa, I wasn't sure – and gave us sad, almost pleading looks. He called for the physio and lay face-down on the ground while the guy massaged the back of both legs. Was he injured? I was busting for the toilet. It was so hot I drank all my water. At the end of the fourth set, I told Teresa, 'I need the toilet.'

She nodded. 'Take your time, *querida*. Nothing can help him now.'

'They're two sets each. It's not over.'

The crowd watched me leave. So did the television cameras. There was a long queue at the toilet. The girl in front stepped aside for me. 'Here, go ahead.'

'Really?'

'Sure. He needs you.'

The next person in line recognised me and gave me her spot. A murmur started up the line and I was waved to the front.

'Thanks, everyone.'

But by the time I'd been to the loo and grabbed another water and returned, the next set had started. Which meant I had to wait until the end of the first game to be allowed back in. I jigged on the spot, watching Emilio on the big screen. He lost that game. The rope opened and I shoved through the crowd, running down to my seat. John the coach gave me his usual filthy glare, adding a head shake in case I didn't get the message.

Teresa was kinder, patting my knee. 'Nothing more we can do.'

From his seat opposite, Emilio looked up at his opponent's team. They sat on the corner, like us, at the top end of the court. I leaned forward so I could see what Emilio was looking at, but I didn't need to. They were front and centre on the television screens. People who looked like parents, sister, family.

Emilio looked at me then, gave me a small smile and I felt something inside me change. A pang of ... what? Pity? Compassion? Yes. I returned the smile, adding a little wave. A few people in the crowd went 'aww' at how cute we were.

The next game started. I turned my head from side to side, trying to relieve some of the tension. Emilio served a pounding ace down the centre line. The crowd erupted. The other guy challenged. I held my breath as the shot was replayed. It was in. I leaped from my seat, screaming and clapping.

Emilio won that game. And the next, and finally, the match. From the edge of my seat, I collapsed back and put my face in my hands. Was I going to cry? Surely not. Teresa put her arm around me. I cried.

God, what was wrong with me? My nerves were wracked. I had a permanent neck ache from being so tense all the time; 24/7 tense. Everything was on my mind, all the time. The missing amulet, my missing gun, Russians, Martin McGann, death threats, attending to Emilio, worrying about Jack and Sharon and whether or not she might kill me. I was over it – all of it – but for some reason, more than anything, I wanted Emilio to win this tournament. It was no longer for my sake, but for his.

.   .   .

DURING HIS ON-COURT interview with Jim Courier, Emilio played the role of relaxed and charming, saying that he really didn't deserve to win that match and that he felt luck, and the Good Lord, were on his side.

Jim talked about the tense moment when the love of Emilio's life vanished after the fourth set.

Emilio laughed. 'Ah, yes, my love, she drinks too much water.'

The crowd laughed and looked at me. I gave a royal wave and shrunk into my seat, my face on fire.

And then later, in the media room, a journo asked Emilio, 'Did you play badly because of your stolen lucky charm?'

Emilio tried to keep the smile on his face and in his voice when he dismissed that with a wave of his hand. 'I do not need it.'

'You were pretty devastated when it went missing.'

Emilio asked for another question. I blew out my held breath.

'YOU CANNOT WIN without *su amuleto*, my darling,' said Teresa.

I jumped in. 'Yes, he can. He can do it.'

Emilio stared miserably at his plate. The three of us ate in Emilio's room while Andrew waited for me in the hotel lobby. I wanted to leave after dinner, but didn't trust Teresa not to say anything more to spook him. I watched television with them. Then Emilio said he wanted to go to bed, and I should leave.

'I am not angry with you, Emily.'

'It will be alright. I promise.'

'I do not know what happened today. I am thinking too much.'

'I know you're worried, but haven't you heard of visualisation? The law of attraction?' I stroked his cheek. 'You attract what you want in your life, darling.' Oh my God! I said darling.

'You are right. I will think about you and me together. It makes me happy.'

'What I mean is, you need to see yourself winning this tournament. See yourself holding that trophy. *That's* what I mean. You can do it, with or without the lucky charm. With or without me.' I gently tapped his head. 'It's only what goes on up here that stops you from achieving anything.'

He frowned. 'I do not think so.'

'It's true. What happened today?'

'Today, I was thinking … I was thinking about my mother.'

'Ah. And she's not here. That must have been difficult for you.' He nodded. 'But you have many people in your life who care about you. Who love you.'

Emilio's eyes got watery. He pulled me close, hugging me tightly, burying his face in my neck, which, after a while, he kissed softly, several times. I patted his back, tried to gently extricate myself, and he took my face in his hands.

'Let me kiss you, *ángel*. I want to kiss you properly.'

I pushed back, hands on his chest. 'No, Emilio.'

'Please, Emily.'

'No. Let's just focus on winning the next round, okay?'

I walked backward, blew him a kiss.

His chest heaved with a sigh.

CHAPTER 59

I found Andrew in the lobby, slouched in a chair with his detective novel, yawning.

'Sorry. I'm ready to go.'

'Great. I'm stuffed.'

We walked toward the exit.

'Are you too stuffed to do something sneaky with me?'

'Yes.'

'If you don't come with me, I'll do it later. I'll steal a car and sneak away.'

'As long as you do it on someone else's shift, I don't care.'

'Yes, you do.'

He gave me a crooked smile. 'Yeah, I do. What are you planning?'

ANDREW DROVE by the small jetty in front of Rod Laver Arena, where I'd seen the twin-hulled boat parked and the fat man emerge from it. The jetty was empty.

'Where would they usually park the boat?' I wondered.

'Docklands, St Kilda, Brighton —'

'St Kilda! It said St Kilda on the boat.'

Andrew nodded. 'Probably there then.'

'Can we go there now?'

He thought about it, staring through the windscreen of his car. 'You'll go there anyway, won't you?'

'Yeah.'

'Alright.'

THE PLACE WAS DESERTED, but brightly lit. We stood at the locked gates, under the arched St Kilda Marina sign.

'I can climb this.' I looked along the length of cyclone wire fence.

'We'll have to.'

We found a part of the fence that was in shadow and climbed. By the time I was halfway up, Andrew was already on the ground on the other side. He held his arms out as I teetered at the top.

'Don't look up my skirt.'

'Not interested.'

'I'll try not to be offended.'

With Andrew's hands on my waist, I found the earth, and looked around again.

'Are there security cameras?'

'Can't see any.'

We walked the boardwalk. Each pier was secured by a locked gate and U-shaped section of fence, making access difficult but, I thought, not impossible. I checked each jetty.

'The boat has a twin hull and two motors.'

'Outboards?'

'Yep.'

Andrew had a small but powerful torch. We walked slowly, looking around. He flashed his light along each row of boats.

'It's called *Iodka*.'

'That one.' Andrew pointed his light at a boat parked about halfway along. It was twin-hulled and twin-engined.

'Could be.' I couldn't read the writing.

I inspected the locked gate. 'Can you get around this?'

'Of course. You're planning on boarding the boat?'

'Yeah. I want to see what's on there. I've got a particular suspicion about the guy I saw.'

'As opposed to a general suspicion.'

'That's right. Can we get in?'

Andrew checked over his shoulder. 'Cover me.'

'What? With a gun?'

He laughed. 'No. Stand in front of me.'

'Oh.' I did so while he climbed nimbly around the fence.

He swung the gate open for me and together we jogged along the jetty. We stood in front of *Iodka*.

Andrew drew his gun. 'I'll go. Wait here.' He stepped silently onto the back deck and disappeared inside the cabin. After a few seconds, he reappeared. 'Clear.'

Inside the cabin with Andrew's torch, I looked around. There were bits and pieces, clothes strewn about – typical messy bloke's pad. I lifted items, put them back. I moved things, looked behind a picture on the wall, looked behind a marine-style barometer and, bingo! Emilio's lucky charm was in a small plastic bag, taped to the wall. I knew it was the fake I'd bought at Chadstone. But this is what I'd wanted to prove: that the man I saw talking to Martin McGann was one of the robbers at the charity lunch.

'Let's go,' called Andrew from the jetty and I gently replaced the barometer, leaving the lucky charm where it was.

I told Andrew what I'd found, explaining about the fake charm and missing real one. But I didn't tell him where I thought the real one was, or how it got there.

'Good work,' he said, and we jogged back up the jetty, through the gate, over the fence and into the car.

'You'd better call Jack. He'll have my balls but he should know what we've done.'

'Don't be mad with Andrew,' I said when Jack answered.

Jack yawned. 'The fact that you need to say that makes me mad.'

'Did I wake you?' Was he alone? Could I hear female snoring in the background?

'Yes. Tell me what you've done.'

I told him.

'Put me on speaker.' I did and Jack's voice addressed Andrew: 'What were you thinking, man?'

Andrew shrugged. 'She's persuasive.'

I butted in. 'I said I'd go on my own if he didn't come with me.'

'Erica, if the police board that boat and find the fake charm, what does that prove? Anyone can buy one.'

'Yes, but it was a fake charm he stole from me and he fits the description of one of the robbers.'

'Okay. We'll bring him in. Maybe he'll confess and then everyone on the planet, including Emilio, will know you were wearing a fake charm that day because you left the real one in a supermarket trolley.'

Oh. Hadn't thought of that. I glanced at Andrew.

'Is that what you want?' said Jack.

'No.'

'So?'

'So, maybe we'll wait another day or two. Until I find the real one.'

'You're confident you'll find it.'

'No.'

'I thought so.' He sighed. 'Alright, we'll watch the boat.'

'Thank you.'

'Andrew.'

'I'm here.'

'If she suggests anything like that again, cuff her and bring her to me.'

'No worries.' Andrew smiled, and a small thrill stuttered through me.

CHAPTER 60

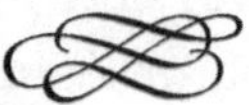

I'd noticed, when I'd climbed the outside of Mrs Booth's house, that Ruth's old bedroom window had been slightly open. I wondered if I'd dare actually break in and snoop around. I wondered if Andrew would come with me. No, he'd cuff me and take me to Jack's. Not that I minded the idea of that. Although at six on Thursday morning, it was Andrew's overnight replacement who was parked out the front, and he might not know he's supposed to stop me from doing stupid things. But anyway, Mrs Booth would be tucked up in bed right now, not away from the house. Or she'd be in the kitchen making cups of tea. Mind you, if she was in the kitchen, I could still climb the trellis and sneak past. God, I'm an idiot.

I showered and went into the kitchen, yawning, and Mum put the kettle on.

'What did you do last night, dear? You were late home again.'

Illegally boarded a boat where I found the fake charm that was nicked at the charity lunch heist. 'I had dinner with Emilio.'

'Well, he's a very good tennis player, so I suppose …'

Suppose what? Suppose it's okay to have dinner with a foreign man if he's a good tennis player? 'I work for Emilio, remember.'

'I suppose.'

I put some bread in the toaster. 'Do you watch the tennis, Mum?'

'Oh, yes, your father and I enjoy it.'

'Sorry I haven't organised tickets for you.'

'That's alright, dear. You're busy, I know.'

Wow. Mum was being nice.

'Besides, Charlotte's invited me to tomorrow's match. She has tickets from work.'

Bitch. (Not Mum.)

'Well, would you like to go to the grand final?'

'I think Charlotte has finals tickets for us.'

I stood straighter. 'What? She can't!'

Mum shrugged. 'That's what she said.' Mum took her cup of tea and the *Herald Sun* into the lounge room, and I went out the back and stood on the bottom railing of the fence, gazing into Mrs Booth's house. Axle climbed the fence and stood next to me on the top railing. He told me that if I didn't stop obsessing and get to work, he'd tell my mother. I went inside and buttered my cold toast.

BY THE TIME I was ready to go, Andrew was back on board. He dropped me off, and I found Charlotte sitting there at my desk with everything under control. This was both good and bad. Good, because Rosalind didn't seem to give a shit that I was late. Bad, because it appeared I was no longer needed. Charlotte held up a basket of scones.

'I made extra for our department to share.'

'Great,' I mumbled.

'Jam and cream?'

'Sure, why not?' I bit into it. It was a good scone.

I called Emilio's mobile phone. Why hadn't he called me yet? Teresa answered.

'Does Emilio want to see me?'

'Not today. He will do the sightseeing with his bodyguard. He will see you tomorrow before his match.'

'Oh. Who's with him?'

'Sharon Stone. Have you found *el amuleto?*'

'Ah, no.'

She hung up.

'If anyone's looking for me,' I said to Charlotte, 'I've got a meeting at the tennis.' I left and said to Andrew, 'What would you be doing if you weren't babysitting me?'

'At the tennis, probably.'

'Bugger. Sorry.' I shouldn't have asked. Now I felt I should take him to the tennis, but I didn't want to go there. I wanted to bury myself in some miserable something.

'It's fine,' he said.

'Can you take me home?'

'Sure.'

At home, I went back to bed and lay there.

Mum came in. 'I'm off to the supermarket. Do you want some pills for your headache?'

'How are you getting to the supermarket?'

'Well, I was going to ask your chauffeur, but Imelda offered.'

I sat up. 'Mrs Booth's taking you to the supermarket?'

'Yes, dear. Do you want some pills?'

As soon as Mum left with Mrs Booth, I changed into my breaking-and-entering outfit – black three-quarter-length leggings, black tank top and runners – and climbed the fence. I ran first to the garage, peeked in and checked there were no cars. All clear. I ran back to the trellis, stood on the vine covering the old basement doors, and there was a loud crack as the timber gave way. I was suddenly sitting among the vine, my leg dangling through the gaping hole. I could feel cobwebs brushing my leg, and this caused me to shoot out of there double time. I gripped the trellis, climbed a couple of feet and looked down. Daylight filled the cavity below. Beyond the cobwebs, waving in the new-found breeze, I could see the old stairs leading down to the basement. I shuddered, repelled by the basement and its potential scary stuff but also guilty about the damage. I wondered how I could make it up to Mrs Booth. Without her knowing it was me, of course.

I climbed another couple of feet and Axle joined me. He scampered up the trellis and sat on the window sill.

'Get home, naughty cat!'

He ignored me and as I pushed open Ruth's old bedroom window, he ducked inside.

'Axle!'

I fell through the window and landed in a heap on the floor. I stood and looked around. The room was very tidy. Everything in its place, women's shoes lined up in a row against the wall. No sign of the ones that looked suspiciously like my high heels. I brushed myself down, and went looking for Axle, who I found on his back in the hallway, swiping playfully at Minx.

'You're grounded, Mister Naughty.'

I crept along the hallway, past the bathroom, remembering where everything was. Mrs Booth's bedroom was ahead on the left, overlooking the street. That's where the lucky charm would be, for sure. I snuck in there and stopped, surprised by what I saw. No rich velvets, purples and maroons, or mirrors hanging from things. It was a "normal" bedroom with a neat floral doona cover, pale pink drapes and white sheers. Well, well, maybe she's really nice and normal after all, in which case … would she have stolen the lucky charm? My stomach turned at the thought of it. If the lucky charm wasn't here, where the hell would it be? I stared out the window onto the street, considering the possibility, feeling sickened by it. I watched Mrs Booth's Kia pull into the driveway. Mum was in the front passenger seat. I blinked at the scene, the realisation that I was about to be caught breaking and entering taking its time to stir me into action.

I heard Mrs Booth say, 'Won't be one minute, Margaret.'

I ran back to Ruth's room, hid behind her bedroom door. Mrs Booth was on the stairs. 'Where on earth did I leave my purse?' And as I stood there, my heart pounding, I saw, not a metre away from me, draped over Ruth's dressing table mirror, Emilio Mendez's famous lucky charm. I let out a gasp and dived on it. But there was a padlock attaching it to the mirror frame. I pulled at it, looking for a way to free it. It was most certainly Emilio's – I could see the inscription. But then I heard Mrs Booth. 'Axle! How did you get in here? Did my daughter leave her window open again?' Mrs Booth's footsteps headed my way. 'I hope you haven't been helping yourself to my gold-fish.' I dashed across the room, rolled over the window sill, gripped the trellis, slid down it a few feet before stopping, clinging to the thin wood and pressing my body flat against the wall. The window above me slammed shut. I heard it lock. I descended fast, jumped the last two metres, rolled like they do in the movies, and raced into the garden where I crouched, puffing, sweating. The back door opened and Axle shot out of it. I waited until I heard Mrs Booth from the front of the house. 'Sorry to be so long, Margaret. Your daughter's cat was in the house!'

I hoped Mum didn't dob on me. I could just imagine: 'Oh, yes, Imelda. Erica's been lurking around your house ever since she moved home. It's a wonder you didn't find her in there, too!'

I lay on my back, listening to the Kia drive away. Axle sat on my stomach. What I really felt like doing was curling into a ball and sucking my thumb. But I had more important things to do for now. How to get the chain off the padlock? It wouldn't be hard, because I could easily cut the chain. I was sure Emilio wouldn't mind if I did that.

CHAPTER 61

 called Jack and told him.

'And where does Andrew think you've been?'

'In bed with a headache.'

'So you snuck out the back door and climbed the fence. Again.'

'Uh, yeah.'

He took a deep breath, whispered something that sounded like, 'God help me.'

'You can come to church with us, if you want.'

'And this means Imelda Booth took the charm, after all.'

'Yes, and gave it to her daughter. Probably trying to make up for being a crappy mother.'

'What are you planning?'

'Do you think I should call the police? Maybe your friend, Bill Lucas? But I don't want Emilio finding out where it was.'

'Erica. Think about it. The charm was found in a supermarket trolley. It wasn't *stolen*, my love.'

Gasp! *My love.* I couldn't speak.

He cleared his throat. 'What do you want to do?'

I shook my head, patted my face. 'I'll go back in there and get it.'

'How will you get in?'

Good point. Mrs Booth had locked the window. But maybe Ruth would open it again. The nights were warm. I could wait until tomorrow. Or …

'Will you help me?'

'Sure. Joe and I'll storm the house while they're asleep. We'll have weapons and wear masks so we're not recognised.'

'Would you?'

'Of course not. You really think I'd do something like that?'

'No. Sorry.' But, bugger, I wish he would. Although it wouldn't be very nice for Ruth and Mrs Booth. They might never get over it. I don't think I would. 'I'll have to wait until tomorrow. The window might be open again. Or I could see if there's another window open.'

'I don't want you breaking into houses.'

'It's only one house. Not like I'm planning a new career.'

He huffed and didn't say anything for a while. Finally, he said, 'Degraves wants me in Bass Strait. There's indication of another attack planned against his rigs.'

'Oh my God! How do you know? Will you go?'

'Yes, if I'm needed there.'

'When?'

'Soon. Next couple of days.'

'But —' I wanted to say *what about me*, but knew I couldn't. Shouldn't. 'What about Emilio's security?'

'Andrew's with you. I'll have others watching Mendez.'

'Joe?'

'He's with me.'

'Sharon?'

Pause. 'With me.'

'Will she fly you out there?'

'Yes.'

Damnit. Why didn't I become a helicopter pilot? Join the Air Force? It can't be that hard to fly those things. Those hornet things.

'Do you think Emilio's safe?' I said.

He took a while to answer. 'What we've learned about the threats against Mendez is that they're pathetic. Minor incidents by inexperienced, frightened people. We've made our presence very clear. I really don't think there'll be a problem.'

'Being shot at by Sharon wasn't minor.'

'It wasn't Sharon, Erica.' He was annoyed.

'How do you know?'

'Your gun was stolen and … I'm working on it.'

I'm working on it … Now I was shitty. 'The armed hold-up wasn't minor.'

'It was in the sense that those guys were all bark and no bite. Their guns weren't loaded. Their purpose was to put Mendez off his game, that's all.'

'*One* gun wasn't loaded. We don't know about the other.'

'Erica.' He sounded fully exasperated now. 'You're here. You're safe. Forget it.'

Yeah, I'm safe if Sharon's with you because then she can't kill me. I hung up. He didn't call back.

CHAPTER 62

On Friday morning, John Degraves wanted to see me in his office. I checked the time. Emilio's semi-final match was this afternoon. When I got to his office, JD asked me to close the door, which meant he wouldn't be discussing Dega Oil business. At least, not *all* Dega Oil business. Originally, when Jack had first recruited me to the Team, he told me that JD would never discuss Team business with me. But JD had broken that rule several times now, and I was getting used to having these secret conversations with him. I always thought about *Get Smart* and the cone of silence, imagining JD and me sitting under it and shouting at each other because the thing never worked, and that thought always made me smile.

'You seem happy, Erica.'

'Always happy to be at work, Mr Degraves.' Especially if Rosalind is sent to Sydney.

JD indicated for me to sit opposite. 'I've spoken to our mutual friend about his visit to Western Australia.' He leaned in, glanced at the door.

I thought about the cone of silence.

'The police have confirmed,' he said in a low voice, 'that the three men killed did, in fact, cause the explosion.'

'How?'

'It was a deliberate attack.'

'Suicide bombers?'

'We assume not. Their boat was thrown onto the rig by the rough seas, and that caused the explosion.' He explained, 'They had explosives on board the boat.'

'But how do you know it wasn't a suicide mission?' I shifted further forward in my chair.

'Because we found evidence on the remains of the boat of another planned attack. We don't believe they intended to die.'

'Where?'

'Bass Strait. I'll be sending our friend and his team to investigate.'

I nodded but didn't say I already knew that.

'Of course, you should just go about your business with Emilio for the remainder of the tournament. He's very fond of you.'

'He thinks he is.'

'And there's been no further harassment, I assume?'

'Death threats, you mean?'

'If you like.'

'No.'

'Very good. Carry on. You're doing a fine job.' And I was dismissed.

LATER THAT MORNING, I was trying to get out of the office to go to Emilio, who'd been calling me every twenty minutes, when Jack called my mobile.

I answered with, 'I can't talk.' Quite apart from the fact I was still pissed off with him, I really couldn't.

'I need to see you.'

You should have thought of that yesterday when you were dismissing my safety, I didn't say. I rifled through the stuff on my desk, trying to find my tennis pass. Charlotte stood in front of me, hands on hips. Rosalind called my name without using the phone. If Jack was calling about Bass Strait or any other Team stuff, I couldn't discuss it here.

'I really can't talk.'

'Can we meet?'

'*Erica!*' The vampire again.

Marcus was there now, flapping his arms. *Now!*

'I've gotta go. I'll call you later.' I hung up before he could speak again, and I hated that, but it was just such bad timing.

IN THE CAR, on the way to Emilio's hotel, Andrew said, 'Jack's going away for a couple of days. He wants me with you, twenty-four-seven.'

'You already are.'

'No, he means *with* you.'

'What about when I go to bed?"

'On the floor in your room.'

'You can't! What if my mother finds you there?'

He smiled. 'I'm sneaky. And quiet.'

Gawd. I imagined my mother, hair in rollers, barging into my room with the latest edition of the *Herald Sun* and coming face to face with Andrew and his gun.

'I think I'd feel a bit ... funny.'

'It's cool, Erica. Just work, that's all.'

Just work. I remembered being in a tree in the jungle with Joe once, evading the enemy, snuggled up to keep safe, feeling funny about having his arms tight around me, and he'd said something like, 'It's survival, that's all.' But being in my own small bedroom with a bodyguard asleep on the floor isn't exactly about evasion and survival.

'Maybe I'll take a room at the hotel.'

'Whatever.'

'I'll get a suite with a separate bedroom. Jack can pay.'

Andrew laughed.

'When's Jack leaving?'

'Tomorrow.'

'And until then?'

'Busy.'

Mr Busy. Mr Too Busy For Me. That's probably why he was calling. To say he was busy and couldn't see me for a few days but he wanted me to stick with Andrew. Why? In case those pathetic criminals come back with their empty guns?

The hotel had an executive suite available on the same floor as Emilio's. I booked it for three nights: tonight, Saturday and Sunday after the finals. I thought briefly about Emilio winning the finals and wanting to rush back to the hotel so we could finally consummate our love. Maybe I would. Bugger Jack. Mr Too Busy. At least it would finally end Emilio's infatuation with me.

ANDREW and I arrived at Emilio's room.

'Will you wait outside?' I certainly didn't want Andrew witnessing Emilio's passion and reporting back to Jack.

'I'll check the room first.'

Teresa opened the door, gave me an exasperated look, pushed past me and left.

I walked in. 'I'm here!'

Andrew followed me, looked around, left.

Emilio was pacing the bedroom, pulling at his hair. 'I don't know what to wear! I can't think!'

'It's alright. Calm down and we'll find something for you to wear.'

'I do not know what is wrong with me!'

I stopped his pacing, took his hands in mine. 'Guess what?'

'What?'

'I'm moving into the hotel.'

His eyes lit up. '*Conmigo?* With me?'

I wagged a finger at him. 'Oh, no, naughty!'

He laughed, relaxed. Better.

'Guess what else?'

'What?'

I leaned in close, stood on tip-toes so our noses were almost touching. 'I found it.'

'*Mi amuleto?*'

I nodded.

He let out a mighty whoop, picked me up and spun me around. 'Where? Where is it? I want to see it!'

'I don't have it yet, but I know where it is.'

'When? When will you have it?'

'Well, I know where the, ah, men who stole it have put it. I just have to get in there and get it.'

'The police, they will get it!'

'Um … no, they won't. They can't.'

'*Por que?*'

'Why? Because, um, because if the bad men know the police are coming, they might do something to it. They might throw it in the river! No, I need to sneak in there.'

Emilio huffed. 'I want it now.'

'I'll have it for the finals, I promise. But in the meantime, I want you to do something.'

'*Que?*'

'Close your eyes.' He did it. 'Now I want you to imagine your precious amulet around my neck. Can you see it?'

'*Si*, I can.'

'And that's all you have to do.'

'That is all?'

'Yes, it will keep you going until I have it in my hand. Can you do that?'

He gave me a suspicious look. 'Maybe, Emily. But it is not the same.'

*E*milio Mendez walked onto centre court for the men's semi-final match of the Australian Open tennis tournament to a standing ovation. Goose bumps sprouted all over my body and I'd never felt more proud in my life. Anyone watching Emilio would never have guessed he wasn't the most confident, coolest guy on the planet. And everyone wanted him to win. Vladimir Vavilov was already through to the final, so the winner of this match would play Vavilov on Sunday evening.

Andrew sat to my right, protecting me from a potential pathetic attack from the aisle. Teresa was on my left, protecting me from a potential lethal attack from John the coach. Below me, where Joe would usually be standing, was some guy I'd seen around but never met. One of Jack's Team guys. I wondered where Jack, Joe and Sharon were. Behind and above me, in the Dega Oil corporate box, were Charlotte Johnson and my mother.

I watched Emilio warm up with his opponent, American John Connor. I wished I could see it all in super-slo-mo, especially when Emilio served and his shirt rode up, exposing his tanned, muscled belly. Not that I couldn't see that gorgeous tum any time I wanted, but it was titillating to watch him like this, knowing I could have him if I wanted. I leaned forward, elbows on knees and chin on my palms. I patted my face, discreetly, because slapping it would have looked strange.

Emilio's habit was to wear his hair out during warm up and tie it back for the match. But not before changing his shirt, which caused every woman in the stadium to cheer. Usually, he'd laugh and wave, but not today. Today he was fully serious. He sat, took a drink, put his hands together, prayer style, and pressed his fingers to his mouth. Eyes closed. It looked like he was praying, but I wondered if he was trying my suggestion of visualisation. When he looked up at me, I patted my chest. *I'm here and I'm wearing your precious amulet, Emilio. Believe it.*

He nodded once.

AFTER TWO HOURS, Emilio and Connor were one set each. Connor was good but I thought Emilio played well. Emilio was younger and it was a hot day. Emilio was good in the heat. I thought about the smell of Emilio when he was sweaty. Emilio in the shower. I did another of those face-patting things.

At the start of the third set, Emilio serving, someone let out a mighty sneeze as he threw the ball into the air. Emilio let the ball drop. Everyone had a little laugh, including Emilio. He started again. This time, someone had a huge coughing fit – it sounded like the same person. Emilio let the ball fall and he turned, peered into the crowd with hands on hips, making a joke of it. Fewer people laughed. Next go at serving, the guy waited until Emilio was a millisecond off hitting the ball before he shouted something. Emilio served a fault. The umpire said, 'Quiet, please!' Emilio's next serve was done without distraction, but he double-faulted. His first for the tournament. A murmur started up in the crowd. Emilio shook his head and nodded to the ball boy for his towel, which he used to wipe the sweat from his face, hands and racquet, then he served the ball. It was a fault. Emilio lost that game. John Connor held serve in the next. At the start of the third game of the third set, with Emilio serving again, the same man shouted out as Emilio served.

People were getting pissed off. Emilio threw his racquet. John the coach shouted abuse at whoever. Security would look for the guy now, ask him to leave. I scanned the crowd, seeking the offender. I saw someone I recognised. I didn't know if it was the shouting guy, but it was certainly the fat man from the boat. I nudged Andrew and pointed. 'That's the guy from the boat. The one I reckon nicked my charm at the lunch heist.'

'You think he's the one making all the noise?'

'It's coming from there.'

Security staff patrolled the back of that section of seating, waiting to spot the disrupting man. Why didn't someone give him up? I said to Andrew, 'Will you go over there? Shoot him or something?'

'I'm not leaving you.'

'But —'

He held up his hand. 'No.'

'Maybe I'll go.'

He put a firm hand on my leg. 'You'll stay.'

'Geez, bossy. You sound like Jack.'

Andrew smiled.

Emilio attempted another serve. Fat man stood fully upright, hollered something nasty in English but with a very strong accent about Emilio's mother. Security were all over him then, dragging him away. Teresa sighed loudly next to me. John the coach quietly threatened to do horrible things to anyone who stood in Emilio's way. Emilio lost that set.

There was nothing I could do but send hand signals and loving, positive vibes. I blew a kiss, patted my chest, nodded my head in the hope he'd interpret it all as *You can do it!* He bowed his head, shaking it, running his hands through his hair. I wished I could have a few minutes with him to give him a motivational talk. Remind him how brilliant he was. But the fact was, his confidence was in pieces, all over the court. Emilio was down two sets to one. If John Connor won the next set, he'd be playing Vavilov in the men's final.

The fourth set started. John Connor won the first three games. It was terrible to watch. I needed the toilet, couldn't wait longer, but didn't bother to explain to Teresa or John the coach what I was doing.

Andrew came with me.

'We have to hurry,' I said.

We arrived at the loos and Andrew said he'd wait for me.

'Don't you ever need to go?'

'Never.' He smiled. 'I'll be right back.' He jogged off to find the men's.

The queue wasn't too long because no-one wanted to miss a second of the match. I stood there pondering my ruined life, wondering about public lynchings, knowing Emilio would ultimately be okay … I mean, as devastated as he'd be, he was only twenty-three and there were plenty more Australian Opens to win; but still, it was awful to watch him throw away this match simply because of that idiot upsetting him.

A woman walked past me and I saw she was wearing a fake Emilio Mendez amulet. I didn't hesitate to leap from the line and grab her arm. She looked at me, horrified, and jerked her arm away. 'What are you doing?'

'Can I borrow your lucky charm?'

'No way!' She backed away.

'I'll pay you for it.'

'No!' She tried to walk away and I followed.

'Please? I'll give you five hundred dollars!'

She started running. I went after her.

'Get away!'

'I need it to help Emilio win this match!'

She stopped and looked at me. 'You're his girlfriend.'

'Yeah.' I nodded.

'What are you going to do with it?'

'Just show it to him. He'll think it's the real one and it might help.'

She hesitated, lifted it and gave it a kiss. 'God, you're so lucky.'

'Yep. Luckiest girl alive.'

'Here, take it.'

'I don't have money with me.'

'Will you give it back?'

'Of course.'

'Okay. We'll meet at the ladies' loo after the match. Go help him win!'

I gave her a quick hug. 'Thank you.' And as I headed back to the toilets, I saw Andrew running through the crowd, panicking, head swivelling.

I waved, 'Here!'

He jogged up to me. 'Sweet Jesus, I swear you'll be the death of me, Erica.'

'That's what Jack always says.'

Someone else jogged up to us. Sharon Stone.

I frowned at her. 'What are *you* doing here?'

Andrew said, 'She'll stay with you for a couple of hours. I need to go pack a bag.'

Don't be long, Andrew, or I might do something I could be arrested for. 'Okay, well, I still need the loo, then I need to hurry back. Look what I've got!'

BY THE TIME Sharon and I reached our seats, Emilio was down five games to nil. This next game was the decider. If Connor won it, that was it. If Emilio won it, he'd then have to win the next six to take the set. It was hopeless, but I needed to try.

Connor served an ace. Barely anyone in the crowd cheered. But, how to get Emilio's attention? He was so forlorn, the match lost, I could see it in his body language. I showed Teresa what I had.

'It is not the real thing.' She shrugged.

I stared at Emilio, willing him to look up at me. Connor won the next two points. Emilio stood in the middle of the court, face to the sky, racquet hanging by his side. *Why, God?* I could almost hear him. I stood, holding the amulet out. I wasn't allowed to call out to him. And then, someone in the crowd shouted, 'Yeah!' and started a slow clap. More people joined the clapping. The ump called for quiet. The clapping got louder. The clapping people were looking at me. The television cameras were on me. Emilio looked up and saw me standing there, holding the fake lucky charm by the chain, letting it swing in front of my face. I gave Emilio my biggest smile and he was transfixed. His eyes grew wide, and a huge smile spread across his face. Suddenly puffed up, seemingly taller, Emilio jogged to the end of the court and waited to receive Connor's serve, which he returned with a fast forehand across court. Connor couldn't reach it. The crowd roared. The ump called for quiet, Connor served a fault. His second was a weaker serve, and Emilio returned it down the line. Connor was shocked.

Emilio won that game. He was so pumped, so fantastic, and his sudden burst of fight infected the entire stadium. The crowd buzzed and the ump found it hard to keep them quiet.

When Emilio served the next game, Connor didn't score a point.

I said to Sharon, 'Not bad, hey?'

She smirked, like she knew something I didn't, and I wanted to slap that smirk right off her face.

CHAPTER 64

Emilio won the semi-finals match against John Connor. Connor didn't win another game after Emilio's fight back. It was the most thrilling thing I'd ever witnessed. And that was all very well and wonderful, but now I had to confess to Emilio that I still didn't have his lucky charm. That I'd borrowed a fake one to trick him into winning the match. I wondered how he'd take it.

I sent a message with Teresa that I'd meet Emilio at his hotel for dinner, assuming he'd want to have dinner with me. Sharon and I met the lucky charm lady back at the loo, and she threw her arms around me.

'I can't believe I helped Emilio Mendez win that match!'

'Yep, you sure did. But don't tell anyone just yet, will you? He thinks I had the real one.'

She zipped her mouth.

Then Sharon handed me back to Andrew. I asked Andrew to take me home so I could pack and tell Mum my plans. On the way, I tried to call Jack, but it went straight to voicemail.

I said to Andrew, 'I ordered a rollaway bed for you. Or are you supposed to be in the actual same bed as me?'

He gave me an exasperated Jack look.

'You can have the big bed if you want.'

'I'm cool.'

I bet he was. If he'd had Jack-type experiences in his whatever-career, that probably included some sleeping-in-the-jungle time, which was rarely comfortable and usually terrifying. I knew. I'd done it.

As we pulled into Mum and Dad's street, Emilio called me.

'Congratulations to the best tennis player in the world!'

'Where are you, Emily? I want *mi amuleto*!'

'Didn't you see Teresa?'

'Yes, Teresa is here.'

'She was supposed to give you a message.'

'She did not.'

I clicked my tongue, annoyed. 'Doesn't matter. I sent a message to say I'll meet you back at the hotel in time for dinner. Okay?'

'Please hurry, Emily.'

I TOLD Mum I was moving into Crown Hotel for the rest of the tournament. 'Just three nights.'

She pursed her lips, trying to find a reason why it wasn't the right thing to do. Well, Mum, it's either that or you'll be scrambling eggs for my bodyguard. She'd probably like that.

'But I'll be back and forth.' Breaking into Mrs Booth's house again. 'By the way, are you going to church on Sunday?'

'Yes, dear. Of course.'

'How are you getting there?'

'Well, I did think your chauffeur could take us, but we've been offered a lift.'

'By …'

'Imelda. Mrs Booth.'

'Yes! I mean, that's nice of her.' So, Sunday morning it would be. I'd have the lucky charm in my hot little hand for the men's final on Sunday evening. Oh my God, it was all nearly over.

. . .

BACK AT THE HOTEL, I stood next to Andrew at Emilio's door and knocked, bracing myself for his anguish. I heard him running. I sucked in a great breath and blew it out. When he opened the door, he looked at me, at Andrew, stepped forward and looked along the passageway.

'Who were you expecting? Vladimir Vavilov?'

'No, it is just …' He looked at my hands, which were empty. 'Where is it?'

I put my hands on his arms. 'I have to tell you something.'

It wasn't so bad. At first, when I told him what I'd done, he'd backed away from me, like I was the most evil thing he'd ever encountered. But I said over and over that I knew where his real one was, that I'd get it, and to distract him, I told him how clever he was – the best tennis player *ever*. I reminded him about his incredible achievement this afternoon. He calmed down, but I didn't think he fully trusted me. If I were Emilio, I wouldn't trust me either.

FOR DINNER, Andrew sat at the table next to Emilio's and mine. I invited him to join us but he shook his head. 'Thanks anyway.'

'You won't listen to the shit we say, will you?'

He gave me a smile, but didn't say "Mum's the word" or anything like that.

Emilio was subdued, didn't have much to say. He was still brooding about the trick. Why couldn't he see the positive in it? He'd won the semi-final, thanks to what he thought was the real lucky charm. He went to the men's and I checked my phone. Still no word from Jack. I leaned toward Andrew. 'Have you heard from Jack?'

'Not today.'

I checked my voicemail again in case there was a new message I hadn't heard. Just an old one from Jack, saying, 'We need to meet.' And that was it. Mr Cool. So unlike me. If *I* was that desperate to see *him*, I'd have left ten messages, each one getting shittier and more panicky.

I went to dial his number but Emilio arrived back at the table, having paid the bill, and now, he said, it was time for bed.

<h1 style="text-align:center">CHAPTER 65</h1>

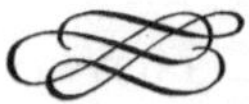

When the hotel lift doors opened for us to enter, Emilio said to Andrew, 'Please, just Emily.'

Andrew gave me raised eyebrows, which were probably about Emilio's request, but could also have meant, *Why are you letting this dipshit call you Emily?*

'Can you follow in the next one?' I waved my arm at the empty lift. 'No murderers here.'

Andrew didn't want to wait for the next one, I could tell, but he stepped back and the doors closed.

Emilio leaned heavily against the wall, rested his head back and closed his eyes. 'Emily, tomorrow is Saturday, and the day after is the men's final.'

'I know, Emilio. You need to get plenty of rest.'

'I'm feeling … worried.'

'I can imagine.'

'I do not know what is happening to me. I do not feel the same.'

'Well, you've already shown you don't need your lucky charm. Just look how well you played today!'

He shook his head. 'Maybe I do need it. *Mi amuleto.*'

'I really don't —'

324

'You do not understand.'

'Yes, I do. I know how important this is to you.'

'No, you do not. All the others. I have beaten them before. I have never beaten Vladimir Vavilov. Not ever.'

'But you will!'

'Not with this.' He pointed to his head and his heart. 'Not with these feelings and thoughts.'

I didn't say anything because nothing useful came to mind. The lift doors opened and Emilio walked out, headed down the passage to his room. I trailed after him, but stopped to wait for Andrew.

Emilio turned. 'Come, Emily. I need you to help me.'

Two more days, I thought. In two days, this will be over. Emilio will have won the tournament and my life will be different, but in a good way. Or Emilio will lose the tournament and I'll be lynched in Bourke Street Mall. My life as I know it is over because of a tennis match.

'Emily!'

'Please don't order me like that, Emilio.'

'But you did not come when I said.'

I walked slowly toward him. 'I'm not a puppet. If you want something from me, then please ask.'

I heard the lift ping and Andrew stepped out. I held up a hand for him to wait.

'No girlfriend has caused me so much problems.' Emilio turned to the door of his suite, pushed the key in the slot. 'Sometimes I wonder why I bother with you.'

'*What?*' As the door swung closed, I shoved it open, stomping after him into the room. 'Emilio, I've done everything you've asked of me. Everything!'

He sat on his bed, put his face in his hands. 'I do not know what is wrong with me.'

There was a knock. Andrew. I ran to the door.

He looked past me into the room. 'I need to check it out.'

'It's clear in here.' I stepped closer and said in a low voice, 'He's upset. I just need a minute.'

I let the door close and returned to Emilio. 'I'll get your charm before Sunday.'

He shook his head, put his face in his hands.

I knelt on the floor in front of him. 'It will be alright.' I meant it.

Emilio took my hand and kissed it. 'Please stay with me tonight, Emily. I do not want to be alone.'

'Uh-uh. No, Emilio. I'm not staying.'

'Then stay with me until I sleep. Please? I do not sleep so well these days.' He made sad puppy dog eyes, squeezed my hand in his strong, warm one. 'Please, my darling, caring Emilita.'

'Alright. Just until you fall asleep. Now, go clean your teeth.'

He smiled, went into the bathroom.

I sat on the sofa, thought about calling Jack. But within a few minutes Emilio was calling out to me, 'I am ready!'

He was in bed, the covers low, exposing that magnificent torso. He opened his arms. 'Come.'

I walked to the other side of the bed and perched on the edge of it, fully dressed, handbag still slung over my shoulder. 'I'll sit here until you fall asleep.'

He patted the bed. 'Lie with me.'

'No, I'm not lying on the bed.'

He pouted.

'Oh, alright.' I kicked off my shoes, threw my handbag on the chair in the corner. Just a few minutes. I couldn't be longer because Andrew would be waiting. I lay facing Emilio, as far from him as I could get without falling off the bed. He flipped onto his side and, with his eyes closed, reached out and softly stroked my cheek. I tensed, but it did feel nice. God, I was tired.

'Ah, *ángel. Mi bonita ángel rubia*,' he whispered.

Emilio stayed on his side of the bed like a good boy. He continued to stroke my face and hair, ever so lightly, and my eyelids fluttered closed as I fought the weariness. Finally, I gave into it, and felt myself sink deeper into the soft bed, my body becoming heavier, my breath deepening, thinking about what Emilio may have just said. *Bonita ángel ... rubia ...* Just a few minutes shut eye...

CHAPTER 66

$\mathcal{I}$'d thought it was Emilio's snoring that woke me, but as I lay there on my back, listening to the bang, bang, bang, I realised it was someone at the door. Thump, thump, thump. Louder this time. And, God, I could hear my phone ringing in my bag. What was the time? I sat up and looked around. Oh, bloody hell, it was 3am. How long had I been asleep? Emilio looked like Adonis, but sounded like the God of Thunder. I shook my head and stumbled out of the bedroom, flicking on the table lamp. I walked to the door, yawning, rubbing my eyes, knowing I'd find a pissed-off Andrew on the other side.

But it was Jack, wearing a suit and tie.

'Oh!' I yawned.

He glanced past me. 'Sorry to wake you.'

'Where's Andrew?'

'He's been calling you and knocking on this door for hours.'

'God, really? I didn't hear a thing.'

'He thought breaking it down should be a last resort. Calling me was the second last. He didn't want you in trouble.'

Okay, I was officially guilt-ridden. Emilio's snoring rumbled around the room.

'It's not how it looks,' I said.

'How does it look?'

Bloody hell. 'Hold on.' I ran to get a room key from the coffee table.

Jack stood at the door, holding it open, waiting for me. I pushed past him and he let the door close; we stood in the corridor. I could see Andrew a little way up, standing outside our room. I gave him a little wave, said, 'Sorry, Andrew,' but I wasn't sure if he heard me. He turned and went into our room.

'You were about to tell me what I'm supposed to think of this.' His eyes flicked over me. My skirt was twisted and my T-shirt wrinkled. I couldn't begin to imagine what my hair looked like. I probably had panda eyes.

I said, waving a hand over my clothes and trying to keep the sarcasm from my voice, 'Obviously, I fell asleep. Fully clothed. I'm tired, Jack. Emilio's not easy to work with.'

'Why? What does he want you to do for him?'

'That doesn't deserve a response,' I snapped.

We faced off. He stared into my eyes and I stared right back. I won.

He looked away. 'Maybe you should have an early night.'

'Yes, I should.'

'I needed to see you.'

'What about?'

He glanced around. 'About my suspicions, which are in line with yours.'

'Really? What?'

He lowered his voice. 'We're watching Martin McGann and the Ukrainians. Like you, I think they're involved in some kind of conspiracy. Against Dega and JD.'

'I don't know, Jack. Sounds a bit pathetic to me.'

He leaned away from me. 'I'll ignore that.'

'Whatever.'

He drew a deep breath, choosing to follow his own advice and ignore my barbs. 'The Russian driver called me with a date to check at the Russian club.'

The angry sparks from us both died down.

'The man who employed the Ukrainians,' I said.

'Yes. There was a visit that night from someone who fitted the description the driver gave me.'

'And?'

'The guy works for Martin McGann.'

'Really? And do you think Teresa's involved?'

'I don't know. McGann could be using her for information.'

We stood there for a while. As we looked at each other, I felt the remaining anger drain away. I didn't want to fight with Jack. I wanted us to love each other. At least, love each other physically, if the other type wasn't possible.

'Are you going to Bass Strait?' I said.

'Yes. I need to.'

I didn't want him to. 'I think JD's making it up to get you out of the way so you won't interfere with Emilio's chances.'

Jack's anger clearly hadn't drained away with mine, and he said, 'I'm not an idiot, Erica.' The expression on my face must have touched him, though, because his tone softened when he said, 'I wouldn't be going if I didn't think there was reasonable cause for concern.'

'When will you leave?'

The lift doors opened down the passage. We both watched as Sharon Stone stepped out of it. Killer dress, heels, nipples, etc, and the purportedly drained anger flooded my body, so much so it prickled my skin. She saw me, gave a small, disapproving shake of her head.

Jack held up a finger, 'One minute. Wait downstairs.'

She walked back into the lift without saying something shitty like, *Please* would be nice' (like I would) and before I had a chance to poke my tongue at her. And before I had a chance to say something snarky about Sharon and ask where they'd been, dressed like that, Jack stepped close, forcing me back. He put his hands on the wall either side of my face, leaned in, mouth right next to my ear. 'I believe something is also planned for the tennis. Something that's likely to emerge on Sunday.'

'During the men's finals?'

'I don't know, but I do know I'm not the only one who'd like to never see or hear of Emilio Mendez again.'

Oh, that was just nasty, and within me, a battle was taking place. Weariness, the green-eyed monster and an anger-induced demon fought to take over my body. Together they pushed him back and forced me to say, 'You know this for sure?'

He gave me a long look. 'Nothing proven, no.'

I yawned. 'Okay, well, if there's anything more I need to know, give me a buzz.' I stepped toward Emilio's room.

'What are you doing?'

'Going back in there to get my things, then I'm going to bed with Andrew.'

'No, you're not.' He took my arm.

I tried to snatch it away but he held on.

'Don't tell me what I can and can't do.'

'I'm taking you to my place and you'll stay there with Andrew until this is over.'

'Like hell, Jack. That's not your call. I'm doing my job, which has nothing to do with you.' I struggled to free my arm. This was a place we'd been before. He wasn't used to not getting his way, and the last time we faced off like this, it wasn't pleasant. 'You're hurting me.'

He eased his grip, then released me. 'I'm not arguing with you. Get your things and leave with me now.'

'Or what?'

'Or I'll carry you out of here.'

I stood taller, squared my shoulders. 'Don't threaten me like that.'

'It's not a threat —'

'I'm not yours to boss around. It's just sex with us, right? I'm free to do whatever the hell I want. As are you.' I pointed to the lift. 'You'd better get going. Your other bed-pal's waiting.'

He took a small step back, like he'd been pushed. His chest heaved and he opened his mouth, but nothing came out. He turned and walked away. And I shut my eyes, so tired of it all. Right now I didn't care what JD or Martin McGann or the Russians or anyone wanted or needed or were up to. I let myself back into Emilio's room. He was now sleeping quietly. I walked across the room and stood at the window, the city panorama before me. I leaned my forehead against the glass. One tear plopped onto the floor and I stared at the small, wet circle. I pushed away from the window and looked out, but the view was gone. Instead, my reflection stared back at me and I was intrigued by the sight of it. My hair was a fright. I didn't have mascara panda eyes, but they were smudged with fatigue. My clothes looked like they'd just emerged from a donation bag.

'What are you doing, Erica?'

Reflection Erica rolled her eyes. *Well, your mother bosses you around, your cat bosses you around, your boss treats you like shit, you're letting a man who calls you Emily boss you around. And you've just let your best friend walk out of your life – the one who you* should *let boss you around to keep you safe. That* is *what just happened, isn't it? Jack just walked out of your life?*

I hadn't thought about Jack like that before. *Best friend.* Lucy was my best friend. Wasn't she? Did Jack just walk out of my life? No. Surely not. It's just a misunderstanding that'll work itself out. Right? *Right?*

I raced across the room, snatched up my shoes and bag. I ran for the door, letting it slam behind me, and flew down the corridor. I pushed the elevator button over and over until it arrived. Inside, I tidied myself: put my shoes on, patted down my hair, pulled at the wrinkles in my clothes, wiped under my eyes for any traces of mascara. I checked Reflection Erica in the mirror.

'It's not worth it,' I told her.

She raised an eyebrow.

'All of this. It's not worth losing Jack over.'

She nodded agreement.

At ground level the lift door opened and I shot out of it, scanning the lobby. There was Jack, striding toward the exit. Why was he only just ahead of me? Had he stopped somewhere? I was about to call out to him, run to him, but he stopped by a lounge chair and looked down at the person sitting in it. Sharon Stone stood and I stopped like I'd just run into a wall. I'd forgotten about her. As Jack held the door for her, she glanced over her shoulder and our eyes met, briefly. Sharon carried on through the door, lightly touching Jack's arm as she passed, and together they left the hotel.

CHAPTER 67

*R*ight. No more Miss Nice Guy. Not that I'd been that nice but anyway, I had a job to do. Emilio needed his amulet to win the bloody tennis, and until that happened, nothing else mattered. I stormed into my suite, waking Andrew, who'd been asleep on the rollaway bed.

'Sorry.'

He looked at me.

'I mean, sorry about everything.'

He rolled over and went back to sleep.

I shut the bedroom door and climbed into the giant bed, feeling extra guilty about Andrew in the skinny rollaway that wasn't even long enough for him. My bed could have comfortably fitted three Andrews. I lay there, staring at nothing, planning my raid on Mrs Booth's until dawn glowed through the blinds of my very expensive hotel room. I hoped someone would reimburse me. I'd been thinking it might be Jack but, well, it appeared there was no more Jack.

I SHOWERED, dressed, and watched Andrew do three million push-ups and a few thousand sit-ups, then we ate breakfast. Rather, he ate and I served him.

'More coffee?'

'No, thanks.'

'Corn flakes? Eggs? Toast? There's jam, Vegemite, peanut butter …' I'd ordered everything on the breakfast menu.

'You don't have to do this.'

I sat, sipped my tea. 'I feel really bad.'

'I know.'

'But I can't promise not to piss you off again before this is over.'

'Try not to.'

'You can have the big bed tonight.'

'I don't want it.'

'I insist.'

Andrew shrugged. 'Jack messaged me.'

I stopped breathing. 'Oh?'

'He told me to forget the plan about taking you to his house until the tournament's over.'

'Really. Well, I wouldn't have gone, anyway.'

'What's happening with you two?'

Tears pricked my eyes. Crap. I wiped them. 'Nothing. As in, nothing further is happening between us. Ever.'

Andrew shook his head. The hotel phone rang and I answered it. It was Emilio, wanting me to come and entertain him. He was bored.

I told him, 'I have a certain mission to accomplish, remember?'

'You will get it today?'

'I'll try, but if not, I know I can definitely get it tomorrow morning.'

He sighed, and huffed into the phone.

'What are you doing today?' I said.

'I will rest. Watch the television. Try to take my mind off things.'

'Sounds like a plan.'

We hung up.

I said to Andrew, who'd finished his scrambled eggs, fried eggs, fruit salad, four pieces of vegemite toast and was now eyeing off the tiny box of Coco Pops, 'I'm going to be honest with you.'

'About fucking time.' He looked up, regret in his eyes.

'I deserved that.'

He snorted a laugh. 'Yeah, you did.'

I sat opposite him. 'I found the real lucky charm. It's in a house behind my mother's.'

'How the hell —'

'Long story, but I need to get it back, so I'm going to do it some time between now and tomorrow afternoon.'

He popped the last piece of crust in his mouth, sat back, tossed his napkin on the table. 'I probably can't let you do that.'

'I thought you might say that.'

'Tell me where the thing is and I'll get it.'

I thought I might kiss him. How come Jack wouldn't offer to do that? Because he doesn't want Emilio to win the tournament? Because he's a meanie? 'I should probably also say that I can't let you do that, but in reality, I'd love you to do that for me.'

He nodded.

'We could go to my mother's today, wait and see if there's an opportunity.'

'Your mother knows about me?'

'She thinks you're my chauffeur. She might ask you to drive her somewhere.'

'As long as you're with me, I'll take her wherever she wants.' Andrew stood. 'Thanks for breakfast. I'm going for a shower.'

'Okay.'

'Should I wear camouflage?' he said.

'You need camouflage for roses and camellias.'

'Who lives there?'

'An old lady and her daughter. We can't do it if they're home.'

'I can't promise no damage.'

'As long as the damage isn't to them, I don't care.'

. . .

WHILE ANDREW WAS in the shower, I went to visit Emilio.

As I approached his door, it opened and Sharon Stone stepped out.

'What are you doing?' I said.

She glanced over her shoulder. 'Checking on my charge.'

'I thought you were going to Bass Strait with Jack.'

'We're leaving in the morning.'

Oh. Which meant Jack was available all day today to see me. But I knew I wouldn't hear from him. 'Okay, well, fly safely.'

She nodded and walked away. And was that another bloody smirk?

I knocked on Emilio's door. He flung it open, wearing his undies, a big smile on his face.

'Ah, it is Emily!'

'Who were you expecting?'

'What are you doing?'

'Visiting you.'

'But I thought —'

'We're about to leave.'

Then Andrew was walking up the passageway, dressed neck to toe in black, hands held out, palms up. 'What part of "with me twenty-four-seven" don't you get?'

'Oops. Sorry.'

I said goodbye to Emilio and we left.

BACK IN CHADSTONE, I introduced Mum to Andrew the chauffeur.

'Perhaps Andrew could run me to the pharmacy? Your father needs cream for his anal issues.'

'Maybe later.' I said.

'I've made scones. Would you like one, Andrew?'

'Um, Andrew wants to see Dad's vegie patch.'

'You know where it is.' Mum waved her hand. 'Your father's pruning.'

We headed for the back door and Mum called after us, 'Why are you taking binoculars?'

'Andrew studies insects in his spare time.'

We stepped through the vegie patch. 'Hi, Dad.' I introduced him to Andrew.

Dad grunted, they shook hands, and we continued on to the fence.

Andrew whispered, 'What will your parents think we're doing?'

'They already think I'm weird. Don't worry.'

'You *are* weird,' he muttered, and I gave him a poke.

Andrew stood on the bottom rail of the fence and looked into Mrs Booth's, binoculars scanning the house.

'It's in the bedroom, upstairs on the left.'

The binoculars flicked up. 'Where in the bedroom?'

'Hanging over the mirror on the dressing table. It's padlocked, but I reckon you'd be able to snap the chain.'

'Window's open up there.' Binoculars flicked down. 'Woman in the kitchen, around sixty. Someone watching TV. Can only see the back of a head.' He handed me the binocs. 'I'm going in.'

'What? You can't!'

Andrew sprang over the fence. I turned and gave Dad a smile and a shrug. Dad scratched his head and went inside. I wondered what he'd say to Mum. He'd probably distract her so she wouldn't know what we were up to. Good old Dad.

By the time I'd worked up the courage to peek, Andrew's feet were disappearing through Ruth's bedroom window. I had instant heart palpitations and felt faint. I sat on the ground, my back to the fence. Axle appeared and crawled onto my lap. 'Bloody hell, Axle. What am I doing?'

He gave a meow, head-butted my boob, which I assumed meant he loves me, no matter how outrageous I am and how neglectful I'd been as a mother. Or it could have meant: Goodbye, you idiot. He jumped over the fence.

I stood again and trained the binoculars on the lower part of the house. I saw Mrs Booth leave her kitchen, walk through the living area and disappear to the front of the house. Where the stairs were. Oh crap, oh crap. I looked up at Ruth's bedroom window. Andrew appeared, quickly, and slid down the trellis. He stayed pressed against the wall of the house. I saw Mrs Booth in Ruth's window. I ducked down, and peeped through a hole in the fence. Mrs Booth turned her head, said something, then slammed the window shut. Andrew crept along the side fence, and then, silently, he was next to me.

'How'd you go?'

'Thing's gone,' he said.

'What? Did you look on the mirror? Behind the mirror? On the dressing table?'

'As much as I could. The old woman came.'

I sat on the ground again. What to do? What to do?

We had scones with Mum. She chatted nonstop, but I didn't hear a word she said. It must be in there. It must! If not in there, then *on* one of them. Mrs Booth or Ruth. What to do?

'What time's church tomorrow?' I asked Mum.

'Nine thirty, same as every other week.' She gave Andrew a look, a little shake of her head. 'If she came with us more often, she'd know what time.'

We drove Mum to the pharmacy for Dad's anal cream, then Andrew and I headed back to the hotel.

On the way, I said, 'Thanks for going in there.'

'No worries.'

'It was really nice of you.'

'Sorry I didn't find it.' He gave me a stern Jack look. 'But that's it. No more. You're not going back there.'

Oh yes, I am. But I nodded, let him see the resignation on my face. 'And it's nice of you to drop everything to look after me for a few days.'

He shrugged. 'It's my job.'

'Have you ...' I glanced at him. 'Have you got someone waiting? At home?'

He hesitated, staring out the windscreen. 'Yeah.'

'Is she —'

'He.'

'Oh.'

We didn't say anything for a minute, and the car was so silent with no radio. Without looking at me, Andrew said, 'You okay with that?'

'Of course. In fact, considering our current arrangements —'

'Better.'

'Yeah.'

I watched out the window, and Andrew turned on the radio, keeping the volume low.

'Does, um, does Jack know?' I said.

'Yep.' He chuckled. 'Probably why I got this assignment.'

'Yeah.' I laughed. And then, because we were getting all honest and cosy, 'I know I don't deserve your respect, but ... but why did you tell Jack about my conversation with Emilio in the restaurant? He knew what we'd been saying.'

'Because Jack needs a kick up the arse.'

His candour shocked me, but also made me smile. 'In what way?'

'He wants to be with you, Erica. He just doesn't seem to know how to say it.'

I shook my head. 'No, Jack doesn't do commitment.'

'He *thinks* he doesn't. I've known Jack a long time. I see the way he is when he's with you ...' Andrew took a breath and blew it out. 'The guy needs a wake-up call. Or he'll lose you.'

I bowed my head, watched my hands wringing themselves in my lap. 'Too late.'

Emilio wanted me to have dinner with him in his room, but I didn't trust either Emilio or me. He might want to cuddle on the sofa, wearing nothing but magnificently fitting, well-filled undies. After the way he'd looked at me with those smoking eyes the other day, and the way he'd *looked* full stop ... With no-one watching, standing in front of the mirror in my bathroom, I was able to give myself a full face slap, followed by a lecture. 'Erica. You love Jack.' It was true. I did love him. But I thought, with a great weighty sadness, that we were probably through. Not that we were really together, anyway. We kind of were. No, we weren't. I thought about what Andrew had said, and decided he was wrong.

I asked Andrew if he'd have dinner with us in Emilio's room.

'I'm happy to wait outside.'

'No, I *really* want you in there with me.' I gave him a pleading look, and he nodded once.

I called Emilio to warn him that Andrew would be dining with us, in case he was planning on wearing only undies. He answered the door wearing only undies, waved us in, and Andrew gave me a look that said, *Really?*

'Are you getting dressed, Emilio?'

'I am comfortable.' He waved at the sofa. 'Please, I have ordered food. Let us relax.' He added, 'Feel free to undress. I do not mind.'

I'D WONDERED why Emilio hadn't kicked up a fuss about Andrew being there with us, but during dinner on our laps I discovered why. There was an SBS special on Emilio Mendez. We watched the story, which included footage of Emilio's finest moments. Fortunately, Emilio could only be comfortable in an armchair, leaning forward, elbows on knees, fully focused on the screen. He admired his beauty and talent, looking to me for validation, and I was sure I heard Andrew utter, 'Wanker.'

At the end of that show, I stood. 'You have a big day tomorrow, Emilio.'

'*Si*. It is a big day.'

I asked Andrew to give us a minute. He stepped through the door, letting it close.

With my hands on his shoulders, I kissed Emilio's cheek. 'Goodnight, sweet, brave, number-one seed. This time tomorrow you'll be the best player in the world!'

He smiled. 'Yes, I think it is true.'

'With so much money!'

He smiled more broadly. 'Yes, that is true also. I will be very happy, this time tomorrow.'

'Good.'

'Because I will have *mi amuleto*.'

'Ah, yes. Yes, you will.'

'And I will have the sexual activity.' He gave me a wink and a naughty smile and adjusted his undies. I backed away before something came over me and I forgot what I was supposed to do. Or what I wasn't supposed to do.

'I'll see you tomorrow.' I blew him a kiss and rushed out the door.

Andrew was standing there. I fanned my face.

'I get it,' he said.

'Thank you.'

And together my new friend and I went home to bed. When Andrew opened the door, I ran across the room and dived onto the rollaway. 'Mine.'

'No.'

'Yes.'

He planted his fists on his hips. I pretended to be asleep, with loud, theatrical snoring.

'Okay.' He disappeared into the bedroom.

I stayed on the rollaway bed until I was satisfied Andrew was tucked up in the big one. I didn't want any fights or arguments about who'd be in which bed because I planned on sneaking out in the morning well before he woke.

CHAPTER 69

I left at 4am. I had to go that early in case Andrew woke up and caught me. He wouldn't have let me go. He would have handcuffed me and taken me to Jack's house. I needed to do it without him. I just didn't know how yet.

I nicked Andrew's car keys, left a note with a huge apology and promises to make it up to him 'for the rest of my life'. I said I was going to see Jack because I was worried that our (so-called) relationship was over. Andrew wouldn't believe me, not really, but I thought it might delay him.

I drove to Chadstone and parked at the end of a leafy cul-de-sac about half a kilometre from Mum's house. I set the alarm on my phone and went back to sleep. There was no point getting ahead of myself. Mrs Booth wouldn't leave for church until around 8:30 or later. I still hadn't decided what to do if Ruth was home.

At six, Andrew called me. I didn't answer and felt really bad. He left a voicemail and I listened: 'C'mon, friend, don't do this to me.' He sounded hurt and worried. It made me cry.

I couldn't go back to sleep; instead I put my phone on silent and sat there staring at the windscreen, listening to the chirping birds. My phone rang a few more times. I didn't look to see who was calling and at 8:30, I turned it off.

In my breaking-and-entering outfit, I trotted down the road, looking over my shoulder, to Mrs Booth's street. I wondered if Andrew had already been there to try to find me. If he had, I wondered how he got there. Nicked a car? I snuck up Mrs Booth's driveway, peeked in the garage. Her car was gone but an old Toyota was there. Bugger.

What to do now? Only one thing. Knock on the door, say, 'Hi, Ruth. Remember me? The one who laughed about you behind your back when we were kids? That's right, the arsehole who lived behind … oh, you do remember …' But what would she do? Invite me in? What would I do once in there? I couldn't just go hunting around the house.

I knocked on the door, deciding to just wing it. If she didn't let me in, then I'd have to think of something else. Set the house on fire or something. There was no answer. I waited, knocked, waited, knocked. It occurred to me then that Ruth might have gone to church with her mother. She might not even be home. I went around the back, looked up at her bedroom window. Wind whistled through the hole in the basement doors. It wasn't windy. I shivered, and stepped onto the trellis.

Ruth's bedroom window was open. With my fingers over the sill, I peered inside, listening. Nothing. 'Hello?' I called out, without thinking what I'd do if someone responded. But there was only silence. I slipped in through the window, landing with a thump on the floor. There was a sudden movement and I gasped, hand over my mouth. Minx the cat appeared. 'It's only you, Minx.' I gave her a pat. 'You're not so scary, really.'

'Oh, but *I* am,' said a voice from the door.

CHAPTER 70

I froze, but didn't look up. I wanted to compose myself, come up with a reasonable explanation as to why I was sitting on the floor in Ruth's bedroom, patting her mother's cat. I cleared my throat, and looked up. 'Hi … Charlotte? Charlotte!'

Charlotte Johnson stood there in the doorway of Ruth Booth's bedroom, wearing my high heels, my wig, a dress that looked suspiciously like mine, and carrying a gun that also looked suspiciously like mine. And which she was pointing at me. Emilio's lucky charm was, of course, around her neck. I stood slowly, hands raised, keeping my eyes on the gun.

'Charlotte, what are you doing here?'

She spat a laugh. 'I'm not *Charlotte*, you idiot.'

'Then ... oh my God!'

'I'm Ruth fucking Booth, remember? The one you laughed at and spied on over your stupid fence.'

'You look so different!'

She turned her head, ran a finger down her straight nose. 'Do you like it? It's new.'

'You've had plastic surgery?'

'Yep.' She glared at me. 'Do you remember how horrible you were? Not Steve. He was nice.'

'I thought he was just as horrible as me.'

'No way! You were so mean.'

'You were a bit weird back then, Ruth.'

'Don't call me Ruth!'

'Sorry.' Oh my God. *Oh my God!*

'Don't you want to know my plans?'

No. Not if they involve burying me in the basement. 'So that *is* my wig,' I said by way of distraction.

'It is not! Okay, it might be. I found it in a rubbish bin.'

'At the tennis?'

'Yeah.'

'It's mine.'

She laughed. 'Who cares! Mine now, stupid. And I'm going to —'

Just then I heard the front door open and close. 'Yoo hoo!' Mrs Booth was home. Footsteps came up the stairs.

Ruth was delighted. 'Perfect!'

'Don't come up here, Mrs Booth!'

Too late. She appeared at the door, staring at Ruth, then at me. She looked Ruth up and down, at the gun in her hand.

'Oh, for goodness' sake, Ruthie, what now?'

'Don't call me Ruthie!'

Mrs Booth tsked and rolled her eyes, just like my mother does if I leave the fridge door open. 'I had a feeling you were planning something today.'

Ruth spat, 'What kind of parents call their daughter Ruth Booth? Huh? Horrible ones, that's what kind!'

'It's not nice to point guns at people, Ru— sweetheart.'

'Don't talk!'

Jack, Jack, where are you now? In Bass Strait? Andrew, why didn't I bring you with me? Why didn't I listen to you? Why didn't I listen to my mother and go to church?

Which reminded me. 'How are my parents getting home?' I said to Mrs Booth.

'Mr Bennett will bring them.'

'Old Mr Bennett? Is he okay to drive?'

'Hello?' said Ruth. 'We're supposed to be talking about *me*!'

Mrs Booth and I shut our mouths.

Ruth waved the gun. It didn't look like the safety switch was on. 'Now, listen up.' She poked Mrs Booth. 'You, Mummy dearest, are going into the basement where you'll die.'

Oh, goody, the basement.

'And *you* …' she pointed at me, '… are going with my mother and I'm going with yours.'

'What do you mean?'

'I'm taking your life, Erica Jewell. Your job, which is pretty much mine anyway 'cause you're shit at it —'

'I am not! You hid my filing and copied my media release!'

'Whoop-dee-do, big deal. Maybe I should let you live so you can do my filing. Anyway, I'm taking your house, which I reckon will be nice after the renovation, and your boyfriend —'

'You leave Jack alone!'

'Not *Jack*, stupid. I don't want *Jack*.'

'You mean Emilio?'

She cackled a long laugh.

Mrs Booth said, 'You can't just go taking over people's lives, Ru — sweetie.'

'Don't call me sweetie!'

'Well, what can I call you?'

'Call me Erica. Erica Jewell. That's who I am now. Besides, I'm through with you, weird old woman.'

'I've tried to be less weird, Ru — swee — Erica. I've tried very hard, as you can see.' She looked around the room to prove her point, and, now that I knew what was going on, I could see that Ruth's bedroom looked very much like mine, but a tidy version. And, come to think of it, Mrs Booth's bedroom was a lot like my own parents'.

'Too late! I'm getting real parents. Proper, normal ones. A *father*. I'm going to be Mr and Mrs Jewell's daughter from now on. They love me.'

'They're not normal,' I said.

'Shut up!' Ruth stepped back, waved the gun. 'Come on, you two, down to the basement.'

'Um, can we go somewhere else? Like, tie us to the railway line?'

'Nope, the basement. Move!'

Mrs Booth and I walked ahead of Ruth, down the stairs with hands raised, past the front door to the basement door. Mrs Booth opened the door, flicked on the light, and I followed her down to the place that nightmares are made of. Actually, it wasn't so bad. There was normal kind of stuff there. Storage cupboards. An old wardrobe that would probably be a bit spooky in the dark. But no bodies, from what I could see. There were two chairs and some rope. I could see where this was going.

Ruth tied us up. Chairs back to back, some distance between us. That's okay, I thought. We'll get away, eventually. Someone will come. It will be alright.

'What are you doing over there, um, Erica?' said Mrs Booth.

Ruth was fiddling in the corner, by the hot water system. She crouched low, reaching behind it. She stood and smiled at us. 'Smell that?'

I sniffed. 'No.'

'You will. Soon you'll smell the gas.' She clapped her hands. 'Oh, this is fun! Wish I could stick around to watch you burn.' She checked her watch. 'But I've got a tennis match to stop. Ta ta!' At the top of the basement stairs, Ruth lit a candle.

Gas. Candle. I wondered what would happen. I wondered how long it would take for it to happen.

Where had Ruth gone now? To Emilio? To watch him play? No, she said she had a tennis game to *stop*. But he wouldn't be able to play anyway if I wasn't there with his precious amulet. Oh, shit. I *will* be there with his precious amulet!

I heard Mrs Booth's chair shuffling around. 'Stupid girl,' she said.

CHAPTER 71

$\mathcal{A}$s I tried to free my hands, I apologised to Mrs Booth. 'When I was a kid, I thought you were a witch.' I didn't mention that, up until half an hour ago, I thought she still was.

'That's alright, Erica. Admittedly, I thought I was a witch, too. I thought I had special powers that could stop my husband running off and that could turn my daughter into a decent human being.'

Mrs Booth grunted.

'What are you doing?' I said.

'Nearly there.'

Mrs Booth appeared in front of me, hands untied.

'How did you do that?' I said as she tugged at the ropes on my wrists.

'Ruthie was a shocker at Girl Scouts, don't you remember?'

'Ah, no. I avoided Ruth at Girl Scouts. Sorry.'

'She used to practise her knot tying on me. Even back then I worried about her. She seemed to get much pleasure out of tying me up. There,' she said, and I released my hands. I rubbed my wrists but they didn't really need rubbing; there hadn't been enough time for any damage or rope burn or anything like that.

'I can smell the gas now. The candle!'

I rushed across the room to the stairs but too late! A flash of blue ignited the space above the candle. A wave of flame rippled across the ceiling.

We ran like frightened rabbits, back and forth, not knowing where to go. The stairwell to the interior of the house was now blocked by fire but the door was locked, anyway.

'Mrs Booth! Where are the stairs outside?'

She pointed. 'Behind that old wardrobe.'

We rushed at it, pushing, grunting from the effort. The wardrobe crashed forward. The internal door, with stairs behind it, was locked.

'Oh, fuck!' yelled Mrs Booth and smacked a hand over her mouth. 'Excuse me!'

'Where's the key?'

'My husband has it!'

'Where is he?'

'Who knows! With Mrs Smith?'

The burning ceiling closed in on us. Bits of it fell. Holes appeared above us, the timber frame exposed. Flames were directly above the hot-water service, the source of the gas.

'Can we shut off the gas?' shouted Mrs Booth.

'Too late!' There were tools at the end of the basement – an axe – and I rushed to get it. 'Stay low! Below the smoke!'

I swung the axe at the basement doors. It bounced off. I swung again, with more gusto. A crack appeared in the door. A shock zapped up my arm and I dropped the axe. There was a small explosion behind me. The whoosh of something big igniting. The storage cupboards. I picked up the axe, swung with all my might. A hole appeared. The rush of air fanned the ceiling flames and the heat intensified. More pieces of ceiling fell around us. I swung and chopped. The hole opened up. Mrs Booth screamed. I threw the axe away and we pulled at bits of splintered door, opening the hole wide enough to climb through.

'Go!' I gasped, shoving Mrs Booth at the hole.

I followed her through, up the stairs and onto the back lawn, coughing, swiping at the cobwebs on my face.

'We can't stay here.' I took Mrs Booth's hand and we ran around the side of the house to the front.

Neighbours were gathering. Some were on their phones, taking photos or making calls. Smoke poured from the basement windows. I heard sirens. 'Everybody get ba —' A mighty explosion ripped through my words. Pieces of Mrs Booth's house fell around us. We ran up the street.

'Minx! Oh, my Minx!' Mrs Booth stopped running.

I took her arm. 'Nothing you can do, Mrs Booth.' She started crying. 'Nothing you can do,' I soothed, leading her gently forward, hoping like hell Axle hadn't been in there, too.

As we rounded the corner into my street, I could see Mum, Dad and old Mr Bennett standing out the front of Mum and Dad's, watching the spectacle behind it. Mum held Minx in her arms, and Axle sat on Mr Bennett's wheelie walker. Mrs Booth rushed at them.

'Minx! Minx!' She took Minx from Mum, crying and hugging.

Mum said to me, 'Did your company cause that explosion?'

'Not this time.'

I needed to get to Emilio but I had nothing. Ruth had taken my bag with Andrew's car keys, my phone, wallet, everything. I needed a car.

'Um, Mr Bennett, can I borrow your car?'

'Erica!' said Mum. 'That's inappropriate.'

Mr Bennett said, 'I can drive you, lassie.'

'Oh, really, I'm in a hurry.'

Mr Bennett turned his walker and Axle jumped off. 'Where do you want to go?' He shuffled across the road to his old blue Commodore.

I looked around for options. What options? If I waited for a taxi, I didn't have money to pay for it anyway. Dad wouldn't give me money – I'd learned that when I was sixteen. And his car was broken. Not that he'd loan it to me anyway.

Mr Bennett arrived at his car. He struggled to open the boot.

'Here, let me help.' I rushed across the road and hooked my fingers under the boot, pushing it up.

Mr Bennett slowly folded his walker. He tried to lift it.

'Here.' I tried to take one side.

'I can manage.'

'Really, I can help.' I didn't give him a choice, snatching up the walker and chucking it in the boot. 'I'll drive if you want.'

'No-one drives old Milly but me.' He wobbled to the driver's door.

By the time he sat in the car, I was buckled in and chewing my fingernails. Maybe I should help him with his seat belt; God, he even did that slowly. Pulled the seat belt like moving fast might detonate something. It was like no part of his body knew how to do something faster than a snail would. I tried to help him with the buckle but he smacked my hand away. I could feel the anxiety growing in my chest. I clasped my hands in my lap, stared out the window, and watched the grass grow.

Mr Bennett started the car. He indicated, checked his rear-view and side mirrors, looked over his shoulder, wound down the window and called out goodbye to Mum and Dad, wound up the window, checked his rear- and side-view mirrors, looked over his shoulder, and pulled away from the kerb.

'Where to, lassie?'

'Rod Laver Arena.'

'Eh?'

'Rod Laver Arena.'

'Eh?'

'The tennis.'

'Eh?'

I put my hands around my mouth and leaned close. 'The tennis!'

He gave me a dirty look, leaned away. 'No need for shouting.'

I continued shouting, but from my side of the car, 'Actually, you can just drop me on Dandenong Road and I'll get a cab. Except I'll need to borrow the cab fare.'

'I can take you all the way. You can pay me later.'

Mr Bennett drove at 50 kilometres per hour in the right-hand lane of Dandenong Road, which has a speed limit of 80 kilometres per hour. Every second car that passed us blew its horn. The driver of every third car screamed abuse at us. Mr Bennett turned on his radio. Elevator music twinkled out of it.

'If you turn up here,' I pointed, 'we can join the Monash Freeway. It'll be much quicker.'

'Not paying those thieving bastards.'

'You mean the tolls? I'll pay for them.'

'Nope.'

'But ...' What was the point? Mr Bennett's saggy old jaw was set.

'You can go in the left lane if you want, Mr Bennett. We don't have to turn for ages.'

Mr Bennett indicated and slowly moved across three lanes of traffic to the left. He checked his mirrors first, but by the time he'd done that and finally made a move, cars were on top of him, screeching, braking, honking and abusing. I sank low in my seat.

It took well over an hour to get to the tennis because Mr Bennett wanted to avoid the tolls on the Monash, and he chose to drive up Chapel Street, the most awesome shopping mecca in all of the universe (next to Chaddy) and where 90% of Australia's population currently was. I had a go at an out-of-body experience, but it's hard to do with the distractions of Chapel Street. The anxiety grew, and I tried to calm myself. To think. What did Ruth say? She was going to stop a tennis match. How would she do that? By luring Emilio with his lucky charm. And that would work, I knew. I checked my watch. Emilio might have gone to the stadium by now. I thought I'd go there first, and if he wasn't there I could track back to his hotel from that point. Maybe Emilio and Ruth were having herbal tea in his room. Maybe they were in the shower together. Good luck to them, I thought, then retracted that. No, I didn't want Emilio to have a shower with Ruth Booth. Emilio wanted to have a shower with me. Just me. Not that I was going to have a shower with Emilio, of course, but it was nice to think I was special to him. I slapped my face and Mr Bennett stared at me.

'There was a mosquito.'

I wondered where Jack was. I wondered where Andrew was. I wondered if they'd been trying to call me. I wondered if Ruth had answered their calls and pretended to be me: 'Erica Jewell speaking ... oh, hi, Jack... no, I'm fine, you go to Bass Strait with Sharon ... Why don't you stay a few extra days? Go on to Tassie and have a romantic time at their wineries …'

By the time we got there, I'd already decided my life was over. Possibly also Emilio's life was over, and maybe Jack's, too. His helicopter might crash in Bass Strait. Mum and Dad's life would be over, too, if they had to bury their daughter. Although, with their new, improved, fake daughter, they might recover and carry on.

I wanted Mr Bennett to park out the front of Rod Laver so I could just jump out, but he insisted on finding legal parking.

'But I'm just going to jump out, Mr Bennett. You can pull up *right here.*'

He crawled past the taxi parking area and drove up Swan Street. I knew there was no legal parking. I knew he'd drive for another hour, trying to find some. The lights changed to red and I pushed open the door before he stopped.

'Thanks heaps, Mr Bennett.' I jumped from the moving vehicle. He was going so slowly I was able to run alongside his car to shut the door.

I ran around the back to the players' entrance. I didn't have my pass. I knew the guy at the door.

'Can you let me in?'

'No, sorry.'

'Please? It's a matter of life —'

'Erica! Oh, thank God, you're here!' Teresa came rushing forward and I took a big step back. She took my arm and pulled me inside, past the protesting security guy. 'Please. I can't find Emilio. He's not at the hotel. He's not here!'

'What have you done with him?' I said but I already knew what had happened. Ruth got to him first.

'I have done nothing! Nothing! Why do you say this?' She stared at me, incredulous and hurt.

I took a big breath. 'When did you last see him?'

'Last night.' Teresa sobbed. 'Oh, *mi carino*, where could he be?'

I put my hands on her arms. 'We'll find him, don't worry.'

Teresa led me through the corridors. 'Let us check his dressing room.'

'Wait. You haven't checked there?'

'Not yet.'

Teresa became suddenly calm as she tried to convince me to walk with her through the smattering of people in the passageway. 'Come along, Erica. We must hurry!'

I held back. With the tournament nearly done, the behind-the-scenes crowds had thinned substantially. I followed Teresa, but at a distance. She entered Emilio's dressing room. There was no security guard at the door, and there should have been. The hair on the back of my neck stood up. From the open doorway, Teresa called to me. 'Come along, Erica.'

I went to turn away, to run, but from behind, someone shoved me through the dressing room door. Inside was the tall, fat man from the boat. Martin McGann's friend. And his buddy, who'd pushed me from behind, Mr Short and Thin. The men from the lunch heist. And Teresa.

'What are you doing —' I started but Tall and Fat rushed at me.

I jerked back. Teresa stopped me with her arms around my shoulders. I spun out of her grip, turned on her, fists raised. I stepped in to fight her but a blow to the back of my head sent me reeling. I lay on the ground, counting the feet around me. I tried to lift myself but I suddenly weighed more. My vision blurred, and, just before lights out, I heard Teresa say, 'She does not know where he is.'

CHAPTER 72

$\mathcal{A}$n engine rumbled and I opened my eyes. Whoa, bad headache. All around me was blackness, with a few pinpricks of light. I stretched, but didn't get far. My legs were curled against my chest, arms folded in front of me. I pushed out with all my limbs. Whatever I was in was mildly stretchy. I held back the panic. There was a pain in my back and with my arm around my middle I felt behind. I fingered the taut criss-cross strings of a tennis racquet. I was in a tennis bag? What else was in here? A soft thing. A towel. Water bottle. Something small, square, hard. Phone. When I picked it up and pressed buttons the light almost blinded me in the darkness of the bag. The screen showed a keypad. I needed a security code. I pressed 0-0-0-0. Ha. Lazy phone owner.

The engine noise changed and grew louder. There were sloshing water noises. I rocked in the bag. I was in a boat? The bag tipped. I rolled forward and my face pressed into something smelly. Sweaty undies was my guess. I turned my head, took a breath, clamped my hand over my mouth to muffle the cough. I dialled my favourite number.

CHAPTER 73

Jack Jones, my beloved, answered my call for help with, 'Emilio.'

'What?'

'Who —'

'It's me.'

Through the phone I could hear the *whup whup whup* of chopper blades.

'Erica? I can't hear you! Where the hell are you? You're with Mendez?'

'No,' I said. 'Is this his phone?'

'For fuck's sake, Andrew's got the police looking for you. Did your parents' house burn down?'

'No, that was Mrs Booth's.'

'Where are you?'

'Are you worried about me?'

'Of course I'm fucking worried! We're heading back.'

'Good, can you hurry?'

'Where —'

'I'm on a boat, and I think I must be on the Yarra. In a tennis bag.'

'*What?* Where's Mendez?'

'I don't know, but I'm pretty sure he's with Ruth – Charlotte. She's got my gun.'

'Jesus Christ.' He shouted instructions to someone.

'We were right about Tere —' Someone kicked my shin so hard I howled and dropped the phone.

The bag was unzipped. Mr Tall and Fat dragged me by the hair. Second time he'd done that to me – grabbed my hair – but this time it wasn't coming off. I clung to his wrist with both hands and he dumped me on the floor, next to Mr Shorty, who was driving the boat and who glanced down at me.

Fatty said something in whatever language. Shorty pushed the throttle; the boat's nose rose high and we surged forward. I lost my balance, rolled backward and landed against the wall of the small cabin. I sat there, trying not to be noticed, and through the window I could see the tops of Southbank buildings whizzing by. The upstairs restaurants with diners on the verandas. One of those was probably where Jack had taken me for dinner the other week. And Emilio. I wished I was sitting there now in a crisp white sundress with a glass of champagne, talking about the tennis and how exciting it was going to be. Not very exciting if the star of the show didn't show. And even if he was saved from Ruth Booth and made it in time to play in the men's finals, he wouldn't be able to play without me there, would he?

I watched Docklands sail past. We were headed for the bay.

Then, as if reading my mind, Fatty said in loud, clear English, 'She said put in ocean with shark.' He grinned down at me.

Sweet Mother Teresa. What was her problem? Why did she want to get rid of Emilio? I mean, I understood where Martin McGann was coming from. He despised JD and wanted to bring him down in any way he could: humiliation, PR terrorism, probably even murder. I wouldn't trust Mr McGann any more than I'd trust his stinky, nasty son. Was Teresa bonking him? Maybe he was paying her for information. But she loved Emilio. Or so I'd thought. Obviously not. He could be pretty annoying, admittedly.

I wondered how far away Jack was. He might have been all the way out in Bass Strait when I called him. He might be hours, I realised, when I heard that beautiful helicopter sound. *Whup whup whup.* Fatty and Shorty peered through the windows, and so did I. Couldn't see a thing. Where was it? And then, like some magical, mystical creature, the chopper appeared in front of us; it spun, faced us, and hovered a couple of metres above the waterline. It was one of those black military ones.

I heard the loudspeaker. 'We are armed. Stop the vessel.' It sounded like Joe.

We were close to the river mouth, Williamstown on the right. Shorty made a wide U-turn at full speed. I rolled to the side, the various pains in my body screaming, head pounding. Fatty and Shorty were fully focused on the helicopter, now in pursuit. I crawled to the back deck and jumped up and down, arms flapping.

The helicopter came alongside. Fatty had me again now, holding me in front of him with an arm around my throat, gun at my head; his human shield. Was the gun loaded? I didn't want to find out.

Jack sat on the floor in the open door of the helicopter, one leg hanging. He had a rifle at his shoulder, aimed at Fatty. Or it could have been aimed at me. Maybe he was that pissed off. The boat sped along and the helicopter kept pace. Jack sat motionless, not taking his eye from the rifle's sight. Fatty's arm tightened around my neck; my breath was a shallow wheeze. I couldn't get air. I clawed at Fatty's arm. My head throbbed. Jelly legs. Jack got blurry. The helicopter sound faded; someone had turned down the volume. I sank against the big man holding me. And then, as I slipped lower, Fatty dropped beside me and I was free. I sucked in air and rolled away from him. Fatty screamed and writhed on the deck. I saw the blood run away from him, lots of it.

I lurched upright and fell into the water. All strength in my body was gone. The concussion, the pain, the lack of air ... I splashed around like a puppy, not getting anywhere, watching the boat make another U-turn and head back my way. I watched the bow grow bigger and resigned myself to my horrible fate.

Something hit the water next to me and pulled me down. The breath exploded out of me. I flailed for the light. Strong arms held me under. I felt the shudder of the boat's motor; the force from the blades thrashed my hair, jerked my head. Then it was gone. Together we broke the river surface and I gulped in great lungfuls of air as Jack held me up from behind.

I coughed, gasped. 'Where's the boat?'

'Joe's got it. You're safe. You're alright.'

I turned in his arms so I could throw mine around him. I wrapped my legs around his waist and he kicked his to keep us afloat.

The helicopter was over us again, line swinging from it. Jack held me with one arm and lunged for the line with the other. He strapped me to a harness, talking to me while he did it, 'You're okay ... nearly over ...' and we were in the air, swinging. A police boat sped up the river, passed under us. There were more sirens from somewhere. Then we were in the helicopter. I flopped onto the floor. Jack released me, sat me on the seat, fixed my seat belt, and was back at the door. I peered through the window. We were over the baddies' boat. The police were there. I wondered if Mr Fatty would be alright. He was probably thinking Ukraine was a better option than Melbourne, after all. Joe was down there, and then a minute later Joe was in the helicopter. He gave me thumbs up, and sat next to Sharon. The helicopter lifted quickly and shot forward. Sharon looked over her shoulder at me. 'Hey.'

'Hey.' I went all blushy and girly. Sharon looked so sexy there, flying the helicopter with her headphones and RayBan sunglasses, chewing gum like they do in the movies.

'Hello?' It was Jack, sitting with his arm around me.

'Sorry, what did you say?'

'Are you alright?'

'Headache.'

He gave me a squeeze.

'Ouch.'

He stared at my face.

'Why are you looking at me like that?'

'You're alright?' he said, again.

'Apart from the headache, yes, I think so.' I searched his face. Something else was wrong. 'What aren't you telling me?'

He leaned close, put his mouth right next to my ear so I could hear above the helicopter noise. 'I got a call from Steve.'

'My Steve? What about?'

'He's found Emilio.'

I pulled back so I could see Jack's face. 'Where?'

He spoke but I couldn't hear. It looked like he said, 'Your house.'

I put my ear to his mouth again. 'What?'

'Your house. Charlotte has him there.'

'Do you know if he's alright?'

'Yes. Police are there. We'll get you to the hospital and I'll go.'

'I'm coming with you.'

'Erica —'

I glared at him.

'We'll see.'

WE LANDED in Gosch's Paddock, where Jack's Merc and a motorbike were parked. Sharon was out of the helicopter before the rest of us. She took off on the motorbike.

Jack frowned after her. 'What the hell's she doing?'

Andrew was there, leaning on Jack's car, arms folded across his chest. Behind his sunglasses, I couldn't see his eyes, but I knew what he might be thinking. I hid behind Jack.

'You can't hide forever,' Andrew called.

I clung to the back of Jack's wet T-shirt, and when he side-stepped, I went with him.

'You need to face Andrew.' He turned, and I released his shirt. 'He'll take you to the hospital.'

'No.'

'Yes.'

'I'm not sick!'

'No argument.'

Jack hugged me, kissed my face ten times. 'I need to go.'

He told Joe to wait with the helicopter and jogged away. Andrew came. He and Jack high-fived as they passed each other. I gave Joe a pleading look.

'Don't look at me.' He climbed into the helicopter, pulling the door shut behind him.

'But I'm traumatised!' I yelled after him.

Which way to run? I looked around. If I went after Jack, I'd have to pass Andrew. I was pretty sure he could outrun me. I ran around the other side of the helicopter and hid there, peeping under it, watching Andrew's legs get closer. I saw Jack running, heading for my house. It wasn't far – five minutes max.

Andrew crouched, and we looked at each other under the helicopter.

'I don't know whether to hug you or strangle you.'

'I choose hugs.'

'Where's my car?'

'Chadstone.'

'Come here.'

'No.'

He walked around the helicopter and I stayed crouched there, pretending to look for worms in the grass. Should I pretend to faint? When I looked up, his sunglasses were glaring down at me.

I stood, threw my arms around his neck. 'Sorry. A million times, I'm sorry.'

He stood there all stiff for a minute, then his body relaxed, and his arms came around me in a bear-tight hug.

'GET IN THE CAR. I'm taking you to the hospital.'

'I don't need the hospital. I'm fine, see?' I spun around and fell over. 'Whoops.' I looked up at Andrew. 'We could go to my house. See what's happening.'

'There's a siege at your house. I'm not taking you there.'

'I'm not going to the hospital.'

'Jesus, Erica, make my life easy for once, will you?' Andrew scooped me up and carried me to the car. I made it hard for him, crossing my arms and legs like I was sitting in a chair. He hoisted me higher. 'You're heavier than I would've thought.'

'Hey!'

Andrew's phone rang. He put me down and with a finger in the waistband of my skirt, to keep me from running off, he answered.

'Mate … yeah … shit … alright.' He hung up and looked at me. 'Police want you there.'

CHAPTER 74

*P*olice were all over my street. It was blocked by police cars and police tape, which reminded me of that stormy night when I first met Jack, when he was on the run from police and dying in my front garden. It seemed strange to see him now, standing there on the corner of my street and Swan, watching for us as we drove through the traffic jam. Andrew gave up the traffic jam fight and parked the car illegally in Swan Street. We jogged the rest of the way.

Jack led us down the back lane, where police let us through.

'What's happening?' I said.

'She wants to see you.'

'Ruth?'

'Yeah.' He scowled, swearing under his breath. He slowed his pace. Up ahead, the back of my house was swarming with people and emergency vehicles.

'And you're okay with that?'

He stopped and faced me. Andrew kept walking. 'No, of course I'm not okay with that. The woman is a psychopath and wants you dead.'

'At least we know it's not Sharon.'

That didn't raise a smile; not that I really expected it to.

'You'll speak to her over the loud hailer, and that's it.'

Bill Lucas met us, explained to me that he was going to fit me with protective gear, bullet-proof vest, blah blah blah. Bill said that Ruth just wanted to see for herself that I was still alive.

'She won't be seeing her, Bill,' said Jack.

'She wants to take over my life, including my boyfriend.' I informed Jack, 'That's not you, apparently.'

'It'll be quick,' said Bill to Jack. 'Erica'll stand in the open for a second or two, satisfy her, then straight back to us.'

'Then I'll be with her.'

'She won't allow it.'

I could see Steve standing by his van, fifty metres or so up the road. Lucy was there, too. She gave me a little wave, looking super worried, and I waved back. No blood or anything on Steve, I was happy to see. Steve's cyclone wire fence was still in place, with the gate standing half open. Ruth had told him to 'scram', apparently, and fired off a shot as he left. The area in the lane directly behind my property was empty, so if you were standing in my house, you'd never know there was anyone out there. But there was. Probably fifty cops and special forces people with police cars and ambulances scattered along the lane.

Bill Lucas had a loud hailer to his mouth. 'Ruth Booth!'

From within my property, Ruth screamed, *'Don't call me Ruth!'*

A police helicopter buzzed overhead.

I said, 'She wants to be called Erica Jewell.'

'Erica Jewell!'

'What?' yelled Ruth.

'We have … the other Erica Jewell here.'

I had on all my black, bullet-proof gear, including a helmet. It was really hot, especially as I was still wet from the river. Phew. I bet I stunk. Bill handed me the loud hailer. 'Just tell her you're here.'

I stepped closer to the cyclone fence but stayed out of sight. Not that Jack would let me go any closer anyway. I felt ridiculous in all the proper gear while Jack stood next to me in wet T-shirt and jeans. I put the thing to my lips. 'Hi … Erica. I'm here. The other … Erica.'

'I want to see you!'

Jack gripped my arm. 'No.'

Bill Lucas held out a clear shield for me to take but Jack shoved it away. 'No.'

I'd seen them before, those shields, on telly during riots. This one was quite small; big enough to cover just the top half of my body.

Bill said, 'Just hold this in front of you. It's bulletproof. Step out, let her see you, step back.'

Jack stood in front of me, facing Bill Lucas. 'No.'

Bill pointed up. 'We've got a sniper on her. She's got the gun to Mendez's head. If she shifts it, we'll take her.'

'Just shoot her, for fuck's sake.'

'No!' I said. 'Don't shoot her. She can't help being weird.'

'Give me a rifle,' said Jack. 'I'll do it.'

'I'll just let her see me so we can get on with it.' Get on with whatever needed to be gotten on with.

'No.'

I took the shield from Bill. It was heavy. Jack tried to take it off me. 'Jack! Stop it!'

He glared at me, but beyond the anger, what I could see was fear. He wanted to say something, but nothing came out.

'It's alright,' I said, gently. His face was so serious, so frightened. I put my hand on his cheek. 'I'll stand there for one second and come back. It will be alright.' I gave him a nod and encouraging smile and he released me, unhappy. I took two steps sideways. Just far enough so she could see me. With the shield up, I took in the scene.

Ruth and Emilio sat next to each other at my dining table on the freshly laid sheet flooring, which I realised I may never get to see finished. Maybe Ruth would live here with Emilio. I wondered why she'd moved the table, then realised it was positioned about where the dining area would be, right under where the old roof finished. Ruth was nesting. Setting up home. On the wall were dozens of photos and newspaper cuttings that appeared to be stapled neatly together. I couldn't quite make out the images, but at least I'd found Rosalind's stapler.

Emilio's hands were clasped in front of him. His head was bowed.

Ruth had an arm around his shoulders, the gun at his temple, force-feeding him scones with jam and cream. Above and behind, on what remained of my roof, Sharon Stone suddenly appeared. She crabbed along the corrugated iron, hands and feet working silently over each other as she inched toward the back of my house.

'Is that you?' said Ruth to me. 'I can't see with all that stuff you're wearing.'

'Now step back,' I heard Jack say.

I took another step away from safety. I realised with surprise that my priority was now to distract Ruth so Sharon could do whatever it was she planned to do. Funny how a person can switch like that, go from wanting someone dead (and buried ten feet under) to putting yourself in harm's way to help them. Having a sudden girl crush didn't hurt, either.

'Erica!' That was Jack. Not-happy Jack.

I glanced sideways. Four cops restrained him.

Bill said, 'Step back, Erica.'

I took another step to the side. I was now approximately two metres from the protection of the neighbour's fence. Still behind the cyclone wire.

Ruth said, 'Let me see your face.'

'Okay, but you have to promise not to shoot me.'

'Actually, I was thinking about letting you live. Because if you're dead, you can't be jealous of what I've got.'

'That's a good idea. I could come over for dinner.'

'Ha! As if. Let me see your face.'

From behind the shield, I removed my helmet and tossed it aside.

'No,' Jack gasped from the sidelines.

'Your hair looks like shit,' said Ruth.

'I was in the river.'

Emilio looked up at me, said with a mouth full of scone, 'Emily —'

'Shoosh, my love,' said Ruth, as she shoved some cream in his mouth.

Sharon was crouched on the roof, directly above them. The cops in the helicopter would have seen her, and relayed the info to Bill Lucas.

They probably wondered who the hell she was; this gorgeous, white-haired woman in black, sleeveless leather.

I took another step, keeping the shield aloft. Jack's struggle with the cops drew my attention. He swore at them. I could see Andrew in the background, watching, hands on his head.

I stood at the partially open gate. Ruth tried to stuff another scone in Emilio's mouth. The lower half of his face was covered in jam and cream. Sharon was waiting, statue still.

'Emilio,' I said, 'you won't be able to play tennis if you eat all those scones.'

Ruth screamed, 'Shut up!' and swung the gun, arm straight, aimed at my face. I gripped the shield. Sharon jumped. The gun fired. The bullet hit my shield and my head hit the pavement. Another headache, I thought, as Jack dropped to his knees beside me. He threw the shield off me and I sucked in air. Andrew arrived, kneeling behind me, gently lifting my head and holding it in his hands. Jack cursed whoever to hell and back; his hands were all over me, looking for bullet holes, presumably.

'What were you thinking!' he shouted.

'Don't yell at me.' But I thought I'd like a dollar for every time he's said that.

He put his hands on his head and looked up at the sky. I patted his knee. Andrew's upside-down face gazed down at me.

'Are you angry or impressed?' I said.

He tried to smile. 'Fully impressed.'

'But I still owe you. Big time.'

'You sure do.'

'I'll do your ironing for a year.'

He smiled some more.

I nudged Jack. 'Help me up.' I inspected his eyes to see if they were watery. Hm. Maybe. With his hand behind my back I sat up, rubbed my head. 'Is there blood?'

'No. You'll live.' His voice was wobbly.

'Does that make you happy or sad?'

He shook his head, couldn't raise a smile. Andrew stood but hovered nearby.

Steve was in front of me now, hands out. 'Hey, buddy.'

'Hi.' He hauled me to my feet. 'Sorry you nearly got shot,' I said.

And then Lucy came, bossing, pointing, wanting me to report straight to the ambos. She hugged me and blubbered on my shoulder.

Police swarmed my backyard, and I wanted to see what was going on.

'What's happening?' I said.

Jack said, 'It's over.'

'Is Sharon alright?'

'Yes.'

'Emilio?'

'Yes.'

'I want to see.'

Jack put an arm around my waist and we approached the scene, cops moving aside for us. Ruth was bent over the table, cop's hand on her head, holding her down. She was handcuffed, and she was screaming. No words, just screams. Scream, deep breath, scream, deep breath, scream.

Sharon Stone wiped the jam and cream from Emilio's face. When she finished she kissed him. A big, pashy one. She released him, they stared at each other, and he whipped her into a deep dip, continuing the kiss.

Jack gave me a squeeze. 'Are you jealous?'

'No!' (A bit.) 'You?'

'Of course not.'

'I wonder how long that's been going on,' I said.

'Longer than today, I reckon.'

'You knew?'

'Suspected.'

So, when Emilio won the semi-final, it was because Sharon was there, not because I had a fake amulet? They were still pashing, but now upright again, arms around each other. Sharon was a fraction taller.

I looked up at Jack, who towered over me a good eight or nine inches. 'I want to be kissed like that.'

He pulled me into his side and I snuggled under his arm. He kissed the top of my head. 'Later.'

When Emilio and Sharon finally broke apart, they gazed all lovey-dovey at each other. Emilio placed his precious amulet around Sharon's neck. She squealed, clapped her hands. I humphed, rolled my eyes.

'You will take me on your motorbike, Sharon? To the tennis?'

'Sure.' She batted her eyes at him.

Sharon. Why didn't he have a problem remembering her name? Why couldn't he call her Sharleen or Shilo or something?

Emilio saw me standing there and grinned. It was a beautiful face; one without guilt at his indiscretion with another woman. 'Emily, look. I have *mi amuleto*. Erica Jewell found it!' He lifted the charm from Sharon's chest and kissed it.

Then, as they jogged into my house and up the passageway to the front door, I shouted after them, 'Hey! I'm Erica Jewell! That's *my* name!'

Ruth Booth screamed.

CHAPTER 75

Jack put his arms around me and, with a relieved sigh, pulled me close. My fingers clung to the front of his shirt like they never wanted to let go; I lay my head on his chest. We stayed like that while police moved around us. From behind I heard Senior Detective Bill Lucas tell Jack he needed to speak with me. Apart from a slightly tighter squeeze of his arms, I didn't know what signal Jack gave to send Bill away.

Jack took me to the hospital. He didn't tell me we were going there, probably in case I tried to leap from his moving vehicle to avoid it. I spent four hours in emergency department with a *lot* of attention from female doctors and nurses, presumably because of Jack, who didn't leave my side, holding my hand, kissing it, stroking my face.

To check for concussion, brain haemorrhages, whatever, every half-hour a nurse shone a light in my eyes and asked simple questions like, 'What's your name?' and I said, 'Emily Jesus' just to be funny but no-one thought I was funny, especially Jack. Bill Lucas stopped by and asked me police questions until Jack thought I'd had enough. Finally, a nurse looked deeply into my eyes with the help of a torch and said, 'Who's the prime minister of Australia?' and I said, 'Some wanker who couldn't give a shit about people or the environment,' and she said, 'Okay. You're good to go.'

The nurse left and Jack sat on my bed, took my hand. 'I'm taking you to my place for a shower. Wash that stinking river off you.'

'You were in the stinking river, too.'

'Which is why I'll be in the shower with you.'

Goody! 'And then?'

'And then I'll tuck you into bed and you'll sleep.'

'Oh, no. They said I'm fine. Really.'

'You're traumatised, if not concussed. You need rest.'

'I'm not!' I sat up. 'I don't need rest and I won't.'

'You do and you will.'

I punched his arm. 'You'll chase me around your bedroom and have sex with me!'

Jack smiled, seemingly unconcerned with the attention I'd drawn from the various emergency department staff and patients.

'For two hours,' I said.

ACTUALLY, it was two and a half hours because after the shower there was a lengthy massage which involved me lying face-down on his bed and moaning so loudly I was glad the windows were closed in case the neighbours got the wrong idea. Or the right idea. I hadn't realised how much my body hurt, and how exhausted I was.

Jack had driven us to his house, taking his time. On the way, in anticipation of any disruptive issues that might arise during shower/bedroom time with Jack, I'd called my mother to remind her I was staying at the hotel and she said that was just as well because Mrs Booth and Minx were now living in my room. I'd also called Rosalind and told her I needed to be on-call for Emilio all night, and so she'd have to attend to my official duties at the tennis. Well, I didn't tell her that directly. I left a voicemail. I told Jack he needed to give Andrew a fat bonus, plus send him and his partner out for a disgustingly expensive dinner somewhere, plus a holiday somewhere nice, plus he had to reimburse me for the hotel room I'd used and he said, 'Why do I have to pay for that?' and I said, 'Because,' and he said, 'Alright.'

I also asked what he knew about Martin McGann and Teresa. 'Do you think they were bonking?'

Normally, he'd frown at my coarse language but he just nodded. 'Yep. All she wanted was money. Didn't care how she got it or from whom.'

'Probably why she was with Emilio's father and then Emilio.'

'Probably.'

'But Emilio didn't pay her.'

'Which is why she needed money.'

'What about Martin McGann? What will happen to him?'

Jack glanced at the clock on the car's dashboard. 'I'd say police are picking him up, right about now.'

'He and Shane have a lot of catching up to do.'

He nodded. 'I couldn't be happier for them.'

'Do you think Martin paid the Russians to blow up the oil rig in W.A.?'

'Yep.'

'What about Bass Strait?' I said. 'Aren't you supposed to be there?'

'Handballed that one back to JD.'

'Nice return.'

Jack looked at me, gave me a small smile. 'My priorities have changed.'

WHEN JACK OPENED his front door and we stepped inside, I turned to him, pouted sexily. 'You know what I want.'

He gave me a questioning look as I backed slowly away, then a big smile spread across his face. 'You get a five-second head start.'

I took off with a squeal, sprinting into the living room, knowing I couldn't outrun him for long. He was behind me in a flash.

'That wasn't five seconds!'

I ran behind the sofa and he stood on the other side, eyes shining with laughter. I edged left and right, and he mirrored me. He hurdled the sofa and I raced into the kitchen, going around and around the bench, then around and around the dining table, pulling the chairs out to block him, and as I bolted for the stairs, screaming with giggles, he caught me, spun me into his arms, whipped me into a dip. I panted, laughing, and he put his mouth to my ear, murmuring something in French, and my heart thumped from the thrill of whispered promises I couldn't understand.

'Did you say something naughty?'

'*Oui.*'

He gently bit my earlobe, and my bottom lip, and his beautiful, smiling eyes gazed into mine while he said more things in French.

'Did you say what you're planning to do with me?'

'Oh, yeah.'

My body quivered with anticipation. 'And that is?'

Jack threw me over his shoulder and carried me up the stairs. I laughed, breathless, whacking his backside, telling him, 'This is not romantic!'

In his room he put me down, and something more serious settled around him. He lifted my palms to his mouth, kissing each one, and each fingertip, the heat from his lips zapping up my arms, swirling around my chest, standing my nipples erect. He lingered with the de-clothing process. The buttons of my shirt – one at a time – the zip of my skirt eased down, straps of my bra carefully slipped off each shoulder. My undies encouraged to the floor. He took my hand and led me to the shower where, standing with an arm around my waist and his body against my back, he held his hand under the water to make sure the temperature was just right. He pushed me gently under the soft flow and in that warm, sensuous space – all soft light and chocolate stone – I let the water wash over me, watching Jack through the swirling steam as he undressed. He was quicker with his own clothes: T-shirt flung over his head while he kicked off his shoes. Jeans, undies and socks discarded together.

When he stepped into the shower I reached for him, but he said, 'No touching.'

'No?'

'Not yet.'

Jack washed my hair, massaging the shampoo then conditioner into my scalp, taking his time, sending equal waves of longing and fatigue through my body, leaving me too weak to do anything but stay barely upright.

'Why are you allowed to touch?' I said.

'Because I'm the boss.'

'Alright. But just for tonight.'

'We'll see.'

He moved me under the water and I closed my eyes, arms limp at my side. He cradled my head in one hand; with the other he worked the water through my hair, rinsing it. With his breath on my cheek and his thigh against mine I was aware of him, how close he was, and I opened my eyes, blinked the water away, held his gaze, held my breath. He stopped all movement except a very light stroke of fingers down my cheek, and in a moment of lost control he kissed me hard. There was a deep, distant groan in his throat and I turned so we faced each other, slick bellies together, my hands on his hips.

He stepped back with a weak gasp. 'Wait.'

He took the soap and lathered my body, massaged my tired and aching arms and back. I leaned against the cool stone wall and watched him crouch, lifting one foot then the other, washing them with a soft cloth and kissing each toe in turn. He placed my foot on his knee; kissed my grazed shin and bruised knee and a deep scratch on the inside of my thigh. He looked up at me and I gave him a big smile.

So now I lay sprawled in Jack's bed, temporarily sated, having finally been allowed to touch as much as I wanted. I was propped up by just enough pillows so I could comfortably watch the tennis. It was a close match. But Emilio was a shining star; Sharon cheering him on from the love seat. I saw Mum and Dad there in Jack's expensive platinum, kryptonite, whatever, seats. I hoped they wouldn't look for me after the match – they'd be looking a long time.

Jack lay with his head on my chest, arm securing my waist; no chance of escape. I twirled my fingers in his hair. 'What are you doing tomorrow?' I said. I, for one, had no intention of going to work, and hoped he didn't have plans either. In light of recent developments, I expected Shazza wouldn't be around.

'I'm locking you in my bedroom.'

'All day?'

'Until your renovation's finished.'

'You don't need to lock the door, you know. I'll willingly stay.'

He rolled away and pulled me on top of him. 'I can't trust you not to run off.'

I sat up, straddling him, admiring his chest and shoulders, running my hands over them, sighing with happiness. 'I won't run off. Unless you're not planning on being here. In which case —'

'I'll be here, feeding you and —'

'Loving me.'

'Yes, loving you.'

With a hand behind my head, he pulled my face down to his, and it was another half hour before I got to see more tennis.

JACK DOZED and I slipped out of bed, walked across the room to his cavernous robe where I rifled through the neatly ironed (by Joe) collection of T-shirts for my favourite. Really, I loved every one of them because they all smelled like him. I pulled on a pair of his boxers.

'Are you running off?' Jack said. He lay on his back now in the expansive bed with an arm hooked behind his head, the sheet low and creamy against his perfect, bronze body. The whole scene looked like an ad for Sheridan sheets.

'I'm getting a drink. You want something?'

'Just you. Don't be long.'

I found Joe in the kitchen wearing tracky dacks, hair messed up, making himself a hot chocolate.

'Aren't you watching the tennis?' I said.

'Yep. In my room.' He checked out Jack's T-shirt with a smile. Joe was happy I was here, I knew. I reckoned he wanted a wedding as badly as my mother.

I put the kettle on. 'Joe.'

'Uh-huh?'

'Will Sharon stay here much longer?'

'She's leaving next week.'

'Really?'

'Yeah. Back to Sydney.'

'Is that where she'll be based with the Team?' I said. 'In Sydney?'

'Yep.'

'Emilio will be happy about that.'

'I reckon.'

'So now Sharon and Emilio are together I can stop worrying.'

'You've never had to worry about Sharon. I keep telling you.'

'But why? Why *wouldn't* I worry? She's so gorgeous and accomplished and —'

'Erica —'

'I thought maybe she was gay but then if she was gay why didn't she —'

Joe slapped his hand on the counter. My mouth snapped shut and I looked at him.

'The reason you've never had to worry about Sharon,' he said, quietly, 'is because Jack's with *you.*'

My jaw dropped. I took a moment to respond while my brain processed that information. I could hear the cogs clunking and wheels grinding. 'He's *with* me?'

'It's pretty obvious.'

'Like, in a relationship?'

He nodded, smiling. 'You haven't figured that out?'

I shook my head, slowly, mouth hanging open.

'Jack's all yours.' Joe gave me a wink, and as he headed to his room, with a smile in his voice, said, 'Hope you can handle it.'

ACKNOWLEDGMENTS

With thanks to my publishing house, Pilyara Press — in particular Jennifer Scoullar, Sydney Smith and Kate Belle — without whom Grand Slam would not have travelled globally.

I am still and will always be grateful to those who made the original edition of this novel possible.

ABOUT THE AUTHOR

In 2005 Kathryn Ledson took a deep breath (whispered a prayer) and left her secure, 25+ year career as a PA in the stuffy, high-stress corporate arena which, admittedly, included a few exciting breaks to travel overseas, work on a tropical island, and tour with famous people like Peter Ustinov and rock bands Dire Straits and AC/DC.

Kathryn returned to study with relief and a great sense of homecoming, and what emerged from that professional writing and editing course was a huge surprise in the form of hapless heroine Erica Jewell, lead character in Kathryn's series of funny, romantic, action-packed novels, which so far includes *Rough Diamond*, *Monkey Business* and *Grand Slam*.

If you enjoyed this book and have a spare moment, please leave an online review. Reviews are of great help to authors.

http://kathrynledson.com/

www.ingramcontent.com/pod-product-compliance
Lightning Source LLC
Chambersburg PA
CBHW030704190726
48286CB00001B/167